JALAPEÑO
REPUBLIC

OTHER WORKS

Other works by Robert J. Alvarado
www.youngpistolero.com

Other works by
Robert J. Alvarado
www.youngpistolero.com

Award Winning Young Pistolero Series
The saga of Rafael Ortega de Estrada, a young Mexican peón on the run riding a stolen Appaloosa stallion after shooting the haciendero who raped his younger sister. Heading north, Rafael enters the United States in 1866 to find life on the other side of the border holds new dangers along with the promise of a new life. This gritty tale is set in the American Southwest as Americans and Mexicans struggle after the Mexican-American War.

Young Pistolero (Book 1) 2013 Sierra Press
> 2018 Finalist for Drama TV Series category, by the Latino Books into Movies Awards by Latino Literacy Now

> #1 Fiction Book for 2015; by The Latino Author, by Corina Martinez Chaudhry

Star of the Young Pistolero (Book 2) 2014 Sierra Press
Death Stalks the Young Pistolero (Book 3) 2015 Sierra Press
> #1 Fiction Book for 2016; by The Latino Author

Legacy for the Young Pistolero (Book 4) 2017 Sierra Press
> #3 Fiction Book for 2017; by The Latino Author

A Reckoning for the Young Pistolero (Book 5) 2018 Sierra Press

Young Pistolero Series (con't)
Dangerous Venture (Book 6) 2019 Sierra Press
Justified Vengeance (Book 7) 2019 Sierra Press
The Black Phantom (Book 8) 2020 Sierra Press

Non-Fiction
Elfego Baca Destined to Survive
2013 Sunstone Press, Santa Fe, NM
2016 Sierra Press, Albuquerque, NM

Fiction
The Jalapeño Republic 2020 Sierra Press
2021 International Latino Book Award Medalist. Insights from the ILBA judges, "It was an interesting book, quite different from most futuristic novels I have read."

Jake Flores Mysterys
Just Vanished 2020 Sierra Press
2021 International Latino Book Award Medalist. Insights from the ILBA judges, "From the moment you start reading it, you imagine an action TV series that keeps you involved."

Zia Westerns
Set in the New Mexico and Arizona territories of the Southwest, these westerns draw from the Southwest's unique flavor. Originally part of New Spain and then Mexico, the Spanish settlers and native Indians forged an informal peace until the years after the Mexican-American War brought them into the Wild West. These stories are set during this chaotic time and attempt to paint a realistic picture of the meaning of the Zia symbol.

The Spanish Sword 2020 Sierra Press
2021 International Latino Book Award Medalist. Insights from the ILBA judges, "This book is carefully crafted and felt thoroughly researched."

JALAPEÑO REPUBLIC

This book is a work of fiction. All of the names, characters, places, and incidents are either the product of the author's imagination or are used fictitiously and any resemblance to actual persons, living or dead, business establishments, events, or locales is entirely coincidental.

A glossary of *italicized* Spanish words is provided at the end of this book, with the exception of words which are equivalent in both languages, such as *importante* = important, *Mamá* = Mama, or words of Latin origin found in the English dictionary. Other words, phrases, and sentences written in Spanish are immediately explained within the text itself.

Printed in the United State of America

ISBN-13: 9780991477791

SIERRA
PRESS

Published by Sierra Press
Phoenix, Arizona
First Printing, June 2020

Cover design by Daniel David Alvarado

Website: www.youngpistolero.com

ACKNOWLEDGEMENT

First and always, I owe more than thanks to my wife, Ellen, for her unending hours of critique and review. Her conviction for this story has brought it to fruition.

The design and creativity for the *Jalapeño Republic* design is pure genius by my brother, Daniel David Alvarado.

Thank you to my friends and family who have encouraged me to explore new adventures in my Hispanic genre. Thank you all.

PROLOGUE

Quetzalcóatl [Kets-ull-koh-ah-tull], a Toltec deity, a God, a myth or legend, has been prominent in pre-Hispanic writings and stories since the Aztec Empire. His name, Quetzalcóatl, in Nahuatl (the Aztec language) is interpreted as – 'Quetzal' meaning beautiful plumage and 'cóatl' meaning snake. Thus Quetzalcóatl is generally represented as a feathered serpent in Aztec paintings and carvings.

According to legend, upon his arrival in the world of humans, Quetzalcóatl wandered the land in human form spreading peace and harmony. At the time, people honored their many gods by offering sacrifices, both animal and human. They believed the gods demanded sacrifices to obtain blessings. However, Quetzalcóatl forbade human sacrifice and brought great joy and prosperity to the land and people. In legend, he is credited for teaching the pre-Hispanic peoples to plant corn, smelt metals, dye cotton, and astronomy. He was revered for his humility, self-sacrifice, and purity of soul.

However his brother, Tezcatlipoca [tes-Kaht-li-poh-kah], was angry with Quetzalcóatl and jealous of his popularity with the people. The people were turning away from the other gods and not performing the ancient rituals and human sacrifice. To Tezcatlipoca's dismay, the people and land were prospering, so he devised an evil plan to disgrace his brother.

Tezcatlipoca disguised himself as an old man and brought Quetzalcóatl a delicious drink or *pulque*. It was a trick. When Quetzalcóatl drank the strong *pulque*, it made him sing, dance, and rage with carnal desire, getting so drunk that he slept with their sister thus breaking his vow of celibacy and purity.

So ashamed by his actions, Quetzalcóatl abandoned his human form, built a raft by intertwining snakes, and fled Mexico toward the rising sun. He promised the people he would someday return to punish the gods for practicing human sacrifice and when he returned the people would be the beneficiaries of a great nation.

By legend, the Aztecs awaited the return of the God Quetzalcóatl from the direction of the rising sun or east. In 1519 the Spanish conqueror, Hernán Cortés, arrived by boat landing on the eastern shore of the continent. He came wearing shining metal armor and rode a horse, an animal never seen in the Aztec Empire. It was no wonder the people believed he was the returning god, Quetzalcóatl. The Aztec king, Montezuma, was so convinced Cortés was the god Quetzalcóatl, he welcomed Cortés and his men into Tenochtitlán [Tā-noch-tet-lan], today known as Mexico City, and thus became an unwitting accomplice to the downfall of the Aztec empire. As Cortés and the Spaniards took control of the Americas claiming the land for Spain, Aztecs scattered throughout desolate parts of the land. They formed or joined other small tribes, many lost to the world forever, or some living in harmony with the earth as their ancestors had done.

In the early part of the twenty-first century, an important discovery occurred in the Copper Canyon area of the Sierra Madre Mountain range, located in the northern state of Chihuahua, Mexico. While traveling, a young Chichimeca Indian happened on an injured Indian boy. Though unable to communicate with words, the young rider was able to follow instructions from the boy. Winding down a narrow canyon wall, the boy led him to his village near the bottom. The rider was swarmed by smiling villagers who touched his clothes, stroked his horse, and chatted excitedly. They spoke in the same unusual language as the boy, but the rider could tell they were happy the boy returned. A man, he assumed was the chief, approached and gave him a small pouch made of leather. Thinking it might be coins or precious jewels, the young rider expressed thanks and rode away. As soon as he was alone, the young man opened the pouch with high anticipation pouring the contents into his hand. Three small unremarkable stones fell into his palm.

Turning the stones over in his hand looking for gold

flecks or some other hidden treasure, he could find nothing. He thought it an odd gift and laughed. Picking up one of the small stones, he flung it away. The stone flew until the rider could no longer see it, as if shot from a high-powered rifle and not a toss of his hand. Stunned, the young rider pocketed the other two magic stones and set off looking for the third. Scouring the barren dirt, he never found the stone, but decided to take the others to the Institute in Chihuahua on his way home. Perhaps they would buy the magic stones from him.

This discovery, a new energy source, profoundly changed the course of history. By 2030, most of the oil-producing world was in turmoil and financial depression after the Oil Wars and a nuclear accident in the Iranian oil fields. The abuse of money, greed, and power had bankrupt most of the global superpowers, particularly the United States of America which was in a deep depression, dragging most of the world down with it. After the financial collapse of the world's superpowers, oil was used as currency.

Scientists at the Chihuahua Institute of Technology analyzed the stones the young man brought, until they isolated the particle that powered the meteor stones. Harnessing the power of the stone, it promised a new power source to replace fossil fuels. The scientists organized a consortium of Mexican entrepreneurs and investors with the determination to bring the new power to the world. Using this new wealth and demonstrating the new energy source, the consortium purchased much of the American Southwest from the bankrupt United States. The acquired states and northern Mexican states were formed into a new country called the United Central Republic. With its strong Hispanic origins and a determined leader, the United Central Republic prospered from the new energy source and helped the world recover from the global depression. This Republic was most often referred to as the **Jalapeño Republic** and Quetzalcóatl's prediction finally came true – a great and benevolent nation was born.

CHAPTER 1

A dusty light green aerovan swooped down into a dark canyon near Presa Rodrigues, a manmade lake northeast of Hermosillo, Sonora, United Central Republic. It landed beside a dilapidated shack with an attached wooden lean-to shed surrounded with brush and tumbleweeds. As the rear of the van opened, a man wearing night vision glasses stepped out holding a weapon in the ready position. Slowly and cautiously scanning the horizon for any signs of life, the man walked toward the shed. Satisfied the area was secure he signaled to the others waiting in the van.

"Check the shed," he barked as two other men walked toward him.

The driver and the smaller man quickly cleared a tangle of brush from the front and opened the shed's door. Inside was a nondescript tan, four-door sedan.

"Good," the leader said taking off his night vision glasses. "Everything is going as planned. You two get the girl out of the van. I'll pull the sedan out. Once you get the girl into the car, one of you put the van into the shed and cover it up. *¡Rapido!*" he barked his commands in a gruff tone.

The two men moved swiftly and efficiently without responding to the *jefe*. They had been warned before this assignment that the *jefe* expected efficiency and had a violent temper. Within ten minutes, the four-door sedan had lifted above ground level then followed the canyon and out across the lake. The leader relied only on his night vision glasses as he flew in the dark. Once past the lake, he sped west toward the capital city of Hermosillo and merged onto a busy aeropath. Lying across the backseat, a young woman, bound and gagged, was oblivious to her predicament.

On the east side of Hermosillo, near the old penitentiary they exited the aeropath. The driver knew the flight would be tracked by the government traffic systems, but nothing about the older model four-door aerocar would trigger any alarm. Flying low and cautiously, the vehicle wound through the darkened streets of a poor neighborhood. The yards of the small adobe houses were mostly neat, but many of the houses needed repaired. A few teenagers hung around on the corners. The tips of their cigarettes glowed in the eerie light. They took little notice of the sedan when it landed on the driveway of a dirty white stucco house. Pushing a button on the dash the garage door creaked open and the sedan maneuvered into the small garage.

"Hurry! Get her into the house," the leader barked. The smaller man pulled the young woman out by the shoulders, while the taller lifted her legs. Taking her into the house, they dropped her on the bed in the largest bedroom. The leader followed behind them with another dose of the sleeping drug. She groaned weakly as the needle stuck her, and then quietly slipped back into a coma-like state.

The two henchmen walked into the kitchen flipping the light switch. The taller man with a sparse black beard, which hid a wide scar across his left cheek, found cold beers in the refrigerator. He got one for himself and handed one to the shorter man. Sitting down they looked at each other, then toasted to their success. The cold beer was gone before the cans hit the table.

"Pendejos," the leader growled calling them idiots as he walked into the kitchen. "We have only just begun, so stop celebrating. I have to go find a public SATComm booth. Stay put and don't drink all the beer!"

Mason Warrick stood about six feet two inches tall. His nondescript bodysuit loosely covered his lean and muscular body. Thinning blond hair hung almost to his shoulders, hidden mostly under a dark blue Chihuahua Cubs baseball cap. Cautiously, he stepped out of the house and walked down the street. He knew a public SATComm could be found near the corner market.

Mason was a cautious man, maybe overly cautious. He carried no Pcom device when he worked. Personal communication device transmissions over satellite links were monitored by the government and easily traced. Public communications on SATComms were too, but gave some level of anonymity and the SATComm pods insured privacy. People on the outside of the pod could not see a holograph or monitor conversations.

Moving slowly, the dark night concealed his movements, though he kept vigilant to any unusual activity. Three teenagers were hanging out on the far corner and Mason could see the tips of their cigarettes. Farther down the street, music blared from a brightly lit house where two men stood in a yard drinking beer and laughing. Mason slowly worked his way along, his left foot dragging a bit from his permanent limp.

"*Mierda*," he cursed tripping over a tree root sticking through the cement on the dark sidewalk. Several blocks later he came to an area illuminated with multicolored lights dotting small storefronts. Mariachi music drifted in the air from the cafe where people were eating and drinking outside at small tables. Staying out of visual light, he watched the people enjoying their food and the music. He thought the strolling Mariachi group was a holograph and was surprised to see someone shake hands with the singer. He wished he could sit and enjoy the music and get a good drink, but he had a job to do. Shrugging, he began looking for a quiet spot with a SATComm pod.

Satellite communications had made cell networks obsolete in the 2050s after the Oil Wars rocked the power balance of the world. At first, the extensive cell networks attempted to survive, but as technology made satellites cheaper, all communications were via satellite. Once a novelty, as the number of satellite links had increased, public SATComms were harder to find. He walked past the market and approached a dark SATComm pod near the shuttle stop. He stepped inside and closed the door and latched it.

Standing in front of the screen, it greeted, "Welcome to SATComm, Thursday April 27, 2075." A robotic distorted voice spoke, "Please state your PIN number."

"Hello," a raspy distorted voice answered the call, but the monitor was still blank in non-video mode. Mason had never seen the face of the person who hired him and it really pissed him off.

"Moonshot," he gave the code.

"Is everything in order?"

"Yes, I have the package. Where do you want it delivered?"

"2225 Echo Park Avenue, Los Angeles, Sunday night. Use a diverted route and do not damage the package or you will not get paid. You will get further instructions later," the distorted voice said.

"I need more money. Those *pendejos* you assigned me are worthless," Mason complained in response, but was cut off mid sentence as the communication disconnected.

"Your PIC will be billed four units," the SATComm alerted.

"Thanks a lot asshole," Mason grumbled to himself hating when anyone treated him with disrespect. All his life people had treated him shitty and he knew why. It was because of his deformed body. "Asshole," he cursed again. It wasn't his fault he was born with a withered arm and one leg shorter than the other. He blamed the whore, the poor excuse of a mother who bore him in Toronto, Canada.

Left to his own devices as a child, Mason learned early on about bullies, bearing more than his share of torment. It taught him well however – bullies always won. By twenty-two, his childhood had honed his vicious nature. After several arrests in the Toronto area, though always managing to escape any serious charges, he left Toronto for good.

Wanting to find warmer locations, Mason finally ending up in Caracas, Venezuela, where the corrupt country appealed to his nature. Starting with small-time jobs, he worked his way up in the Venezuelan oil and drug cartels called the Petroleros Venezuelan or PLV for short. Life with the cartels reminded him of his youth. It reminded him of the bullies who tormented him, but he survived with grit and a vicious reputation.

Now almost forty, Mason would do anything for the right price. He was offered one and a half million Bolivars, about one hundred and fifty thousand if converted to Federated dollars, to pull off this job with half up front.

He and his cohorts made two previous attempts to kidnap the woman, but each time something interfered. The buyer insisted the job must be untraceable by the government tracking systems. "The young woman would be chipped and monitored closely," the buyer told him and reviewed every detail of the plans. Today's plan worked perfectly, allowing him to circumvent the Jalapeño Republic's tracking systems or so he believed.

Muttering to himself, he limped his way along the backside of the markets in the dark. Originally the job sounded easy. The target was a young woman who worked for the Republic's EQA department, the agency that managed use of the energy particle. When they kidnapped her, she was in her uniform and had official documents and identification.

Mason believed he was tapped for this job because he had knowledge of aerocars and the Republic's flight tracking systems. Some thirty years behind the new technology, Venezuela still used internal combustion engines, as oil was still plentiful in Venezuela. Many of the PLV's operatives were not as knowledgeable with the new technology.

He learned to fly aerovehicles in Toronto when he was younger. Over the years, he studied the global flight tracking systems and had thwarted it on numerous occasions while pulling other jobs in the Jalapeño Republic and Federated States of America for the PLV. The flight control systems were thorough, but predictable. Kidnapping the woman in Los Angeles relied upon this predictability.

He believed he had covered any footprint linking the Venezuelan PLV to the kidnapping. According to their plan, he kidnapped the girl in Los Angeles. The Republic's security analysts would suspect the Federated States of America was at fault or some internal faction of discontented *políticos* in the Republic. Animosity still simmered in the American Southwest after the Jalapeño Republic purchased Arizona, New Mexico, Southern California, and parts of Colorado and West Texas after the United States' financial collapse in 2035.

Now however, he thought it odd they were to return to Los Angeles with the woman, but assumed it part of the plan's treachery. At a minimum, it would take the Republic's government tracking systems some time to put the pieces together and likely not at all.

As he walked back to the old house, he squelched a desire to bump off the young woman and split. This job was annoying, as were the two Venezuelans the PLV cartel assigned to him. He wanted to tell the distorted voice to forget it several times, but he needed the money. He still had over fifty thousand Republic dollars of the down payment, but the other half was a lot of money. His thoughts wandered to how he could rip-off the two Venezuelans. He might have to kill them, as there was no way he was going to split the final payment.

When he opened the door to the small hideaway, the two men were watching soccer on an old media display unit and drinking beer. Mason gruffed at the shorter man. "There better be more beer in that fridge. There should be some preserved dinners in the cabinet. Go zap three of them and make it snappy. Bring me a beer now," he ordered.

"Fuck you," Rico replied. "You're so hungry, you go do it."

Mason whipped out his X9 laser and pointed it at the shorter man. "Go get the food asshole."

The two men looked at each other and then at Mason. They had been warned the blond-headed cripple was crazy, a real *loco,* and his reputation as the best assassin for the Venezuelan PLV organization was well known.

"All right, all right," Rico retorted. "Keep your pants on, *jefe.*"

While the three kidnappers ate dinner, Mason explained the next step of the plan.

"Back to California! We just came from there?" Silvio complained. "This is stupid. Why didn't we just stay there?"

"We take orders and don't ask why. We lie low here and go to L.A. after dark Sunday night. No contact with anyone; you fucking understand? You make any fucking mistakes . . . " Mason patted his weapon to finish the sentence. "We'll sleep in shifts. The girl should be out until morning. If you hear her wake, come get me. Now, keep that video down while I study these maps," Mason growled before he walked to the kitchen.

Rico, the shorter man elbowed the taller in the arm and whispered as Mason walked out of the room. "I got me a cousin in L.A. When we get back there I'll call her and we can go to Sunset Strip and party." Rico smiled showing a gap from a missing front tooth.

Silvio grinned and nodded his head in agreement with the idea, feeling somewhat immune to the blond cripple's threats. Silvio's brother, Armando, was a kingpin in the PLV and Mason would not dare to shoot him.

CHAPTER 2

A silhouette of a man on horseback shimmered in the morning sun at the edge of a nearby mesa. As the image came into focus, the rider appeared to be an Indian warrior riding a large dark horse. With no warning, the horse reared back on its hind legs. A loud, wild scream disrupted the morning serenade of the desert quail.

The horse and rider lunged down a small mesa at full gallop smashing the desert growth, creating a trampled path and a dusty cloud. Through the dust I saw the black horse snorting, puffing, its mouth snarled as it thundered down the mesa heading directly toward me. Mesmerized, I watched the scene unfold, unable to react.

Clad only in a short, white loincloth the warrior carried a long lance. A leather band across his forehead held a crop of coal black hair away from his painted face. Three eagle feathers were flowing freely in the wind attached to the right side of the leather headband. Black and red war paint formed a mask defining the warrior's face in a menacing scowl. On his chest, I saw the profile of a black jaguar, its mouth open showing long sharp teeth.

Suddenly I heard and felt the pounding of my heart in rhythm with the horse's pounding hooves. The warrior screamed and raised the lance above his head, shaking me out of my trance – I started running for my life.

Cat claw ripped at my shirt as I ran and blood trickled from my legs, lacerated by the spiky shrubs and prickly cactus. Suddenly I found myself out in the open, heading toward a wide river. My lungs were screaming and when I glanced back to look for the Indian warrior, he was about to overtake me. The huge black horse puffed steam from its nostrils and flung white foam from its mouth. The wild Indian was laughing and yelling unintelligible words. I struggled to demand more from my body, and picked up my pace until I stepped on a loose rock and fell face first in the dirt. As quickly as I hit the ground, I somehow popped to my feet again, running, running.

Fighting hard to fill my aching lungs, I reached the bank of a river. Frantically I scanned for a way to cross the swift running water. White caps broke everywhere on the reddish brown water, giving no sign of the river's depth. On the other side of the river, I could see a grinning old man bent over in laughter apparently enjoying my

*predicament. Between spasms of laughter, the old man would motion
for me to cross the river.*

*A wild scream pierced my ears and I turned toward the sound.
Only a few meters in front of me, the powerful black horse came to a
dusty halt on its hind legs. The Indian threw the lance directly at my
chest and I knew I was about to die.*

Drenched in a cold sweat the dreamer's foggy brain
swirled between the dream and reality. As he tried to open
his eyes, his body felt paralyzed to the weight of the air
around him. The nightmare was one which came to him
often, manifesting in many ways. It always ended with a
vision of his *Nino,* his godfather, wanting to help him
escape the warrior ready to take his life. Though familiar,
the recurring dream always shook him to the core.

CHAPTER 3

Waking from the dream and disoriented, Francisco Salaz crawled slowly out of bed, his senses overloaded. In an unstable gait, his feet took him through the bedroom and across his living space toward the back of his house. He pushed his way out the eastern patio door. After months in an enclosed artificial atmosphere, the sounds and colors of Earth bombarded his dulled senses.

Orange and pink hues blazed the thin gray morning clouds on the eastern vista. The sight delighted him, and then the colorful morning panorama blurred like a surreal painting as his eyes began to water. His body felt heavy and his chest labored to breathe the cool morning air. Unsteady, he slowly walked across the deck and down the backyard's hillside trying to orient himself while his aching body complained with each step. Gravity weighed so heavy, picking up each foot took concentrated effort. The struggle to acclimate to Earth's gravity seemed more difficult with each space mission or perhaps age was just catching up to him.

Standing at the end of the path and looking south, the apricot and peach orchard his father helped him plant five years ago was alive with activity. Bees worked the maturing tree's pink and white blossoms nestled between intensely new green leaves. He breathed deeply and the blossoms' scent permeated the air with a sweet aroma. The chirps and calls of spotted towhees and a variety of warblers flitting in and out of the blossoms filled the morning with a sweet music.

Francisco watched as the blazing eastern sunrise gradually faded to only a slight tinge of pink etching the underside of the clouds. The sun continued to rise above the mountains until the pink faded completely and only a scattering of thin white altostratus clouds lazily floated in the teal blue sky.

Gradually with each breath, the fog in his head began to clear as his body adjusted to Earth's level of oxygen.

Quietly standing on the lower patio, Francisco breathed deeply with a satisfied sigh. Home, he was home, high on the eastern slope of Monte Tecanachic in the Sierra Madre mountain range northwest of Dublán City, the capital of the United Central Republic.

He caught a cargo freighter from the Mars Space Port yesterday morning and landed at the Chihuahua Space Terminal last night. The trip was uncomfortable, with the old freighter rattling and scaring him on reentry, but at least it arrived safely. The normal reentry routine seemed especially slow and meticulous because the space medics stuck to standard protocol. Usually, he could sneak out of the reentry routines early since he knew most of the medics, but not last night. Armed guards stood at all of the doors. He asked why security was so tight, but the medics denied knowing the reason for the high alert status. Finally cleared and released, it was after midnight by the time he secured a shuttle to bring him home.

With shaky legs and painful breathing, he began his morning exercise routine trying to work his soft muscles with Ukidokan Karate stretching exercises. *"Qué desgracia,"* he groaned aloud feeling the painful resistance of his aching muscles. Every part of his body hurt, reacting to the change in the oxygen levels and gravity. Scientists tried to emulate Earth's atmosphere in space, but it was not the same. The complex human body actually adapted quite well in the artificial environment, but acclimating to the Earth's atmosphere was always a struggle.

Facing the morning sun, Francisco continued stretching. Working slowly and methodically, he worked from his hamstrings up to his shoulders feeling the muscles loosen a bit. He breathed deeply, filling his lungs with natural oxygen. With even a minimal effort, sweat began dripping profusely. Stripping his shirt displayed his usually bronze-colored skin had faded to a sickly beige from the lack of natural sunlight in the Mars colony domes. A cool breeze stung the moisture beading on his chest.

As he pushed the stretching routine, each muscle screamed with any increased movement. He knew it would take several weeks, maybe more, to regain his normal strength and flexibility. Extended space travel in an artificial environment meant depleted muscle mass. It was a problem scientists were yet unable to resolve. Many believed there was a connection between gravity and muscle absorption of oxygen – some undetectable synergy where gravity supported the body's ability to absorb oxygen properly.

Worse yet, was the artificially grown food in aeroponic bays of vitagreen. It was all they ate in space. Chemically enriched air fed the plants without water, a necessity for space colonies. Other products were not grown, but created from enriched fillers such as cornhusks and beet fiber.

The research started here on Earth to increase food production to an ever hungry world. During his college years, Francisco gave little thought to grabbing a vitashake for breakfast or a burger made of soybeets for lunch. Artificially generated food made from fillers and vitamins was continuing to increase for mass consumption in most parts of the world – cheap, tasty, and readily available. His parents, especially his father, argued against the artificial foods and growing up Francisco thought his parents were just old fashioned.

Then he got his first entry-level job after college as a chemical analyst with the Global Food Administration. There he read the research and performed testing suites. His job was to mitigate or disprove any negative test results of vitagrown foods. World governments and the medical community discounted contrary research. It was a global policy to minimize scientific proof of the long-term effects of vitagrown food. Better to feed people crap than to let them starve. Francisco understood the principle, but knew most vitagrown food was not good for the body. After a year he quit, changed forever to both his view of food and the GFA's push of synthetic food for mass consumption.

Continuing the karate routines, his body slowly responded and the stiffness began to ease slightly. The stretching exercises evolved into more vigorous kicking and punching of the air. Even though the morning was cool, the sun was warm and sweat began to soak his dark hair and trickled down his face.

At the end of the exercises he gracefully, but with authority, danced the Ukidokan Kitsuni Kata, deliberately performing the ancient movements as if in slow motion. Each movement defined a defensive position or an attacking move against an imaginary opponent, while paying particular attention to form and timing. At the end of the ancient karate dance, his mind and body relaxed a bit and he finished the workout with deep breathing exercises trying to fill his lungs to capacity with natural oxygen.

Walking back into the house and grabbing a towel, he headed to the west-facing sunroom. Pulling the cover off the hot tub, he ran his hand through the hot water before stripping his sweat-soaked pants. Gingerly he stepped in. *"Ahhh, qué suave,"* he murmured to himself. The hot water felt amazing, a luxury definitely not available in space. Hot bubbly mineral water, fed by a natural hot mineral spring tickled his aching body as he settled into the tub. Leaning back and relaxing, he let his mind wander.

The last six months on Mars was his third trip to the Global Meridian Bay Colony. The colony was located near the geographic center or meridian of the planet. The colony of permanent scientists and robotic workers were verifying the Earth-like properties of ice, iron, magnesium, and other minerals found in the rocks and soil. They tested growing cycles and long-term exposure to the Mars environment. Their work preceded hope a permanent Mars colony could be established.

Staring out the sunroom's windows to the bright teal blue sky peppered with small white clouds scuttling along the mountains, a smile spread across Francisco's face at the view. Living in the enclosed artificial domes for six months depleted human senses and returning to the sights and sounds of Earth was pure joy. Releasing a deep sigh, he sank up to his chin in the water.

At least the extended six-month space assignment earned him an extra two weeks of recovery time. First, he wanted to see his parents and get some personal business in order. He imagined the last week of vacation would find him fishing for black marlin at Keno Bay off the Sea of Cortez. He hoped he could talk his father into joining him. Closing his eyes and the thoughts from his mind, Francisco drifted into a deep relaxation, allowing the mineral water to soak his weary body.

Suddenly a sound resembling an electronic cricket chirped him out of meditation. It took several chirps before his foggy brain recognized the sound. *"Mierda,"* he cursed at the interruption from the communicator. He thought about not answering, but slowly pulled his dripping body out of the hot tub. Leaving a trail of water, he followed the sound and found his Pcom chirping on the kitchen table.

The indicator showed the call was from Guardian 90 on a secure link. Approaching the Pcom, he voiced his secure id and password. The voice recognition pattern took only a few seconds before a feminine image popped up and her voice said, "Cisco! Welcome home."

"Thank you. How did you know I was back?"

"We got your report from the reentry center this morning. Did you rest well?"

The soothing voice irritated him. The female's image and voice were artificially programmed to display human emotions, but none of it was real. Her holographic image was simply a computer program designed from a database of what the techno-nerds thought were your wants and desires. For him the image usually had long auburn hair, greenish eyes, and an athletic-build on the thin side. Extensive studies determined human responses to individually pleasing images resulted in a positive outcome. Every available piece of data on a person's life was stored and analyzed into a profile. The masses did not understand and probably thought the Pcom holographs were real people. They might even be embarrassed standing naked talking to what looked like a real person. Knowing the technology, he found it obnoxious, yet the image reminded him of several old girlfriends, particularly his high school sweetheart Vivian.

He wanted to say, "Cut the crap," but responded more correctly, "Yes thank you, why are you bothering me?"

"Republic Security Headquarters apologizes, but you have been scheduled for a meeting at seventeen-hundred today. Please meet your department director by sixteen-forty-five at the Security Headquarters facility," the woman's voice explained sounding more official.

"Hold on. I'm on leave. What's going on?" Irritation rang in his voice, but it fell on deaf robotic ears. The artificial communications did not react to human emotion, only the words spoken. So far, the techno-nerds had only figured out how to adapt the artificial voice to speak with a proper emotion, not to react.

"The nature of the meeting is classified," the robotic image replied. Then in a softer tone she smiled and said, "Have a nice day Cisco."

"But . . ." he started to respond as the image faded and the Pcom disconnected leaving him staring at empty space in disbelief. Normally the agency was careful to allow ample time for rest after a long job. His fatigued brain struggled to make sense of the G90 call. Classified? It was easy to discount the high alert status last night at the reentry building, but now a classified meeting. It made no sense. As a scientist, he worked for EQA, the Evaluation and Qualification Agency. His department and the jobs they worked on typically were not classified. He and his peers, although often called agents, were scientists working on peaceful projects. There must be some mistake.

Standing naked and dripping on the kitchen floor, he barked at the communicator, "Office." An automated voice answered with the date and time, "Saturday April 29, 2075. Please start your message now Cisco." Realizing it was not a workday he responded, "Shutdown."

Grumbling, he walked back to the sunroom. Stepping into the tub, he sank into the hot water and reflected on the call. His recent assignment was to give technical aid to the Federated States of America's scientists. The FSA was spearheading the global effort to land human colonies on

Mars. Scientists from around the world were working together to explore and build suitable outposts in space, modeled after the Betazona project on the Moon.

It was the discovery and application of the energy particle that empowered both space travel and the ability to sustain a space colony. As an EQA representative for the United Central Republic, Cisco's job was to evaluate and verify the use of the powerful energy source derived from the particle. At the Mars site, it provided the energy source to fuel the oxygen and gravity generating engines for the colony domes and all necessary energy to sustain life. Francisco was impressed with the American ingenuity in their newest artificial environment designs. The interconnecting domes were to be a showcase for future large colonies on Mars.

Slowing his breathing, he tried to let the soothing hot water envelop him, forcing his mind and thoughts to fade until he had no thoughts at all. A short time later he awoke refreshed and clear headed.

CHAPTER 4

Rummaging through the closet for a favorite blue sweatshirt, he was glad to be free from wearing the official uniform made of synthetic materials, a requirement during missions. He loved the feel of his old sweatshirt made of pure Argentine cotton, even though it was starting to fray. Synthetic materials made from recyclables were lightweight, form fitting, and durable. Though he believed in the reuse of materials, he preferred the feel of soft cotton on his skin. Sliding the well-worn sweatshirt over his head, he then pulled on a pair of jeans.

Finally feeling awake and thankful to be home, he could almost taste his mother's cooking. It was the first thing he wanted after any long mission. In her last communication several weeks ago, she was thrilled his father had been offered a consulting position as horticulturist in the food-producing region of Sinaloa near the coastal city of Mazatlán. His father was overzealous when it came to growing food and tending plants. It was his passion and he loved teaching the subject.

His father's expertise in programming agrobots used in modern food production kept him out of retirement. At sixty-seven he still worked for AgriCorp, a consulting firm specializing in agriculture production methods. His passion drove him to work long hours, though his last trip to Australia was followed by a bad coughing spell. Francisco's mother fretted about his father's health, but he doubted the old man would quit.

The display on the kitchen media unit blinked 8:10 AM. If he wanted breakfast as his parent's, he needed to get going. He walked across the concrete kitchen floor to grab his Pcom when small puddles of cold water shocked his bare feet.

"*Mierda*," he cursed and grabbed a nearby hand towel. Throwing it on the floor, he used his foot to mop it haphazardly around hoping to dry the puddles, and then threw the towel in the sink. A pair of loafers sat near the back door. He slipped them on and said, "Secure Main," to the house monitor as he walked out.

The exit unit on the monitor pad beeped. In thirty seconds the house monitor would lock and secure the main house. As Cisco walked across the back patio he noticed last year's wildflowers needed pruned around the garage. Though he encouraged natural plants, his mountainside home showed evidence of his six-month absence. Mentally he put several tasks on a to-do list as he walked to the front of the garage and commanded, "Open." Sunlight filled the garage as the large double doors slid open. Inside, light illuminated a covered vehicle.

Fine dust flew as he pulled the cover off his Corvette XA200 aerocar. Walking around it, he caressed the shiny surface with his fingers. The silver convertible was his 'baby' and most prized possession. It was a luxury he allowed himself in an otherwise minimalistic lifestyle. Sliding into the custom fit driver's seat, his six-foot one-inch frame fit perfectly.

"Startup!" he said.

The onboard computer replied with "Saturday, April 29, 2075."

Automatically the startup sequence completed the pre-flight check. A short clicking sound signaled, before the seat restraints gently grabbed his body.

"Operation mode?" the system asked.

"Manual."

Taking control of the steering stick, he pulled back very gently and floated the convertible out of the garage. Elevating just above tree level, he circled his property just to get the feel of the powerful machine. Lazily circling three times, he inspected the farther ends of his mountainside home. The orchards were green, but one of his two small greenhouses had a rip on a top panel. On the south end, his pond looked as full as he had ever seen it. His mother had communicated to him several months ago about the exceptionally rainy spring.

As he circled the third time, the feel of the powerful aerocar under his control brought a silly grin to his face. He

missed a lot of things about life on Earth, but driving his
XA200 was one of the things he missed the most. His
mother's home cooking was on top of the list.

Glancing at the vehicle's Comsys monitor, no other
vehicles were visible. Goosing the accelerator to maximum
speed, he headed east toward Dublán City's Aeroway
interchange. The sudden force pushed him back against the
headrest as the powerful machine responded to his touch.

Here on the far outskirts of Dublán, Chihuahua,
manual driving was still allowed. As a kid, he listened to his
father and uncles tell stories about the early aerocars. The
world changed dramatically after gas-powered internal
combustion engine vehicles became obsolete. Modern
vehicles utilized a derivative of the particle for the power
source. Once the particle was activated, no effort was
needed to control lift or accelerate to any desired speed.
The particle provided a clean, non-depleting power source.
Early technology originally developed uses of the energy
particles for space travel and energy production. By the
time Francisco was a teenager, it was widely used for
household utilities, cars, planes, and many other
applications.

Since the mid twenty-first century, air quality and
pollution were no longer a political or environmental issue
in most of the world, but replaced by traffic control issues.
With particle powered cars, drivers could fly anywhere at
any altitude and just zip through the sky. In the early days
of aerocars, accidents were deadly and frequent. Sometimes
aerocars and aeroplanes collided. Finally, the multinational
Global Traffic Control Administration was established. The
GTCA and a satellite network brought control over the
chaos. All aerocars came equipped with an onboard
communications system, or Comsys, connected to the
global traffic control system. The GTCA controlled speed
and altitude on all major traffic patterns through the
vehicle's Comsys.

As the Vette sped along, he watched a light wind
push some puffy white clouds south. They gathered at the
top of Picacho del Diablo Peak. It was a sight familiar to

him and today it piqued his soul as it cemented he was finally home. In the far distance, the outline of Dublán City's tall glass towers became visible and he knew he was almost out of manual control space. It was possible to take a remote mountain pass to his parent's house, though Cisco decided against it as he fought fatigue.

Approaching the outskirts of the city, Comsys warned him, "Comsys automatic control imminent."

Nearing the entrance to the busy Dublán aeroway interchange, a click signaled the loss of manual control and Comsys brought the Vette to a hover.

"Destination?" Comsys asked.

"Exit 1452."

Although it was Saturday morning, the aeroway was busy. A number of years ago the traffic system added the ability to fly multiple levels for rush hour traffic, but this morning there was only one level of vehicles. A dark green pop-top Jaguar FX hovered in front of him. In it, an elderly lady with bluish-white hair was putting on lipstick as she waited. Behind her a single-seat Mitsubishi wing interceptor from the Traffic Control Department and the rider, a GTCA officer, looked much like an overgrown insect. Built for speed and maneuverability, the wing interceptors patrolled the traffic ways.

Cisco knew the Mitsubishi wing interceptors used a modified particle allowing them to exceed any aerocar. Aerovehicles were limited to about two hundred kilometers per hour, while the wing interceptors had been clocked at over three hundred. Cisco thought flying one would be a pure kick.

Suddenly unintelligible music blasted the aeroway interchange. The reverberation from the bass echoed in the air. A sleek XKE Supercharger with five young men laughing, jiving, and hollering to the music pulled up behind him. Cisco glanced back and shook his head. Drunk driving problems ceased to be a crime since automated Comsys control of vehicles eliminated a driver's need to be sober or even awake. Many commuters slept or worked on their personal devices while their vehicle flew to its destination.

The car's system signaled a clearance to enter the aeroway lane as the Vette was positioned inline going south. Under Comsys control, the Vette smoothly accelerated to the proper speed. Cisco perused the music menu. Skipping the popular synthesized selections, he picked a classical rock channel and leaned back into the seat.

About 10 minutes later, Comsys alerted him. "Arriving exit 1452. Direction?"

"South."

"Destination?"

"Parents," he replied. The Vette exited the aeroway, turned south, and merged onto a southbound aeropath. His parent's home was located about forty-five kilometers southwest of Dublán City, nestled at the base of Sierra Pamachi near Rio Urique. Knowing the location was programmed into Comsys, he leaned back, closed his eyes, and listened to the music.

"Arriving at destination," Comsys stirred him from a slumber about fifteen minutes later.

CHAPTER 5

Landing on the parking pad, he knew he would find his parents in the kitchen having breakfast and viewing the morning news. They were predictable and this was their Saturday morning routine. Quietly, he walked into the kitchen until he could see his mother's back leaning over the sink. Surprisingly his father was not sitting at the kitchen table and Cisco thought he was out tending the garden.

"Mamá," Cisco snuck near and whispered in her ear.

"¡Mijo! Dios mío," his mother cried out turning to face him with joy written all over her face. "What a surprise. Let me look at you, Francisco," she said grabbing him in a bear hug. "When did you get back?"

"Late last night. It's great to be home."

"Oh, I wish you had told me you were coming today. Your *Papá* left early this morning for Sinaloa. They asked him to go and preview his new job. You know what he is like when he feels needed. He will not refuse even on a Saturday. I am worried he is working too hard at his age, but now you are home, thank God."

"Sounds just like *Papá*. When will he get back?"

"He is supposed to be home tonight in time for a late dinner. If only he had known you were back, maybe he would have stayed home."

"Don't worry so much about him, *Mamá*. You know it does no good and only upsets you. I'm here and I'm craving a chorizo and egg burrito. All I've eaten for the last six months is synthetic space food and right now I want some of your delicious home cooking," he said putting his arm around her shoulder.

"Por supuesto, mijo," she responded, of course, smiling broadly, and then ordered him off to the garden to bring her some onions and several ripe tomatoes.

As he walked out the kitchen door following a path to the large greenhouse, Cisco thought it looked bigger than the last time he visited. It would not surprise him if his father added a new section. The greenhouse had been larger than the main house for years, providing his parents with year round fruits and vegetables. His father experimented with vegetable hybrids of his own breeding – some good and some bad, but he never stopped trying. Entering the greenhouse the smell of newly turned dirt and the sweet smell of blossoms was thick in the humid air.

Curious about the latest addition, he walked to the newly added section where the sound of bubbling water gurgled in a large pond. On top of the pond, blooming lily pads covered one end. Through the clear water, he saw medium size rainbow trout swimming lazily in and out of the lily pads and rocks. Smiling to himself, he was never surprised by his father's love of nature and self-sufficiency.

Walking back to the front of the greenhouse, he gathered several onions and three tomatoes from the prolific vines. The tomato plants grew on a vertical trellis, which could be lowered for picking – another invention to maximize growing space.

When he returned to the house, the kitchen was filled with the sweet, pungent aroma of frying chorizo. "That sure smells good!" Cisco could hardly wait and stole several bites right from the pan almost burning his fingers.

"Stop that," his mother said and grinned as she shooed him to the kitchen table to wait for the tortillas to be cooked.

"I see father built a trout pond in the greenhouse," he said speaking to his mother's back while she chopped the onions.

"Yes, he says fish are getting polluted by the agrifood waste in the water system. He is monitoring these fish and comparing them to commercial samples to prove his theory."

"So they are not for dinner?"

"Well, only after he completes the test. You know nothing goes to waste in this house."

Smiling, he knew what she meant. His parents were unusual in many ways, perhaps a throwback to previous generations when excess was a luxury. They lived almost self-sufficiently in this remote spot. Between his father's gardens and orchards, they grew most of the food they consumed. The chicken coops and composting pits provided the organic fertilizer for all the plants. Cisco often wondered how his father had enough energy to manage all his pet projects.

"I was thinking about asking *Papá* to join me on a fishing trip for black marlin next week, but maybe he won't want to."

"No mijo, I am sure he would love to. It would be good for him to have some fun. He has been working too hard."

As his mother scrambled the eggs into the chorizo and potato mixture, Cisco's stomach rumbled loudly in anticipation. Standing, he took the spoon from her hand and said, "I'll stir while you roll those tortillas. My stomach just can't wait."

A few minutes later, she filled two large burritos placing the plate on the table in front of him. The first burrito he downed in five bites, with the chili and chorizo flavors bursting in his mouth. No synthetic food could ever taste this good, no matter what they did to it. Slowing down he savored bites of the second burrito filled with sausage, mixed with red chile and spices and fried with sliced potatoes and onion.

Victoria Salaz sat across from her youngest son as he devoured the simple breakfast. He looked so much like her husband, Emilio, when he was younger. Both were a little over six feet tall with a lean build. She remembered Emilio's hair as a bit darker than Francisco's, but both heads were topped with unruly wavy, though not what you would call curly hair. Francisco had his father's hazel brown eyes and his infectious grin.

Cisco wiped his plate with the last piece of tortilla. His mouth still wanted more, but his stomach was full. *"Qué delicioso Mamá,"* he said as he pushed the empty plate aside.

"Tell me about your mission, *mijo.* Has the Mars colony grown since you were there last?" she asked him always interested in his adventures. While she scientifically understood space travel, the thought of leaving earth unsettled her. To be truthful, it scared her.

"It's amazing how much progress has been made," he responded. "They're preparing for over 500 colonists to be settled on Mars and survive indefinitely by the 2090s. The new dome design is much larger and the agrodomes are thriving. Father would be so intrigued with the use of the growing spaces. Oxygen generation seems to be resolved, but they are still struggling with water production."

"Indefinitely?" she grimaced. "They will not send you, will they?"

"No Mamá, you can stop worrying. I'm not a colonist," he laughed at her knowing exactly what she was thinking.

"I'm amazed at the progress they're making though. It's fascinating to ponder living on Mars, but I love the Sierra Madre Mountains too much to leave forever," he said.

"Oh, what about me?" she teased him pretending to pout. "What about my home cooking?" Pushing out her chair, she picked up his empty plate and turned toward the sink.

Cisco laughed knowing his mother's humor and grabbed her in a hug swinging her around several times. When he set her down on her feet, they were both laughing hard.

"Do you know your next assignment?" she asked.

"No. Right now I get a nice long rest and plan on eating more of your home cooking."

"So you're on vacation for several weeks?"

"I have almost a month off. Like I said, I want to take Papá fishing."

"Oh yes, I wanted to tell you I ran into Vivian's mother, Florencia, at the store last week. Florencia says Vivian is a big shot for the Department of Health living in the city and she's not married. She asked about you," she said trying to sound nonchalant. Actually, Vivian's mother had asked about Francisco, but Victoria hoped bringing up

Vivian might spark her son to think about his old flame.

She turned and looked at her son directly. At thirty-four, she thought he needed to get married, instead of being content to live on an isolated mountainside and accepting remote missions from the government. She meddled several times, instigating blind dates or inviting a young woman to dinner, but nothing seemed to change him.

Victoria always thought Francisco and Vivian were a perfect match. Both were smart, educated, and seemed interested in similar things. They were so in love and it had reminded her of how she and Emilio fell madly in love practically overnight. She was disappointed when Francisco and Vivian's relationship dwindled.

He chuckled under his breath knowing his mother thought he needed a companion. An image of Monica flashed in his brain. She was an FSA scientist and arrived on Mars several months ago. Petite with perky breasts and a tight ass, Cisco was immediately enthralled. They had spent his last two months in either his bed or hers during off hours.

"You should call Vivian and ask her out." she continued the onslaught.

Vivian Bejarano was Francisco's first teenage love and only serious girlfriend. They attended high school together. Toward the end of their senior year, they fell madly in love. Inseparable, they planned for a future together. Then college started with Francisco at the Chihuahua Institute of Technology and Vivian at La Salle University. By Christmas of their freshman year, he knew they were growing apart and while they tried to keep it together, the relationship quickly dwindled to a friendship.

"*Mamá*, don't start with the match making routine," he grumbled. He had not seen Vivian for many years after they split. She left the country and after La Salle enrolled at Harvard for her doctorate degree. He assumed she might have stayed in Boston or be married by now. Still, an image of Vivian's teenage breasts crossed his mind. A distant memory, but he remembered how awkward he was when he pulled her blouse up and saw them for the first time.

"I am not pushing, just thought it might be nice to see her and catch up since you have some free time. She might like to see you, too." Victoria looked directly at her son with a determined look in her eyes. "I updated the PIC with her new number," she said with a happy grin. "Give her a call, *mijo*. Go on."

"*Mamá* stop pushing. I'm home on leave and just want some peace," he grumbled putting up his left hand to stop his mother's verbal assault.

Victoria turned toward the sink and crossed herself, placed her hand on her heart, and looked up silently asking the Lord for his help. "I'm sorry *mijo*. You know all I want is your happiness."

"No, you just want some more grandchildren. You should bother Eduardo and Celina. They are both married and could give you more grandchildren. Anyway, I have a bunch of errands to run. I'll see you at church tomorrow. Call me when *Papá* gets back. *Te amo,*" he told her he loved her and gave her a big hug.

Victoria kissed him on the cheek. "*Te amo, mijo.*"

As Cisco walked down the long hallway toward the front door, he passed pictures of his brothers, sister, and himself at various stages of youth. He and his siblings laughed at the various school pictures and hilarious achievements their mother kept framed on the wall. Toward the end of the hallway was Cisco and Vivian's prom picture. His mother refused to take it down after they split saying it was part of his life. He stopped and looked at it. They were young and happy. Vivian was beautiful in a mauve low-cut dress, he in a matching tie. It was a time when they had so many plans and dreams.

CHAPTER 6

Valentino Torres, the President of the United Central Republic, sat alone waiting to begin the meeting. He felt every bit of his ninety-two years and perhaps it was time for him to step aside.

Yet it seemed like only a few years ago when he and his assistant, Salvador Salaz, discovered the power of the particle. Their quest and diligence changed Mexico and the world. He felt blessed for having been able to rid so much of the world of strife and poverty and to guide the United Central Republic to its place of dominance in the world. He prided himself that peace was always his objective, not war. Now that peace was in jeopardy.

His mind slipped back to his memories of the quest to find the particle. Those vivid recollections were part of his soul. He and Salvador were geologists at the Chihuahua Institute of Technology in 2027. One day a young Chichimeca Indian man brought two small unremarkable stones in a leather pouch to the Institute. The shy ragged young Indian told them the stones had magic.

To amuse the young man, Valentino and Salvador asked him where he got the magic stones. He said they came from Barrancas del Cobre, an area where the running Tarahumara Indians lived. He was on his way to Atachi from Creel, because he had been told the gold mining operation at Atachi was looking for workers. On the trail to the gold mine, he found a Tarahumara boy with a badly broken ankle. Loading the young boy on his horse, he returned the injured boy to his tribe. In gratitude, the chief gave him this small pouch with three stones. Expecting gems or gold, the small plain stones seemed of no value. He threw one away thinking it was worthless. Then he explained how the small stone flew as if shot from a rifle when he merely tossed it away. Desperate for money to feed his family, the young man begged them to buy the remaining two magic stones. Though skeptical of any magic, Valentino was intrigued and gave the young man two hundred *pesos* from his wallet.

He and Salvador worked diligently to identify the composition of the stones over the next months. They found them nonconforming to anything found on Earth or previously studied. When put into motion by a small force, thrown or shot, the stone would sail for extended distances. When placed on the ground, the stones remained motionless. In an antigravity chamber, Salvador modeled the flight distance to be infinite when the stone was not affected by any gravitational pull. The most interesting characteristic – it never lost energy. There was no depletion of its power and no emission of any substance generating the power – an infinite, pollution-free, energy source.

Realizing the stones great potential, he and Salvador formed a bond of trust and secrecy to find more of the powerful stones. They packed geological equipment and took the train to the end of the line at a small village named Creel. The Rio Oro Gold Mine near the village of Atachi was well established and Valentino asked about local Tarahumara villages. Hiring two horses and mules for the trip, they followed crude instructions to find the Tarahumara village.

Winding through the canyons, they finally found a secluded pueblo. About twelve shabby houses made of random rocks and crudely cut logs surrounded a central plaza, where women were grinding corn under a ramada. A group of six boys were kicking a small brown ball, yelling and screaming with delight in their game.

Winding through the village to the far end, they stopped in front of a better built home. At the entrance, a colorfully woven blanket covered the doorway. Respectfully, they stood outside the door and Salvador called out a greeting in Spanish.

Soon the door covering moved aside and an old man stepped out. *"Kuria,"* he greeted them in the Tarahumara language. A bright red loosely fitting shirt covered part of faded jeans. He wore a straw hat and adjusted rimless eyeglasses. Although his greeting was cordial, his face was drawn and concerned.

"Do you speak Spanish?" Valentino asked him.

"*Sí, soy Cacique Corosia.* Are you with the gold mine company?" Chief Corosia asked suspiciously eyeing the equipment on the mules.

"No, we are with the University in Chihuahua. We are visiting the area on a research project," Valentino responded. Valentino remembered how he pondered ways to approach the chief about the stones. "May we camp at your pueblo for the night?"

The scowl on the chief's face had lifted when Valentino said they were from the university and he invited them to stay. "Yes, follow me. I will show you where you can camp."

As they followed the chief, he walked with his chin high and wore *huaraches* with rubber tire soles. Valentino remembered how the chief and the tire prints in the sandy dirt path had tickled him at the time. The chief led them to the north end of the pueblo where there was a clearing by a stream.

"Tonight is *Omawári.* It is a celebration for the end of the drought and to ask the Gods for a cure to the sickness plaguing our children. You are welcome to attend," the chief told them.

"What sickness?" Valentino asked about the curious comment.

"My grandson and several other children have been ill with odd symptoms. Our *sukurúame* is treating my grandson and says he can cure him. I am not so sure. The illness comes and goes. He is worse again today," the chief said.

"What is a *sukurúame.* Is he a man of medicine?" Salvador asked.

"He is a shaman. He has been treating my grandson with *híkuli,* peyote, to bring the Spirit into him to cure him."

Valentino studied Biology and pre-Med before switching to Geology in his studies at the university. Treating an illness with peyote did not seem prudent.

"What are your grandson's symptoms?" he asked.

"He has headaches. Sometimes when he stands up, he says the world spins around and he falls down and vomits. His skin is flushed red with a rash."

"I am a man of medicine. Maybe I can help. Would you allow me to see the boy? I will not interfere with your shaman," Valentino said respectfully.

While Salvador setup their camp by the stream, Valentino followed the chief. They reached a hut where the boy slept. The shaman chanted and blew incense over the boy's body. The chief told the shaman to allow the stranger to look at the boy. After a few minutes, Valentino motioned for the chief to go outside with him.

"You said other children have been stricken with this illness?"

"Yes, eight other boys have the same sickness in the past several weeks. Why do you ask?"

"By the looks of his skin, I would say your grandson has been poisoned. Can you tell me if the boys were together when they got sick?"

"Yes, they are the same age and are together most of the time, playing and doing chores."

"What were they doing when the illness started?" Valentino asked.

"I believe they were swimming at the pond just above the canyon to the north of here. It is not far."

"I will go to the pond and see what I can find," Valentino told him and went looking for Salvador.

"What is wrong with the boy?" Salvador asked when Valentino returned to the campsite.

"He is weak, dizzy, nauseous, and has a rash. Apparently several boys have similar symptoms."

"That's odd. Were they together when they became ill?" Salvador asked.

"Yes, they were swimming at a water pond north of the village. It is a favorite place for boys to swim and stay most of the day."

"We should go there and have a look," Salvador said.

Valentino and Salvador saddled up and followed the

directions the chief gave them. Just north of the village, in an upper canyon, they found a clear deep blue pond fed from a thin waterfall on the north canyon wall. As it was late in the afternoon, no one was there.

After scouting the perimeter of the pond, Salvador said. "There are no animal tracks. That seems odd for such a pond."

Salvador got down to the pond's edge and tasted the water. It had a slight bitter or acrid taste on his tongue. "Valentino, come down here and taste the water," he called out.

"What do you think?" Valentino asked after he too tasted the bitterness of the water.

"We need to see what is feeding this waterfall," Valentino said. "Let's go back to the village for the night and tomorrow we will go up to the next level of this canyon and see what's up there."

CHAPTER 7

A door in the anti-room opened disturbing the president from his memories. A uniformed guard entered and saluted him.

"Are they ready for me?" Valentino asked.

"Not quite sir. We are still waiting for two Protectors to arrive, but Comsys shows them to be nearby. It might be another ten minutes. Do you need anything before the meeting, sir?"

"No. Thank you. Let me know when everyone is ready."

As the uniformed officer retreated and closed the door behind him, President Valentino Torres sighed. Leading this great country had been a privilege. However, the days spent locating and testing the power in the meteor rocks had been his true life's work.

Those days so many years ago at the village deep within the Copper Canyons were still vivid in his mind. He never envisioned how those months spent there would change not only the country, but his life in so many ways.

After finding the tainted pond, he and Salvador attended the *Omawári* celebration. At dusk a bonfire was lit in the center of the village. Wooden flutes and horns sounded and dancers came out of homes all dressed in traditional *Rarámuri* costumes. Men wore turkey fathers bunched on top of their heads held by red, blue, green and other colorful bandanas. Their entire bodies, including their faces were dotted with a white paint. They wore loincloths with a cloth skirt covering their backside to behind their knees. Each carried a decorated stick resembling a primitive weapon. They danced and pantomimed around the bonfire while the villagers clapped.

He and Salvador sat on a large rock watching the ancient spectacle. Several older Tarahumara women offered them the local corn beer. They told them it was called *tesgüino* and it had a bitter aftertaste.

After breakfast the next morning, Valentino and Salvador gathered their camping gear. They rode to the pond and headed around to the top of the canyon wall to find the source of the waterfall. They followed a stream north, losing it at times but finding it again after careful searching. By nightfall, they heard rumbling sounds of heavy equipment in the distance. Too dark to travel, they settled in for the night.

An explosion woke them early the next morning. It came from another part of the mountain and was followed by several others. When they reached the top of a rise, the Atachi gold mining operation spread out across the mountain. Large bulldozers worked to move the mass amounts of rubble. Above the bulldozers and large earth moving equipment, large buildings with smokestacks spewed gray smoke into the sky. They could see streams of water haphazardly cutting paths through the sandy soil.

It was Salvador who remembered studying gold mining in a Metallurgy class.

"They use cyanide in the refining process. If I remember correctly, it is one of the main chemicals and it must be leaching into the water. We must go and talk to them. They will have to stop," Salvador said.

Valentino shook his head sadly. He knew the ruination of a small village of Tarahumara Indians would not stand in the way of the large gold mining operation. On the way back to the village, Valentino pondered the dilemma. They went directly to find Chief Corosia and the shaman.

They explained the problem to the chief. "We believe some of the chemicals used by the gold mining operation to the north of here are leaking into a creek which feeds into the pond. Each time the boys swim, they are hurt by the chemicals. Soon it will affect everyone, as the chemicals will leak into the water you drink. With your permission, we can send for the proper authorities to deal with the mine management. I believe they can find a way to ensure your water supply is not tainted," Valentino told him.

"And if they do not?" the chief asked.

"Either you and your village must move or you will all die," Salvador told him.

It was not unexpected that the chief refused to contemplate moving from the location where the tribe had lived for centuries. He gave Valentino permission to contact the authorities.

It was not as easy as it sounded, but a number of months later the gold mine relented and built a retaining pond for their runoff. The authorities tested and retested the village's water supply. Valentino stayed in the village most of the next six months working with the authorities and the chief, while Salvador returned to Chihuahua.

It was during these months, having gained the trust of the chief and the shaman, he was allowed to find the meteor site. The location had been a religious shrine for the tribe for over several hundred years as explained by the chief.

"In our tradition, when a young warrior comes of age they must prove themselves worthy. They must live off the land and suffer cold nights or hot days to find their *tonalli*, their destiny. They eat the belladonna berries to seek their vision. Many, many years ago, a young warrior was on such a quest, as our ancestors have done for hundreds of years. He ate the berries and prayed to our Gods. On the fifth night into his journey, a gigantic light crossed the moonless night sky, from the north toward the south. Many brilliant colors danced along its tail and its light illuminated the dark sky before it disappeared into one of the canyons. The young warrior realized the dancing lights were his quest. Searching for the source, he came upon a spot on the south end of a small canyon blackened and cratered by an impact. There he found the magic rocks, some big and some small. He returned to the village with a pouch of the stones with great power. Since then, we honor the rocks in our religious ceremonies."

Valentino explained the source of the light was a meteor burning up in the atmosphere as it fell to earth. The meteor rock could be a piece of a star from a distant solar system. The shaman called the event, Spirit of the Dancing

Lights.

The shaman, who called himself a *nagual* or a sorcerer, believed Valentino had been sent by the Gods, as was his belief. Valentino had saved the village from the terrible curse. With the chief's blessing, he and the local shaman, Genaro, spent many months testing and gathering the meteor rock.

While Valentino stayed in the Tarahumara village for almost six months, Salvador returned to Chihuahua and began tedious testing. Valentino found the meteor fragments spread over a wide area. As the meteor crash had happened in the late 1700s, natural brush and soil had reclaimed the ground. The shaman and several men from the tribe helped Valentino dig, sift, and bag the rocks. Once a month, Salvador would make the journey to the remote site and take it to a secure site near Chihuahua.

Valentino developed a deep friendship with Genaro and revered his knowledge as a shaman. It was during those months, he found himself fascinated in the rituals and beliefs of the shaman. On the surface they seemed simple, but the centuries of his belief system was anything but simple. Genaro took him as a student and taught him the ways of *naguals* of ancient Mexico. He found himself having visions. At first he thought them just dreams, but Genaro helped him to sharpen his meditation method to allow his spirit to soar.

Shaking his head, Valentino cleared the memories from his brain. It was a long time ago and much had changed. The Republic and the world were in danger from an unknown entity, but his visions were again clear.

The door opened again and the uniformed guard saluted and told him the group was ready. Valentino stood and walked into the waiting conference room.

CHAPTER 8

Emilio Salaz, Francisco's father, sat in a private conference room at the top floor of the United Central Republic Security building in a confused anticipation. An encrypted call late last night alerted him to this meeting of the Protectors, as they called themselves. Once again Emilio lied to his wife, telling her he was going to Sinaloa to check on the consulting job. Instead, here he sat at a large table with the other Protectors of the Republic awaiting a meeting with the president. While several of the Protectors chatted while they waited for everyone to arrive, Emilio was deep in his own thoughts.

The Protectors were a secret, elite group of men and women who had sworn to protect the United Central Republic's sovereignty over the peaceful use of the energy particle. They were the protectors of the faith so to speak and the inner circle of the president's most trusted allies. Some of the older Protectors worked with President Torres to form the Republic in August of 2044. Emilio looked at the graying heads around the table. With the exception of himself, General Roberto Castillo the Republic's Commander of the Military, and Miguel Arias the Head of Security the group were well up in their late seventies and eighties. Both he and Roberto were sons of the original members.

Emilio's father, Salvador, instilled every detail of the history of the energy particle. A geologist, Salvador worked under Professor Valentino Torres' tutelage at the Chihuahua Institute of Technology. Together they traveled to the remote Indian village and located the meteor crash location. In a secret trust, Valentino and Salvador retrieved and learned to harness the power of the rocks. It was their effort which developed the meteor rock into an energy source.

Emilio learned the story and the secrets from his father years ago. The discovery and development of the new power changed the world in so many ways. It was

during the Oil Wars and the world was on the brink of
disaster. When Valentino, now the president of this great
Republic, and Emilio's father were finally allowed to enter
the sacred canyon, they began painstaking experiments. It
was 2029 and the world was diving headlong into turmoil.
After a global virus pandemic in the early 2020s, the
resulting global recession was barely recovering before
disaster struck. Pushing their nuclear capabilities, Iran had a
catastrophic nuclear accident in March of 2027,
contaminating most of the Middle East and killing millions
of people immediately. Most of Iran, Iraq, Syria, Jordan,
and Israel were unlivable.

The nuclear fallout affected about a billion people. A
massive migration of people from the region swarmed into
other parts of Europe and Russia. The European Union
quickly went bankrupt trying to absorb the immigrants. In
addition to the loss of life, much of the precious oil
producing region was destroyed. Underground fires burned
the available oil further polluting the environment.
Radiation contaminated the ground water and land. Much
of the Middle East became a wasteland.

Without OPEC oil, the Oil Wars began. Although
electric vehicles had vastly replaced fossil fuel burning
vehicles by 2030, the electric power generation plants were
maximized to provide the electricity and that meant oil.

Desperate for the petroleum to power the world, oil
became the single most coveted resource. For a while, the
shortage helped countries like Canada, Venezuela and the
United States of America to prosper, as they had oil
reserves underground and in the form of hydraulic
fracking. However, the United States and Canadian
governments were heavily in debt from rampant financial
recession and years of living on spiraling debt. The United
States went essentially bankrupt in the year 2036. The law
of the Wild West gun returned to the streets of America as
chaos shook the country. People shot first and asked
questions later. Gang wars broke out in the larger cities,
pitting one ethnic group against another. Canada fared only
a little better.

Mexico was not spared from the growing crisis of its neighbors to the north. People in the larger cities suffered more than the rural areas, which had always lived simple and off the land. The only economy that rebounded in South America was Venezuela, which emerged from a deep depression after many decades under a Socialist dictatorship. Oil was valuable and oil-rich Venezuela was the recipient of renewed wealth.

Emilio remembered when his father moved the family to a remote piece of land on the east side of Sierra Pamachi near the Rio Urique River. His father worked at the University in Chihuahua, but felt the mountainside property safer for the family. At first living in the hastily built wooden house was fun for young Emilio. He was fifteen and thought hunting and exploring the mountainside was a great game. As the oldest, he helped his mother home school his younger brother and sister, though some winter nights he remembered going to bed cold and hungry as his father studied and worked long hours.

It was not until years later when Emilio learned his father was working with Valentino Torres on the energy particle. Theirs was a sworn camaraderie of trust and exhausting work. Emilio remembered many long months when his father was not at home. The second autumn, Emilio helped his father build a covered greenhouse to keep the plants safe and warm. Looking back, those years helping in the greenhouse cemented Emilio's love of growing food. It was his home now, high up Sierra Pamachi and the home and greenhouse his pride and joy.

In 2042 Valentino and Salvador, along with a small group of hand-selected scientists, finally perfected a method to harness the energy particle from the meteor stones. Encased in a titanium vessel, a minuscule piece could be controlled.

The first application provided the necessary energy for power plants to generate electricity in Mexico. As technology of the particle advanced, Mexico's prosperity grew. Large power plants were converted to the particle and uses of the particle became available for other commercial uses within Mexico. After the Oil Wars, the once global super powers clamored for the technology.

It was Valentino's vision and wisdom, which led to the creation of the United Central Republic. It was his vow to create the new Republic encompassing some northern states of Mexico and to purchase the American Southwest as part of a deal with the United States for access to the new energy technology. He was elected almost unanimously as the first president of the Republic, a position which he held since the beginning. The people of Mexico heralded the new Republic, which was often referred to as the Jalapeño Republic. Though mostly peaceful now, tensions between the people once living in the United States and people from Mexico were heated for many years after the realignment of the territory. All out war broke out on the streets of Los Angeles and El Paso, with both countries trying to restore calm.

Emilio's family was subject to the tension directly. His wife, Victoria, grew up in Santa Barbara, California. He met her at the university there and they wed in 2033. After the purchase of Southern California by the Republic, her family disowned her. Though now they all lived in the same country, the United Central Republic, Victoria's family never spoke to her again. When her parents died, she was not invited to attend the funerals.

The United States, now known as the Federated States of America or FSA, had recovered and prospered. Relations between the governments of the FSA and the Jalapeño Republic were good, though many people, like Victoria's family, still carried bitterness.

As technology began to apply to varied uses for the new energy, the Republic created the Global Energy Core to administer the use of particle. Within a few years of cooperation, the greatest scientific minds had transformed the world, finding unlimited uses for the non-polluting, non-depleting energy source.

At first, the Republic simply allowed the energy to be used under their control without reimbursement from the financially broke superpowers. Within a few years, economies were thriving again as the energy particle brought peace, cooperation, and economic global recovery. As the world economies flourished, the United Central Republic became the world's largest super power.

The Republic maintained the stockpile in a secure location, known only to these few men and women surrounding the table. President Valentino Torres swore never to allow the particle's power to be used for war or weapons.

Several times over the years, that policy had been tested, but the group assembled in this room and the Global Energy Core quelled the attacks. Emilio sat pondering why the Protectors had been called together and wondered if the peaceful use of the particle was again under attack.

When his father, Salvador, was near death, he confided the sacred trust of the Protectors to him. "You and your offspring are forever intertwined with Valentino and the power of this new energy. It is a sacred trust and bond between us to never let the power source be used for anything but peaceful purposes," his father told him. Emilio took his father's place with the Protectors upon his father's death.

Someday he would confide this sacred trust to his son, Francisco. Although not his oldest son, he knew in his heart Francisco would proudly carry on the tradition. He knew it when he held his tiny son shortly after birth and why he asked Valentino to be the boy's godfather.

The door swung open and President Valentino Torres walked into the room. The buzzing of conversations abruptly stopped. The old president looked all of his ninety-two years, though his eyes were still sharp and his step strong.

When President Torres walked to his place at the large table, the room became quiet. He looked at the graying Protectors; these men and women were like his brothers and sisters. With their diligence and secrecy, the energy source had changed the world.

"Gentlemen, ladies," he began. "Once again we are under attack. Unfortunately, this time I believe the attack is internal and not external." A collective mutter filled the room.

"Is the stockpile safe?' General Roberto Castillo asked immediately.

"Yes, the stockpile is safe, as is the Republic," the president replied. "It is I who is under attack. My great-granddaughter, Maya, has been kidnapped and the ransom is the control of the Republic. They will kill her if I do not step down within the next two weeks and abdicate power."

CHAPTER 9

The sun was directly overhead and shining brightly through a cloudless blue sky when Cisco lifted the Vette from the pad at his parent's home and headed to Dublán. The bright sun stung his face and eyes and he knew he should use his helmet or put up the convertible's top, but the feeling of natural sunlight was too gratifying. On sunny days, Earth's pollution free atmosphere intensified the sun's radiation, but after six months in the enclosed domes of Mars, the feel of wind on his face was a simple joy. The Corvette zipped back toward the aeroway and caught the southbound loop corridor heading into the city.

"Destination?" Comsys asked.

"Old Town Plaza Parking."

The Vette's navigation smoothly guided the convertible toward a multilevel parking lot near the town square and after engaging the landing tripods gently set it down beside a parking meter.

"Arriving, Old Town Plaza Parking Garage," Comsys announced.

Climbing out of the Vette he commanded, "Lock." After a few clicks, the Comsys and the vehicle's display panel turned red.

Stepping out of the dark parking structure at street level, the plaza in Old Town was alive with Saturday morning commotion. Street vendors lined the sidewalks with their carts, parents brought their children to watch the puppet shows, and musicians played for coins. The older town of Dublán had changed little since he was a boy and remained much as it was around the turn of the twenty-first century.

Old Town Dublán did not have the modern sanitized look of the steel and glass Dublán City, the capital of the United Central Republic. Here the buildings were made of brown adobe, concrete, or lumber, most covered with stucco facades. None were over three stories high. The large grassy plaza teemed with children and dogs. Mothers, fathers, and grandparents sat on benches in the shade and watched them play. The old Iglesia Santo Niño Church sat on the north end of the plaza. It had been built in the late 1800s, burned down, and rebuilt and enlarged several times over the years. The bell tower was the tallest structure around the plaza, pushing upward into the clear blue sky.

The Plaza Hotel constructed of white stucco under a rustic red tile roof, set it apart from the rest of the town. In a courtyard, bistro tables with small red umbrellas provided an outdoor eating area. Today almost all the tables were full, the people smiling and talking.

As he turned the corner, he noticed two military vehicles parked near the busy plaza, while two armed soldiers stood guard. They seemed to act casual, smiling at the children. It was odd to see any armed soldiers in Old Town, which was generally considered a neutral zone. Old Town functioned like its name. Off the plaza, smoke-filled pool halls, a couple titty bars, and some rowdy pubs allowed gambling and other vices. Street vendors sold black market goods, locals were allowed to sell homemade and homegrown items, and cash was still accepted. Authorities from the government mostly looked the other way, unless there was a killing or a young politician or security officer made trouble trying to drum up votes. These skirmishes left Old Town with a few bumps and bruises, but then life went on as usual.

Cisco had been coming to Old Town as long as he could remember. His father brought him here for haircuts and on shopping trips. On Christmas Eve before midnight Mass, the entire family would come to Old Town to admire the beautiful display of *farolitos*. Thousands of paper bags, half-filled with sand holding a lit candle illuminated the entire town. The *farolitos* outlined rooftops, lined walls and sidewalks, and turned Old Town into Christmas magic. This past Christmas Eve, he watched computer images of the *farolito* lined streets alone from his small pod in a Mars dome.

Saturdays were market day on the plaza. Vendors setup carts with fruits, vegetables, empanadas, ice cream and other sweet treats, flowers, and a variety of other fresh handmade items. You could readily buy non-manufactured food from a number of small farmers. The Global Food Administration, GFA, tried to shutdown independent farmers, forcing them to sell out to the large industrial food brokers, but thankfully the farmers' independent spirit prevailed. However, Old Town was the only place in Dublán City where farm fresh foods were still sold commercially.

When he was a boy, he enjoyed exploring Old Town on his own while Rudy Garcia cut his father's hair. He hunted through the toyshops looking for small antique cars called Matchbox. A Matchbox 1977 silver Corvette still sat on his dresser at home, most likely the reason he decided to buy the XA200.

One summer day when he was about eight, he came with his father to Old Town. His father gave him a few dollars to spend on the plaza while he was at the barber. Today, as always, coming to Old Town brought back an old memory. He had been walking on the plaza with an ice cream, when a pair of *maldito* street boys pushed him into a small alleyway. "Give me your money," the taller boy said. The second boy was not as tall, but held his fists tight and ready to fight.

Cisco refused and tried to hold his ground, but they left him with a bloody nose, a welt under his eye, and without his money. By the time he got back to the barbershop to find his father, Cisco's eye was already turning black. It was not long after that incident his father enrolled him in the Ukidokan Warrior School of Martial Arts here in Old Town.

It was intimidating at first, watching the other boys at the karate school punch and kick at each other. He sometimes wrestled with his older brother, but was not generally the aggressor. The teacher explained how karate was generally a defensive sport. He patiently taught Cisco the importance of balance and how to find one's center of gravity.

"You are stronger when your body is in balance," the

teacher told the class over and over. By the time Cisco earned his orange belt he was hooked and earned his first black belt when he was seventeen. Karate was now just a part of his being, like breathing or eating.

As he passed by the two military guards on the corner of Piedras Street, they glanced briefly at him without expression. Strolling down the sidewalk, he turned into Garcia's barbershop expecting to have to wait for a chair. Instead, the barbershop was empty. Pedro Fuentes, a short man with a round jolly face, was sweeping around the barber chair singing an old Mexican drinking song. Pedro bought the barbershop when Rudy Garcia retired many years ago, but never changed the name. When the door jingled, Pedro looked up. His face lit up with a bright grin.

"Ese, Panchito. ¿Qué tal chico?" the barber greeted Cisco using Spanish street slang. "Good to see you again sonny! Come, take this chair by the window. You came at a good time."

"Hola Pedro," Cisco greeted the barber. "Why is business so slow on a Saturday morning?"

The barber's face beamed with excitement and his voice lowered as if someone would hear him. *"Ese,* something is happening in the Republic, something big. *La RSPA* is everywhere. No one here knows what's happening." The Republic's Security Police Agency, known as *la RSPA,* was a part of the Republic's military, higher in rank than the local police department. It was highly unusual for *la RSPA* to be patrolling in Old Town. The barbershop was the center of gossip in Old Town, so if Pedro did not know what was going on, it was pretty clear the government was being tight-lipped.

"It's probably just drills. You always think the government is up to something, Pedro." Cisco shifted uncomfortably in the chair as Pedro draped a cover over him. Trying to act nonchalant, Cisco internally wondered what the hell was going on. First, the high security alert last night at the reentry center, then his G90 meeting this afternoon, and now Old Town was under surveillance by *la RSPA.*

"I just saw a couple of military jeeps parked by the plaza and a couple soldiers walking around," Cisco replied keeping his voice indifferent.

"Yes, they have been here since Thursday and people are getting nervous. What about you *Panchito*? I have not seen you for a while. Where have you been?"

"I was on assignment," Cisco replied vaguely not wanting to start a conversation about his time on Mars. If he told Pedro about going into space again, the barber would ask him a million questions.

"You want a shave, too?" Pedro asked.

"Yes, you better clean me up good."

Pedro whistled while he snipped. Cisco never worried much about a style. A basic chop at his unruly mop was fine. Vivian used to nag him for coming to the Old Town barber and wanted him to go to a hair salon in Dublán City for a 'style' though Pedro's cut was more to his liking.

"What about your *Papá?*" Pedro asked. "He has not been here lately either."

"*Papá's* fine. He is in Sinaloa working on an agrofarm for the food growers. I haven't seen him since I've been home."

The doorbell tinkled and a middle-aged man walked in. *"Hola Pedro,"* he greeted the barber.

"Hola, Gonzalo," the barber said. The man sank into a well-worn sagging seat against the wall.

"Pedro, did you hear *la RSPA* rounded up a couple of the local *vatos* last night and they are still being held. The Republic doesn't push muscle in Old Town unless it's something really big," Gonzalo said talking to the barber.

Gonzalo's use of the term *vato* was common in Old Town referring to members of the local lowrider club. It was old *Chicano* slang from the 1950s. While *vato* could mean 'dude' or 'guy' it was commonly used in Old Town to refer to the locals who spoke street slang and dressed in gang styles. Not really gangsters or outlaws, the local *vatos* were more like a throw-back to an earlier time and added local color, driving unique lowriders around town.

Pedro's attention turned completely to Gonzalo and

the scissors stopped clipping Cisco's hair.

"No way, *ese*," the barber said in street jargon. "Was it that gang of lowrider *vatos* from up north? I heard they moved into Los Rosas Motel, you know that one out at the edge of town. The local *vatos*, they don't want no new muscle in town."

"Maybe *la RSPA* is here to stop another gang war," Gonzalo said. "I heard their rides are really sharp."

Pedro stopped cutting again and walked around to look directly at Cisco. "You heard anything *Panchito*?"

Cisco shrugged his shoulders. "It sounds serious, but I have no idea what's going on. I just got home yesterday. Anyhow, I'm on rest and relaxation for a couple weeks and all I want to think about is fishing."

The barber's dark eyes frowned at him. He knew Cisco worked for the government, for some agency, but not the police or military. Pedro assumed Cisco knew more than he was telling and wanted to pry.

"Hey," Cisco changed the subject. "Have you seen my *tío* Charley? He hasn't left town has he?"

The barber's face lit up with a mischievous grin. "*¡Caramba! Ese carajo.* I meant to tell you right off. Your uncle is a sly one. *Qué macho, ese vato. El Charley, tiene tanates grandototes.*"

The jolly barber's assessment of the size of his Uncle Charley's balls tickled him. Charley lived life to the fullest, perhaps could be considered a *picaro*, engaging in gambling, drinking, and chasing women. More than once he spent time in jail for some offense, but only minor stuff.

"Let me tell you what that *cabrón* did, *ese*. They say he played poker with those Española, New Mexico outlaw *vatos* who moved in over at Los Rosas. He won a bunch of their money and stole one of their *ranflas,* you know one of their lowriders. It was the leader's best car, *ese*. Those *vatos* are after his ass big time."

"*Sí,* it's a good thing he has lots of friends here. Those *vatos* from Española are bad news," Gonzalo chimed in.

"*Sí* and it gets better, *ese*. I guess the *vato's* girl friend took a shine to Charley. He fought his way out of the pool hall and took off in the *ranfla* with the *chica*." The barber chuckled as he told the story.

"So, that's why those outlaws from Española are still here in Old Town? They want her back?" Cisco asked.

"Maybe, *ese*. Some people in town are mad at Charley because the *vatos* are causing a lot of trouble, but you know your *tío, ese*. He won't give her or the *ranfla* up. The local *vatos* are on his side and are protecting him and the girl. Me, I think the local *vatos* like having a reason to cause trouble."

"Do you know where he is?"

"Word is he's holed up at the El Cortez Hotel. You be careful if you go there *Panchito*. I heard he has big-time protection," the barber warned.

Pedro finished Cisco's shave and wiped all the soap from his chin. After the barber dusted the back of his neck with a scented powder brush he said, *"Bueno Panchito*. You are handsome again, *ese*," and handed him a small hand mirror.

"Perfecto, gracias Pedro. Charge it to my account."

"Adiós, ese. Remember, you be careful if you're going to see Charley."

"I will, thanks."

CHAPTER 10

When Cisco walked out of the barbershop, the Saturday farmers' market was in full swing at the plaza. A line of children stood at a street vendor selling ice cream treats, while their mothers watched quietly enjoying the warm spring day. He grumbled for not bringing his Blocray sunglasses to protect his sensitive eyes from the bright noon sun. Nevertheless, the light breeze, warm sun, and the open sky invigorated his space weary body and soul.

On the far side of the plaza, the two armed military policemen strolled slowly in the crowd, their rifles slung over their backs in a non-threatening way. Children were playing a game of tag-your-it in the central plaza. Their childish yells and screams were a delight to his ears. Two *ranflas* slowly drove along the road on the east side of the plaza. The drivers of the brightly painted lowriders were playing music and entertaining the people.

Around the Old Town plaza, obsolete parking meters stood watch on the scene in which they participated when gasoline cars roamed the streets. The city voted to force all aerocars to use the modern parking garage. Antique and retrofitted *ranflas* could drive on the ground. They were allowed to drive on tires and park at street level anywhere in town. It added to the charm of the area.

Some of the local *vatos* retrofitted modern aerocars with tires and the ability to travel on both the ground, as well as in the air. The cars were elaborately painted in bright colors, with shiny chrome adornments. Many had been chopped and rewelded into unusual shapes and sizes. They called this new breed of aerocars, riders, though most people interchanged the term lowrider and rider, for short to mean any car that embraced the Chicano style. Locals called them *ranflas*.

The owners of the cars were also referred to as lowriders or *vatos,* in reference to a tradition started by Chicano gangs in Los Angeles in the 1950s. On Saturday nights, the lowriders paraded around the Old Town plaza taking young girls for rides as spectators enjoyed the show. It stemmed from an old Spanish custom when *señoritas* rode in decorated carriages and *caballeros* strutted on horseback to catch the young unmarried *señoritas'* attention. The ritual had only changed the mode of transportation.

The *vatos* were part of the local life here in Old Town. Not criminals, but the local tough guys mostly flexed more muscle than brains. They worked for the local businesses by day and drove the colorful cars around town at night. Cisco always thought the two ruffian boys who accosted him for his money when he was eight, possibly now ran with one of the local groups of lowriders. He chuckled when one of the brightly painted cars sounded a loud rhythmic horn blast as they neared the armed guards, making one of the guards skip a step. Pedro was right when he said the local *vato* gang would not like the presence *la RSPA* in Old Town, especially if they arrested one of their *vatos*.

The old plaza clock showed 1:10 PM, if that was correct. The G90 meeting was at 4:45 PM and he needed to get home for a quick shower and change of clothes, but was intrigued by the barber's story about his uncle. His mother's youngest brother had always run with a different crowd, lived in Old Town, and embraced the past. His mother called her brother a *picaro* although Cisco knew she loved Charley dearly. Deciding he had time for a quick trip to check in on Charley before heading home, he bought two ripe melons he knew his uncle liked.

The El Cortez Hotel sat a few blocks off the main plaza. The building was old and the lobby somewhat shabby. No longer a tourist hotel, it now was available for permanent guests. Cisco wondered why Charley, who lived in a small house on Encino Avenue not too far away, was staying in the hotel instead. It was quiet as he walked into the dim lobby. Behind the counter a clerk hunched over paper work. His face was unshaven and his blue shirt looked slept in.

"*Hola,* can you tell me what room Charley Arambula is in?" Cisco asked startling the clerk.

There was redness in his eyes and his hair was oily and unkempt. The tired young man took a quick glance and responded as he continued shuffling papers. "Who are you?"

"Charley's my uncle."

The clerk looked up suspiciously sizing him up for a long minute. Dressed in the old sweatshirt and jeans Cisco did not look like a *vato*.

"Well, he's rented the entire top floor. That *cabrón* won't let anyone up there, not even the maids. I'm not supposed to let anyone go up, but it's your funeral," he said with a shrug.

Cisco chuckled to himself waiting for the antique elevator. The old pulley elevator groaned to a stop and the doors opened. Pushing a button for the third floor, the doors slowly closed. With a loud ding, the elevator stopped and the doors opened. A large man with tattoos on his arms and neck came to his feet and stomped toward the elevator with a seriously mean look in his eyes as Cisco stepped out.

"*¿Ese puto, qué ghingado quedes aqi?*" Mean Look yelled at Cisco asking what the fuck he was doing here.

"*Ver a mi tío,*" Cisco replied he came to see his uncle. Mean Look grumbled something and made a move to push him back into the elevator.

By instinct Cisco dodged the large hand of Charley's mean-looking guard. The many years of karate allowed him to deftly respond to the man's actions. The guard took an awkward swing, missing Cisco's face, but caught the grocery bag. With a smack it fell to the floor.

"I only want to see my *tío,*" Cisco told him again, but the man seemed bent on his mission. No doubt Charley hired him to stop anyone trying to come up. Mean Look sprang forward again with a right cross. Easily sidestepping the punch, Cisco responded by chopping Mean Look across the side of the neck with a right hammer fist. The large bodyguard fell to his knees, before hitting the floor face down.

"Some bodyguard," he chuckled to himself picking

up the bag of smashed melons.

The door to the penthouse stood slightly ajar. Cisco slowly pushed it with caution. His uncle might be armed and might shoot first and ask questions later. Stepping into the room, Cisco called out, *"¡Tío!"*

Suddenly a pair of large muscular hands grabbed him in a painful headlock. *"Pinche* space cadet!" the owner of the hands said. While the large hands continued applying pressure on the headlock, the owner of the hands laughed.

"Tío. . o. . o," Cisco croaked under his uncle's grip.

Charley Arambula laughed enjoying Cisco's predicament. Finally, the large hands let go of the headlock and grabbed Cisco in a bear hug.

"Good to see you space cadet," Charley said teasingly with a huge grin. Charley was always happy and good-natured, with a huge zest for life. It was a quality Cisco thoroughly enjoyed about him.

Charley looked down the hallway to where Mean Look was lying on the carpet. "I hope you didn't kill Chuco, space cadet," Charley said.

"He'll have a headache when he wakes up, but he'll be okay. Not a very good body guard."

"Lucky for me the *vatos* who want me dead are not as good as you," Charley chuckled. "What's in the bag?"

"They were your favorite melons." Charley took the bag and set it on the counter.

"Why are you living here? I heard a story from Pedro the barber about a run in with some *vatos* from Española."

"Mercedes, come out here and meet my nephew," Charley hollered at the closed bedroom door.

"Is that the girl you took from the Española outlaws? Pedro said you stole a *ranfla* and took off with a girl. You really know how to stir things up."

"Pedro likes to gossip. I won the *ranfla* fair and square. Mercedes was looking for a way out of the gang and jumped at the chance to leave. I didn't force her, she begged me to protect her. I decided to stay here until things blow over. It's harder to protect her at the house, though I guess I might need another bodyguard. Mercedes, come out here and meet my nephew," he hollered toward the closed door. "She doesn't like to be seen without makeup and her hair done," Charley explained shrugging. "She'll be out when she's ready."

"Tell me, space cadet, how's your *mamá*? I haven't seen her in a while." Charley picked up the leaking, wet grocery bag and dumped it into the kitchen sink. "I want to see her, but you know your mother. She always lectures me on how I'm wasting my life away and that I should be married with a family. If she knew this latest adventure, she'd never get off my back!"

"Yes, I know what you mean *tío*. *Mamá* is doing it to me now. She's trying to get me married." They laughed knowing Victoria enjoyed fussing over her younger brother as well as her youngest son. Charley put his arm around Cisco's neck and pulled him to the bar where he poured two shots of tequila.

"*Salud,*" they toasted and downed the shot in unison. The smooth *añejo* tequila seared Cisco's throat as it went down. He was not much of a drinker, mostly beer, and held back a grimace hoping his uncle would not notice. Charley laughed, slapped him on the back, and poured another round. Charley downed the second shot in a single gulp, while Cisco let his shot glass sit on the bar.

"When are you going to grow some balls and drink like a man?" Charley chided him. "You, a big-time space cadet and you drink like a girl."

"I have a meeting later this afternoon, *tío*. I . . . I can't get drunk. Tell me what happened with the lowrider *vatos.*"

"Well, let me tell you. A bunch of lowlife outlaws from Española, New Mexico, came to town to make trouble. They took over Los Rosas Motel. The locals were mad, but those chicken shits wouldn't do anything about it," Charley began. "So I went to Los Rosas to see if I could take a little money from those *pendejos.*"

"And probably start a little trouble," Cisco interjected knowing his uncle well. Charley chuckled and gave him a wink.

"Word on the street was those *vatos* considered

themselves good poker players, so hey I was more than happy to let them show me how good they were." Charley poured himself another shot before he continued.

"You know how it is, space cadet. I played them for a while letting them win. They were convinced they had a real sucker. One of their pretty *vatas* made sure I always had a full shot of tequila trying to get me drunk and you know how I don't like this stuff!"

He chuckled again and saluted with his tequila shot glass. Cisco had seen his uncle drink a bottle of tequila once and not seem drunk at all. When it came to tequila, Charley could drink anyone under the table.

"I acted like the tequila was getting to me and made the *vatos* drink me shot for shot. I let them win some and lose some, you know the game I play, space cadet." Cisco nodded knowing his uncle was a gambler with the best of them.

"When I thought they had enough tequila in them to even the odds, I started taking their money. Finally, the leader put up his *ranfla* on a hand he thought he had me beat. He threw the key fob on the pile of money." Charley stopped the story long enough to down another shot.

"I had four queens," Charley chuckled. "They came after me, but the two big *vatos* were staggering from the tequila. Hey, I was ready. I grabbed the money and the key fob, overturned the card table, had one of those smoke grenades in my pocket, and threw it toward the exit. As I headed for the door, someone grabbed my arm. I whirled around ready to smack whoever it was, when I saw it was a young girl. She pleaded with me to take her, grabbed the key fob from my hand, and started running."

"Pedro said you stole her from the outlaws. It sounds like she stole you."

"The *vatos* were right behind us. I ran behind her and we jumped into a red *ranfla* and took off." Charley poured another shot into his glass. "There was a hell of a chase, but I lost them by zigzagging around the old buildings here on the west side of Old Town."

Cisco knew Charley was familiar with every street,

alley, and hiding spot in Old Town.

"I didn't want to take her, but there was no other choice. Finally, I got my chance to escape to the mountains. We holed up near Rio Urique for a couple days."

It was exactly the type of trouble his uncle always seemed to attract. Charley was really a good man, a bit of a cad, a gambler, but not a criminal. Cisco often thought Charley should someday write a story about his life.

"What about the girl?" Cisco asked.

"Well now. That's an even more interesting story. Mercedes told me how the outlaw gang had taken her. It happened during a big gang fight at the Taylor Ranch Shopping Mall on the west side of Albuquerque over a year ago. Her parents had taken her shopping for school clothes when they were caught in a vicious crossfire. When her father tried to help a boy who was wounded, they shot him for no reason. She seems to have a mental block about what happened next, but evidently they kidnapped her. She doesn't know what happened to her mother."

"*¡Ghingado!* Those stupid outlaws," Cisco cursed.

Charley nodded in agreement taking another shot of tequila. "After a couple days in Rio Urique, I took her back to Albuquerque to look for her mother. We finally found her at a private mental clinic. It was awful. Her mother didn't even recognize her. Mercedes told me her mother was about forty-four years old, but when we saw her, she looked like an eighty-year-old zombie. Mercedes went crazy."

Charley stared out the window and appeared to be pondering something. "The whole situation was sickening," he went on after the pause. "I didn't know what to do for her or with her. She said her life was worthless and not worth anything to anybody. She has no one, except a distant uncle in Minnesota. She mostly stayed in bed and would not eat. I tried to be understanding, but I was getting restless and needed to get back here to Old Town. Finally, I told her to get herself together or I'd leave her behind. She told me to go away, but how could I just leave her?"

Cisco tried to think of something to say, but there

was nothing. Charley's dark eyes were sad as he spoke of Mercedes' kidnapping and finding her mother. It was an emotional side he seldom showed.

After another small pause he continued, "I finally promised to find her a safe place, so we went to Keno Bay for a few days. We took long walks where the beach is still deserted. We swam naked in the surf and made love on the warm sand." Charley stopped to smile. "You don't want to hear about that. Anyway, we fell in love. What do you think of that, space cadet?"

The story amazed Cisco and he found it hard to believe his uncle was finally in love. Charley was the family *cabrón,* and no one thought he would ever settle down.

"Why did you come back to Old Town? Obviously the Española gang is still here and just waiting for a chance to get you."

"I had to come back. Everything I own is here. This is my town and I have protection. Besides those *bandidos* will tire of this game and move on. The local *vatos* will take care of those outlaws."

Just then the bedroom door opened and a beautiful young woman entered the room. The makeup on her face was perfect, her long brown hair falling over her shoulders glinting golden in the sunlight of the room. Her mysterious green eyes studied Cisco as she floated toward Charley. "Mercedes," Charley said tenderly, "This space cadet is my nephew Francisco. Cisco this is my love, Mercedes."

Cisco stood, took her hand, bowed, and kissed her hand gently in an old fashioned way. "I am honored to meet you Mercedes. My uncle is a lucky man."

"I am the lucky one," she responded putting her hand on Charley's shoulder. Charley blushed a shade of red visible through his bronze skin.

"Why does he call you space cadet?" she asked smiling. Her voice was melodic and her smile lit up her face.

"He's been calling me that since I graduated from the Space Academy in Houston and because I do a lot of space travel. As a matter of fact I just returned from a six month mission on Mars."

"Oh, I could never leave Earth. I don't think I could survive without all our conveniences and I hate those *pinche* space suits!"

Charley swatted her gently on her butt laughing. "Yes, Mercedes is not the space suit type."

Glancing at the clock on the wall it was almost three. "I gotta go. I have a meeting at my office."

They walked to the hallway with Charley's arm wrapped over Cisco's shoulders. Chuco the bodyguard lay snoring softly on the carpet.

"I think you need a better bodyguard."

CHAPTER 11

As he flew home to change for the meeting, Cisco's Pcom chirped and Vivian's image popped up on the dashboard. Shocked at first, he then chuckled thinking Vivian's mother gave her the same story about meeting his mother at the grocery store. Still, he was surprised by Vivian's call.

"Cisco, I heard you were home from Mars," she said.

"Vivian? Uh . . . hi. How are you?" he stammered shocked at the call. Her face had matured and her hair styled with golden highlites. She did not have the carefree smile and long, free flowing hair he liked. However, she was beautiful by any standards.

"I'm great. Busy. How are you?"

"Just back from a six month stint. I heard you have a big job here in Dublán. Congratulations."

"Thanks. We should get together and catch up. How about later tonight?"

Her request startled him. He wondered if his mother had meddled again, as Vivian's call was completely unexpected. He could not believe she wanted to see him after all these years. Without thinking he stammered a reply. "I . . . I have a meeting this afternoon, but maybe later, I guess. I don't think the meeting will run very long."

"Great, I'll plan a little supper here at my place. Come anytime after six," she said. "Twelve-o-two La Condesa, number 1864. It's a high rise in the city."

"Okay, see you then." Cisco's mind swirled. He and Vivian had a history, a good history, but that was long ago. Seeing her again seemed so natural, but then there was hurt too. He had loved her and she broke it off. The hurt lasted a long time. Pondering whether seeing her again would dredge up the old feelings, he quickly tried to convince himself it was only dinner and not sex.

The car turned off the aeropath and in a few minutes it touched down on the parking pad at his home. Throwing the Pcom on the kitchen table, he hurried to shower and change for the G90 meeting having stayed a little too long with Charley.

About forty minutes later, dressed in his formal EQA uniform, Cisco hovered beside the security force field at the main entry gate to the Republic's government complex of buildings on the north side of Dublán City. He waited for the security clearance to open the gate. From behind the glass encased guard shack, a robotic scanner hummed as he and the Vette were checked for weapons and an image captured by the online system was verified.

The system seemed slow to complete the check, while Cisco tapped his fingers nervously on the steering stick. Finally, the force field released the car and the Vette hovered to the covered parking area. The afternoon sun was dropping lower, but at least this time Cisco remembered his Blocrays. Locking the Vette he walked toward the main entrance.

Security was obviously at high alert. At each access point, his physical appearance was scanned and compared to the image taken at the main checkpoint and his file. Cisco had been working out of this complex for over eight years and had never seen security this rigid. A security officer at the final checkpoint escorted him to a large conference room on the top floor.

More intrigued by the heightened security than worried, Cisco's mind swirled with questions for his boss for not following protocol and allowing him time to recover from reentry before calling him back to the office.

Alirio Martinez, director of the Evaluation and Qualification Agency, sat at a holographic workstation with a privacy headset on his head. He looked up as Cisco entered and motioned with his index finger to wait. When he completed talking into the headset, Martinez stood up, walked toward him, and shook his hand.

"Thank you for coming. I know you just got back, but you have been summoned by the president. The meeting will start shortly. I just told them you arrived."

His boss' words stopped Cisco in his tracks. Summoned by the president? President Torres was Cisco's

Nino, his godfather, but this was official business and not some family event, like a wedding or funeral. What had he done? Cisco searched his memory for any discrepancy on the last mission. He was not a perfect EQA agent, sometimes verbally obstinate, but he always completed the jobs and had won a number of honors. He could think of nothing, which would bring him before the president for either an award or a reprimand. His nights with Monica on Mars flashed through his brain. It was not against regulations, but not condoned, given the circumstances of life in the close-quartered domes.

"How is the Mars complex coming along?" his boss asked, obviously trying to make small talk to pass the time. Again, Monica came to Cisco's mind and he gulped.

"The dome construction is moving right along. The new oxygen system is working well." His boss knew all of this information so why was he stalling and trying to be nice. Cisco was about to blurt out a demand to know what was going on, when a large opening in the front wall opened to another room and an armed guard exited and stood beside it.

"They are ready for you," Director Martinez said. "Good Luck."

Cisco felt frozen to the floor. What the hell was going on? Suddenly feeling sick, it felt like he was going to a firing squad. With effort he moved his feet forward, slowly walking through the guarded door. The guard stood at attention as Cisco went into a secure conference room he never knew existed. It was not as large as the exterior one, but elaborately decorated. A large screen filled the front wall. The walls were paneled in a rich wood and a huge conference table filled the center of the room. About a dozen people sat around the table, their faces a blur in his vision.

His heart beat loudly in his ears, seeming the only sound in the room. The president sat at the far end of the table. The faces at the long conference table all looked expectantly toward him as he walked in. Why are you all looking at me, he wanted to scream. Then he caught his father's face sitting on the left side of the table. His father? Why was he here? He should be in Sinaloa. Cisco's stomach soured and sank. Was he here to watch him be arrested for some indiscretion?

"Francisco, please come in and join us," President Torres said kindly. He pointed to an open chair at the table. "Gentlemen and ladies, this is Francisco, my godson," he introduced him.

Nervously stumbling, Cisco managed to get to the chair and sank down. His *Nino's* kindly voice put him slightly at ease. Looking around the table, he recognized a few faces, high-ranking members of the government, like General Castillo and Benjamin Aguilar, but besides his father and the president, he did not know the rest of the men and women sitting at the table.

"Please ask your questions," the president addressed the group.

"Francisco, have you ever felt you were in any danger while performing your duties, particularly when you travel to the repatriated parts of the Federated States?" General Castillo asked the first question. The general was well known in the Republic. Castillo was a fully decorated general from a family with a long history of military leaders. One of them was a hero who was instrumental during the liberation of Chile from Spain. The obviously robust man looked about fifty-five years old with a full head of graying hair.

His demeanor was gruff and the question was not the one Cisco expected. He did not know what to expect, but certainly not that. Standing up he uncomfortably replied, "No, our jobs are peaceful and scientific. I am accepted with great enthusiasm and appreciated by those I work with. My role as adviser is not a security threat to any party. I deal mostly with computers and scientists. I have travelled numerous times to the FSA and never felt threatened in any way."

"Do EQA agents have any security guards assigned to them for a project's duration?" a women sitting near his father asked.

"No." Cisco tried to sound calm as he replied to their questions. "We usually work alone and we are in constant contact with our agency, either by voice or through the satellite computer networks. We do all the modeling and system analysis through the network. We are guests of a foreign state and the prospective governments treat us with respect. They often go overboard to make us comfortable. They give us access to their best laboratories and computers. I suppose if there was a need for security, we would be protected by their agencies," Cisco explained.

"Mister Salaz," a man in a grey uniform spoke. "Do you make your own arrangements or does the department know your whereabouts at all times. I guess what I am asking is whether you are ever off-the-grid, so to speak." The man in the grey uniform had many ribbons decorating his chest.

Cisco did not recognize him. His mouth went dry at the question. Had his rebellious nature finally caught up with him? Had he pushed the rules too far? He thought about the times he and Monica scrambled their chips so they could enjoy their nights uninterrupted.

"Ah, . . . well, you know we are chipped."

Everyone knew most private individuals in the Republic were embedded with a personal identification microchip. Cisco remembered when he was six and the doctor inserted the chip before he started going to school. When he started with the EQA, his chip was upgraded to a global beacon microchip. All government officials, airline pilots, police, bus drivers, and any other public servants were chipped so they could be located at any time. Everyone hated the thought, though realized the importance of the information for the public good. It was now just a part of him, like hair or skin, but there were ways to scramble the locator signal. Pretty much everyone he knew went off-the-grid from time to time.

"Have you ever purposely disengaged the chip mechanism?" the man asked looking directly at Cisco.

Cisco's tongue stuck in his dry mouth and his mind swirled trying to make a decision. Should he lie? Catching his father's eye, suddenly he knew what to say.

"Everyone I know, including me, wants some privacy. It is pretty well known how to scramble the locator signal to prevent detection. I would never do so while on a contract. That would only be to my detriment should something happen, but at home here in the Republic, yes I sometimes go off-the-grid."

He had answered almost truthfully, as Monica's image came to mind. Ok, well this was it. His career at EQA was evaporating. He waited for the hammer to drop. How would they fire him? Right here, right now?

"Thank you for your honesty," another man responded.

The president's chair squeaked as he leaned back and turned slightly. He activated the flat wall monitor behind him. An image of a young woman filled the front wall. Several different shots of the same young woman were shown and Cisco thought she looked familiar, but did not immediately recognize her. In the last photo, a beautiful young woman wore an EQA uniform similar to his.

The president spoke directly to Cisco while viewing the monitor. "That, *mijo,* is Maya my great-granddaughter. You probably have not seen her for several years. After she finished her studies, all she wanted was to be an EQA agent. She used an assumed identity and we thought that identity was a secret. We assumed wrong. She has been kidnapped."

He remembered Maya as an awkward pre-teen at her cousin's wedding a number of years ago. Could she be this grown up?

"I . . . I," Cisco stuttered at a loss for words. "Kidnapped? Where? Why?" Stammering the questions, he felt stupid and lost in the room of high-level officials.

"We were afraid this might happen and for that reason she has been working under an assumed identity and keeping a low profile, but the kidnappers must know who she is," General Castillo interjected.

"She wanted to be an EQA agent more than anything," the president continued sadly. "She worked so hard in her studies and was accepted into the agency on her own merit. This was her life's dream. She did not want any help from me or anyone else. I am very proud of her," he spoke with a choke in his voice. "But I was an old fool to think she was safe."

"Do not blame yourself, sir. We, around this table are all to blame," General Castillo said and most heads nodded in agreement.

The lights brightened and the image on the wall faded. "Please leave us alone," he said looking at the group surrounding the table. As if on cue, everyone rose, except Cisco's father. The president waved Cisco to come closer.

Quickly heading toward him, President Torres rose and gave Cisco a tight *abrazo*, then releasing him from the hug said, *"Mijo,* your father and I have much to explain. Come sit next to me."

It had been a couple years since Cisco had seen his godfather in person. Everyone looked better on the media or perhaps they fixed the image. Over 90 years old, the president's body stooped a bit, but his eyes had the sheen of a young man's eyes. Remembering those intense eyes and the powerful voice Cisco saw often as a boy when his godfather visited his grandfather, tonight those eyes were reflecting pain.

"¿Nino, cómo está?" Cisco asked how he was, feeling his own face flush from the love he felt for this man and the respect he felt for his position. His *Nino,* his godfather, had pledged to take him as his own, if anything ever happened to his parents as well as guiding this great Republic to become a world power. For over three decades, the entire Republic had enjoyed his benevolent guidance.

"I understand you returned last night from the Mars Colony. How was your trip home?" he asked seeming to change the subject.

"The return trip home was a bit rough. I missed the commercial shuttle, but managed to catch a cargo transporter. Not the most comfortable ship, but it got me home. I'm looking forward to some time off to spend with my family." Cisco wondered why the small talk. Looking directly into his *Nino's* eyes, he saw the pain again. "What's happening *Nino?*"

It was his father who spoke. "Cisco, the men and women who were just sitting around the table are the Protectors. It is an elite group of people dedicated to the survival of the Republic and the protection of the particle. They have sworn their life to that purpose, as I have and as your grandfather did before me. It is a sacred position to protect the particle from aggressive uses and to protect the integrity of the Republic's work. The identity of the group is the highest secret of the Republic, a sort of super secret service to the country."

Cisco heard his father's words but they made little sense. His father was a horticulturalist. His grandfather, a scientist who was instrumental in figuring out how to harness the particle along with the president.

"*Mijo,*" the president spoke to Cisco like his son. "When your grandfather and I found the power in the meteor rocks, we swore to find a way to harness them for the global good and to make sure they were never used for weapons of war. It was something we could not do alone. We selected a few elite people we could trust with our very lives. It is the group you just met. They are the protectors of the cause and the Republic's control of the particle."

"*Papá?*" He turned to his father. "I don't understand. Does mother know?"

"No son, she doesn't know. All of the Protectors have normal jobs and families. It is part of the secrecy. Only the people in this room know the identities of the others. We do not often meet together, such as today."

"But why am I here?"

"It is time to pass this sacred trust onto the next generation. From the time you were born, I knew you were the one. I could sense it in you in the same way my father sensed it in me. When your grandfather died, I took his place in the Protectors."

"Father, are you ill?" Cisco asked.

"No son, but none of the Protectors can do this

mission. We are all too old. Valentino and I know we need to start passing the torch to the next generation who will protect our country."

Cisco's mind swirled with his father's words still disoriented from the space mission and the sudden revelation of the Protectors. Nothing made much sense.

"Francisco, the kidnappers are ransoming Maya for my presidency. Their demand for her safe return is for me to step down within two weeks. They are threatening to kill her," the president spoke. "We believe the kidnappers are associated with the opposition party here in the Republic, though it could be an external source, such as the Federated States. There are factions in the FSA who want to control the particle and others who resent the repatriation of the Southwest. If my presidency is lost, the security of the particle will be in jeopardy. The opposition party has openly demanded more use of the particle for weapons and external governments would destroy our world with the particle. My granddaughter Maya is our future. I know she carries the spirit of my ancestors. The spirit within me, which has guided me all these years, is also within her. I have always known she would be the next leader to carry on this great Republic. And now, I am afraid for her." Tears welled in his eyes, but there was still a presence of pure strength about him.

Moved by emotion, but still confused Cisco responded, "What about the generals? Can't they find her? Can't they arrest the opposition leaders and interrogate them?"

"It is a very delicate situation. No one knows of the kidnapping. If we move on the opposition they will act offended, innocent of any charges. I have contacted the President of the Federated States and he denies any involvement. We are monitoring many of the higher ranking opposition members and the communications chatter from the FSA, but if we make a move it might put Maya in greater danger," his father explained.

"It is why I asked for you Francisco. We are negotiating with the kidnappers. The generals and the

Protectors are analyzing the situation. I want you to go undercover. I feel in my heart you are the one who can find her," the president said.

"Me?" Cisco blurted out stunned by his words. "I . . . I'm a scientist, not a . . . a secret agent. I wouldn't know where to start."

The president looked intensely at him. "I . . . we don't trust anyone. I believe they may kill her even if I meet their demands, which would be disastrous for the Republic. If they kill her, my heart will break and the Republic will be lost. *Mijo,* my visions have shown me you are the one who can find her. You must find her!"

Everything in the room swirled, their faces blurred, and Cisco's brain screamed, *"Don't ask me to do this. I can't."* Maybe this was another dream, like the one with the screaming Indian trying to kill him. In the dream, it was his *Nino* who always helped him escape. Now he wondered if it was a dream or a vision of the future.

Cisco heard his voice speaking, but did not know how the words came out. "Tell me where to begin."

CHAPTER 12

Emilio reached his arm across his son's shoulder as they walked from the headquarters building. Cisco wanted to start immediately, but the president insisted he go home and get a good night's sleep, knowing he was still space weary.

"We will continue the negotiations and will stall as long as we can. We are gathering intelligence constantly," the president had told them.

It was dusk as Emilio and Cisco walked out of the building and into the parking lot. Part of a rising moon peeked over the southeastern horizon, barely visible in the early evening sky. Normally Cisco would appreciate the sight, but tonight his mind was reeling. He could not refuse the president, but felt he had little to offer, only his life. No doubt the kidnappers were intent upon their goal. If they planned on killing Maya, his life would not be a second thought.

His father finally broke the silence. "I'm proud of you son."

Nodding, he seemed too numb to respond.

"You have many questions," his father said the obvious.

"Yes, like why the hell you didn't tell me you were a secret agent?" he blurted out not able to control the anger in his voice.

"That kind of negates the secret part, doesn't it?" Emilio chuckled.

"I'm sorry. I didn't mean that, Father."

"Yes you did. I understand. I felt the same when your grandfather enlisted me many years ago."

"*Papá,* everything is so confusing. It's like I don't know who you are."

"No son, I'm your father, but the president has counted on me for more than just growing crops all these years."

Cisco turned to look at him, barely comprehending

what he was saying. "What about mother? How could she not know?"

"We, the Protectors, are very good at covering the tracks of our deception. She thinks I'm just a workaholic." Emilio chuckled again and smiled at him.

"Father, why me? I'm not trained to do anything like this. There must be someone else."

"I spent most of the day with the president who believes the kidnappers are from inside the Republic, possibly attached to the opposition party. General Castillo thinks the Americans may be to blame. He feels they are emboldened now that their economy has recovered. He believes they want to rekindle their world superiority by controlling the particle. Since we do not yet know who is responsible, there is no way to assess how badly our government has been infiltrated."

"But . . . this is incredible *Papá*. Who in our government could be responsible for this? The president is beloved by everyone. We have been at peace with the FSA for years and are trusted allies."

"Son, peace or war, politics is always a tricky business. Those in power are always at risk from those who are not. The Republic is no different. However the president controls the world's most powerful energy source. He has always been a target. Now, they finally found a way to get to him. Can you imagine what the world would be like if the particle is used for war?"

"What about the president's security service? Surely there is someone better trained than me?"

"In the past, the Protectors might have handled this internally. Unfortunately, most of us are older than we care to admit. We should have been grooming replacements years ago, but we have been stubborn old fools. Besides, if it is the opposition, our faces are known in the Republic. The president believes you can infiltrate whatever group is behind this without any suspicion."

"Yes, but unqualified. What if I fail? I'm not sure I could live with that, even if I do manage to survive."

"The president has faith in you and so do I. You

know he is a very spiritual man and he has had visions. The visions tell him you will save her."

Cisco shook his head. What about his visions or dreams? What about the screaming Indian always chasing him with the lance ready to strike?

They reached his father's car. "Don't worry about it tonight. Tomorrow will take care of itself." Emilio grabbed him in a strong *abrazo,* wrapping his arms around his son tightly.

A few minutes later, his father's car hovered and then sped toward the sky. Now, the half full moon was shining brightly through the pollution free sky, giving the landscape a blue-white cast with sharp shadows as the vehicle disappeared into the night. His time unit blinked 6:13 PM. Vivian was expecting him for dinner. He no longer wanted to go, but did not want to go home either. All he wanted to do was run and keep running. His life had turned upside down in the course of a couple of hours. His father was a Protector. It seemed impossible and now they wanted him to pull off some miracle of an undercover nature to save Maya and the Republic.

He walked in zombie mode toward the Corvette. "Unlock," he said as he approached. Slowly easing into the custom seat, Cisco sank into it closing his eyes. None of this was real. It was all a dream – a crazy, crazy dream manifested in his space weary mind.

"Destination," Comsys asked after the several minute preset time delay elapsed stirring him back into the present.

"Twelve-o-two La Condesa," he responded with Vivian's address.

The seat belts adjusted automatically around his body and the door lock clicked. Slowly the vehicle lifted, hovered, circled part of the parking lot, and headed south toward Dublán City. Minutes later it parked at the apartment building's lot. Grabbing the lightweight linen suit coat he threw on the passenger seat earlier, he closed the door and issued the lock command. On the way to the elevators, he shrugged on the suit coat over his gray EQA body shirt. He called for the 18th floor.

Stopping at door number 1864, Cisco ran his fingers through his unruly hair and took a deep breath. He stood there for several minutes, numb, wanting to leave, then pushed the welcome button.

"Cisco," Vivian said as she opened the door. She grabbed him in an awkward hug. "You look thin," she scolded him, holding him at arm's length.

Vivian Bejarano glowed in a rose-colored bodysuit made of Zortex. The synthetic material clung to her lithe body showing each curve. Her brown hair framed her radiant face with tendrils of curls and accented her hazel eyes. She looked younger and more beautiful than he expected, making him more tongue-tied trying to form words, but it also stirred his manhood.

"Viv, you look great."

CHAPTER 13

She took his arm and pulled him into the apartment. The eighteenth-floor corner unit was everything he expected for Vivian. Back when they were dating, she dreamed of a home of glass and steel decorated in an ultra-modern style. She would hate his wood and stone home in the mountains. A low sleek gray sofa faced a large picture window overlooking the city lights. Stainless steel floors reflected the ceiling lighting giving a weird feeling as he walked to the picture window.

"You have a beautiful view," he mumbled observing the city lights and the half full moon hanging above it.

"I love it," she replied. "Look I can see the top of Patriarca Torre."

Cisco stared out at the millions of city lights twinkling in the early evening. Could one of those lights be where Maya was being held captive? An overwhelming feeling of dread crept up his back. How could he possibly find her? Vivian let go of her grip on his arm and pointed to the stars.

"My mother says you just got back from the Mars Colony. Look, you can see the red planet up there." She pointed out the large window into the night sky to a pinpoint tinged red. Vivian knew exactly when Cisco had reentered late last night. Her high-level security clearance at the Department of Health gave her access to all his records. She chuckled internally thinking she even knew about his affair with a woman named Monica on Mars. His chip records tracked his every move and the security data on Mars was extremely detailed.

"Yes, I got back late last night. I guess I'm still a little fatigued from reentry." The conversation felt stilted and he wondered why he had come. Vivian was a beautiful woman. She most likely had many well-connected suitors, no doubt all with high-powered jobs. He would not blame them after seeing her in the skintight body suit.

"A good hot meal and a glass of wine will relax you,"

she said softly. Linking her arm in his, she pulled him away from the window, away from his thoughts, and toward the kitchen bar. Her touch was warm and he fought the fatigue away.

"White or red? Do you still go for the Zinfandels?" she asked remembering he liked a hearty red Zin.

"Yes, red. I guess I haven't changed much. Do you still like Chardonnays?"

"Oh Cisco, you aren't on this planet are you? Chardonnay is so old fashioned. Everyone drinks Velado."

Actually he drank little wine anymore at all. Had tried Velado, but found it had a bitter aftertaste. It was mostly full of chemicals with a little juice of the grape to give it color and flavor. "Oh, I guess I'm out of the mainstream."

"Way out." She laughed a bit as she poured a glass of red for him and white for herself and they sat at the bar. It seemed surreal to be here talking to her. It had been ten or eleven years since they split, and they had not been in contact.

He hated to admit how heartbroken he was when they split. It took him some time to even contemplate dating anyone else. Now she was here in front of him again in a sleek bodysuit hugging her curves and the stir in his crotch nagged at him. At thirty-three, she was a role model for achievement and success. Graduating with a doctorate in Global Health from Harvard, she commanded an enormous salary to afford this fancy apartment.

"What about you? Living on Mars, what is it like?" she broke into his thoughts.

"Mars? Well, I guess you would call it confining. The domes are getting bigger as they have figured out how to control oxygen, but it is like living on a small island and you can't get off," he said with a bit of a grin. "It's good to be home."

"Dinner is ready," a pleasant voice alerted from the kitchen. Pour us another glass of wine and I'll go get dinner."

Cisco poured the wine and took it to the table, which was set with two places sitting across from each other.

Vivian returned with plates. Each held a piece of breaded fish and bright green broccoli with a small grilled tomato. He knew the foods were synthetic and found it amusing how the agro masterminds decided people would eat broccoli if it maintained a bright green color when cooked.

"Looks good," he lied.

This was Vivian's world – high-rise apartment, modern conveniences, and synthetic food. She was living completely in the modern world, not at all like his world. He thought she would hate his mountain top retreat. They ate and made small talk. Thankfully, the wine numbed him a bit from the day's revelations and the dread of what tomorrow would bring.

He caught her watching him eating the meal. She seemed interested in his conversation and his mind found her alluring in her rose-colored bodysuit, which clung to her rounded curves and glowed in the ambient lighting complimenting her hazel eyes. He felt her eyes studying him. Why now? Was it real or just an act of being curious about an old friend? More to the point, what were his feelings toward her? Could he ever feel anything for her again?

Her curves and beauty did arouse him. He remembered their passionate lovemaking of their youth. She was a tiger in bed, screaming and clawing at him, wanting to take all of him deeply into her. Monica was a decent lay, but nowhere near Vivian's zest.

"Why did you come back to Dublán? I thought you might stay in Massachusetts or get a job in the Federated States?"

Vivian rubbed her thumb up and down the stem of the wine glass. There was a quiet pause as she seemed to ponder what to say.

"I decided to go to Harvard after *Papá* was killed. I was bitter about his death as it was so senseless. They should have known the mine was dangerous. . . ." her voice grew angry and she did not finish the sentence.

"I'm so sorry. I know how much you loved him." Cisco was on assignment when the accident happened and was not able to return for the funeral. He never had the chance to console her. Vivian and her father were very close, more than close. They adored each other and Cisco could imagine the hole left in Vivian's heart by his early and terrible death.

Tears brimmed in Vivian's eyes as she fought the pain and bitterness she had for the accident. Her father was a metallurgy expert for the Department of Mines and Engineering. She blamed the government officials for sending him into a mine, later determined to be unsafe. Several high-level officials lost their positions and two went to jail over the incident, but nothing could bring her father back or ease her pain.

"Harvard was great, but I guess you could say I was homesick. I missed the Republic. I missed the way the people still have ideals here and still have a sense of family," she said softly twirling her wine glass. She looked pensive, a look he remembered meaning she was not being truthful and wondered what she really wanted to say.

"I'm thinking of changing jobs to work in children's health," she changed the subject abruptly.

"Really, I thought you liked the Global Health stuff?"

"Well it's still in Global Health, but directed at children specifically."

"Sounds good," he responded.

She put down her fork and looked directed at him. "When I went to Harvard, I lived near the town of Peabody. Peabody is a child-free town."

"What do you mean?"

"It is adults only and they are working on procedures to improve adult longevity. It is one of the places in the Federated States where abortions are mandatory or you have to leave. In Peabody when an adult leaves or dies, there is a waiting list of others to come in. They believe the world is overcrowded and it is why we can no longer control many deadly illnesses and starvation." Vivian paused, waiting for Cisco to make a comment, but he stared into his wine glass.

"At first, I was fascinated by the concept. It fit with

the horrendous problems I dealt with everyday in my Global Health job. I had been working with countries where drug-resistant viruses and even childhood diseases could not be controlled. Many of my professors at Harvard taught mandated family size control and child selection is the future. For a while I even began to believe the world is overcrowded and the only way to control it was through forced abortion and sterilization."

Her hands rubbed the wine glass stem up and down. She looked at her hands while she spoke. Cisco was appalled by the concept, but this was Vivian's life work and he listened not wanting to offend her.

Cisco knew most of Europe and Asia aborted many pregnancies to control population. China had limited a family to one child for years. It had become normal in many parts of the world where food production and land was scarce. Children in the womb who did not meet basic health criteria were aborted. Down Syndrome, Microcephaly, Spina Bifada, and most other major birth defected babies were considered a drain on society and aborted regardless of parental approval. He thought that was a good thing.

"I suppose it's an interesting theory," Cisco said not knowing what else to say.

"It's not interesting, it's awful," she blurted back at him out in frustration. "Children are our future, Cisco."

Vivian paused for a moment to take a sip of her wine. "Aborting children to control the population is terrible. I found out in Peabody there is a clinic where some of the women get pregnant on purpose, carry the fetus to eight and a half months, then abort it live to harvest the organs. The clinic is doing research on how the harvested organs can keep adults alive and rejuvenate their bodies. It's terrible what they are doing to those babies." Vivian's eyes grew moist as she talked, her voice filled with passion.

"That sounds barbaric and selfish," Cisco said.

"The Harvard professors embraced it, calling it part of a global health initiative. They touted it as the only way to control disease, but in class they also called it population weeding. Survival of the fittest, only the fittest was determined by politics and money. At first I bought into their belief, but after I learned about the clinics in Peabody . . . " her voice trailed off.

Vivian touched Cisco's hand. "Sorry, I'm getting too serious." She kept her hand on his and did not move it for a few moments. He felt the warmth of her touch and it sent tingles up his arm. Her body seemed to glow brighter in the rose-colored suit. He could see her nipples under the material were aroused.

Suddenly, she changed the topic. "Oh, I saw you check in at Republic Security Headquarters today. Are you in trouble?" she asked. He reacted slightly to the question, thinking it odd she was checking up on him.

"Ah, no. No trouble. Just a routine meeting." The answer was all he could muster, trying not to react enough for her to notice something was amiss.

Her eyes flicked slightly at his use of the word, routine. Vivian knew routine meetings were not called for people who had only arrived home from space within the last forty-eight hours. It was highly irregular and she wanted answers.

"Hey Cisco, it's me, Viv. You don't need to keep secrets from me. If you're in trouble, you can tell me about it," she assured him looking into his eyes and squeezing his hand.

Her question took him off guard. Of course he could not tell her about the meeting and he found her interest odd, but the wine and his fatigue was fogging his thoughts.

"It's late Viv. I'm tired and should go," he said.

He rose from the table and sighed as he did. He was tired, exhausted. She stood up near him and grabbed his hand. Her greenish-hazel eyes glinted in contrast to the rose body suit. She was all woman and he could tell she was willing. Gently pulling her into his arms, he kissed her. Tender at first, then harder as she responded. Breathless, they parted and looked into each other's eyes, then kissed again.

After several minutes, Cisco ran his hands down her

bodysuit and felt her perked nipples and let his hands stop at her hips. Vivian took his right hand and led him to her bedroom.

At breakfast, Cisco was mesmerized watching her working at the cooktop. The sway of her hips were driving him mad and only his ravenous appetite was keeping him from grabbing her and taking her here right on the countertop. He tried hard to control his lust, but he felt insatiable after their passionate night. If sex was good when they were young, it was now fantastic. She roused something in him he thought was lost.

"Will you be at church this morning?" she asked.

Suddenly, reality came crashing back on him. It was Sunday and it all seemed confused. What time was he supposed to be at the Security Headquarters this morning? He could not remember.

"I think so."

"Well, I'll see you then. Maybe we can go for a drive after church."

"Ah, sure."

Vivian kissed him passionately at the door before she let him leave.

Cisco's knees felt like rubber as he left and walked down the long hallway of her apartment building. Getting to the Corvette parked in the garage, he sank into the seat and let Comsys take him home. He was completely exhausted.

CHAPTER 14

At 9:30 AM Sunday morning Cisco's Pcom chirped. He had just gotten out of the shower and the Pcom showed a voice message waiting.

"Your meeting is at eleven hundred," was all it said. No location, no person's name, nothing. Shaking his head, he wondered why the message was so cryptic, although nothing about the Protectors and yesterday's meeting made much sense. Only the night with Vivian remained in his immediate memory.

Climbing into the Vette he said, "Start." Normally Comsys performed the start sequence and then asked for a destination. Today it startled him and replied. "Good Morning Cisco. Estimated time of arrival at Central Headquarters is ten-fifty."

He sat back trying to relax and allowed Comsys control to take him to headquarters. Less than fifteen minutes later, he was circling the security entrance and the car slowed at the security force field at the main gate. Expecting the same tight security as he experienced at the security gate yesterday, to his surprise the gate released immediately as the Vette approached.

The parking lot was mostly empty and the Vette touched down close to the main doors. Locking the car, he walked briskly to the building. Looking down at his jeans and T-shirt, he now regretted not wearing his uniform. He wondered if he was already bucking the assignment. He wanted to laugh, but could not. Reaching the security pass-through, he again expected to be stopped, searched, and questioned. Instead the guard said, "Take any elevator to the seventh floor. General Castillo will meet you there."

As the elevator zipped up to the seventh floor, his stomach danced with butterflies. *Mierda*, this was not a dream; it was real. The doors opened and General Castillo was waiting.

"Good morning Francisco," the general said.

"Call me Cisco."

"Okay, come along and we'll join the others." He followed the general into a small conference room. Five people he recognized as Protectors from yesterday's meeting sat at a conference table. There were no introductions. On the far end of the room, a holograph of Maya in her EQA uniform was displayed. The image looked so real it startled him. The general pointed to a chair at the table.

The four others, three men and one woman, stared at him quietly as he sat down. General Castillo began, "I have to be honest, we don't have much to go on. As best we can determine, Maya was kidnapped Thursday from the CalEd parking garage in Los Angeles."

The general pointed at a button and the screen on the wall behind Maya's holograph came into focus. It was her itinerary for last Thursday. She traveled to the Dublán Aeroport and boarded a shuttle to Los Angeles. Her initial meeting with Yamamoto-Rockwell Space Company was a presentation of a derivative of the particle. She was scheduled to make a courtesy call on CalEd Power Systems later that day, and to return home at 3:30 PM. It seemed like a normal EQA agent's itinerary. Cisco noticed the name on the itinerary was Cecilia Juarez, her assumed identity.

"We know she boarded the flight to Los Angeles, arrived, and rented a vehicle. She completed the appointment at Yamamoto and was scanned out of Yamamoto at 11:10 AM. The security cameras at the Yamamoto parking lot and her autosensor chip show she left the parking lot and requested Comsys to go to the CalEd building near Burbank. We have confirmation of her arrival at the CalEd building's parking garage at 11:31. The rental car was recovered at that location." The general paused in his presentation as if thinking about how to continue.

"From this point on, nothing is for certain," he said. "The CalEd security cameras show a confused accident in the parking garage at 11:33:14 near where Maya parked her vehicle. We see her near the accident, heading toward it as if she wanted to lend assistance. On the audio of the recording we can hear someone yelling for help."

The general commanded the video unit and a holographic video replaced Maya's image. First, the crashing sound of vehicles was followed by several pieces of car parts flying in the air. It looked as if a car took the corner too fast and then crashed into several parked cars. As the images played, Maya could be seen moving toward the commotion and a voice was yelling for help. A baby cried in the background. Maya ducked down as if looking into the window of the wrecked vehicle, then suddenly the image went dark although the audio continued.

Castillo paused the video. "We think the kidnappers were able to stop or somehow disable the security monitors at this point, which is why we lost the images. The audio continues for a little over three minutes, and then the image returns shortly before the police arrive. By that time, Maya is gone."

"What about her chip?" Cisco asked.

"It is why we asked you about the chip yesterday in the meeting. Her chip stopped transmitting at 11:34:48. Whoever kidnapped her knew how to disable her chip," the general said then added, "permanently."

Cisco felt completely foolish. Of course they thought about the chip. She would be easy to find if her chip was working.

"In front of you is written the security access code to the case documents." The general pointed to a white piece of paper with '2942TIXB4' written on it. "Memorize this code and then destroy it," the general said.

"You will also have access to all files related to this case and personnel files of the opposition leaders, known sympathizers, criminals, etc. It is imperative you speak to no one about the true nature of your mission and always refer to Maya as Cecelia Juarez. She is a missing EQA agent, nothing more. The security of your mission is at the highest level."

"Speaking of security, why is security so light here at Headquarters?" Cisco asked.

Castillo and several others laughed. "We are virtually on lock down. You were monitored from the time you left headquarters last night and were expected this morning. Security already knew exactly where you were. However, we have scrambled your movements and any record of your attendance at this meeting. We have to assume the kidnappers can tap into our databases. If they determine who you are, your effectiveness will be minimized."

Shocked, Cisco remembered the Vette's Comsys was preprogrammed this morning for this meeting. Then he thought about being at Vivian's apartment last night.

Before he could ask anything more, the general continued. "That's why we need you to go undercover, alone and un-chipped. We can't trust anyone outside of this very elite circle and a few key intelligence people. We have arranged with a contact in EQA to cover you with bogus assignments for the agency to account for your activities and limit any suspicion. We will place work credits you might need into your EQA account, but you should not contact Director Martinez or any other EQA agent over ordinary channels. If asked, detained, or otherwise interrogated, you are simply doing your job as an EQA agent. You will only contact us as necessary over a priority encrypted channel," the general continued to describe how Cisco should proceed. He was describing everything, except how to find Maya.

A thin man in a blue uniform picked up as the general stopped talking. He had beady eyes and a hawkish nose and for some reason gave Cisco the creeps.

"We are going to have to feed you information as we go and likewise you need to keep us informed. You will be fitted with an encrypted priority communications device to contact us. No one else can use the priority channel except you. It will be monitored twenty-four, seven. Never speak to anyone else about it and never use your personal Pcom."

"Who will answer the encrypted device?"

"The less you know about the people the better . . . plausible deniability," General Castillo interjected. "Just know they are working very hard behind the scenes to assist you to find Maya."

"I am supposed to be on leave. I don't understand what EQA jobs I will be assigned."

"Your official EQA record will verify you are on leave. As you determine where you need to travel, phony EQA jobs will be assigned. We don't think the kidnappers will be looking for someone like you. The records will be disjointed, so they will not be able to resolve the discrepancies. We believe they will be following and watching our security and secret service personnel very closely. We will be sending off agents on assignments as subterfuge, trying to keep the kidnappers off your trail," the general explained.

The words – priority, encrypted, plausible deniability, phony, and subterfuge rang in his ears and he was starting to feel a bit dizzy.

"I arranged to have you checked out on some new personal weaponry. These weapons are very small, easy to conceal, and powerful. We know you were trained in firearms at the Space Academy. Do you still feel comfortable carrying a weapon?" he asked.

Cisco nodded numbly. It was all beginning to sink in. Undercover meant – espionage, covert operations, deception, special weapons, secret agent stuff. He was a scientist. He wanted to shout, "I'm not a secret agent," but he kept nodding his head and wondered if he had a choice.

"Okay," the general said. "We know you are still space lagged. We can give you today to get rested, organized, and to review all the known information, but time is of the essence. You will be escorted to the infirmary and outfitted with a priority channel device and then to the weapons laboratory to practice with the equipment. Then Monday morning . . . . well you are on your own. Good luck son," the general said sticking out his hand. Cisco pasted a confident smile on his face and shook it.

As if on cue, a door opened. President Torres and his father walked into the room. All eyes turned toward him. He walked directly to Cisco and gave him a long tight *abrazo*.

"*Nino,* I will do my best to find Maya and bring her home to you safely."

"I know *mijo.* I have seen it in my visions. Those who want the Republic's political power to achieve global control have managed to operate in secrecy. I believe they are emboldened because of my advancing age, and because I have not named a successor. The Republic is vulnerable. It leaves some in the Republic unsure of the future or hungry for power. Either way a power struggle is inevitable."

"Many of us have worried what would happen if the president is no longer able to lead," Emilio said. "He has been protecting Maya until she attained an age to be acceptable to lead this country."

"Maya is the peaceful future of the Republic, *mijo.* You must find her and bring her home safely."

Embracing his godfather, Cisco's father signaled to him and they walked from the room.

CHAPTER 15

After the meeting with General Castillo, Cisco and his father walked down a long hallway and turned into a room, which looked a bit like a hospital surgery clinic. The bright lights made Cisco squint. A woman in a white coat greeted him and asked him to sit down. She gripped his arm lightly and held a scanner over his chip for several seconds.

"There, I've disabled your chip completely. You'll have to get it reactivated when you return," she told him.

The doctor walked to her desk and picked up a device, which looked somewhat like a tiny wasp.

"What is that?" Cisco asked.

"This is the latest G2000 microcom. It might be uncomfortable until I get it sized properly, then you will not be able to feel it," she said. She brushed hair away from his left ear and inserted the device into it. It took several tries before Cisco could no longer feel it in his ear. Then she asked Cisco to repeat certain words and phrases as she recorded them.

"Okay good. It's calibrated to your voice and auditory nerve. You can leave it in at all times, even when you shower. It's almost like having a Pcom inside your head," she chuckled. "Well, you almost do. It's connected to the government's secure satellite. Only top-level security cleared officials have access to that satellite channel."

"How do I activate it to send a call?"

"Oh yes, just say "open secure channel" to activate it and then speak normally. Based upon your voice match and your physiology, your call will be answered twenty-four hours a day."

"Will it receive calls?"

"It is a one way communications device and only works if it is close to your auditory nerve. We cannot call you and no one else can use it externally, even you, so you don't have to worry about security."

"Anything else I should know?"

"No, I guess that's about it. Like I said you should just leave it in your ear and forget about it," she said.

Cisco jumped off the table, turned, and walked toward the doorway where his father waited. They walked down the hallway until they reached an elevator. Cisco watched his father as if seeing a stranger. He seemed completely at ease with the internal workings of this secret part of the government. His father placed his palm against a flat panel near the elevator and the doors opened.

"Weapons Lab," his father said after they entered the elevator. Cisco heard a slight whirl and then the doors closed. In a few seconds, the doors opened to a hallway. It had no markings, only closed doors with no differentiation.

Emilio led Cisco to a unmarked door where he placed his hand over a security pad. With a click it opened and they walked into a large brightly lit room. A middle-aged man stood near a table and looked up when they walked in.

"Cisco, meet Javier Alvarez," his father said. Cisco shook Javier's extended hand. "Javier is our weapons expert."

"So you were trained at the Space Academy?" Javier asked. Cisco could only nod in response, after he had mumbled a greeting. His father's smiling confident look gave him little assurance.

"Good, but we have a new weapon that you will not be familiar with." Javier walked to a counter in the middle of the room. Lying on the countertop was a tiny black device. Javier picked it up.

"This is the latest in laser weaponry. I helped design and test it myself. This laser reacts quicker and with more options than any other on the market today. Even quicker than the best French M88 laser. Small and lightweight, it's my favorite." Holding out a sleek, shiny black device about two inches long, Javier handed it to him. The tiny device looked much like a large black beetle.

"Here," Javier said pushing the laser over Cisco's index finger where it was held with a flexible thin loop. The tiny laser tucked under his fingers and was almost invisible from the top of his hand.

"See that small depression? That's the power regulator. The harder you press, the more lethal. A light tap is stun. The button is very, very sensitive. Let's see what you can do."

"What about this slim bar behind the button?" Cisco asked.

"Yes, I was going to tell you about that. It is a butterfly lever. When you push the level forward, the weapon becomes totally stealth. It will not emit the typical laser point beam. No one can see where any shots are coming from and they are silent. If you push it back, it shoots a wide spread blast, but the distance is cut in half. Almost like an old-fashioned shotgun. However, the spread is flat and about eight feet wide. Good if you are charged by a group, as it is possible to take them all out at once."

"And the neutral position?" Cisco asked.

"That is the typical laser function with a single shot and a targeting beam. All the features work together with the pressure you use on the button. It's extremely versatile as well as powerful," Javier explained.

Cisco noticed his hands were shaking. Although trained in weapons at the Academy, he preferred old-fashioned hunting rifles and even played around with a cross bow from time to time. He thought he would make a complete idiot of himself with the modern weapon. Turning, he tried to shake off the feeling of dread churning in his stomach.

After dimming the lights, Javier pushed a button and holographic targets began to appear across the room. He showed Cisco how to use his thumb to touch the firing pad on the tiny laser.

"You just point and fire." Javier demonstrated. The device seemed much like a child's imaginary finger gun, like he used to play with his siblings. It was awkward at first, but he started to feel more comfortable. Javier changed the holographic images to pop up and then disappear, creating moving targets. With each practice round, Cisco got a little better on his hits.

"The device can be so powerful, you only need to hit any part of the target to be effective," Javier explained. "You don't have to make a direct hit to disable or kill an opponent, if you even use marginal power." Seeing the lost look in Cisco's eyes, Javier patted him on the back. "You're doing just fine, let's try again."

Javier let Cisco try the different features of the tiny device. At minimal power, the targets lit up, but at full power they burst into flames. The power was amazing.

Emilio stood quietly watching his son finish the training. At the end, they walked out the door of security headquarters together and walked toward the parking area. The sun was high in the sky and Cisco realized the entire morning had passed by quickly.

"*Papá*, mother expected me at church. She'll get suspicious if I don't come around. She knows I'm on leave."

"Leave your mother to me. I will think of an excuse she will believe. Trust me I have been doing it for years, *mijo*," his father chuckled.

"*Papá*, what do you think? Is it the opposition? What about a foreign government?"

"My gut feel says that it is internal because of their demand. A foreign government would want the stockpile of the particle, but would care less if the president steps down."

"Why doesn't the president order all the opposition leaders arrested?" It seemed an obvious question, though he knew it sounded stupid.

"That would be a death sentence for Maya and cause chaos in the Republic. Besides, there are millions of people who follow many of the opposition's political opinions. They have a large voice in the government as it is. They disagree on many things, but have never threatened the Republic. I think there might be a new and dangerous group behind this. One thing is in our favor," Emilio continued. "We believe they know she is the president's great-granddaughter, but would not know she is to be named his successor. I'm worried they may have already harmed her."

A part of Cisco wanted to reply, "What about me? Why aren't you worried about me, father?" He knew the answer in his heart. However, he also knew this important task was way out of his league. It was something for a trained military person or special operative. Cisco was neither and his only skill was Karate and a lot of scientific knowledge. He had nothing in his past to prepare him to be a secret agent. Nothing to help him take on this dangerous mission. He would most likely only last a few days and fail or be killed.

"What a fucking mess!" His inner voice yelled out in his mind.

His father held him in a long and hearty hug, then pulled back saying emphatically, "Remember this. Trust no one."

CHAPTER 16

Putting the Vette into Comsys control Cisco tried to relax as it flew home, but found himself nervously watching behind him. He wondered if G90 was following his every move or worse the kidnappers. The small wasp-like communicator device and tiny laser were in his pocket. Javier explained to him that the laser would not activate if not on his finger.

By the time he arrived home, it was after noon. Even in the bright midday sun, he found himself drawn to his thinking spot, an outcrop of rock facing east at the end of the orchard. He often went to the spot to meditate and today he tried to clear his mind using Ukidokan meditation techniques. It was impossible. Too many thoughts swirled together as he tried to sort out his feelings. Ultimately they all came back to one – fear.

His father and *Nino* had faith in him, but he had no faith in himself. Nothing in his life prepared him for this task. What if he failed? Of course he would fail. Everything was stacked against him. He was no secret agent. He did not even know where to begin. Suddenly, an image of kissing Vivian's breasts last night flashed across his mind. He had not let himself ponder their sexual encounter, but now it ran through his brain.

Their lovemaking was both fierce and tender. She had developed from the young naive girl he once knew into a mature woman. She aroused him with tender nips around his groin and her tongue found places that drove him crazy. Even his space-weary body responded in kind and now he hoped he had pleased her. Just thinking about her made his penis react.

They made no plans when he left her apartment this morning. Perhaps she was testing his resolve or perhaps it was just one of those momentary flings, curiosity about their old love affair. As he thought about it, he was sure she instigated it. She came on to him.

After a while he walked slowly back up to the house,

made a cup of coffee, and sat down in the study. Golden shafts of sunlight crept across the desk. He forced the images of Vivian out of his brain and decided to start from the beginning. Entering the memorized password, the case documents opened on the monitor. The first several pages were a dossier on Cecilia Juarez with pictures. Maya's fictitious life was laid out from a birth certificate to EQA badge. Her itinerary, flight confirmation, meeting appointments, and the aerocar rental forms for last Thursday were next. All the documents used Maya's fictitious name.

She had taken a typical commuter flight to L.A. The Comsys itinerary of her rental car's movement listed her route from the aeroport to Yamamoto on several of the L.A. aeroways. She was at Yamamoto for forty-eight minutes. It then detailed her flight from Yamamoto's parking lot by a verbal request for the California Edison Building in Burbank, California.

Starting on page twelve of the report, an exact timeline of the kidnapping and a transcript of the audio portion from the security system at the CalEd parking garage were included.

Page twenty-three started the police report of the accident scene by a Lt. Henry Johnston. It appeared to be cryptic, addressing what seemed like normal questions and reporting. The names of the individuals who owned the vehicles, who was at fault, comments, including the time of the accident. No injuries were reported and no mention of a Cecilia Juarez.

Following the police report was a security dossier on each individual at the scene of the accident. If the accident was staged to kidnap Maya, then some or all of these people named in the police report could be involved or were the kidnappers. Reading each page carefully, he thought the people's resumes seemed normal and none had criminal backgrounds. No doubt the Republic's security team had already scrutinized the people looking for clues.

Several pages near the end of the report were pictures of Maya's Dublán apartment and the pictures showed it was neat and not apparently searched or ransacked. Another picture showed her red micro aerocar sitting locked at the Dublán Aeroport's parking garage. A traffic control system flight timeline showing her flight that morning from her apartment to the aeroport.

General Castillo was right, there was little to go on. She seemed to have vanished from the accident scene inside the CalEd parking garage without a trace. It nagged him how the kidnappers could have known her itinerary. The event reeked of internal people or very highly trained computer hackers. Knowing her pre-defined itinerary was one thing, but how would they know where and when she would park? That seemed purely by chance.

Cisco stared out the window watching some clouds building up along the horizon. Watching as one changed shape overtaking another, he could see the trees bending gracefully as the wind blew across the orchard. It all seemed so normal, just any other day on his mountainside house, but the task before him seemed impossible. He felt ill equipped.

Why him? The thoughts continued to run through his mind. If all the great security and police investigators cannot find her, how the hell could he? His *Nino* had faith in him. Why? He said the spirit gave him a vision.

Cisco's grandfather, Salvador, told Cisco stories about President Valentino Torres. Stories about the time they were looking for the source of the meteor rocks. Valentino spent many months at the remote site with the village's shaman. Cisco's grandfather said the experience profoundly changed Valentino into a very spiritual man. He learned many secrets from the shaman and used meditation to see visions. His grandfather used to say, the president had the spirit in him.

"I sure hope the spirit or whatever it is, is not fooling the president. Or I am a dead man," Cisco grumbled to himself.

Growing up Cisco sometimes spend time at his godfather's house. He would take Cisco hiking on obscure trails, which his *Nino* said were only known to him, because they led to places of power. Cisco took it all in, hoping to see what power looked like. He never did see it, but was sure his godfather did.

Trying to shake the disquieting thoughts, he forced himself to concentrate on the information in the dossier. Near the end of the documents were instructions to access videos. Tapping the access pad to view the accident video, it began to play.

The holograph he saw earlier at headquarters played. Maya's rental car came into a security camera's viewpoint. She parked and exited the rental car just before the accident. He watched the replay of the accident, then the several minutes of darkness listening closely to the audit feed. After a few minutes, the video portion resumed and the police arrived. It was exactly as he remembered from this morning. Maya was there and then was not. Watching the holographic video three times, he paid close attention to Maya's image going toward the accident area. There had to be something there, something everyone was missing.

Switching the monitor from holographic mode to watch the video in 2-D, he replayed the video over and over. Using Ukidokan training he focused on the images, trying to allow his mind to see the images without thinking. On the third time, something caught his eye. In the image of Maya walking toward the accident, there were a number of empty parking spaces along both sides of the parking area. After the dark portion of the video, there was one extra empty spot.

Catching his breath, he replayed the video. Before the accident, an older commercial aerovan came into view immediately before Maya's silver rental car turned the corner and parked in an empty spot. After the accident, it was gone. The police would not have allowed anyone to leave the scene of an accident, so the aerovan must have left during the blacked-out part of the tape. Taking out a piece of paper, Cisco watched the video and made a quick drawing of the location of all the vehicles, putting the type and color of each on the drawing.

His brain went wild with possibilities. If the person

or persons in the aerovan kidnapped Maya, they could have moved to a different spot, waited, and then left the garage at any time. As long as Maya was subdued, any timing was possible. However, his gut feel made him contemplate the kidnappers would want to escape from the area as soon as possible. Most likely before the security system was restored.

Tapping the list of security images for the CalEd Parking Garage, Thursday, April 27, 2075, Cisco requested a start time of 11:00 AM. Vehicles moved up and down the access way, a few passing and a few parking. Finally, a rusty colored service-type van preceded Maya's rental car as it turned the corner. As she parked in a spot without a car on either side, the van turned the next corner and parked in the first empty spot. It was almost out of the security camera's viewpoint. Watching it, nothing seemed abnormal, except no one exited the van. After about a minute, Maya exited her car. The familiar video of the timeline of the accident began to play, but he kept a close eye on the van. No one exited while the video portion played, then after the video blackout period the aerovan was gone.

If the van was the kidnapper's vehicle, it meant there were several well coordinated events, not just one. Someone disabled the video security cameras to the parking area. Was the woman who crashed the car part of the plan?

Selecting the police report again, he searched for the van in the list of vehicles and ownerships identified in the report. No aerovan was listed, but then perhaps it seemed parked too far away to be pertinent to the police. Then he realized the van was already gone when the police arrived.

Stretching, he walked to the kitchen, his mind swirling with scenarios. If Maya's itinerary was known, the kidnappers could have surmised she would park in the parking garage. It was the logical place for anyone familiar with Comsys. The GTCA system was absolutely predictable, automatically parking in the most convenient garage, if it had available spots. Knowing her destination, the parking garage would have been the logical destination. Anyone with half a brain could have figured that out.

But, the aerovan preceded her. It had not followed her into the garage as expected. His brain tried to understand. It would have been easy to follow her there or to lie in wait near the garage until she arrived. Pulling off the accident, required several vehicles, not just whoever was inside the van, and practically perfect timing. This was no random kidnapping or mugging. This was a well-orchestrated event by disciplined people.

Grabbing a glass of water, Cisco returned to the study. It took him over three hours to finally find a security video showing the date and time the aerovan entered the garage. It clocked in at 9:32:16 AM. It parked on the ground level where it had full view of all incoming cars. No one exited the vehicle. The license was AV4531 996-2106. Rolling the video of the entry, he could clearly see the company logo on the side of the rust colored service vehicle – VAN NUYS PLUMBING REPAIR & SUPPLY. Finding the security video of the van's exit was easier. The van clocked out at 11:44:47 AM, minutes after the accident on the fifth floor.

Entering the name of the plumbing company into the secured database, a number of entries popped up. The most recent was a police report of a stolen company vehicle on Thursday morning. According to the police report, the company vehicle was stolen about 8:45 AM. Two plumbers were on a service call in suburban Burbank. The service call at 14562 N. Vista Barranca was legitimate. When one of the plumbers was getting parts from the company van, three armed men wearing ski hoods subdued him, took the keyfob, the aerovan, and fled. No major harm came to the plumbers. There were no other witnesses. Van Nuys Plumbing Repair reported a business address on Kester Avenue, Van Nuys.

Playing the security video at the point when Maya entered the parking garage, he watched the rust colored van pull out of the spot where it was parked and precede her car. It hovered slowly in front of her as she entered the gated parking structure. Checking several other videos as the vehicles moved from floor to floor, Cisco watched as the van drove slowly in front of Maya. When she parked, the van almost simultaneously parked nearby. All of the van's actions would appear to be typical and coincidental.

Leaning back, he put his hand on his pocket where the secured communicator was resting. He should tell headquarters what he found. Then his thoughts changed. Why had the security people missed this? Had they? Perhaps they were only looking for a vehicle following her, not preceding her.

The thin man with the hawkish nose who explained the secure communications setup had given him the creeps. Torn, Cisco vacillated on what to do. His father's last words kept ringing in his head, "Trust no one."

CHAPTER 17

Cisco wandered outside for fresh air as his eyes hurt and his lower back ached from sitting and staring at the security reports and videos. As he walked through his orchard alive with bees buzzing at the spring blossoms, he tried to organize the thoughts in his head. The Protectors selected him to be inconspicuous, not someone the kidnappers would suspect was looking for Maya. Well that described him pretty well and also untrained. However, he believed he found a crucial piece of evidence.

The kidnapping was well planned, more than well planned if you believed they had no prior knowledge of Maya's exact parking spot on the fifth floor. How could anyone know that information? However, the aerovan was waiting for her. It waited hours for her to arrive then tracked her to the parking spot. The van did not cause the accident, so how then do you stage an accident at just the right spot? The accident baffled him. It seemed so much easier to kidnap her from her apartment under the cover of night.

The plumbing company's aerovan was stolen, but at least it was a start. He was absolutely sure the aerovan carried Maya away from the scene during the video blackout. He searched and found no police report in the files saying the stolen aerovan had been located. Was it possible the security gurus working for the Protectors missed this crucial piece of information or was it possible they were in on the kidnapping?

"Trust no one," kept replaying over and over in his mind. His father believed the kidnapping and demands came from a new and dangerous group, not necessarily tied to the opposition party. He trusted his father and the president, of course, and General Castillo, but the others he met yesterday he did not know. They were Protectors, his father called them, a most trusted and elite group, so surely they could be trusted.

After Saturday's meeting, he had been obviously

tracked. His chip gave his coordinates, but how else had they tracked him – his Pcom, the Vette's Comsys, satellite, was his home bugged? His brain tried to work out if it was a good thing or bad. If the security team could track him so closely, then maybe so could the kidnappers. In truth, it nagged at him how they kept him under surveillance, tracking him since last night, and maybe even before then. No doubt, they knew he spent the night at Vivian's. Someone knew when he got home this morning. His Comsys was pre-programmed. How then could Maya have slipped through their surveillance? Surely Maya was monitored as a high priority person.

He needed to get under everyone's radar, really undercover, and he needed help. There was only one person who came to mind. It was crazy, but his uncle Charley knew more about staying one-step ahead of the law than anyone he knew.

Striding back to his house, Cisco opened a Pcom channel to Charley. When he heard a click on the receiver and saw his uncle's face he said, "*Hola tío*. What are you doing up so early?" he asked knowing his uncle often slept late after staying up all night.

Charley's face smiled in a big grin. "*Horale*, space cadet. I'm a changed man. No late night gambling for me," he said and laughed.

"*Tío*, I need a big favor."

"Sure, anything. What's up?"

Cisco thought about the tracking and knew all his transmissions would be monitored, so he made a vague statement, "I'll just come over, if that's okay."

"Anytime, space cadet. We're just watching soccer."

It was late in the afternoon when he parked the Vette in the Old Town parking garage. On his way to Charley's hotel, Cisco wandered into a military surplus store. Picking up a set of night vision glasses, an old hunting knife, long-range binoculars, a water canteen, a small pick, and a camo-shirt and cap, he dumped the bundle on the counter.

"Going camping?" the clerk asked as he looked over the items Cisco put on the counter. "You got a good sleeping bag? It's still cold up in the hills."

"Ah, no. Give me the best you have and a tote bag," Cisco replied.

He paid with his digital bankcard credits. If anyone was tracking him, the items made it look like he was going camping. It seemed like a good subterfuge for items he might need.

Slinging the bulging tote over his shoulder, he walked the short distance to the El Cortez Hotel. His uncle was expecting him, so the desk clerk and watchdog downstairs ignored him as he got into the elevator.

A kick came fast and without warning as Cisco came out of the elevator door preoccupied with thoughts about Maya and carrying the large bag with the surplus stuff. Instinctively he threw his right arm in front of the kick. The foot caught his arm above the elbow and pushed it into his ribs. Moving with the momentum of the kick, he stumbled to his left. Chuco, the mean looking bodyguard, snarled and threw another punch toward his face. The punch whizzed past Cisco's nose as he instinctively ducked.

"Hijo de puta! Got you this time," Chuco cursed, calling Cisco a motherfucker.

"CHUCO!" Charley yelled as he came out the door. *"¿Qué chingado tienes baboso?"* Charley cursed, calling Chuco a fucking drooling idiot.

A glare in Chuco's eyes told Cisco the matter was not over yet. With a low guttural grunt, he returned to his guard position near the elevator door.

"Sorry," Charley said. "I got on his case when he let you deck him yesterday."

"I take back what I said about him," Cisco said shaking his stinging elbow. "You should keep that one."

Charley was watching a soccer game on the media center. Mercedes sat on the sofa scanning a magazine reader. "What do you need that you had to come over?" Charley asked.

Cisco swallowed hard and said, "I need to borrow that *ranfla* you won in the poker game."

"What? A space cadet driving a lowrider?"

Cisco swallowed even harder then said, "I'll let you borrow my Vette in exchange, but no stunts."

"¡No me digas!" Charley responded with a surprised look. "Are you sure you want to drive the ranfla? I can't believe you would let yourself be seen in one of those machines."

"I have a special project in Los Angeles and I don't want to take the Vette. It will stand out too much," Cisco lied, although the part about the Vette standing out was true. He decided assuming a very low profile, a split identity, might give him the ability to travel in different circles. One of his trainers at the Space Academy stated when asked about the possibility of meeting space aliens, "Then, you must think and act like an alien." The trainer was joking, but Cisco thought it a good point.

"Sure, you can have it for as long as you like. It will give me a break from those pinche Española outlaws. We've been holed up here too long. Those vatos keep watch for the car in town and would be on me if I took it out."

Mercedes must have been listening to the conversation. "Can we go back to the coast?" she asked. "I'm sick of being cooped up here."

"Sure honey, anywhere you want to go," Charley replied to her. "Mercedes will love the Vette convertible, except it will mess up her hair," Charley whispered to Cisco.

A big play on the soccer field was announced by a loud cheer filling the living space with noise. The Durango Diggers had kicked a goal. Charley turned down the sound of the holograph unit.

"I can't believe you want the ranfla. Are you sure?"

"Yeah," Cisco laughed. "It'll be fun."

Charley walked over to the bar. "Tequila?"

"No, I gotta go."

"You always gotta go," Charley said. "Here have a shot. What you got in the tote?" Charley asked.

"Oh, just stuff I need for camping. I'm hoping to get some downtime and thought I'd go hiking up in the hills after this next job," Cisco lied. He wanted to change the subject before Charley asked too many questions about the gear and he needed to get other information from his uncle.

"*Tío,* can you give me the name of your InfoAgent? I might need some help on this next job." Cisco tried to keep his voice nonchalant.

Charley boasted many times about his InfoAgents – hackers, trackers, computer gurus who worked undercover of the electronic snooping devices. He boasted the Old Town InfoAgents were the best in the Republic.

Cisco was relieved when Charley did not directly question the request. "No *problema,* space cadet," he responded. "I work with two guys. One is a lightweight and the other is a real heavyweight expert. Which one do you want?"

"What do you mean?"

"The lightweight does simple stuff like document research or credit analysis or missing persons. He mostly works with public domain information. The heavyweight expert can get any information from anywhere, anytime. He knows how to access any database through any network around the world and then some."

Cisco jumped in a little too quick and said, "Heavyweight."

Charley scrutinized Cisco and narrowed his eyes, but only shrugged. "His name is Agustín de la Garza. You can find him at Edificio Obregon on Calle de Nogales. It's not too far. Ask for Gus. I'll send him a message and tell him you are on the way. He doesn't work cheap."

"Can he be trusted?"

"Trusted? I trust Gus with my life and have a couple times."

"Oh . . . okay thanks," Cisco said.

"You in some kind of trouble, space cadet?" his uncle asked sensing something was not right.

"No *tío,* nothing like that. I just have a weird job to do in Los Angeles." It was not an understatement. Weird, crazy, scary, and all of the above. He wished he could tell his uncle more, ask him for help, or just talk over ideas.

Pulling out a keyfob to the Vette, he put it on the bar top. "The password to override the autosensor is Vette2069."

"What kind of a stupid password is that for a space cadet?" his uncle laughed.

"I guess I'm not all that creative," Cisco responded. "You take good care of it!"

"I know, I know," Charley said, "No funny business. No loopty loops. You'll find the beast at Peralta's garage on El Centro. Ask for Pete at the back door and for God's sake get it out of Old Town quick."

"Gracias tío, I have to go. You two have a good time at the coast." On his way to the elevator Cisco skirted Chuco. The bodyguard gave back a mean glare.

CHAPTER 18

A few cold raindrops fell on Cisco's arms and dotted the sidewalk when he walked out of the hotel. A patch of low dark clouds hung in an otherwise bright sunny sky, but it did not look like the rain would stick around. Cisco walked several blocks toward the plaza, which was beginning to come alive with families carrying picnic baskets and lawn chairs for a Sunday evening concert. They too were taking a chance the clouds would move on.

He found Edificio Obregon several blocks off the plaza. The older looking adobe facade concealed a modern interior. It was not an apartment building, but a small office building. Pushing in the main doors, flowers, plants, and three small trees grew in areas where sunlight was brought indoors by a series of reflecting mirrors. The lobby was empty, but he spotted a monitor located on the far wall. Cisco activated the monitor and a robotic voice vibrated at him.

"Please state your business?"

"I'm here to see Agustín de la Garza," Cisco answered nervously.

"One moment please," the robotic voice replied. There was a short pause, before the monitor displayed a young man with shaggy hair. His brown face was unshaven and his eyes were somewhat blood shot."

"What do you want?" the shaggy young man said.

"Charley Arambula told me you could help me. My name is Francisco Salaz."

"Yeah, he told me you were coming," the shaggy young man said with more enthusiasm. "Go to the elevator. I'll have it programmed to bring you to my suite."

The elevator moved fast. It was difficult to tell which direction it was going, up or down. Suddenly the elevator doors popped open into an empty area. Cisco stepped out and the elevator closed behind him. The room was completely empty except for two odd pieces of framed artwork. There were no visible doors except the elevator and Cisco stood there scanning the room feeling a bit uneasy.

"Drop the tote on the floor and step away," a voice came from behind him. As a few minutes of silence ticked by Cisco felt sweat pop out along his brow. What the hell had he been thinking? He was trapped in an office building with no way out.

An invisible panel in a wall opened and the shaggy young man came out the opening. He held out his hand and said, "Glad to meet you Francisco. Your uncle is a good friend of mine. Come on in. Sorry for the scrutiny, just part of my work you know." Gus picked up the tote of supplies and led the way through the opening.

Gus' office did not reflect his shaggy appearance. Everything was both orderly and tasteful. He had sleek furniture and interesting art and sculptures. Video monitors filled the main wall of the living area. It had the look of the control room at the Space Port on Mars. Each video monitor displayed a different image and several small holographs were playing on the wraparound desk area. To Cisco's left a modern kitchen and a partly open door led to a bedroom. Gus not only worked here, but obviously lived here as well. Gus noted Cisco assessing the area. "I work twenty-four seven," he said explaining his home office.

Gus motioned Cisco to follow him toward a couple chairs near the desk area. "Charley said you must be in some kind of trouble. How can I help?"

Cisco tried to process Gus' appearance and Charley's confidence in this man. He was obviously successful, but could this man be trusted?

"Please call me Cisco. I'm not in any trouble, not legal trouble anyway. First, I have some questions. What exactly do you do? I mean what kind of things can you do? What are the rules?" Cisco's cheeks reddened. "I guess you've figured out I've never used an InfoAgent before."

"Relax Cisco," Gus replied. "It's a very simple agreement. Basically, I get you the information you need and you pay me an hourly rate plus expenses. Since you're Charley's nephew, I'll skip all of the yucky stuff about what happens if you don't pay. Everything is strictly top notch confidential. A good InfoAgent knows enough information to topple governments, but that's not what we do. Whatever information you need I can get it."

"How can I be sure the information is correct?" Cisco pressed further.

Gus leaned back in his chair and laughed. "If it wasn't, I'd be out of business. I can tap directly into any government or business system. Sometimes a system is deliberately modified, but I have many sources that I run my crosscheck algorithms. Believe me, I love this job and I'm good at it."

The wall with the monitors was almost visually blinding as the twenty or so monitors and holographs all played different visuals. Cisco stared at the wall trying to get over a feeling of panic. He sensed this man would not work for him unless he knew the truth.

"Well, what do you need me to do?" Gus asked again.

Cisco swallowed hard and said a silent prayer. "An agent for the Evaluation and Qualification Agency named Cecilia Juarez was kidnapped last Thursday. I have to find her," Cisco said.

Gus turned and voiced a command. A picture of Maya popped up on one of the monitors with some information beneath the picture.

"*Madre*, the president's great-granddaughter. The Republic is sure keeping a lid on that one."

Shocked, Cisco replied, "Yes. Her identity is supposed to be a secret."

"I told you I have very good sources," Gus replied. "What does this have to do with you? All I could find on you is your EQA identity."

"I need to go undercover to find her.

Gus whistled. "You got a big job. Why you?"

Cisco paused and didn't know exactly what to say. Why him? It was a question he still could hardly process.

"The president thinks the kidnapping is an inside job and doesn't trust anyone. We're afraid she'll be harmed if the kidnappers detect the secret police or government is on their tail. The president is my godfather and since I work for the EQA they think I can be . . . invisible."

"Nobody is invisible, but they may have a point. If they use any typical government operative, it would be obvious. Tell me what you know."

Cisco spent several hours relating all the known details. He explained about the CalEd parking garage, the missing video segment, and the stolen van. He tried to leave nothing he knew or surmised out of his narrative.

"Have the police found the van?" Gus asked.

"No. At least there is no police report," Cisco replied. "I thought that's where you could start."

"I'll get you the make and model of the aerovan from the plumbing company records. I can get the footprint of that model from the manufacturer. Then I can scan the traffic control database to match that footprint with anything that resembles it in the area of CalEd. I'll check the police report and follow up," Gus explained how he would get started.

"How undercover are you supposed to go?" Gus asked.

Cisco hesitated. "I'm not sure what you mean by that?"

"Why aren't you chipped?" Gus asked.

"I am, but they've disabled it. The head of security for this project had me fitted with a secure channel microcom."

"I scanned you before I let you in and you're clean. Where's the device?"

Cisco dug into his pocket and pulled out the wasp-like communicator.

"Has it ever been used? Have you made contact using it yet?" Gus asked.

"No. They fitted it to me and did some stuff, but I haven't used it yet."

"Good. Once activated, they can track you and monitor any digital frequency, phone calls you make, stuff like that. I think they don't trust you and are using you as bait," Gus explained.

"Bait?"

"Well, maybe not exactly bait, but they are putting you out on the front line to take the fall while they work behind the scenes and will only tell you part of what you need to know."

Cisco shuddered and anger churned in his gut. He knew the thin man in the blue shirt, the security guy at headquarters, gave him the creeps. "Can it be disengaged?"

"Yes, give it to me. Do not turn it on. I can run a debugging program to disable the tracking. They will never know it has been modified," Gus assured him and began to fiddle with the communicator.

"What if I'm not wearing it? They said it doesn't work if it's not in my ear," Cisco asked him.

"The communication only works calibrated to your voice and if it is close to the auditory nerve. If it's in your pocket or just in the car you can't send calls, but the tracker still works unless it's disconnected like I'm doing," Gus explained the wasp-like G2000 microcom device.

"So, how do we communicate?" Cisco asked.

"No problem. You can't use your personal Pcom. They'll have that tracked too." He pulled open a drawer and pulled out a small Pcom device with a wristband. We'll use normal channels, but this Pcom has a scrambler which will jumble the database so our conversations are garbled and misdirected in the government communications databases. Only someone actively listening to our conversations could listen in. That is highly unlikely unless they are sitting right next to you with a listener device. I think you'd notice that," he said and chuckled.

"I'll program it to your voice and I'll answer day or night."

"Can I use this to make other calls?" Cisco said turning the Pcom over in his hand.

"You can use it like a regular Pcom, but I wouldn't unless you have to. Calls other than to me would be open to the database. Oh yeah, and it only does voice, not video." Gus explained. "Is that all?" Gus added.

"I guess that's all I have to start with," Cisco said.

"It shouldn't take too long to pick up the trail of the van," Gus said. "When are you leaving?"

"In the morning, and oh yeah I'll be driving Charley's stolen *ranfla.*"

"You are living dangerously," Gus laughed then continued, "Actually, that's not a bad idea. Your Vette could be a big fat target. They no doubt have it on special tracking."

"How did you know about my Vette?" Cisco asked.

"I told you, I'm good."

Gus stuck out his hand and Cisco took it. The handshake sealed their agreement.

CHAPTER 19

The rain stopped and the sun was low when Cisco emerged from Gus' home office. He felt somewhat more comfortable after meeting Gus and now did not feel so alone. Heading across the park, he walked five blocks before he crossed El Centro. Down the street, he could see the old sign for Peralta's garage.

It was Sunday and getting late. The place looked closed. The faded old gas pumps stood like aged guards, long ago dried up. He went around to the back and knocked on the door.

"Sorry we're closed," a voice shouted.

"I need to talk to Pete," Cisco shouted back. "I'm here to pick up Charley's *ranfla.*"

From somewhere inside the building he heard a loud clang and Mexican music filtered to his ears.

"Just a minute," the voice yelled.

After a short wait, the door swung open and an older man wearing jeans and holding a sandwich said, "I'm Pete. Charley sent me a message, but I wasn't sure when you were coming. So you want the beast?" Pete looked at Cisco and chuckled. "You don't look like the lowrider type," he said and motioned for Cisco to follow him.

Parked in one of the bays, a sparkling candy-apple red aerorider's frontend stared at him. At first glance, Cisco was shocked at the sight of the ghastly machine. Tires had been obsolete for years, but *ranflas* were modified to be street machines, with tires and wheels. The exterior of the normally streamlined aerocar design sported large wheels and wheel covers. Each side rail was trimmed with small lights that illuminated down toward the street. The car's paint job was shocking. The bright red hood was airbrushed in the center with a large yellow circle. In the center of the circle was a red Zia sign, the traditional symbol used for New Mexico. Depicting the sacred symbol, each direction from a center circle had four parallel lines radiating in four directions. An image of the Virgin de

Guadalupe was airbrushed on the trunk. Inside, the seats were covered with white fur and the dash was wood.

Cisco swallowed hard. He had not expected the *ranfla* to be so . . . so noticeable. Suddenly, he questioned his plan. Loud music blasted from powerful speakers. A young *vato* was bobbing up and down with the music sitting in the front seat.

"Jose," Pete shouted, "shut that thing off. This man is here to take it, *ese.*"

Jose gave Cisco a curious look and said. "You don't look like no *vato.*"

Cisco stared at the car as the young man turned off the music and crawled out. He was about Cisco's size. The image on his faded black t-shirt was indistinguishable. His black cotton pants hung low around his hips, torn in several places. Around his head, a black and yellow banana covered his forehead topped by a baseball cap, which he wore backwards.

Cisco wanted to tell Pete he was not going to take the car after all, but chuckled. If the government wanted him to go undercover, how better than somebody they could not imagine.

"Jose, I'll give you a fifty if you sell me those clothes," Cisco told the young man.

"Fifty! You got yourself a deal, *ese.* For fifty I'll even throw in my sticker. You might need it."

Behind him Pete was laughing. "You one crazy son of a bitch," he said, "but then I guess you're related to Charley. Nothing ever surprises me about him."

While Jose went to find something else to wear, Pete showed Cisco the unusual knobs and buttons on the console of the car. Pete handed Cisco a heavy gold chain. Hanging off the chain was a keyfob shaped like a gold cross.

"I know. It is pretty crazy," Pete said with a laugh.

Jose came back with a pile of clothes and handed them to Cisco.

"Oh ah, thanks," Cisco said putting the stack into the car. He crawled into the driver's seat and sank down low in the car. He inserted the keyfob, but nothing happened. Jose reached through the window and pointed to a button on the console. Cisco pushed it and the engine started, lighting the console up like strands of Christmas lights. Jose opened the large garage doors. Gently pushing on the steering stick, the aerorider jerked forward.

"It takes some getting used to," Pete yelled to him. "Use a real light touch when you're ground level."

Cisco barely touched the control and slowly drove through the large doors. Driving the car on tires was a crazy sensation. Cisco could feel every bump in the Old Town streets. He could not imagine a world where all cars drove this way, although he found it intriguing to navigate corners. The street glittered from the tiny lights running around the base of the car. Surprisingly, the ghastly vehicle handled well.

Once he was several blocks from the central plaza, he pushed the button Pete showed him and heard the engine whirl as the *ranfla* lifted off.

"Destination," Comsys asked.

"Monte Tecanachic," Cisco replied.

Comsys followed the aeropath from Old Town and merged onto the aeroway skirting New Dublán. When it exited the aeropath just south of the mountain, Cisco took manual control of the *ranfla* and flew home. Knowing that his house would be watched, he landed about a half a mile away in a wooded area. Hiking to the back door of the house, he let himself in. He assumed everything he might do inside the house would be monitored, but he hoped to keep the *ranfla* hidden.

CHAPTER 20

Sunday evening, as the darkness of the Earth's shadow overtook the orange glow on the western horizon, a nondescript tan sedan pulled out of a dirty white stucco garage in an older section of Hermosillo, Sonora. Blending in with traffic the tan sedan headed north. Mason Warrick flew the sedan with Maya, drugged and bound, slumped in the front passenger seat. The two Venezuelan *pendejos* were goofing around in the backseat telling each other stupid jokes. Grumbling, Mason hoped to find some way to get rid of the two assholes before the job was finished.

Heading north they cruised toward Phoenix, Arizona. Flying the aeropaths under GTCA control, the sedan crossed the Maricopa quadrant and skirted the west side of the mega city heading northwest. As the lights of greater Phoenix disappeared behind him, Mason followed a line of aerocars going to Las Vegas.

Mason planned the route with precision. When he saw the lights of Kingman, Arizona in the distance, he turned west recalculating to Laughlin, Nevada. He had calculated the time and distance from Kingman to the California border. Fifteen minutes west of Kingman, he saw the lights of Bullhead City and Laughlin up ahead. Just past the two cities on the Colorado River, the empty desert was dark in every direction. He dropped to under 100 feet above the desert and put on his night vision glasses. He knew the trick should evade the global traffic tracking sensors, though it was risky to fly so low in the dark. This section of desert had small hilly sections, leftover from when the land was the bottom of a huge ocean covering the American Southwest. Even with the glasses, he might not see the unusual terrain.

As the sedan sped low above the Mohave Preserve, Mason had few visual pointers once the lights of the river towns faded and he crossed into the California desert. About twenty minutes later, ahead and south, he saw the ribbon of lights from the I-40 aeroway crossing the sky south of the small town of Goffs. Staying north of the aeroway, he continued west. Thirteen minutes later, the lights of Lancaster, California, popped on the horizon and as he reached the outskirts of the town, he lifted to a cruising altitude. Comsys beeped as the car was recognized by GTCA's radar. If his planning and execution was accurate, the gap in the trip would be untraceable.

Mason listened to Comsys east of Lancaster until he heard the traffic control system acknowledge the vehicle as it entered metropolitan Los Angeles. "You have entered Los Angeles metropolitan airspace. Destination?" Comsys prompted.

"Santa Clarita," Mason replied. Following the Los Angeles tangled aeropaths toward the west, the tan sedan flew across miles of lights. The aeropaths utilized quadruple multi-lane layers, something only very large cities used. Eight lanes, four deep, went in each direction. Mason removed the special night glasses and leaned back in the seat, finally relaxing.

He found this job tedious. His package, the semiconscious young woman, was an unusual job. Babysitting the girl with the two stupid goons the PLV insisted he take along grated him even more. His work was usually, make the kill and disappear. His instructions however were clear – they were not to harm the girl and to keep her alive. For how long, he did not know.

The two goons were idiots and Mason could not understand why the PLV sent them along. The only logical reason was the buyer did not trust him. It meant at least one of the goons was not what he appeared. A fake, a plant, making sure Mason performed the job per instructions and possibly instructed to eliminate him if anything went wrong.

One of the goons was Silvio Leoni, the younger brother of Armando, a PLV kingpin. Mason kept a sharp eye on him, wondering if Armando sent Silvio along on this mission and just how personally involved Armando might be in this deal. He thought Silvio was the plant, but both men seemed just goofy or very, very good at their job.

Either way it worried him.

ʼ Leaning against something hard along her right ribs, Maya felt the drug starting to wear off. She learned over the last few days to ignore the woozy feeling she felt when the drug wore off. Through her closed eyelids, lights flashed around her and she was sitting, not lying down. She told her foggy brain to focus. It was difficult as the drug they gave her worked quickly and wore off slow. Over the past couple days, when they would come into the small bedroom to check on her, she pretended to still be under its effect, so as to have more time with a clear head. She worked hard trying to remember every detail and listening to conversations, not knowing if some tidbit would help her escape.

She remembered hearing church bells earlier today when she was locked in the small bedroom and thought maybe it was Sunday, but was not sure. As she listened to the sounds around her, she heard Comsys tell the driver he was entering Santa Clarita airspace and realized they were moving. Forcing her eyes open, Maya tried to concentrate on her current situation.

She knew she was kidnapped last Thursday from the CalEd parking garage in Burbank. Her EQA assignments had taken her to Los Angeles numerous times, but she had never visited CalEd. California Edison was California's largest utility company.

On her way to the CalEd meeting, she parked the rental aerocar in the parking structure. It was a little before noon and she thought she would have enough time before the meeting to have lunch. Suddenly a small aerocar zipped around the corner and crashed into several parked vehicles. It happened so fast. Now the accident was a blur in her mind. What was clear in her mind was the sound of a woman's voice yelling for help and what sounded like a baby crying.

Of course, she responded and ran toward the accident to see if she could help. It was instinct. Dropping her briefcase near the crashed aerocar, she knelt down to peer into the open window. Suddenly a smelly rag was pushed against her nose. The pungent smell was the last thing she remembered until she awoke in a little bedroom. Where, she did not know.

There were three kidnappers. The leader was tall with stringy blond hair and walked with a limp. She only saw him a few times. He injected her with a drug of some sort. The two others, one tall and the other one shorter and stockier, fed her and watched over her. The shorter one was nicer and untied her hands so she could use the bathroom. The blond leader groused at him, but the shorter one stood up to him.

The blond leader spoke Spanish with an odd accent though Maya heard him curse in English. The other two spoke only Spanish. She had a feeling they were not a collective gang. The leader seemed to dislike the two men, yelling and cursing at them often. She heard names. One was named Silvio, but she was not sure which one.

Except for the times she was allowed to use the bathroom, her hands were bound tightly in front of her, though often her feet were free. At night they cuffed her to a bed post. They fed her and gave her water. Yesterday, the shorter man shared a coke with her when the blond leader went out. He asked her name and she told him, "Cecilia Juarez." It was her assumed name. The name she lived with, not her real name, Maya Angelina Torres, great-granddaughter to the President of the United Central Republic. When she said her name was Cecilia, he did not react to the lie, giving her hope this was not a political kidnapping.

Her great-grandfather was her inspiration and all she wanted as she grew up was to serve him and the Republic. He had developed the particle, which allowed the world to recover from financial disaster and founded the Republic. She always felt a strong connection to him, maybe even stronger than with her own father or mother. She often dreamed of him in strange dreams, and it was always her *bisabuelo,* her great-grandfather, who spoke to her or helped her in those dreams.

Earlier today, the kidnappers gave her food, a

synthetic premade meal tray. It tasted like turkey, but Maya knew it was not. Then sometime later, the mean blond man came into the room with the needle. She tried to resist, but knew it was hopeless. The drug acted quickly and she had no recollection of being put into this car. Slowly, the drug's effect was wearing off and Maya fought for control over her mind.

Leaning on the right-side passenger door, Maya forced herself to watch the sky outside. She could see other vehicles flying near them and heard Comsys chirping. The traffic continued to get busier and busier. She had distinctly heard it say, "Santa Clarita airspace." It was in the Los Angeles quadrant, not far from the city of Los Angeles.

Though she was kidnapped in Burbank, she had heard the video unit this morning giving the Hermosillo newscast. There was no doubt in her mind she was in that city in the United Central Republic this morning. She thought it odd they kidnapped her in California and now brought her back. For just a moment, she wondered if they might be taking her back to release her, here in Los Angeles. Perhaps it had all been a mistake and they realized it.

"Where are we going?" a voice grumbled from the backseat.

"Shutup, Rico. I didn't ask for you two *pendejos* for this job. Just do what you're told and don't ask questions," the driver grumbled in response.

The blond man was driving. From the tone of his voice, she realized she was the job and they were not returning to Los Angeles to release her. She heard the hard edge in his voice. Her heart sank. Their job, no doubt, was to kidnap the great-granddaughter of the President of the United Central Republic. No doubt there was a huge ransom. She wished she could tell her great-grandfather not to pay it.

"Entering Los Angeles central quadrant," Comsys said. "Destination?"

"Elysian Park," Mason replied. The park was four blocks from the address in Echo Park. He hated knowing his movements were now tracked, but there was no way to circumvent the Los Angeles Comsys.

Maya listened storing the words in her foggy brain. They were going to a place called Elysian Park in Los Angeles.

CHAPTER 21

Settling at his desk, Cisco logged into the security network and pulled up the documents pertaining to Maya's kidnapping scanning for anything marked as a change or newly added. Finding nothing, Cisco reread the records containing all the accident information with newfound enthusiasm.

Pulling up the video monitor he watched the accident video again, and again, in case he missed anything. Cross-referencing the police report, there seemed no connection of the people involved in the accident and the kidnapping, and yet the coincidence seemed unbelievable.

The police report took the following statement from Alexis Groves, age 27, 3456 West Covington Apt 215, Van Nuys. She was driving the small blue aerocar which appeared to take the corner in the parking garage too fast and lost control crashing into two parked vehicles.

"I was trying to find a place to park. I came around the corner of the parking level. I dropped my Pcom and I swerved. These old-style parking garages are so tight, you know. Navigating them is hard. It wasn't my fault."

The information from the security people on Alexis Groves showed she worked at a small company in Van Nuys, had a nine-year-old daughter, and a clean record. If anything raised a red flag, the government security people could not find it.

Cisco watched the tape looking for the distraction the young woman described, but the angle of the camera was not good. Still, she was the most likely person to be involved with the kidnappers. She caused the accident. Her security bio however was clean – nothing to make anyone think she was a criminal or involved in something diabolical like this high-level kidnapping. The car was in her name, was insured, and she did not leave the scene with the kidnappers. It made no sense to him, yet he believed she must be somehow involved.

Next was the driver of a second aerocar that crashed

into the rear end of Alexis Groves' vehicle and some debris from the first crash. The driver's name was Philip Conner, age 31, 672 West Covina Drive, Building A, Unit 12, Burbank. The second car crashed after the video blackout.

"I came around the corner of level 5. I was putting my parking fob back in my glovebox when I looked up and the lane was blocked by an accident. I know it's stupid, but I just didn't see it in time or expect it. I was just coming back from lunch. I work at CalEd."

Cisco thought an employee of CalEd seemed unlikely to be involved and just unlucky. Besides his security bio confirmed he was a financial tech for CalEd and had been employed for over six years.

The police also took a report from Richard Gomez, age 44, 1214 E. Deever Street, Burbank.

"I was coming back to my car after paying CalEd to turn my lights back on. Some idiot crashed my car. You better put that in your report, so her insurance will pay. What am I supposed to do?"

None of the three people questioned at the scene mentioned the van, Maya, a kidnapping, or anything helpful. Cisco pondered how Alexis Groves could have known exactly when to stage the accident. He thought about wading through the video from the parking structure's other cameras, but decided he would let Gus do it. Maybe Gus could connect Alexis Groves to the kidnapping.

Exhausted, he stripped and eased into the hot tub. He chuckled to himself wondering if the security police were bugging his house and wondered if they watched him slip naked into the tub. He decided to act as normal as possible, doing only expected things.

Leaning back in the hot mineral water, he closed his eyes. His muscles relaxed. Surprisingly, his body no longer ached in Earth's gravity and he wondered if the adrenaline boosts over the past two days helped restore his strength faster. Slowing his breathing, Cisco cleared his mind and sank up to his chin in the bubbly water. Drifting into sleep, the familiar dream scene appeared.

The river before him churned deep and the current was strong. Across the river stood his Nino, his godfather, and next to him stood a young girl. He saw them clearly. She looked about ten years old with short black hair and big black eyes. He recognized her right away. It was Maya. The expression on Maya's face was sad and tears were flowing down her cheeks. She raised her hand to him, motioning him to come across the river in the same way his Nino usually did in the dream. Was this her way of asking for help?

Water touched his lips waking him with a start. His *Nino* and Maya evaporated from his mind. Disturbed, he wondered if he had fallen asleep or was it truly a vision. Confused, Cisco pulled himself up out of the water and dried off.

It was only 9:10 PM, but he felt the exhaustion kick in. Heading to the bedroom, he tossed aside the towel wrapped around his waist and stretched out on the bed with the media device on his lap. He started reading the case reports carefully, one more time. He was in the middle of rereading the accident report when his Pcom chirped. It was Vivian.

"Hi Cisco," she greeted him. "I was just thinking about you." The holograph of her casually perched on her sofa wearing a soft black sweater looked staged. Was she trying to look suggestive? His lap was covered with his media device, but it tickled him to think she might find his nakedness alluring.

"I, ah, just got home and have been going over some reports from Mars. I was going to call you later. Last night was great," he replied.

"Yes, it was great. I was wondering if you'd like to go with me to the new exhibit at the Museo de las Culturas on Thursday. We'll have dinner and come back to my place."

His brain clicked through something to say other than a snarky comment like, *"No, I have no idea where I will be on Thursday because I have to find the great-granddaughter of the President for the Protectors who expect me . . . to save the country."*

Instead he said, "Viv, that sounds fun. I'm going camping with my father for a couple days. Just some time to readjust to having sky over my head and spend time with dad. I'm not sure of his schedule. Can I call you later in the week?"

"Sure," she replied sounding a bit disappointed. "Well, call me. Call me anytime Cisco, but next time make sure you're dressed," she laughed lightly and her holograph image disappeared.

He stared at the Pcom. Was Vivian getting serious? She was beautiful, even more beautiful than when they were dating. When they were young, they had been so in love. They could talk about anything and sex was terrific. She was everything he wanted back then. Last night seemed normal and yet, something left him feeling weird. He lived on the side of a mountain and she hardly seemed the type of woman who would enjoy his way of life. Certainly, he could not fit into hers. However, he was not oblivious to the erection he hid under his media device during the call.

Vivian terminated the video call to Cisco. She had not wanted to call, but his beacon locator was not working. Her high-level security clearance gave her access to location data, however he was not tracking. She wondered about his excuse for Thursday. His father was in Sinaloa at an agrofarm. Vivian was tracking him too. She knew Cisco was space weary, but her plan to entice him had not worked. She voiced a PIC number into the Pcom and waited for an answer.

Sometime later Cisco woke in the middle of the night from a deep sleep. The evening's chill was gently blowing through the window, so he pulled up a blanket and rolled on his side. Trying to regain a peaceful sleep, his brain started working. Any additional sleep came only in fitful ten-minute spurts. At 5:30 AM he crawled out of bed dreading the sunrise.

The morning was cool as he performed the karate exercises on the back patio. The crisp spring air hinted of rain with heavier clouds gathering along the eastern side of the mountains. Somewhere during the exercise routine, he realized it was the first of May. It was a holiday in the Republic for workers and most government offices were closed. Today was not a holiday for him however; it was the first day of working as an undercover agent for the

Protectors.

As he continued his workout, orange and pink tinted gray clouds on the eastern horizon, announcing the sun's daily ascent. Stopping, he watched the sun rise to its full glory turning the sky an intense crimson along the edges of the clouds. Staring at the miracle spread out before him he thanked God. *"Gracias a Dios."* Surely God would help him with the unbelievable task. Surely God would let him see more sunrises here on his mountainside.

He worked through the morning routine, his body knowing what to do without thought. He was in the middle of roundhouse kick, when his brain snapped to attention. The police report did not mention the woman who caused the accident, Alexis Groves, had a baby in the car. A baby was crying on the audio as Maya could be seen walking toward the accident. The woman was yelling for help and the child was crying. Cisco could hear a replay of the audio in his mind. Surely the police would have noted a baby in the woman's car in the police report, perhaps checking to make sure the child was not hurt. What happened to the child?

Excitedly he finished the workout. The beautiful sunrise and his revelation filled him with hope replacing the knot of dread in his stomach. By the time he finished the karate workout, the sunrise's colors had faded and the sun was starting to warm the chill in the air.

CHAPTER 22

Back at his study, Cisco replayed the video and audio portions of the crash. The audio recording of the woman yelling for help and a baby crying were as he remembered. It was a small detail, but important. Hurriedly he scanned the young woman's bio. All it indicated was she worked in Van Nuys, had a nine-year-old daughter, and a clean record. Cisco tucked the information in his brain and decided to ask Gus to find out more about Alexis Groves.

Staring in the bathroom mirror, the face looking back at him looked tired. The dark brown unruly hair was sticking up around his face and his chin stubbly. He activated the shower, deciding to let his beard grow.

Cascades of hot water poured over his head. He started humming a tune. Vivian's call last night inviting him to the Museum and dinner bothered him a bit, but in the light of morning it seemed like a fine idea. Why shouldn't he want to spend time with a beautiful sexy woman? After all, Monica was still on Mars and besides Vivian was much better in bed.

Perhaps it was the lie he told her, saying he was going camping with his father. Perhaps he should have told her he was going hunting, because it was more to the truth – hunting for Maya.

He realized the dream did not come to him last night. Hopefully it did not mean Maya was already dead, not able to summon him in the vision. She was kidnapped on Thursday. Today was her fourth day of captivity. Looking up into the cascading water, he asked God for help, "Please send *San Cristobal* to watch over me and Maya."

Ten minutes later, he stood naked with a cup of coffee. He smiled thinking perhaps someone in the security police might be watching. If they were, well they had already seen his dick in the shower. Walking to the back patio, his voice activated the Pcom waiting for Gus to answer.

"Cisco, I found the van. *Chingado,* I have to tell you it

wasn't easy. Those boys are good and understand how to
confuse the GTCA's tracking. You were correct. I think
this is definitely an inside job. They're good, but not good
enough for me," Gus gloated.

"Here's what happened. After stealing the aerovan in
Burbank, it flew to the parking garage. It entered the garage
at 9:32 AM. You already know that. Anyway, it left the
garage at 11:44:47 using a prepaid digital card to pay the
bill. I'm still working on tracking that purchase. It flew to
Vanalden Park and landed. Vanalden is a large recreational
park in the Northridge area. The aerovan is not there
anymore, so I assume the police finally found it even
though there is no report. I had to process a three hundred
sixty degree scan to pick up all traffic leaving the park. I
figure they would not want to drag or carry her too far and
perhaps had another vehicle waiting. About ten minutes
later another smaller aerovan left that area. I tracked it
heading into a canyon near Presa Rodrigues northeast of
Hermosillo. I'm one hundred percent sure it was the
kidnappers. I was able to verify all the other vehicles from
the park and their destinations seemed normal, like mom's
taking their kids home."

"Great," Cisco replied. "At least that's a start.
Anything else?"

"There's more," Gus said. "Presa Rodrigues is a really
desolate area with very little traffic. This is one of the
kidnappers' mistakes. The aerovan never came out, but
about fifteen minutes later, a Ford sedan left the same area.
I'm sure they switched the aerovan for the sedan near the
lake. I followed the sedan to an address in Hermosillo.
They stayed put in Hermosillo until last night. I tracked the
sedan to outside of Kingman where I lost it in the desert,
but I have a trace going. Whoever is controlling this
kidnapping understands the GTCA and is definitely making
it impossible for the police to track. Where do you want to
start?"

Cisco was impressed with Gus' findings. He certainly
was living up to Charley's description of a heavyweight
InfoAgent.

"First I need to tell you something. In the audio portion of the kidnapping, there is a woman yelling for help and a baby crying. It seems to be coming from the car which caused the crash. Maya is seen walking toward it, probably lured thinking the woman and baby needed help. However, the police report does not note a baby, only the driver, an Alexis Groves. I think she's in on it and I need you to check her out."

"Good work. I missed that too. Have you decided where you'll start?"

"I want to follow the trail," Cisco replied. "Maybe I can pick up some clues along the way. I'll start at the Presa Rodrigues location and then go to Hermosillo."

"Good idea. Are you ready to leave?"

"Just about. I've got to pack and shut down a few things here."

"Okay, call me on your way and I'll download the coordinates." Gus disconnected.

Cisco tried to clear his mind while he packed. He decided to wear his favorite sweatshirt and jeans, though he should have run them through the wash last night. He stuffed a small duffel with two EQA shirts and pants, a couple t-shirts, socks, underwear, and his shaving kit and a few other things.

Walking into the kitchen he picked up his EQA lab toolkit from the kitchen table and a handful of space meal packs and placed them on top of the clothes and zipped the bag. The stack of *vato* clothes sat on the kitchen table. He stuffed them into a grocery sack. He decided not to wear the *vato* outfit even though he might look out of place driving the *ranfla,* at least not yet. Picking up a baseball cap and stuffing the laser and communicator in his pocket, he ordered the security system to lock as he walked out of the house.

Exiting the back door, he took a circuitous route to where he parked the cherry red car. Inserting the keyfob, he instructed it for manual mode. The morning sun was still low behind him as he headed the *ranfla* west over a dip in the northern Sierra Madres.

He activated the communicator for Gus and got an immediate answer.

"Gus, I'm driving the *ranfla*. I left the Vette parked in the Old Town garage for Charley to use."

Gus whistled and laughed. "Okay, give me a sec to set a beacon on you," he said.

"Ok, got you. I'll download the coordinates of the location in Presa Rodrigues into your Comsys. Call me when you get there."

Putting the car into Comsys automatic control, Cisco glanced behind him seeing only blue sky and puffy clouds. He leaned back into the seat.

A half mile away, a blue *ranfla* was parked near the base of Cisco's property. The blue car had followed Cisco from Peralta's Garage in Old Town last night, when they got an alert the red *ranfla* was active and moving. It flew and parked near a house in this remote location. Three men spent a chilly night on the mountain, waiting for the driver of the red *ranfla* to get up. Oso and Flaco snored in the back seat. Arturo, the owner, dozed in the front waiting for the blip to show on the scanner.

Arturo was sure the man driving his red car was not the *vato* who stole it and Mercedes from the poker game, but hoped the man might lead them to him. The man, named Charley Arambula, bested him at poker on a hand Arturo was sure he had him beat. In the mayhem, Mercedes escaped with Charley in the red *ranfla*. According to his sources, Charley had a home and many connections in Old Town. After almost a week, the red car was spotted back in Old Town at Peralta's Garage. His contacts said they were holed up on the top floor of the El Cortez Hotel surrounded by bodyguards. Then last night the car was on the move.

"Wakeup, he's leaving," Arturo grumbled at the two sleeping in the back seat.

Hovering, before accelerating, the red *ranfla* circled then flew off west over the mountain. The image blipped on the simple scanner held by the driver of the blue car. As

Cisco flew west, the blue car lifted off and followed, staying a few kilometers behind.

CHAPTER 23

Circling around the coordinates programmed by Gus, Cisco hovered near the lake. Gus was right Presa Rodrigues was desolate, beautiful but desolate. Cisco crisscrossed the manmade lake several times then hovered over the spot indicated by Comsys. Below him, a small shack was partially obscured by a tangle of trees and brush. Carefully he landed the car nearby. Gus said the kidnappers exchanged vehicles here and all looked deserted, but he proceeded with caution. Shrieks from several hawks circling in the sky broke the silence as he slowly got out of the red car. In the distance, he saw a flash of blue, but it disappeared.

Standing near the car, the quiet rang in his ears. Nervously he studied the building and surrounding hills. The wooden structure looked old. Across the reservoir were the dam and a few service buildings. Otherwise, all he could see was emptiness. Typical of the Sonoran desert, only creosote bushes and squatty mesquite trees, along with cholla and prickly pear cactus dominated the terrain. On the south side of the building, a large tangle of mesquite trees and branches covered the side of the almost hidden shed.

Slowly he walked toward the old shack with the laser on his finger. Dread soured his stomach. The front of the shack looked deserted and undisturbed.

Cautiously he walked nearer. "*Hola,* is anybody here?" he called out loudly into the wind. Only quiet rang in his ears. He rounded the side of the shack and noticed fresh footprints and broken pieces of mesquite branches scattered on the ground near the shed. It was obvious the branches had been moved, and then replaced to cover the door. Tucking the laser in his pocket, he moved the branches and opened the shed's door. The front-end of a green aerovan glowed dimly in the morning sunlight. Suddenly he felt sick to his stomach. Maya could be dead in the back of the van in this desolate place.

Activating the Pcom he waited for the connection. "Gus. Talk to me. I found it! I'm on the eastern side of the lake. I found the van hidden in a shed next to a deserted shack."

"Okay, hold your position and I'll get a visual on you." A few seconds later Gus' voice continued, "Okay, I've got you. Have you checked the van?"

"No, I'm doing it now. Can you stay on the line?" Slowly he approached the van. He concentrated on every move trying to forget what he might find inside. His heart pounded in his ears. "Please let it be empty," he prayed. Holding his breath, he carefully opened the driver's door.

The keyfob was still in the startup system. Looking in the back, he saw to his relief an empty rear seat, with one side pulled forward. On the floor in the rear cargo area, he saw a dark blanket in a heap. Pulling it out he noticed a faint perfume smell to it and a small glass vial fell to the shed's dirt floor. Stooping he picked it up and a small amount of residue flowed to the bottom when he turned it right side up. The label read SedaPan.

"*¿Qué pasa?*" Gus' voice interrupted. "What's in the van?"

"Oh, yeah," Cisco said startled back to reality by Gus' voice. "It's empty. I found a used vial of SedaPan. What is that?"

"A pretty strong sedative," Gus replied.

Pocketing the small vial, he walked out of the shed and out into the sunlight. Taking a few deep breaths, he tried to calm his pounding heart.

"Give me the serial number and I'll run a search," Gus prompted him.

Cisco walked back toward the van. "It's an older model Hyundai, light green, and the serial number is KH207055-984."

"I'll get right on it."

"I'm going to check out the area and then follow the sedan you saw leave this location," Cisco replied.

"The address in Hermosillo is downloaded. The sedan is a 2058 four door Ford. I don't know the color, but something nondescript, like tan or silver."

"Good," Cisco said. "I'm going to leave this place like I found it and get back to you when I reach the Hermosillo address." He carefully replaced the blanket in the back of the van, closed the shed door, and arranged the shrubs much like he found them. If the kidnappers returned for the van, he did not want them to know anyone had been here.

The quiet of the place and knowing Maya had been here gave him the creeps. Something else bothered him. He felt like he was being watched. Carefully he scanned the hills again, but saw nothing. Shrugging off the nervous feeling, he walked back to the car.

From the top of a nearby hill three men in the blue car watched Cisco's movements. From there the shed looked like a large pile of bushes. It was obvious the man driving the red car was hiding or looking for something.

"What are we waiting for, *Chingon*" Flaco asked. "Let's just go pop the *pinche pendejo* and take back your car. Nobody is around to hear nothing, *ese.*"

Flaco made his comment to the driver, a clean-shaven man with his black hair slicked back on the sides and tucked under his cap. His amigos called him *Chingon,* with respect, because he was a tough fighter and he was the leaders of their gang. His given name was Arturo Perez.

"No, *ese.* He is not the man who stole my *ranfla.* I want to know what he's up to."

Arturo was not a man to be argued with and Flaco did not ask again. Arturo knew the man driving his car was not the one who stole it after the poker game. He was not the man named Charley Arambula who stole Mercedes.

"He's leaving now," Flaco said watching the red car lift off. Arturo's small hand-held scanner began beeping as the red car lifted and sped off across the lake. Once it was out of sight, they got back into the blue *ranfla* and lifted to the sky following the blip on the scanner at a safe distance.

CHAPTER 24

Cisco checked the address Gus downloaded into Comsys against a visual image of Hermosillo. The address, 45 Calle Santa Rita, displayed a location east of the city in an older part of town near the old state prison. He took one last look at Presa Rodrigues Reservoir as he lifted the red car into the air. Speeding across the desolate lake, he did not see the blue car lift off the nearby hill.

Leaving the main aeropath Cisco wound his way into the older part of Hermosillo passing over the old prison. The grounds of the brick penitentiary with broken windows, overgrown with weeds and the fences falling down, looked sinister. Slowly he turned onto Calle Santa Rita and passed the white stucco house marked 45. Turning two blocks away, he put down where he could still see the house. Children playing in a nearby yard waved at him.

"Great, so much for being inconspicuous in a candy-apple red *ranfla,*" he muttered to himself. From where he parked, he did not notice a blue car touch down at the other end of Calle Santa Rita.

"Gus," he said into the Pcom.

"Yeah," Gus responded almost immediately.

"Are you sure they left here?"

"Well, the car left last night. Hold on a second, I'll check the electric records. The power records had a spike for a couple days, but nothing since last night. You're probably okay," Gus reported.

"Probably? . . . Okay, thanks, talk to you later." Picking up his Chihuahua Cubs baseball cap, Cisco stepped from the car and walked toward the house. An elderly woman was watering some flowers planted along the fence next door to the white house. Opening the short gate to number 45, he walked up to the front door. He knocked. Nothing. He knocked again louder.

Walking back down the sidewalk, he glanced at the neighbor. She was watching him closely. Strolling across the dirt yard, he greeted her.

"Buenos días Señora."

"Buenos días," the woman responded with a curious look in her brown eyes.

"I am looking for a friend. I was to meet him at this address. Have you seen anyone lately?" he said pointing to the white house.

The neighbor woman only glanced at the house, *"Nadien vive en esa casa,"* she said no one lived in the house anymore. "A man told me last year it belongs to a big company." She shook her head. "I think it belongs to *drogueros,"* she whispered the Spanish expression for the drug cartel. "People stay there from time to time. They don't take care of it," she said in Spanish.

Cisco looked at the dirt yard on the one side of the fence and her well tended yard with flowers and a bit of grass on the other. Thinking fast Cisco said, "My friend is a reporter for Channel 15. I think he's working on a story about drug dealing in this area."

"Ah sí," she said and her face brightened a bit. "A few nights ago on my way home from the corner market I noticed the lights were on in the living room. While I was unlocking my door, a blond man came out of the house. He walked with a limp," the neighbor woman said. She stepped a few feet to the right to water other flowers.

"Sí, the blond man with a limp. That's my friend," Cisco agreed with her. "Do you know if he is still here?"

She looked down at the water and pondered her answer. *"Quien sabe,* I don't know. People come and go. I can't keep track. I haven't seen anyone today."

"I think his wife was coming with him. Did you see a young dark haired woman?"

"No se." The woman turned back to her flowers breaking eye contact. Perhaps he overstepped his bounds by asking the woman so many questions.

"Muchas gracias Señora," Cisco called to her brightly as he turned and walked away. There was no response from the woman.

From his watchful position, Arturo saw the man

knock on the door of a house and then talk to the neighbor woman until she turned away.

"*Chingon*, do you think that's where that gambler *vato* has Mercedes?" Flaco asked tired of following and waiting. "Cause I'm hungry." Arturo only glared as a response wishing he had left his two friends at home, but the gang always traveled in packs for safety.

Arturo studied the man driving his red car talk to a neighbor woman. The man was tall and trim, definitely Hispanic, but not a *vato*. The *pinche vato* called Charley who stole it must have sold it to this man, but the man was definitely not the type to own a *ranfla*.

His movements at the lake and now at the small house made no sense. Arturo watched him climb into the red car and hovering low near the ground, he circled around the neighborhood. Finally, the red car flew down the street and Arturo followed. Several blocks away he parked at a small strip mall and Arturo parked on the far end of the parking lot. The red car gleamed brightly in the sun where the man parked it nearer the cafe. At least the *pinche vato* who stole it had taken good care of it.

As they watched the man go into the cafe, Oso complain, "I'm tired of following that *baboso*. *Chingon* I don't think he is going to lead us to the Mercedes. I think he's doing something else. Let's go home. Alexa wants me to take her to the movies, *ese*."

"You two just shut up. We're staying with him," Arturo grumbled. He would do anything to find Mercedes. He would not admit to his *amigos* how much he loved her. The macho in him made that hard to admit to anyone, even himself. All he wanted was to get her back. If he got the car back too, better yet.

Oso rolled his eyes at Flaco who nodded his head slightly in agreement, but kept his mouth shut. Flaco knew Arturo was a man not to rebuke.

"Oso, go down there and get us a couple of sandwiches and see what he's doing," Arturo said. Jumping quickly out of the car, Oso hurried to the cafe. About fifteen minutes later, he returned with three bags and a grin on his face.

"I think he's getting ready to leave. He's paying his bill, *jefe*."

Cisco paid the bill, and walked toward the parking lot. The sandwich and Coke had revived him and given him time to mull over the morning's search. Hopping into the car, Cisco activated the communicator's link to Gus.

"Gus, the house was empty. The woman next door says there was a blond man with a limp there for a couple days. That's all she knew. I couldn't get inside."

"A blond man with a limp, huh? I'll see if I can profile him."

"Gus, did you find the sedan yet?" Cisco asked.

"Whoever is orchestrating this is really good, but they can't fool me, Cisco. The sedan left the main aeropath west of Laughlin, Nevada. They must have ducked under the traffic scanners, but I picked them back up west of Goffs, California. Once past Lancaster they got onto the I-40 aeropath heading west. I followed the footprint to Los Angeles near the Echo Park area." Gus' voice was pumped with enthusiasm. "I'll download the address where they parked the car. It left that address about 8:30 this morning and flew to a grocery store on Sunset, then returned to the same location. Looks like they are laying low near there," Gus explained.

"Where is Echo Park?" Cisco asked. He knew Los Angeles was a huge city, previously part of the United States, and now the largest city in the Jalapeño Republic. He had been there on several jobs, but spent little time exploring.

"It's near the old baseball stadium, not far from downtown. It's a pretty rough area, lots of turf wars and they don't like outsiders," Gus responded.

"Okay, keep monitoring them." Cisco disconnected the call.

It was 1:15 PM and Cisco decided to call in on the secure device before heading north. Why he felt so uneasy with the security people assigned by the government made little sense, but he could not shake his father's words, "trust no one."

He inserted the wasp microcom in his ear and said, "Open secure channel."

"Francisco, where are you?" a voice in his ear asked almost instantaneously.

He could not tell if it was the thin man in the blue uniform from the meeting or someone else. It was just a voice. He decided to test a theory wondering if they had tracked him or the red *ranfla*.

"I'm just leaving home. I'm headed to Los Angeles. It seems like the place to start. I'll check out the parking garage and the rental agency. Do you have anything new for me?"

"No, our people are working on it, but nothing new. We'll keep you updated," the voice said.

"How often do you want me to check in? Cisco asked.

"Twice a day, but if you find anything call right away. Good Luck," the voice said and then Cisco heard a small beep and then quiet in his ear.

If the government was tracking him or expected the wasp-like microcom to pinpoint his location, the voice gave no indication. Surely the best people were working on this crisis, though they offered nothing new to help him. How was that possible or was he bait as Gus surmised? Shrugging, Cisco took the device out of his ear and stuck it in his shirt pocket.

Assessing the situation, his stomach churned on the lunch. Gus said the kidnappers were holed up in an area called Echo Park, a rough neighborhood near downtown Los Angeles. The car they believed carried Maya was still there. Cisco grabbed the small sack from the back seat and crawled out of the car heading back to the cafe.

In the cafe's bathroom, Cisco shed his jeans and sweatshirt for the *vato* outfit he purchased from Jose at the garage. The baggy pants hung low on his hips, almost feeling like they might fall off. The t-shirt smelled of rank BO from the armpits and was well worn around the collar.

He wrapped the bandana around his forehead and topped it with the baseball cap turned backwards. It was as close as he could remember how Jose had looked. Satisfied he looked the part Cisco stuffed his clean jeans and shirt into the small bag and headed for the cafe exit. No one in the cafe seemed to notice the change.

Watching the cafe from their vantage point Arturo, Oso, and Flaco watched as the man returned to the cafe. About ten minutes later, they stared in disbelief as a *vato* emerged from the cafe and walked toward the red car and got in.

"Who's that *pinche vato?*" Oso growled pointing to a gangster exiting the cafe into the sun dressed in a black t-shirt and low hung black pants. The three men watched the *vato* climb into the red *ranfla.*

Arturo barked at Flaco, "Go check the cafe for the other man." Shaking his head, Arturo tried to make sense of what happened. In a few moments, Flaco returned to say the man who drove the red car was not in the cafe. "Did you check the bathroom?" Arturo demanded.

"Sí Chingon, he is not there."

Arturo lifted the blue car following the blips on the scanner. He matched the red car's movements, but well behind. Ahead of him, Cisco merged onto the busy aeropath, heading north. Unaware he was being watched, Cisco requested Comsys for a path to Los Angeles from Hermosillo to the address downloaded by Gus. As the car merged onto the I-1711A aeropath heading north, he leaned back and tried to clear his mind of all thoughts.

CHAPTER 25

Luis Jimenez tapped his fingers on his desk in the government security building after disconnecting from Francisco Salaz. Something did not add up. He had worked long enough for the government to know when he was being left out of the loop. They always expected him to be on top of his game, be the man behind the scenes, and then the glory went to one of the special agents. "Shit, the *pinche* agents would be lost without me," he grumbled.

He had been tracking Francisco since last Saturday, when the order came down from his boss, Director Arias. An EQA agent was missing and Francisco was engaged to find her. The missing EQA agent was going by the name of Cecelia Juarez. It was the name the director told him, but his sources indicated she was Maya Torres, great-granddaughter of the president.

Luis had done a full security panel on both Francisco and Cecelia. Cecelia graduated two years ago and was a Class 2 agent. She was young and inexperienced, with only a small EQA footprint. She graduated top in her class from Chihuahua Institute of Technology.

Francisco was a ten-year veteran, a Class 7 agent, with numerous awards. Nothing seemed out of the ordinary in his work record. He was an exemplary worker, but he was a loner, lived off-the-grid on some remote mountain northwest of town on the eastern slope of Monte Tecanachic. Luis had scanned images of Francisco's mountainside home. It was a medium-size rustic building with a large patio and several acres of trees. A separate garage and a landing pad stood several yards from the end of the patio. Both the house and garage were in good repair, though looked a bit overgrown. It was obvious he lived alone.

Luis investigated the Salaz family, looking for details. Francisco was Emilio Salaz' youngest son. Emilio was a well-respected horticultural scientist for the Republic. He and his wife, Victoria, lived in a modest home at the base of Sierra Pamachi near the Rio Urique. The elder Salaz' work was well documented and he was considered one of the top agricultural gurus of the Republic. His work on agrobots was revolutionary in the 2060s and the subject was still taught at universities as the model for agricultural success. His wife, though educated at the University of Santa Barbara, had little work record and raised the couple's four children. They belonged to St. Mary's Catholic Church and attended regularly.

Typically, twenty-four seven monitoring of this type was reserved for high-profile security agents on special ops missions. Luis was given the task, but not extensive particulars. Something did not add up. The choice of Francisco Salaz bothered him. A job requiring constant tracking should have been left to the internal police or the Republic's top security agents. Surely, there was someone more qualified than this joker.

He complained when told about Francisco, but as usual his complaints were ignored. His superiors often treated him with disrespect. They glorified the field agents with awards, medals, and bonuses. It really pissed him off, but his job paid well and usually garnered him a raise each year.

Luis had tried to make the cut for the Republic's security agent training school. He passed the written exam with flying colors only to be cut for his slightly shorter right leg. It had been badly broken in a bicycle accident when he was nine and the butcher doctor botched setting the leg properly. A year later it had to be re-broken and reset, leaving Luis with the slight limp. What did that matter? He was as good as the best agent, maybe better, but he was now stuck in this thankless desk job.

All his years of working as a security analyst piqued both his curiosity and his skepticism over the choice of Francisco Salaz. Besides being unknown, the Republic's security team had little time to vet or train Francisco properly. They were going to have to rely mostly on the standard GTCA records and standard global satellite intelligence. At least Luis was able to get him fitted for one of the new G2000 security microcoms. The tiny wasp-like device had global tracking and it should be operating now that Francisco had initiated the first call.

Luis' monitor chirped as the fifteen-minute report popped up. The XA200 Corvette had not moved from the Old Town parking garage where it parked yesterday afternoon. Francisco said he was just leaving, so why was the car still parked in Old Town? Luis grumbled reviewing the reports. Francisco's EQA chip had been disabled at 11:54 AM Saturday morning. Since then, Luis had been unable to track him, except for the Vette's GTCA footprint monitoring. Scanning down the report, he stared at the final page. The transcript listed the microcom message from Francisco, but with no coordinates.

"What the hell is going on?" he grumbled as he scanned the records from yesterday and checked the serial number for Francisco's G2000. It was the latest model with global tracking, so why was it not registering? Stupid doctor must have fumble fingered the device setup. Luis was surrounded by that type of incompetence and it infuriated him. Entering his security code into the encrypted satellite database, he setup a trace on Francisco's microcom serial number.

Getting up from his desk, Luis stretched his back. He was on 24-hour call and would be eating and sleeping here at the center. Though the government provided hotel-like accommodations and a pretty good cafeteria, even the overtime pay did not make up for these shifts. They cared little for the disruption to anyone's life or family. Tomorrow was his daughter's tenth birthday, but he would not be there.

Walking down the hallway, Luis wound his way to the cafeteria and picked up a sandwich and a soda. He took the time to have them make him a fresh sandwich to his exact liking, instead of accepting one of the premade ones. He had it cut and wrapped as separate halves.

By the time he returned to his desk with the sandwich, the next fifteen minute report was displaying on the monitor. Francisco's Vette was still parked in the Old

Town garage and nothing showed on the microcom's tracking report. "Where the hell is that asshole?" Luis grumbled.

Staring at the missing tracking information, Luis wondered if Francisco was not what he seemed. He had surmised Francisco was possibly a red herring, a plant, a decoy by the government for some reason. Now he was not sure. Perhaps Francisco was a rogue agent, one of the ultra secret agents no one but an elite few knew about. Not even security gurus, such as himself, could trace a rogue.

Francisco fit the model – single, well educated, living off the grid, a model employee at a government agency, a perfect record, and little history. His record was lean and might have been scrubbed. In addition, Francisco had one very unique and very interesting piece of information in his record. He was the president's godson. His grandfather worked with President Torres at the university and was instrumental in isolating the energy particle.

Luis took a bite of sandwich and shook his head. He told his superiors this was a bad plan, but they ignored him. "Fuck," he grumbled. Now if things went wrong, they would blame him.

CHAPTER 26

In the dream, the desert was quiet and peaceful. She and her bisabuelo were walking near a wide river. Cooler air blew across the river and fanned her face from the warmth of the desert. They talked of many things but she could not remember the words, only a feeling her great-grandfather seemed to be reassuring her, telling her not to worry. Across the river a young man waved frantically at them. Maya's drugged brain drifted from the dream to semi-consciousness, as she slept and awakened several times in the night from the dream as it replayed over and over.

A loud thump jarred her awake and angry voices shouting startled her into awareness. She tried to move, but her body felt heavy. Several small rays of light crept through the edges of a blanket that covered the single window in the room. She had no sense of time or place, but this was a different room from the last one. Concentrating, images of the blond man sticking her with a needle replayed in her brain. It was her last memory. She was so tired and just wanted to drift off. The voices in another room shouted again.

"Big deal, so I made a call," an angry voice said.

"Shut up," another voice yelled. "You'll wake up the girl."

As Maya concentrated on the voices, her head began to clear slightly. Struggling to understand her situation, she listened to the voices trying to commit every word to memory. Slowly she stretched her legs, but not without effort and some pain. Somewhere in a fog, she vaguely remembered a short man helping her eat soup and crackers. He washed her face. Bits and pieces of events wandered in her mind, like puzzle pieces on a table.

"Cálmate jefe, cálmate," Silvio told Mason to calm down. "He only wants to see his cousin because he hasn't seen her in six years. It's not like he went to the police."

"I don't care," Mason yelled at the short Venezuelan. "I told you not to contact anybody." Lunging, Mason put his fist into the short man's belly. Rico doubled over and grunted. "You fucking asshole, I ought to kill you," Mason growled.

Silvio grabbed Mason's arm before he landed another punch. "He didn't mean it *jefe*. It won't happen again."

"If you idiots fuck up this job . . . " Mason left the sentence unfinished with a look at the two Venezuelans meaning big trouble.

"Okay, we get it," Silvio said placing a hand on Rico's shoulder to stop him from retaliating.

The angry voices in the other room stopped. Maya recognized the blond man's voice. One of the other men had a cousin here. Where was here, she wondered. In the dim light Maya studied the room. Only the small bed she was on, an old-fashioned dresser, and a chair made up the sparse furnishings. The door was across from the bed. A light fixture hung overhead, but was off. A soft, fuzzy blanket covered her. Slowly she rolled onto her back and stretched her legs. Her hands were bound, though not tight. Moving from side to side and stretching, except for some sore spots, she seemed to be okay.

"All we do is sit here and watch videos. We're going to be here a while and all the girl does is eat and sleep. All I wanted to do was see my cousin before we leave town. This is Los Angeles, nobody knows us here," Rico complained to Silvio after Mason left the room.

"You're going to get us killed. That man is *loco.*" Silvio told Rico. Both worked as muscle for the PLV, but never with the blond *loco* named Mason. They heard stories about the crazy hit man and even the big *jefes* were scared of him. Silvio doubted Mason would actually kill them, knowing he would have to answer to the PLV, still the blond *loco's* evil reputation nagged at him and he did not understand why three of them were needed to babysit the drugged girl.

"*Pinche pendejo*," Rico growled under his breath calling Mason a dumb fucker.

"*Cálmate amigo,*" Silvio told Rico to calm down.

Mason Warrick walked into the kitchen stinging from the stupidity of the two assholes. He did not need them for this job.

Mason carefully watched their back trail and monitored the police bulletins. No alert or alarm was posted for the girl's kidnapping and he was sure they were not followed. The kidnapping was pulled off without a hitch, thanks in part to Alexis, an old friend now living in the Los Angeles area. Alexis waited near the parking garage until the target showed. She followed, waited for Mason to signal the floor number, then caused the accident. Alexis was happy to crash her old blue car for the money Mason gave her. With that and some insurance money she could get a new car. It was just an accident, nothing to get her into real trouble with the police. Since all the other cars were parked, there were no injuries. Alexis used a recording on her Pcom of a baby crying and yelled for help to attract the young woman to come to her aid.

Mason promised her another five thousand if she kept her mouth shut. It was insurance to keep her quiet, but he also planned to stiff her for it. Once this job was done, he planned on disappearing someplace on the coast. Maybe he would go to Chile or Costa Rica or anyplace warm. Somewhere the PLV could not find him. He was tired and he was done. This job would give him enough money to buy a little place and a boat, but only if he did not have to split the money with the two assholes in the other room.

Walking back to the living room Mason barked, "Silvio, go check on the girl. See if she's awake. She needs to eat."

Maya heard the man's voice and closed her eyes and turned her head away from the door. She heard the door handle squeak and the hinges creak as the door opened. A few seconds later she heard the door close again. She was hungry, but allowing them to think she was sleeping gave her an opportunity to overhear more of their conversations.

"She's still out. So how much longer do we stay here in Los Angeles?"

"I don't know, yet," Mason replied. "I'm just

following orders. When I know, you'll know."

"She must be some hot commodity for all this effort," Rico grumbled.

"Yeah, she's probably worth a lot, *eh jefe?*" Silvio said using the term *jefe*, calling Mason the boss to appease him.

"I don't even know who the girl is. I wish I did," Mason admitted. He did not know and it bothered him. The buyer of this job was keeping him in the dark, so he had no idea who or what would be after them. Could be a jealous husband or fucking anybody for all he knew. If you did not know your enemy, it was much harder to protect yourself, let alone the package.

"She don't look like anyone special to me, except for that uniform," Silvio said.

"The uniform is for the EQA division. She's some type of scientist for the government. Maybe someone wants to keep her quiet about something. When she wakes up, I think I'll use a little muscle to see if she'll talk," Mason groused.

Listening to the conversation, Maya locked into three separate voices. The last voice was the mean blond who stuck her with the needle containing the drug. She recognized the hard edge in his voice. One of the other two sounded like the man who helped her eat the soup and crackers. He was nicer. It was his voice saying they were in Los Angeles, or perhaps they had never left Los Angeles, although she had a memory about a dingy house somewhere else and thought she remembered being in a car.

She was sure she was kidnapped because she was the president's great-granddaughter and there would be a huge ransom. However, the three kidnappers seemed unaware of her true identity. She heard the mean blond man say he was going to make her talk.

"They won't find out who I am," she swore under her breath.

CHAPTER 27

Heading into Los Angeles, Cisco activated the channel to Gus. "Gus, what do you have for me? I'm fifty miles east of downtown Los Angeles."

"*Nada.* I don't have an exact address yet, but I'm working on it. The old area is setup weird with common garages on the street," Gus responded. "I know it's near Sunset and Echo Park. The area will be like Old Town. They can still drive on tires there."

"Traffic is crazy. I've had some weird looks from people. This *ranfla* sticks out like a sore thumb."

"Oh yeah, something you need to know. I'm getting cross-reference blips from some source I think is trying to track you. I can't get to the source because it keeps moving around, but will keep trying," Gus continued sounding a bit worried.

"Is it security headquarters?" Cisco asked.

"No. It is some other source, a low-level old-fashioned scanner. I can't isolate it."

"Keep trying Gus."

The news that someone was tracking him was not a surprise, however it made him uneasy. When Comsys alerted him to his destination, he descended from the aeropath and found himself hovering over the dilapidated baseball stadium. The open air baseball stadium with blue seats sat in a large ravine surrounded by an empty parking lot. A weathered large blue and white sign was still legible as Dodger Stadium. The Los Angeles Dodgers were big rivals for the Chihuahua Cubs and Cisco had seen them play at the Chihuahua stadium numerous times. Apparently, this was the old stadium and no longer in use.

Flying west, Cisco caught his first view of the older area of Echo Park. Surprisingly, he found it hilly with lots of green vegetation. Small houses dotted the tree covered hills. Circling the area again, Cisco looked for a place to touch down. He got lucky and a spot opened near a busy eatery. Parking the red car not too far from the Pioneer

Chicken Ranch on the corner of Sunset Blvd and Portia Street, he sat watching lines of people waiting at the restaurant for their food.

The gaudy neon lights of the Chicken Ranch were lit even though it was daytime. Reflections from the neon lights sparkled on *ranflas* parked around it. They all had a similar style, though very different than the red one he drove. Six or seven *ranflas* were parked near the restaurant and dozens of young men dressed in an unusual style were standing nearby.

Arturo and his gang tailed Cisco into Los Angeles, keeping close as they followed the blip from the red car. They saw him park near a busy corner, but they had to park around the corner and down several streets.

"Flaco, go keep an eye on him," Arturo demanded. The area worried him. Perhaps the driver had brought the red *ranfla* to L.A. to sell.

Flaco jumped out quickly, heading in the direction of the red car parked several blocks away. The intersections were busy with people, and he was surprised by functioning traffic signals for both pedestrians and ground-level vehicles.

Sitting in the red car Cisco activated the Pcom and heard Gus pick up immediately. "What's the matter?" Gus asked.

"I hope you got something for me, cause it is not good here."

Gus had told him the area was rough, though this was not what Cisco expected. The Chicken Ranch seemed a hangout for gangbangers and lowriders. Small groups of young men gathered at the corner whistling and yelling at passing cars and flashing hand signs. A row of decked-out motorcycles were parked near each other and several men in heavy boots and jackets stood near them. They were definitely Hispanic and all wore the same color bandana tied around their foreheads.

Another group of young men were dressed in karate-style clothes. Two were pushing each other, while several others egged on a fight. The situation made Cisco cringe. When Gus said it made Old Town look like Disneyland, he was making an understatement.

"I'm in the middle of a biker and lowrider convention and it doesn't look good for me," Cisco said.

"Oh, those must be some of the gangs that control that area. During the financial collapse of the United States, gang wars started in most of the large cities. Los Angeles was overrun by several ethnic gangs who sectioned off the city, running drugs, and taking protection money. The gangs or locals invented names for themselves. The bikers are the Mayans, if they are Hispanic," Gus explained.

"Yes. I can see that name on one of the biker's jacket. The lowriders look different. They look more Asian to me," Cisco said.

"Those may be the Kudo kai, a minor arm of the Japanese Yakuza syndicate. Lots of people just refer to them as *japovatos*."

"*Japovatos?*"

"The Japanese word for mixed is *japa,* so the locals just started calling the downtown Asian gangs, *japovatos*. Mostly they are a mixed race of Hispanic and Japanese families who have lived in the area for ages," Gus explained. "They speak some weird mixed Spanish and Japanese slang."

"How dangerous are they?" Cisco asked.

"The Mayans are more dangerous. The *japovatos* can cause trouble, but now the gangs in Los Angeles are more like our Old Town gangs and most of it is show. They usually don't make serious trouble outside of their area," Gus told him.

"Well I hope not, because here comes four of them." Cisco terminated the call.

Cisco watched four *japovatos* approaching quickly. They wore skin tight shorts with gray silk tops that resembled karate tops. Two wore an orange silk belt wrapped around their waists, another one wore blue, while the man in front had a black sash.

Cisco briefly thought about lifting off and leaving, then decided to get out of the car to meet them instead. In an instinctive move, he removed the Chihuahua Cubs baseball cap.

"Ano, ese, doko vienes?" the black belted *japovato* asked Cisco as he walked up. His speech was deep and guttural. He pulled at Cisco's t-shirt saying something else to his friends and laughed. Cisco figured they wanted to know who he was and were he came from. The one wearing a blue belt walked around the red *ranfla* nodding his head up and down.

"Española, New Mexico," Cisco lied forcing a wide grin. At least the car was from Española.

As Flaco rounded the last corner, the neon sign of the Pioneer Chicken Ranch blazed in the afternoon sun. Parked on one side of the restaurant were a line of motorcycles. Bikers dressed in leather jackets and black boots stood nearby. On the other two sides, odd looking *ranflas* gleamed in the sunshine. They were nothing like the lowriders of Española or Old Town Dublán. These were sleek and streamlined. Young men wearing tight-fitting outfits milled nearby. Four of them were talking to the driver of the red car. Turning around, he walked quickly back to where Arturo had parked.

Leaning in the window he said, "Crazy shit, *ese*. There are crazy-looking *ranflas*. Some of their gang are talking to the *vato*. This is not so good. We need to get out of here."

"You're a *culón*," Arturo called Flaco a chickenshit. "Go back and keep an eye on him," he growled.

"I'm telling you, we got to get out of here. There is a biker gang and a bunch of weird looking *ranflas*. There are four of them talking to the driver of your car."

Blackbelt's dark slanted eyes turned into long slits. *"Nani ases koko?"* He demanded to know why Cisco was here, making hand gestures when he spoke. Cisco noticed calloused formations on the first two knuckles of each hand.

As Blackbelt continued to express his displeasure at Cisco's presence, his three cohorts walked around the car making comments and touching it. Cisco was not sure if they liked it or thought it was weird.

"Mi primo vive aquí en Echo Park, ese" Cisco told him he was he here to visit his cousin. Very slowly he slid his right hand down to the side of his pants and felt for the tiny laser in his pocket. *"¿Ese, tienes problema con eso?"* he asked calmly if that was a problem. He tried to speak in street slang like a lowrider and made no threatening moves.

Blackbelt's lips tightened and his right hand retracted to his side into a fist. *"Anata wa koko no eres bienvenido aquí debes irte"* he hissed in his lingo near Cisco's ear. The odd mixtures of Spanish and Japanese slang told Cisco he was unwelcome and should leave, now.

"No problema," Cisco assured him, "I'm just visiting my cousin, *ese*. I'll be gone in the morning."

"Horale mishiranu hito," BlackBelt hissed. *"¡Ano ne, vamonos!"* Blackbelt called to his friends to leave.

As the four *japovatos* strode away, Cisco watched them jump into a sleek silver and black aerorider. It lifted and headed west above Sunset Boulevard. He got back in the red car and sank low into the seat. Slowly he breathed in and out, trying to relax after the encounter with the strange *japovatos*. He activated the channel to Gus.

"Hey Cisco, you okay?" Gus asked.

"Yes, so far. The *japovatos* spoke in a mix of Japanese and Spanish, good enough for me to understand. They told me to leave now. I need a place to go."

"The car is still parked on Echo Park Ave. I just can't figure out for sure which house they might be in. I'm searching the utility records and stuff like that to try to figure it out. Is there a shopping center or parking lot where you could chill for a while?" Gus asked. Cisco thought and remembered the empty Dodger Stadium parking lot and told Gus about it.

"Good. Go there and I'll call you as soon as I know something."

Cisco started the *ranfla* and drove ground level on

Alvarado Street. Staying on ground level seemed like a good idea with the *japovatos* patrolling the sky. Shortly, he found Stadium Way and wound toward the stadium parking lot. The parking area's gate was ripped from the hinges and hung as a twisted reminder of a bygone time. The asphalt was cracked with humps of pavement buckled in a long ridge across a wide area. Weeds and small bushes pushed up through the cracks. Cisco wondered why the old stadium had not been demolished. Parking in the shade of a large tree, he opened the windows and stretched out his six-foot frame as much as possible and tried to relax.

Flaco headed back toward the corner of Sunset and Portia. He was a block away when he realized the red car was gone from the parking space. "*Mierda*," he cursed. Running back to Arturo, he was out of breath when he jumped into the blue car.

"He's gone!"

Arturo glanced at the scanner, which had not blipped. "Fuck, he's on the ground. You fucking let him get away you idiot," Arturo cursed.

"He can't be far, *ese*, he's tire level. We'll find him," Flaco whined.

Arturo lifted the blue car and headed down Sunset Blvd hoping to spot the red car driving on ground level. The hand held scanner showed nothing. Not a very powerful scanner, it could only locate the beacon if it was airborne and within about ten miles. He crisscrossed Echo Park Lake, flew back over the Chicken Ranch, and hovered over a large park. The red car was nowhere. Arturo lifted higher and flew off west on Sunset Blvd.

A sleek black and silver *ranfla* came up behind him and one of the passengers made hand signs. Arturo knew the signals were not friendly, but there was no way he was leaving without finding his red car.

"Hey," Flaco said. "I saw that *ranfla* at the chicken place. It's the same guys that talked to the *pinche vato*."

Flying above street level, the late afternoon traffic was getting heavy, forcing Arturo's car to slow down. The silver and black *ranfla* was on his tail. After several blocks, Arturo grinned when he saw Comsys light flash red to indicate an impending stop. Accelerating, he deliberately flew through the intersection and made a sharp left turn. The traffic infraction set off an alarm on his Comsys. The black and silver *ranfla* tried to follow, but was stopped in the middle of the intersection.

"With luck the police will get them and not us," Arturo said hoping the traffic control police were the same here in Los Angeles as most of the rest of the Jalapeño Republic. With any luck, the traffic police would assume the local gang was the source of the problem. Arturo circled another corner and landed on a street not too far away.

It did not take long for the LAPD's traffic control officers to recognize a familiar *ranfla* stopped in an intersection. The LAPD officers forced the Comsys of the black and silver car to land. The *japovatos* were not surprised by the turn of events. They knew the procedure well.

"*Baka, pinche vatos, los mataré,*" the driver swore, vowing to kill the fucking *vatos* in the blue car.

Cisco groaned bumping his knee on the dashboard as his body stretched on the uncomfortable seat. Disoriented, his brain thought he was back on Mars in his small sleeping pod. The single bed in the pod was barely enough for his large frame and how he and Monica managed to have sex took a bit of contortion. Dozing off again, he pictured Monica's face, but it quickly morphed into Vivian's. Images of stripping the rose-colored bodysuit from Vivian's firm body were etched in his brain. Her body had only aged in a good way from when they were teenagers. Her breasts and hips slightly plumper, while her body tone was tight and muscular.

Suddenly the Pcom chirped him out of his visions. "Shit," he cursed shaking his head as he opened the channel on the Pcom. It was after 6:30 PM and deep twilight shadows cut across the Dodger Stadium parking lot.

"Did you have a nice sleep?" Gus asked and laughed. "I was going to wake you, but not much is happening, so thought I'd let you sleep."

"You got the address for the sedan yet?" Cisco asked trying to shake the sleep from his brain.

"The car is parked in a single garage on Echo Park Avenue between 2225 and 2227 on the west side of the street," Gus answered. "It's moved twice today, but always comes back. I checked the satellite records. The satellite signal from 2227 had 97 calls for 245 minutes, 2225 had one. My guess is that's the house, but you'll have to check it out from the ground."

"You sound groggy," Gus said.

"Still a little space weary, I guess. Have you picked up anything from security headquarters?" Gus had told Cisco he would monitor the secure channels of the Republic for any chatter about the case or anything he thought odd.

"No. Nothing much. They sent out two operatives in opposite directions, maybe as subterfuge or maybe on legit assignments. Not sure. I saw your report to headquarters go through. The beacon is not working, so they are most likely confused."

"What about the tracking signal you noticed?"

"It stopped. It was probably nothing."

"Thanks. I'll call you when I get to the location. I just want to get the girl and get out of here."

Starting the car, he lifted from the old Dodgers Stadium parking lot and turned northwest. Flying low he told Comsys the address and let it map the route. According to Gus, it should not be far.

Arturo had almost given up finding the red *ranfla*. It was like finding a needle in a haystack without the use of the scanner. They had been cruising for several hours and the rush hour traffic was getting crazy and busy.

"This is stupid, *Chingon,*" Oso whined. "It's getting late and I'm hungry."

"Me too," Flaco chimed in. "Drop me off and I'll pick up some chicken. That place on the corner is always busy, so it must be good."

Turning back toward the Pioneer Chicken Ranch, Arturo landed nearby and Flaco jumped out. About ten minutes later, he returned with three bags and sodas.

"Damn this is good," Oso said as he devoured the crispy chicken. The breading of the fried chicken had a spicy kick.

Suddenly the scanner chirped. A blip was moving and it was nearby. Throwing his bag of half-eaten chicken on the seat, Arturo lifted the blue car and headed toward the blip. "I got you now *vato*," he grumbled.

CHAPTER 28

Hovering over the houses on Echo Park Ave, Cisco could not see much from the air as the evening shadows were deep in this old, hilly neighborhood. Hundred-year-old trees and overgrown bushes graced the old houses. Careful not to park too near, he brought the car down to street level and parked it across the street under some large trees.

In the twilight, he studied the houses. The house marked 2227 was close to the street with the front door on the side. Several lights shone in the windows. The house to the left, an equally old two-story house perched at least fifty steps up a steep slope from the street, was mostly dark. Cisco could not see the house number.

At street level, three single garages faced the street. They were newer, pre-fab construction, consistent with aerocar requirements. If the house up the hill was where Maya was held, escaping down the steps to the car seemed an impossible task, but there was nowhere else to park near these old houses and Gus said the sedan was parked in a single garage.

He stared at the two houses hoping for someone or something to give him a direction. His brain swirled with ideas. Two teenagers came walking down the street. They were young, but dressed in gang-style clothes. Cigarettes dangled from their lips. As they passed him, Cisco saw one had a thick chain hanging from his belt. The other looked tough and unfriendly. He held his breath as they walked by the red *ranfla*, hoping not to draw their attention. As they walked on down the sidewalk, Cisco rethought his situation. Cautiously, he got out of the car.

Arturo spotted his red *ranfla* just as it landed, and flew overhead and up the street. "There's the *cabrón*," Oso said pointing below. Arturo cruised north on Echo Park Ave and made a u-turn hovering, then landing just far enough away to keep the red car in sight. They jumped out, but stayed out of sight behind a parked truck.

"*Chingon*, what's he doing?" Flaco asked.

"Shut up, keep out of sight," Arturo hissed. It was almost fifteen minutes before he saw the *vato* get out of the red car.

Looking up and down the dark street and seeing no one, Cisco hopped a low fence and stood near the garages. Above him, the two-story house mysteriously loomed. Concrete steps, crooked from numerous earthquakes, snaked up the steep slope to the house. It had a large front porch, which seemed to wrap around the side and out of his vision. His stomach churned as he looked up the steep steps. He patted his pocket and felt for the laser, slipping the loop around his finger.

He tried hard not to think about the situation. He was here and if Maya was here, all he had to do was disable the kidnappers, grab Maya, get to the car, and they were home free. It would be easy he told himself.

Standing behind tall shrubs, he assessed the pathway to the house. The house had a metal gate entrance from the sidewalk, with a low metal fence circling the narrow but steep yard. From his position, Cisco could not see the back of the house. The concrete steps had low growing bushes and weeds on either side. A light from the neighbor's window dimly illuminated the yard, but it was impossible to see the front porch area.

Pulling out the Pcom he whispered, "Gus."

"Hey, what's going on?"

"I'm at the house and I'm not sure what to do. What if this is the wrong house? What if the kidnappers have already left?"

"Nope, they haven't left. The sedan is in the garage." Cisco jumped away from the garage as if spooked. "What about a security system?"

"Let me check. Hold on." Less than a minute passed in silence, but it seemed like an eternity to Cisco. "Good thinking," Gus said. "There is an old electronic security alarm. I don't know if it still works, but I can try to disarm it. I'll scramble it and it should be neutralized, but you may have to break a lock."

"Okay. I don't see any guards. It's really quiet. I'm going in now. I'll contact you as soon as I get out," Cisco said and paused, "Gus?"

"Yeah."

"If I don't make it . . . ." The words hung in an unfinished sentence.

"You'll make it. I'll keep you visibly on the scanner as best as I can. Good luck," Gus said.

Luck? Yes he needed luck, more than luck, maybe a miracle to pull this off. Fear manifested as sweat dripping under his arms. He thought about calling in to the Feds. The security communicator was sitting in the car. "Why not call them and let them come and rescue Maya?" he asked doubting himself.

Even if he did not feel completely comfortable with the security guy, he was one of the Republic's people. Supposedly, he was one of the trusted people at headquarters. All he needed to do was make sure Maya was here, call the special ops to come get her, and go home. But was Maya here? He had to be sure before he called in.

Sneaking behind shrubs Cisco practically crawled up the steep yard staying off the concrete steps. All was quiet and nothing about the house changed. Crouching behind a low bush, he contemplated the next move. From his position, he had a better view of the house. A faint light distinguished the glass pane in the middle of the front door, but the front porch was very dark. The side patio was overgrown with vines. Lights shone from windows to the side of the house. The second floor was dark.

He sucked in a couple of deep breaths and quietly sprang up the concrete steps of the front porch and crouched in the dark.

Arturo saw the dim figure of the man creeping up the yard to the house on the hill when he and his friends moved closer. It was obvious the man was not aware he was being followed.

"You stay here," Arturo hissed at Flaco when they

reached the garages. "Don't let him get back to the *ranfla*."

Arturo and Oso hopped over the low wall and slowly crept up the yard beside the crooked steps. They could see the *vato* faintly on the front porch. Arturo held onto Oso's sleeve to stop him as they crouched about halfway up.

At the front door, Cisco spied through the small glass window. In the dim light, there was no sign of anyone guarding the entryway. Lights shone down the hallway toward the rear of the house and opened to the kitchen. He could see a table and chairs and could hear the sound of a media unit, laughter, and a man's voice. The stairs leading to the second floor were dark. Very slowly he turned the door handle. It turned a little, but stopped.

"Aren't you supposed to be watching outside?" Mason grumbled at Rico who was standing in front of the open refrigerator door.

Rico was tired of the blond asshole giving the orders. "I'm thirsty. There's nothing out there but the neighbor's cat." Earlier the cat made friends with him as he sat on the back patio. It let him hold her for a long time. She was a young skinny tabby and she purred really loud.

"Get your drink and get outside. Keep your eyes open," Mason groused at him. "You two will take four hour shifts all night." Mason turned toward Silvio, "You, go check on the girl. She needs to eat."

Crouched on the front porch, Cisco heard voices. Peeking through the front door's window, a dark haired, fairly tall man became visible moving across the area near the table. Cisco's heart pounded in his chest.

Rico grabbed a soda and headed out the back door. The kitten was not curled up on her favorite chair. He wandered toward the side of the house, looking for it.

Cisco aimed directly at the door handle and took a shot. With a pop, the handle glowed brightly. Trying the handle again, it slowly turned and he pushed the door in. Expecting an alarm to sound, he released a sigh when there was no sound except for media voices coming from the back of the house. He eased into the entryway leaving the front door slightly cracked.

Rico heard a pop. The sound came from the front of the house. Forgetting the cat, he rounded the house to the front.

"Come on," Arturo said seeing the light from the opening front door. "He's going in the house. Move it!" he said letting go of Oso's sleeve.

In a small bedroom off the kitchen, Silvio was struggling to undo the girl's nylon ties. She said she needed to use the bathroom. The stupid *loco* always pulled the ties too tight.

Carefully Cisco stepped into the small living room and was inching toward the back of the house when he heard a female voice cry out, "Ouch."

"Stop pulling," Silvio told Maya trying not to hurt her.

"¡Mierda!" Rico yelled when he rounded the corner and saw the dark shadows of Arturo and Oso near the top of the steps. Drawing his laser, he fired two shots at the front shape.

Arturo saw the man coming around the side and dropped flat beside the concrete steps. The air crackled with shots near his head. Oso felt a burn on his left leg buckling it beneath him. *"Pinche pendejo* shot me," Oso groaned as he went down.

Rising up slightly Arturo could see Rico's shape in the flash of the laser. As Rico aimed for a third shot, Arturo fired spinning the kidnapper around as a blast hit his arm. Rico dropped to his knees and fired back. The night air hissed with the laser shots.

"What the fuck," Mason cursed in the kitchen hearing the laser blasts outside.

Cisco froze in the hallway when he heard the blasts. He heard a man's voice in the kitchen say, "What the fuck." Too late for surprise, he thought. With the laser drawn, he leapt toward the lighted kitchen. A tall blond man stood beside the kitchen table fumbling with a laser gun, then turned limping slightly toward the back door.

The sudden bright light in the kitchen forced Cisco to blink as he approached the doorway. The blond man had his back to Cisco. Maya stumbled out of the small bedroom on his right, wobbly on her feet from the drugs and groaned. The sound made the blond man turn.

All three of them, Mason, Cisco, and Maya froze for what seemed like a minute, just staring at each other. From behind, Silvio pushed Maya through the doorway not realizing the scene in the kitchen. Cisco could not tell if the man behind Maya had a weapon. Maya cried out causing the man at the table to shift his gaze just for a second. Cisco raised his laser and fired at the blond man, but not at full power.

"Mother fucker," Silvio yelled as Mason took a hit to his arm. Cisco saw the man behind Maya reach for his pocket. Not wanting to hurt Maya, Cisco aimed and stunned Silvio who fell to the floor.

Mason grabbed Maya and held her like a shield. She struggled in his grasp, but had little strength from the drugs. His disfigured arm stung like a son of a bitch from the laser shot and it took all his strength to keep his hold of the struggling woman.

Cisco wanted to fire, but the blond man held Maya firmly in front of him. In his excitement he had barely tapped the tiny laser giving it only minimal power. Mentally he cursed himself. He remembered the trainer at headquarters say he did not have to hit his mark directly with the powerful laser on full power. Now, with Maya used as a shield, taking a full shot could easily hurt or kill Maya even if she was not hit.

The blond man backed up with Maya in front of him, pulled her out of the back door, and into the night. Cisco heard the back door clang shut, scrambled to it, but the blond man and Maya were swallowed by the dark.

Outside, Arturo and Rico exchanged shots, though neither seemed particularly willing to make an aggressive move. Arturo could hear Oso groaning somewhere in the dark. From the direction of the house, several laser blasts hissed, but not in Arturo's direction.

Coming toward him, Arturo saw a man pulling a dark haired woman by the arm, running down the hill on the south side of the old house. "Mercedes!" he yelled, but there was no answer.

Rico saw Mason pulling the woman down the steep yard and realized he was escaping. "Hey *jefe,* you can't leave me here you bastard," he yelled at Mason. "Hey, wait for me," Rico yelled, rose up and started running.

Arturo trained his sight on the man and took a shot. He saw it explode in a circle of light on the man's back. A guttural scream pierced the night. From below him, he heard a shot and then a young woman's voice scream, "Help!" A loud creaking from the garage broke the temporary silence. Almost immediately, a tan sedan hovered out of the small garage, flew off and disappeared.

Arturo was so engrossed in the scene from the street he did not hear the man coming up behind him. "Drop the weapon and don't move a muscle," a voice said. "I don't want to have to kill you." They both heard a groan from Oso in the dark. "Who's that?"

"Don't shoot, *ese,*" Arturo said. "It's Oso, my friend."

"Tell your friend to hold still or I'll blast you."

"Don't move Oso," Arturo yelled.

"Okay," Cisco said. "Get up and move over to the steps, no tricks." In the dim light Arturo's image became clearer and Cisco grabbed his arm. The man was a *vato,* dressed in a typical style familiar of Old Town. "Who are you and what the hell are you doing here?"

"Don't shoot, *ese,*" Arturo pleaded as Cisco's shape became clear in the dim light. "I only want to find my woman, Mercedes. I was hoping you would lead me to her. We've been following you from Old Town. Don't shoot me, *ese.* I wasted that *vato* for you."

Cisco shook his head in amazement. These outlaws had been following him since Old Town and he had no clue. "You've been following me, how?"

"You're driving my red *ranfla,* the one that *vato* won from me when he stole my woman, Mercedes."

Cisco wanted to argue with the man about who stole who, but decided it was useless.

"Well Mercedes isn't here. I don't even know where

she is," he lied. Cisco pocketed his laser and let go of the man's arm.

"What kind of trouble are you in here? Oso and I were following you when that *vato* up there started firing at us." Arturo stood up realizing the man was not going to shoot him.

Cisco picked up the man's laser and said, "Go check on your friend. I'll see about that guy up the hill." Cisco carefully edged up the steep steps. A dark lump lay at the top. He poked at the form, but nothing happened. He kicked the man's fallen laser weapon a few feet away.

Arturo walked up beside him. "Dead?"

"I'm not sure. What power did you hit him with?"

"Nine, but my laser is kinda old. Oso got hit on the leg, it's pretty bad. Who are these guys?

"I wish I knew. There's another one in the house."

"I gotta go check on Flaco, okay?" Arturo said pointing toward the street.

"Okay."

As Arturo ran down the steps, Cisco activated the Pcom and waited for Gus to respond.

"Hey man, you just gave me a light show. Did you get the girl?"

"No, some lowrider *vatos* from Old Town followed me here and shit it's a mess. A blond guy took her in the sedan. You need to start tracking the sedan's footprint again."

Gus whistled. "What's the damage?"

"Well, there are three down, two kidnappers and at least one of the Old Town guys is hurt. Can you get these guys some medical help?"

Gus' police scanner tuned to the Echo Park area, bleeped suddenly. "Shit, the police are on their way. I'm surprised they aren't there yet," Gus said. "You better get out of there before you get tangled up in this mess."

Cisco hopped the steps two by two stumbling twice on the crooked steps in the dark. Near the bottom of the steps, he saw the *vato* kneeling over someone doubled-up on the sidewalk. He could hear sirens in the distance.

"I tried to stop them, *Chingon*," the fallen man said. "It's okay Flaco," Arturo told him. "He took me by surprise, *ese*. I didn't want to hurt Mercedes."

Arturo looked up at Cisco. "He's hit in the hip, but I think he's okay."

"The police are on their way. I've gotta go." Cisco hesitated a moment then added, "Look I can't tell you what this all about. All I can say is Mercedes is not involved in this. I'll try to get in touch with the right people and keep you guys out of this trouble, okay?"

"Okay . . . thanks," Arturo mumbled as Flaco groaned.

CHAPTER 29

Hopping into the *ranfla*, Cisco jammed the keyfob into the slot. Activating the link on the Pcom, he waited for Gus to respond as he lifted the car above street level. Flying away, he saw the first police lights coming into view at the far end of Echo Park Avenue.

"That was quick," Gus responded. "I'm still working on the sedan's footprint. The L.A. database is huge and it's taking longer. When I get the first tracking ID, I can follow it quite easily. Where are you?"

"I'm just leaving the site. Gus, I can't let those lowriders boys get arrested with two dead kidnappers to explain. Can you contact the police and get them off the hook?"

"Hey, the law is out of my league. Remember, my line of work is not entirely, well . . . legal," Gus reminded him.

"Oh, yeah. Well, I'll have to think of something else. Oh, shit!" Cisco cursed. A low slung silver *japorider* was coming right toward him. They zipped past and turned the corner toward the Echo Park house.

"What?" Gus asked.

"*Japovatos* just turned the corner. This is going to get real messy."

The driver of the silver and black *japorider* hovered over the house on Echo Park for only a second, then flew down the street keeping its distance as the police turned the corner nearer street level.

"*Eh Chingon,*" Flaco said seeing the silver and black car hovering above. "Maybe those guys can help us."

"I don't think so," Arturo replied. As the lights from the first police unit turned the corner, he suddenly realized their dilemma. "Flaco, the medics are coming. I have to find that *vato*. He is the only one who can clear us of this mess. I'll come back for you, *ese*, and Oso." Gently he laid Flaco's head on his jacket.

Running down the street, he jumped into the blue *ranfla*. Pushing the accelerator, he quickly sped off on street level. Only after several turns did Arturo lift off leaving his hurt friends behind. The scanner blipped on the seat beside him picking up the red car's signal going west.

Three *japovatos* in a Japanese-style *ranfla* hovered at a safe distance from the incident. This part of Echo Park was their territory. Assuming a drug bust gone bad, the leader cursed the stupid fucking assholes, *"Baka kuso pendejos. Mierda!*

It had been a long time since a rival gang tried anything in his turf. The gangs of East Los Angeles made sure their turf was protected, but earlier today the out of state lowriders cost him a traffic violation. Swinging around, the *japovatos* saw several well-armed cops start scanning the area.

The *japorider* circled west away from the scene. A couple blocks away, it rose above hover level. If a rival gang was causing trouble in their turf, the driver wanted to know why and he believed those two old-style lowriders from New Mexico were at the heart of it.

Traffic on Sunset was heavy as Cisco flew the congested streets leaving the Echo Park area behind him. Until Gus could find the sedan, he flew aimlessly, waiting. Comsys beeped at him wanting a destination.

"Van Nuys Boulevard, two miles south of the aeropath I-101 interchange," the computerized voice said. "Please set course?"

"Santa Monica," Cisco replied. It was the only place in Los Angeles he could think of at the moment. His brain was in a blur of images. He had found Maya only to have lost her. The blond man with a limp, the one described by the neighbor woman in Hermosillo, took her. At least she appeared unharmed.

Cisco joined a steady stream of traffic heading west along the I-101 aeropath as Comsys navigated through the Los Angeles metro area. The traffic was five levels in multiple directions, with more lanes than Cisco had ever seen. He leaned back in the seat happy to have the car under Comsys control.

The Pcom blipped and Cisco answered.

"Gus, did you get them?"

"Yes, the sedan is heading southwest. It seems to be making a lot of evasive turns, like he is trying to get the GTCA confused, but I've got him."

"Gus, he's got Maya."

"Yeah you said. Was she okay?"

"Yes she seemed unhurt, but did not recognize me. It was the blond man with the limp. The one I told you the neighbor in Hermosillo described. There were two others. I think one might be dead and not sure about the other."

"I'm watching the police scanner from the scene. I'll be able to pick up something on the goons that might help us. How are you holding up?" Gus asked.

Ever since Cisco came to him needing assistance to find the president's great-granddaughter, Gus felt a special connection to the young inexperienced man, Charley's nephew. Though Gus spent his days circumventing the law and hacking data in government databases, it was not because he was unpatriotic. Nothing could be further from the truth. He loved the Republic. He spent six years in covert special ops before he took a laser blast to his head. No one knew that about him, no one, not even his parents knew his secret covert identity.

He was good, very good at what he did in special ops, but he was discharged after his injury. He bumped around trying to find something to do, before he started doing what he was trained for, espionage, but working for himself. Now, someone kidnapped the president's great-granddaughter. Gus knew it was not for fun and not for anything good for the Republic. The fact the government was using Cisco, an unknown entity, to find her meant they did not trust anyone on the inside, even special ops. That thought was particularly unsettling.

"I'm okay, only shaken," Cisco's voice interrupted Gus' thoughts. "She was right there not more than five feet from me and I couldn't save her." He should have taken a shot, should have tried. The blond man was using Maya as a shield, but still he could have tried. Did he freeze? Was he too scared?

"Don't worry. She's still alive and not hurt, then that is how they want to keep her. Otherwise, she'd already be dead."

Gus' practical assessment of the situation made him feel only slightly less than a failure. He had seen her. She appeared disheveled, but otherwise okay.

"You did a good job to find them. Sometimes things just go wrong. Stay in the area until I get a confirmation on the sedan's path," Gus encouraged him.

"Okay, I'm going to try to pick up something to eat." Cisco disconnected.

Gus' words helped to bolster his confidence slightly. He tried to assure himself, if he could find her once he could find her again. The next time he would not hesitate to act, but now the kidnappers knew he was on their trail. Cisco knew it would only get harder from here on out.

CHAPTER 30

Cisco was both exhausted and starving. The cafe in Hermosillo seemed days ago instead of noontime today. Reaching the outskirts of Santa Monica, he asked Comsys for a fast food drive through near him. It offered several options and he chose a place called, The Hat. It said 'World Famous Pastrami' on the sign. He hovered through the drive-thru line and ordered a Pastrami sandwich, fries, and a Coke. Taking the food, he flew to a spot well behind the restaurant. Before he unwrapped the sandwich, he inserted the wasp-like microcom into his ear and said, "Open secure channel."

"Francisco, where are you?" Luis Jimenez asked almost immediately. The sudden beep of the secure microcom startled Luis who had been waiting impatiently monitoring the link. Cisco had not communicated for over seven hours and the reports were not providing any GPS coordinates.

"I'm in Los Angeles," Cisco replied. He had been trying to figure out just how much to tell the security people back in Dublán. "I was following a lead from the parking garage and got attacked by a *japovato* gang here."

"A japo what?" Luis asked.

"*Japovato*. They are a mixed Japanese and Hispanic gang here in Los Angeles."

"Do they have Cecelia? Are they involved in this?" the voice asked.

"No, they didn't kidnap her. It was just a big mess." Cisco thought about telling him about the blond man and Maya, but still felt uneasy.

"This is really uncomfortable," Cisco said. "I don't even know your name."

There was an odd silence on the other end of the communication link. "It is better you don't know," the voice finally replied.

Luis wanted to tell him, but it was against protocol. Francisco said he was in Los Angeles, but Luis was tracking him blind. The microcom's global positioning was not giving any coordinates. He could be anywhere. No one knew how to disable the G2000 microcom's GPS signal, supposedly not even top secret agents.

Luis tapped his fingers on his desk pondering what to do. Using every possible cross-reference, Luis was trying to find him. All the data showed Francisco's Vette still parked in an Old Town parking garage. His personal Pcom records showed no activity. Luis did not like any of it and neither would his boss. He was about to pose some questions when Francisco suddenly said, "I gotta go," and abruptly disconnected.

"Damn him," Luis muttered.

Two lights shone brightly in Cisco's rearview mirror as a blue *ranfla* landed close by. Cisco pulled the secure communicator from his ear as the driver approached. Before he could undo his seatbelt, Arturo was banging on the window.

"Hey, you can't leave me holding the bag for what happened back there, *pendejo,*" Arturo yelled through the window.

Cisco opened the door of the car forcing the man to step back. "I won't let you take the blame. I just can't go to the police right now," Cisco said. "How are your friends?"

"The police were just arriving. I had to leave them to find you. You have to go to the police and tell them what happened," Arturo begged him. "Flaco and Oso both have records in Española."

"I told you I will handle it, but not right now," Cisco tried to reason with the man.

Before Arturo could answer, lights flashed nearby as a black and silver *japorider* touched down blocking Arturo's car. Three men jumped out. Cisco recognized the *japovato* black-belt leader from the Chicken Ranch.

"*Ano ese,* I told you not to make any trouble on my turf. You don't listen so good, *baka-yaró,*" the leader yelled at him quickly closing the distance to where Cisco stood with Arturo. Cisco did not know what *baka-yaró* meant, but it was pretty easy to figure out it was not good.

"I don't want any trouble with you." Cisco replied making no sudden or aggressive movements.

"Your friend here got us another ticket from the traffic cops. That's two work units. It's going to cost you a whole lot more," the leader threatened. Cisco decided against trying to deny Arturo was his friend. Maybe there would be safety in numbers. Besides, the *japovato* would not believe him anyway.

"What were you doing in Echo Park, *ese*? You *drogueros* need to stay out of our territory." Cisco understood why the *japovato* thought the skirmish in Echo Park was a drug deal gone bad.

"Show him," the black-belted leader ordered a companion standing beside him.

In a flash, the man threw a kick in Cisco's direction. Cisco's many years of training in the martial arts allowed him to deftly spin and return a blow to the man's ribs.

"*¡Chingado baka-yaró!*" Bluebelt cursed when he regained his balance. He circled Cisco pulling a thin blade in his left hand.

"Careful, he's got a knife," Arturo yelled. Cisco threw a reverse roundhouse kick hitting the man's right hand and the knife skittered harmlessly away on the parking lot.

Arturo did not know karate, but was not afraid of a fight. He also understood gang mentality and knew they would fight for their leader. As they circled Cisco, Arturo moved away to one side.

"*Hijos de su chingada madre,*" Arturo cursed at the men belittling their mothers as whores in an old Spanish curse. He hoped it would divert their attention from Cisco. "Come and try to take a piece of me," he yelled at them.

"*¡Chuy! Kiko!*" Blackbelt ordered the others. "Take them."

"*¡Aaaahhhhiiiiii!*" Bluebelt screamed as he cocked his leg for a thrust at Cisco, while the other one turned toward Arturo.

Chambering his left leg Cisco jumped straight up as the Bluebelt's front thrust fell harmlessly on his chambered leg. On the way down Cisco caught Bluebelt on the nose with a right punch.

"*Ahhh* . . . " the man groaned as he hit the pavement.

"*Daijóbu, ese,*" the leader praised Cisco for the move. "Now it's my turn."

Arturo looked around and saw the man with the blue belt on the ground. Blackbelt took a fighting stance, fists ready. The third man was circling him. Arturo thought the yelling and karate posturing amusing. When the young man set up for a kick, Arturo caught him off guard and gave him a street brawlers kick in the groin. The man stayed down, folded over holding his crotch. Turning, Arturo watched the black-belted *vato* attack Cisco.

"*¡Aaahhii!*' Blackbelt yelled as he threw a front wheel kick followed by a spinning heel hook. Cisco deflected the wheel kick then grabbed Blackbelt's leg and spun him around before throwing him against the silver car. The man groaned when he hit the car and made no move to get up.

"Hey, you're good," Arturo grinned. Suddenly the little scene in the parking lot lit up as three more *japoriders* descended. Cisco knew the odds were against them.

"*Vamonos,*" Cisco yelled grabbing Arturo and pulled him to the red car. They hopped in and Cisco barked instructions into Comsys.

CHAPTER 31

Maya slumped on the passenger front seat of the tan sedan looking out the window. The blond man was going in circles. She saw the same large dark reservoir several times. They were in Los Angeles. Someone had found them, or at least she hoped the man who looked like a *vato* was there to save her. It was not what she expected. She expected the cavalry, her great-grandfather's special operations agents to come save her in a blaze of laser blasts.

The *vato* said nothing to her. It seemed to her, he wanted to kill the blond man and hesitated because she was used as a human shield. She kicked herself for not fighting harder. Perhaps if she had kicked him, the blond man might have loosened his grip and she could have escaped, but the drugs made her lethargic and her muscles did not respond well. At least now there was only the one kidnapper, so she thought her odds were better than before.

As Mason flew through the night, a raging anger was building. This job was getting out of control. Who the hell was that guy in the kitchen? The two Venezuelans were dead, injured, or in police custody. He heard police sirens as he left the house.

He had followed the buyer's demands to the letter and then some. The plans were carefully followed, so he could not believe someone found them. The man in the kitchen looked like some local gang banger, except for the fancy laser. Had the Republic's security police found him or was it a drug deal or were they looking for the girl? He wanted answers and he wanted more control over this job.

"Don't move bitch," Mason growled at Maya. "You're nothing but trouble. You try anything funny I'll be happy to use this," Mason said pointing a laser at her.

Maya nodded at him. While her body was stiff and sore, her mind was clear. She flashed back to the scene in the kitchen and tried to focus. When she had stumbled out of the bedroom, the bright lights in the kitchen blinded her making the faces blurry. A man who looked like a Mexican gangbanger was pointing a small weapon. The blond man was holding his wounded arm. It all happened so fast, but she remembered the face of the gangbanger. He looked somewhat familiar, but then maybe she was only imaging someone was trying to save her. If he was someone looking for her, surely he would have yelled her name.

Finally the blond driver flew to a public SATComm in a busy parking lot. Turning to Maya he growled. "I have to make a call. You try anything funny you die. Do you understand?"

Maya nodded her head. She knew he was not kidding and would have no problem killing her. Dragging her with him, they squeezed into the SATComm pod.

Mason voiced the buyer's number into the SAT unit keeping a hold on Maya. After a short wait, the familiar blank screen appeared and the same distorted voice answered.

"Moonshot," Mason snarled.

"Why are you calling again? I have no new orders for you," the distorted voice sounded pissed.

"Well I have some orders for you," Mason spoke to the blank screen. "We have big problems. Some local druggy gang broke into the house and blew our cover. My two men went down and I had to leave them. I grabbed the package and escaped. I'm getting the hell out of the country tonight."

"Wait! You can't do that," the distorted voice yelled.

"Bullshit, I'm giving the orders now. I'm headed to the Long Beach docks where I have a friend who'll get us to Caracas," Mason yelled backed at the blank screen, then shut it off.

Not caring what the buyer thought, Mason took control. It was the way he usually worked, alone and making the decisions. Once in Caracas, he could call Armando. Armando Leoni owned a big, heavily guarded ranch near Lake Maracaibo, well suited to lying low and well protected. However, Armando was Silvio's older brother. He would be furious that Mason left his brother, but Mason knew the PLV was up to their necks in this mess. Still, Armando would be mad about his brother and Mason hoped Silvio was not dead.

Returning to the aerocar, Mason barked instructions to Comsys. Requesting the Long Beach docks, he watched his rearview monitor carefully in case anyone followed.

Maya had listened to the one-sided conversation in the SATComm pod. She was obviously the package and they were going to Long Beach, then on to Caracas, Venezuela. Leaving the Republic worried her. It would only make it more difficult for her great-grandfather's agents to find her. She somehow had to get away before the kidnapper got her onto the boat, even if it meant death.

CHAPTER 32

Cisco and Arturo flew off and left the *japovatos* at the parking lot. Merging onto aeropath I-101, Cisco felt safe in the busy traffic. Only after they were on the aeropath did he speak.

"How the hell do you keep finding me?" Cisco turned and asked Arturo.

"We always bug our *ranflas*, because they get stolen, *ese*. In Española, we build great machines, everybody wants them. We've been following you from Old Dublán. That's how we found you at the house in Echo Park. Why are you driving my *ranfla* anyway?" Arturo had realized back at the house in Echo Park, this man was no *vato*, just dressed like one.

"Why didn't you stay with your friends? I told you I'd send help and keep you out of trouble," Cisco answered his question with another.

"I don't know who you are, *ese*," Arturo complained. "If you don't go to the police and fix this, my friends will end up in prison."

Instead of answering, Cisco activated the secure channel to Gus.

"Hey Cisco, where are you? The police scanners are going crazy back at the Echo Park site. Did they follow you?" Gus' voice sounded concerned.

"I'm okay Gus. I had some more trouble with the *japovatos*. Did you find the sedan?"

"I tracked it to Long Beach and have an ID on the two kidnappers you left behind. I'm loading the visuals to your Comsys. Here they are." An image displayed a dark face with a smile that betrayed a missing front tooth.

"This one is Ricardo Avila. Born in Cabimas, Venezuela. Goes by Rico. Age thirty five. Lives in Caracas and is a member of the Petroleros Venezuelan terrorist organization, better known as PLV. He has two priors for kidnapping, but I guess his career is over, he's dead."

Another image on the monitor portrayed a lean, younger-looking face with dark eyes and wild black hair. On the left cheek, a scar ran across toward his ear. "This is Silvio Leoni," Gus said. "No known priors. The only thing I can find on him is he is the youngest brother of Armando Leoni, a well known cartel kingpin and mercenary. They were both born in Maracaibo, Venezuela, and still live there. Silvio was alive when the police got there," Gus said.

"Yes, that's the guy I shot in the kitchen," Cisco replied recognizing the face.

"Just a second and I'll pull up Armando, Silvio's brother." A few seconds later the display image showed a handsome chiseled face with brown hair and a lighter complexion than Silvio. "Armando Leoni," Gus said. "This one is very dangerous and well connected. He runs both an oil and drug cartel out of Maracaibo. He seldom leaves his estate there, allowing his mercenaries to do his dirty work. However, he is one bad dude. Two other injured guys from the Republic were taken to the hospital. They must have been the lowrider *vatos,*" Gus continued. "I thought you said there were three of those guys?"

"Yeah, there are three. One of them is sitting in the passenger seat."

Gus whistled. "*Caramba*, you picking up hitchhikers?"

Turning to Arturo, Cisco asked, "What's your name?"

"Arturo Perez," he answered. "You sure my friends are okay?" Arturo asked Gus.

"Yeah, they'll be okay. I still don't have any positive ID on the one that escaped with the girl. I have a number of searches working trying to pick up some more information. I'm thinking he is also from Venezuela, so I'm going on that angle."

"Okay, I'm going to set a course for Long Beach. I'll call when we get there."

Arturo whistled. "What are you? Some kind of secret agent, *ese?*" he asked.

"Not really," Cisco replied. "Just trying to find somebody."

"I saw a man drag a girl down the hill at that house. Is she who you are looking for?"

"Yes, it was her, but then you guys fucked up the rescue. By the way, my name is Francisco, but I go by Cisco."

"I'm sorry *ese*, I thought the girl was Mercedes," Arturo told him. "But I saved you from those gangsters, didn't I? We make a good team, Cisco. I can help you."

"I don't want your help," Cisco replied. "I just want to get you and your friends back to Dublán or Española or wherever the fuck you came from."

"Seems like you need help, if those guys with the girl are as bad as they sound," Arturo said.

Cisco thought Arturo was right. If the Venezuelan drug cartel had Maya, this was big trouble. Within a few minutes, they approached a Long Beach exit. Cisco activated the Pcom channel. "Gus, I'm entering Long Beach. I just took the first exit off the Harbor Aeroway. Do you have the coordinates on the sedan, yet?"

"The sedan is parked near the docks on San Pedro Avenue. I've downloaded a picture and GPS location into your Comsys. Because of the connection with Armando, my guess is our blond friend is taking Maya to Venezuela. I checked the schedule and found two ships scheduled to depart before morning. One is headed to Venezuela and the other to Columbia. The Carabobo left about a half an hour ago for the port at Maracaibo, Venezuela. The other is a cargo ship that leaves in the morning for Barranquilla, Columbia. I suspect the kidnapper is headed to Venezuela on the Carabobo to meet up with Armando."

"Do you think it's worth checking out the other ship?" Cisco asked Gus.

"I would say no. I checked on the captain and he is respectable. Not likely he'd be mixed up in anything like this."

"Can you get a passenger list for the Carabobo?"

"I'm trying, but it's unlikely they will be listed. This would be strictly a cash deal. I figure the kidnapper knew there would be too much security at the aeroports. It would be easy to stowaway on a ship, especially if you knew the captain or someone on the crew. If I'm right, you, my friend, are in deep *mierda*. These men are professional killers."

Cisco's heart skipped a few beats. If Maya was on that ship, she was heading straight into danger. "Thanks for the warning, but I can't quit. I'll check out the sedan, but I want you to find out where and when the Carabobo is scheduled to land. Then get me a flight from LAX to Venezuela. I'll call you when I get to LAX."

Comsys lowered the car to street level on San Pedro Avenue, across from the tan sedan.

"Stay here," he told Arturo. "I need to go check out that car." The street was completely empty, but he held the tiny laser at the ready. Slowly he walked across the street and peered into the sedan's windows. It was empty, but he checked the doors anyway. They were locked.

"Nothing?" Arturo asked when Cisco returned.

"Nothing to help me."

Cisco voiced LAX Aeroport into Comsys and the car lifted off.

"Take me with you," Arturo said calmly.

"What!" Cisco turned to look at him in disbelief. "Are you crazy? You heard how dangerous those men are."

"*Mira ese,* I can help you. Those assholes hurt my friends and besides that Armando *vato* sounds mean and crazy. I can help you take him," Arturo explained in a calm voice hoping to convince Cisco to take him along.

"All I'm going to do is give you this car and send you back home," Cisco replied. "When I get this sorted out, I'll get your friends out of the trouble in Los Angeles and that's all."

"And what if you don't come back?" Arturo's straightforward question staggered him.

"Maybe the media will be interested in a secret agent running off to Venezuela after some missing girl, *eh ese?*

How about this Armando guy, maybe he'd like to know you're headed his way. Maybe I could sell my story, *ese*. Either I go to the police now or take me with you," Arturo warned him.

"*¡Cabrón!*" Cisco cursed at Arturo calling him a fucking asshole. "Why would you even want to go?"

"I want to help you, *ese*. Nobody will notice a *vato* like me down there and I'm pretty good with a weapon. Don't let my street slang fool you, I can speak perfect Spanish when I want to."

Cisco grumbled, but Arturo had some good points. If he blabbed to the media it would spoil the mission.

"*Por favor*," Cisco pleaded again. "Please just go home, keep quiet, and don't try to help me, okay."

Arturo knew he had nailed Cisco's fear and went in for the kill. "*Nel ese*, send me back and I'll tell anyone who will listen or take me with you. You choose."

Cisco sighed. "Gus."

When Gus answered he started giving Cisco an update. "Okay, here's the data on the ship. The Carabobo is a third-class aerovessel. It is scheduled to port at Panama City. Then it will sail to Venezuela and port at Maracaibo at five tomorrow morning. I booked you a seat on AeroLinas de Venezuela departing LAX International at two-fifteen on the red eye flight. You will arrive at Maiquetia International at four-thirty. Your ticket is waiting for you at the Executive Class Club."

"Gus I have a problem," Cisco replied. "I need two tickets. I'm taking Arturo with me."

"What?" Gus asked sounding both confused and astounded.

"Yes. I need to arrange for his paperwork and tickets."

"You're crazy?" Gus chided him.

"Maybe," Cisco said with a nervous laugh. "I'm going to need all the help I can get to go after Armando. Just book another ticket, okay," Cisco said with a sigh.

"Okay. I guess it's your neck. There will be two tickets at the aeroport."

Arturo grinned, but neither man spoke on the way to LAX. Comsys landed and parked the car at LAX's long-term parking lot. Waiting for the shuttle, he quietly mulled the new situation over, but Cisco had no ideas.

CHAPTER 33

LAX, the busiest aeroport in the world lived up to its reputation. Cisco worked his way toward the AeroLinas counter while Arturo tagged along behind him. Once settled in at the Executive Class Club waiting area, Cisco told Arturo to stay put. Closing himself in a SATComm booth, he activated a call to his father. Hopefully the call would not be traced.

"Hello," Emilio answered.

"Dad, it's me."

"Son, are you okay?"

"Yes," Cisco replied. "I . . . I . . everything's okay. I can't talk on this line. Just know I love you and *Mamá*," Cisco stammered the words almost choking on them. He desperately wanted to ask for advice and help, but who was listening? He just wanted to hear his father's voice, as it might be the last time.

"How are things at home?" he asked.

"Not much to report, except I'm having concerns about one of the old crop protectors I've been working with for so long," his father responded with the odd comment.

"That's too bad. Hope you can fix it. You might get a call from a man named Gus. If you do, he can help you with the problem," Cisco replied. *"Te amo, Papá,"* he signed off telling his father he loved him.

Sitting in the SATComm booth, his father's odd comment rumbled around in his brain. Perhaps his father was trying to make small talk knowing the link might be monitored. Pulling out the G2000 microcom, he inserted it into his ear. It worried him to use the security people, but he needed a cover to enter Venezuela.

"Open secure channel."

"Francisco, where are you?" the voice demanded.

"I'm at LAX. I'm booked on the two-fifteen flight to Caracas and need an assignment in Venezuela."

"Venezuela? Then you've found something?" Cisco

heard the sound of the man's voice perk.

Cisco debated how much to say. Should he say he saw her and lost her again? "I followed the trail to Los Angeles, to a house in Echo Park. I believe Cecelia was held there. Things got crazy. If you check the police report, two men from Española and two from Venezuela got hurt or killed. The two from Española were just innocently caught up in this thing and need to get back home. I left before I could clear them. Can you take care of that problem?"Cisco asked.

"Sure I'll get on it right away. So you think there is a connection to Venezuela?" the voice asked.

"Yes, at least I think so, maybe. I need to go and check on it."

"I'll make sure you have an EQA assignment waiting at immigration," the voice said.

"And don't forget about the two from Española, okay? They had nothing to do with this."

"Okay." When the link dropped, Cisco put the tiny microcom in his pocket. He sighed hoping the voice, whoever it was, would take care of Arturo's friends. He suddenly realized he had forgotten about Arturo. He would also need paperwork.

He activated the secure channel to Gus again.

"Hey, I see you're all checked in," Gus said.

"Yeah thanks. What happens when we get there? I will have an EQA assignment to cover my travel, but what about Arturo?" Cisco asked.

"I've created all the entry paperwork you both need. I guess you'll just have to make it up as you go. By the way, I think I have a line on the blond man with the limp. I should have something by the time you land. If he's who I think, he's another bad character, not to worry you or anything."

"Hey Gus . . . um . . . if anything happens, call my father and tell him everything, okay? Tell him we did our best."

"You got it, but everything's going to work out," Gus replied trying to sound more lighthearted than he felt.

Cisco walked back to the waiting area. Arturo was sitting next to a young family talking to the children, while the parents laughed. Arturo was teasing the kids, showing them simple magic tricks with a coin. So much for not calling attention to himself. His baggy blue plaid shirt and low-slung black pants looked clownish beside the normal sleek, skintight body suits worn by everyone else. His dark hair was slicked back on the sides of his temples and he wore a bandana around his neck like a cowboy. Then suddenly, Cisco remembered he was still dressed in the street clothes of Old Town, which explained a few funny looks as they entered the Executive Club.

"Hey," Cisco called Arturo. "Let's go get something to eat."

Cisco grabbed his bag and Arturo followed. Several shops at the concourse sold clothes. "Go find yourself some decent clothes, while I go change and get us some food. I'll be back to pay. Make it something business-like or touristy."

Arturo smiled and walked into the men's store. Cisco headed for the bathroom.

About twenty minutes later, dressed in his EQA uniform, Cisco walked back toward the men's store carrying a sack with two sandwiches, two salads, and two sodas. A young man in khaki pants and a collared synthetic golf shirt lounged near the door. His dark hair was combed down on the sides topped with a Panama hat and sunglasses. Cisco almost walked by him.

"Did you get me some food?" the young man asked and grinned as Cisco reached him. The voice had no sound of street slang.

"Wow," was all Cisco could say.

"This okay?" Arturo asked.

"Yes," Cisco choked. He could not believe the transformation.

They had about an hour before the flight boarded. After eating the sandwich and salad, Cisco closed his eyes. It seemed like only a few minutes before the loud speaker roused him.

"AeroLinas flight 1344 to Caracas, Venezuela, is now ready to board," a loud announcement blared in the Executive Club.

"That's us."

Standing in the line to board, Cisco's Pcom beeped.

"Gus, I can't talk now we're boarding."

"Okay, so just listen. The third man is definitely Mason Warrick." Gus started. "He's forty-two and has dual Canadian and Venezuelan citizenship. At eighteen he was employed as a security guard at George Brown Institute of Technology in Toronto. A couple years later he tried to join the Toronto Police, but was rejected because he was born with a slightly deformed arm and an obvious limp. At that point, his record seems to go downhill. After several arrests for petty stuff, he left Canada and ended up in Venezuela. It seems he made his home in Venezuela for the last fourteen years. He's a mercenary, however his record is clean on the surface, possibly scrubbed, but I can see ties to Petroleros Venezuelan, the PLV, the same Venezuelan oil cartel run by Armando Leoni. He has piercing blue eyes and has blond almost white hair."

Cisco could still picture the twisted looking man holding Maya in the kitchen at Echo Park. He remembered the cold blue eyes staring at him, just before the man disappeared with Maya.

"Yes, that's him. Thanks," Cisco responded.

"Cisco, I'll do my very best. I'll have your back." Gus meant every word. It had been a long time since he felt needed as he did now, needed by his country. His years of Special Ops service were not dead and gone. His country needed him again and it felt good.

"*Gracias* Gus. I'll contact you from Venezuela."

Cisco tucked the Pcom in his pocket and stepped up in the long line waiting to board Flight 1344 to Caracas.

After Francisco's call saying he was going to Venezuela, Luis searched and pulled up the police report on the incident in Echo Park earlier that evening. Two men from Española, New Mexico, were in the hospital with injuries, as was one Venezuelan born man. Another Venezuelan was dead, a Ricardo Avila.

Luis searched the names of the Venezuelans. Both were associated with a Petroleros Venezuelan terrorist organization. The surviving man, Silvio Leoni, was the youngest brother of a well-known Venezuelan mobster, Armando Leoni. At least the information Francisco relayed to him was accurate.

Luis opened a channel to his boss, the Director of Security. "Sorry it's so late, sir, but you said to keep you informed," Luis apologized.

"Yes, have you heard from our boy?" the director asked.

"Yes sir. He tracked the kidnappers to Los Angeles. Apparently there was a confrontation. The Venezuelans have fingerprints on this one, sir," Luis said.

"The Venezuelans? And the girl?" the director asked.

"Francisco believes one of the kidnappers escaped and is taking her to Venezuela. Francisco is on his way to Caracas."

A moment of silence hung on the line. Finally the director responded, "Are you tracking him?"

Luis swallowed hard. The director would fire him if he knew the G2000 had not been properly vetted before sending Francisco out. It was the only explanation Luis could surmise for the malfunction of the G2000. Still, the director would blame him and not the medical technician.

"Yes sir, we're tracking him," Luis lied. "And he's keeping in touch. Anything else sir?"

"I want an update regularly, night or day," the director demanded.

CHAPTER 34

"Please sit back and enjoy our short flight to Caracas," the holograph said finishing the pre-flight instructions. Arturo's smile reached from one side of his face to the other as he watched the lights on the ground quickly turn into pinpoints.

"Haven't you ever been on an aeroplane before?" Cisco asked.

"Yes, but only local flights. This is great!"

Cisco smiled at Arturo's childlike exuberance. The young New Mexican was a puzzle. At first he seemed a lowlife *vato*, a gang member. The young man sitting next to him spoke proper Spanish and now looked like a pleasant young traveler. The change was profound.

Perhaps it was just the clothes, but if Arturo was coming with him, Cisco wanted to know more basic information about him.

"Were you born in Española?" Cisco asked.

"Yes. Did you know that Española is the lowrider capital of the world? The best looking *ranflas* come from there. The *ranfla* your uncle won from me has won several best in show awards. Not like those weird looking rides of the *japovatos.*" Arturo's voice conveyed his pride.

"What aerocar did you start with?" Cisco asked.

"I started with a 2056 Chevy Monte Carlo, stripped it down to the frame, then rebuilt the body from scratch and added the wheels. Oso, you remember Oso? He's the best painter in Española. He put on four coats of primer, then seven coats of the best candy-apple red acrylic. He did all the airbrushing by hand. I shouldn't have bet it in that stupid poker game. It was the tequila," Arturo said.

"I was surprised how well it handled," Cisco said. "It's a very creative piece of work. Where did you learn about cars?"

Looking down at his hands, Arturo thought about it before he answered. "It started at Española High when I turned sixteen and learned to drive. I took a class in motors and flight. It's one of the best vocational-tech schools in the Republic, but I had to quit." After staring out the window for a minute he explained. "I left home at seventeen and I've been on my own ever since. *Mi pinche* father was a wino. Our house was a mess. I left behind four little brothers and two little sisters, but I sent money home when I could."

Cisco detected a slight choke in Arturo's voice as he continued. "I couldn't take it anymore. The old man was always drunk and didn't give a damn about anything except the bottle. He was always just a drunk asshole and he treated my mother badly."

Cisco shook his head. What could he say? He looked down trying to avoid looking Arturo in the eye.

"After dropping out, I kicked around for a couple months and then convinced my mother to sign the legal documents I needed to join the Army. I figured it was a way out, but I was only seventeen and needed permission. Sometimes I think I don't have any luck," he said shaking his head. "The Army took me alright, but I got the worst the job the Army can give. Since I hadn't completed high school, they put me into a construction division. That meant I got to carry a shovel and hammer instead of a weapon."

Again Cisco wanted to say something, but did not know what. His childhood and education was superior. His life so much happier, normal, or was he just one of the lucky ones.

"We were the rejects, *muy tontos,*" Arturo laughed when he called himself one of the dummies. "But at least I had a decent place to eat and sleep. I met a lot of badass dudes during those Army years, but I also learned a lot of good things. I kept my nose clean and finished my GED. During my last year, I earned the stripes to enroll into a mechanics course with the motor pool."

"Is that where you learned about aerocars?"

He nodded his head up and down. "I really got into it. I saved most of my money and got my first car before I got out. I worked my heart out on that Ford aerocar. Some of the soldiers had never seen a *ranfla* before. A lot of them laughed, but I didn't care. That car was my pride and joy."

"Why did you get mixed with the gang in Española?" Cisco asked him.

"Pinche suerte, I swear I must be the unluckiest person," he replied shaking his head.

"When I got home with my *ranfla*, it was the talk of Española. Way better than anyone else had. I went back home, cause my mother needed me to help with the younger kids. My father was drunk practically all the time. I got a job at a car repair shop. Pretty soon the local *vatos* were bringing their *ranflas* to the shop. They assumed I was one of them and they were okay guys. I helped them make their cars better. It was about two years later when the local aerocar factory representatives in Albuquerque put on a huge aerorider competition. Cars came from all over. I won first place with my car in the *ranfla* category. My friends took trophies at all levels. Our style was voted the best in the show."

Arturo's face flushed with pride, then he continued, "The day before we left for home my friends wanted to go to the Taylor Ranch Mall to find some local girls they met at the competition. We just wanted to have a good time. Those girls were real pretty and my friends started talking with them." Arturo turned and looked out the window into the darkness. Cisco thought he might not finish the story.

"Then without any warning a gang of *vatos* from the westside of Albuquerque jumped us. I guess they didn't want any competition with their girls. Anyway, it started with *chingasos,* you know fisticuffs, then one of their *vatos* brought out a photon blaster. All hell broke loose after that."

Arturo's face darkened with emotion as he continued with his story. "They had us out numbered, shooting at us from across the mall. Innocent people were running and hiding. I didn't even have a weapon. My friend *el Cheuco* was shooting at anyone who moved. I watched as an older man tried to help a young boy who had been hit. *Cheuco* shot at the old man. It was stupid, but *Cheuco* was scared. We were all scared. I saw a teenage girl crying over the man's body. Then she looked at me and started screaming that I had killed her father.

"I swear I didn't kill anybody. All I wanted was to get out of there, but the girl came running after me screaming, I had killed her father. I knew she could identify me, so I grabbed her and took her with me. At first I was scared because I didn't want to go to jail for her father's death, so I kept her. I couldn't prove anything. That was over a year ago. I've been on the run and I hang out with the Española gang and wear their colors." Arturo leaned back in his seat and seemed to relax. It was as if he was glad he could tell Cisco his story.

"Was that young girl Mercedes?" Cisco asked even though he knew the answer.

"Yes, she's been with me ever since. I'm in love with her and always treat her good, but she'll always hate me for taking her and I don't know if she believes that I didn't kill her father. I know I can never have her. Those *pinche babosos,* those westside idiots, really screwed up my life."

Cisco had no words to respond to his new friend. Arturo was not the person he originally appeared to be. His story was both believable and crazy at the same time.

Closing his eyes Cisco thought about his own problems. It was circumstances which caused so much trouble in Arturo's life – circumstances outside of his control. Was it any different in his own life? Exhaustion soon took over and Cisco fell asleep thinking about what he would do once they got Venezuela.

CHAPTER 35

"¡Mira! allí va otro," Maya said pointing at the black object as it popped out of the reddish brown water. Every time one popped up, she excitedly pointed it out to her great-grandfather. She delighted in the game to catch sight of the shiny black objects as they popped out of the rushing river at random intervals. Sometimes several would pop out at the same time. "How does it happen, bisabuelo? What makes those black rocks pop out of the water like that?" little Maya asked.

Valentino smiled at his ten-year-old great-granddaughter. "It is a wonder of nature that causes such a sight. Rocks are carried downhill by the rushing water only to collide with big rocks under the water making the smaller ones pop out. Enjoy it mijita. This show of nature is just for you," he said enjoying the look of wonder in Maya's eyes.

Maya's black eyes were sparkling with delight and her shiny white teeth filled her big smile. She was watching the river's show when she noticed a long cloud of dust across the river. Watching the dust cloud as it neared the other side of the water, she saw a young man running wildly toward the river. Dust spewed from the hooves of a huge black horse chasing him. Atop the horse sat an Indian warrior screaming in an unfamiliar language. Three feathers in the Indian's braid were flying in the rushing wind.

Maya watched spellbound as the scene across the river unfolded. Time seemed to pass in slow motion, hanging on each move. She caught her breath when the young man tripped, but he quickly popped up and stumbled wildly toward the river. Running up to the riverbank the young man was trapped. The Indian reined the horse to a stop behind the young man, cutting off his retreat.

Suddenly, she heard her great-grandfather quietly say something as if talking to the young man. She could not understand his words, and was sure the young man across the river could not hear him either. Maya pulled on her great-grandfather's sleeve, but he did not respond.

The young man waved wildly, frantically at them. She could feel his plea for help in her soul. 'Help him,' her heart pleaded. Rising up on the horse the Indian warrior threw his lance directly at the young man and she screamed.

Her scream woke her from the dream, but her eyelids were heavy with the drug. Sweat from the humid air and the fright from the dream soaked her olive skin. She could clearly see the frightened young man across the river in her mind. He reminded her of someone, someone she had seen recently, maybe. The drugs confused her memory. A bell sounded in the background, then another. Two bells rang. A voice yelled in the distance and another responded. Maya's mind fought for control, but the gentle swaying of the room cradled her back into a drugged sleep.

Maiquetia International Aeroport looked like the reception room of a once luxurious hotel. Only the AeroLinas de Venezuela counter was open at four o'clock in the morning and manned by a weary clerk. Except for the customs and immigrations checkpoints, the rest of the Maiquetia terminal was dark. Once expensive, but now tattered furniture told of the bygone opulent era when oil ruled the world. Oil rich Venezuelans used Maiquetia to travel to and from Miami or Los Angeles for business and shopping trips. During that time the running joke amongst Venezuelan tourists was *"¿Quanto vale? Oh, está barato dáme dós?* How much is it? Oh, that's cheap. I'll take two."

Cisco and Arturo wearily waited in line. Most of the early morning travelers were business men and women taking the overnight flight for morning meetings. Several families with small sleepy children appeared to be traveling home from a vacation in Los Angeles. One small child held a Mickey Mouse doll in her arm. Cisco prayed the security people had provided the EQA assignment for him as requested. They would know nothing about Arturo, and Cisco had not invented a plan on how to explain him. Perhaps they would refuse Arturo's entry and send him back to the Republic. He thought it would be the best outcome.

"Ah, Señor Salaz come with me," the tired immigration agent said after he read the monitor displaying Cisco's passport. Cisco and Arturo followed the agent to a small, dimly lit office located to the right of the

immigration checkpoint. *"Por favor quédense aquí por un momento,"* he told them to stay put for a moment and closed the door.

After the agent left them alone Arturo asked, "Hey, what's going on?"

"Immigration. Remember we don't have proper paperwork, so keep cool and let me do all the talking," Cisco advised him. "Now just sit and stay calm."

About five minutes later, the immigration agent returned and asked them to follow him. Down the hall, he opened another door leading into a larger well lit office. An immigration officer, his uniform neatly pressed with sparkling gold buttons down the front, was sitting at a desk reading a newspaper and drinking coffee. A small plaque sat on the desk with his name, Capitán Manzano.

"Señor Salaz, welcome to Venezuela," the officer said gruffly.

Cisco saw a vertical wrinkle appear on the officer's forehead when he looked up. Frowning, the man assessed the situation before him while looking at Francisco then at the passport on a monitor. His dark expressionless eyes studied Arturo looking awkward with a Panama hat in his hand.

Working the midnight to six in the morning shift normally suited Captain Manzano because he liked to be in charge without government interference. Two hours ago, he received orders to allow these Republicos entry. The man named Salaz had documentation, but the other one was without proper papers. He did not like it. No, he did not like it at all.

"Señor Salaz, why are you here?" the captain asked.

Cisco's mind was blank. He had absolutely no idea what type of job had been authorized to cover this bogus EQA trip. The immigration official's monitor would have the information sent from the EQA office.

Before Cisco replied, the captain changed his question. "What do you do for the Republic Señor?"

"I am a scientific representative for the Evaluation and Qualification Department. I specialize in applications using the energy particle. I'm assigned by the Republic to assist your government," Cisco lied with the only vague excuse he could muster.

The captain nodded. The data on the monitor identified Francisco Salaz as a Republic EQA agent. Captain Manzano loved Venezuela and was well aware of the country's general animosity toward the United Central Republic. The Republic had ruined Venezuela after the discovery of the particle. Having his country slowly grind into depression and decay grated him. Now this *pinche* EQA agent from the Republic arrives in the middle of the night and some bigwig at the Department of Energy wanted him allowed entry. Something stunk.

"Who is he? I only have papers for you," Captain Manzano grumbled nodding in Arturo's direction.

"This is Arturo Perez. He is traveling with me on this trip in training," Cisco thought it was the best lie he could come up with. He stared directly into Captain Manzano's gaze, trying not to blink.

"I cannot allow Mr. Perez to enter the country without proper documentation. My information approves you but not him," the captain said after a long minute of silence. Cisco felt Arturo stiffen behind him.

"Surely this is only a mistake. I will be able to provide you what you need when my office in Dublán opens in the morning."

The captain had his orders and methods. No one was allowed into the country, especially from the Republic, without proper documentation. "Your department should have provided the proper information with a visa. Are they incompetent in the Republic?" Captain Manzano asked. His voice was full of sarcasm and Cisco actually felt sorry for the man. After all he was only doing his job.

As Cisco was about to answer, the door to the office opened. A man dressed in a white shirt with an insignia on the left side entered the room.

"My name is Freddy Mendoza from the *Departamento de Energia*. Welcome to Venezuela, Señor Salaz," he said sticking out his hand to Cisco.

Freddy turned to the official and said, "These men are here to work with my department. *Señor Salaz* is a government representative for the United Central Republic."

Captain Manzano knew he was about to be overruled. These bigwig government types always pushed immigration around when the need suited them.

"Why are they here? They do not have proper documentation, especially him," he grumbled pointing to Arturo.

"Our department needs their help," Freddy broke in. "There was no time for us to arrange for their visas before they left Los Angeles."

Knowing this was a losing battle, the captain looked at Freddy. "Sign here then. They will be your department's responsibility."

"Gracias Capitán Manzano," Freddy thanked the captain crisply after he signed

"Come, follow me," Freddy said to Cisco and Arturo.

Once in the hallway Cisco apologized, "I hope we didn't cause too much trouble."

At about midnight, Freddy Mendoza had received a call from his superior telling him to meet two men at immigration. His assignment – get them into the country and help them in whatever way he could. No questions. Stick with them and make sure they had everything they needed. His department did not want any problems with official representatives from the United Central Republic.

"De nada amigos, I was sent here by my superiors to assist you in any way I can. The majority party in my government wants a solid relationship with your country. We are ready to fully convert our power systems to new energy, but a very powerful petroleum consortium wants to keep things the way they are." Freddy said wanting to impress Cisco with his knowledge. Considered a progressive in his country, Freddy Mendoza was looking forward to converting to the new energy. It was the way of the future and Freddy thought it would greatly help his lagging country.

"Do you have a vehicle, a hotel, *Señor Salaz?*" Freddy asked.

"Call me Cisco and we have neither. This is Arturo Perez." Freddy shook Arturo's hand.

"My car is in the parking lot. Follow me."

Freddy navigated toward an exit sign and through the turnstile. As glass double doors opened automatically, Cisco and Arturo were bombarded with hot humid air. Across a wide deserted street running in front of the aeroport, a large parking lot was filled with cars on wheels. Freddy led them to a white four-door sedan with a Department of Energy insignia on the side. Leaving the parking lot, he headed for a multiple lane freeway. From a distance, Cisco caught sight of the tall buildings of the city of Caracas shimmering in the hazy morning sun.

Soon Freddy was speeding down a nearly deserted expressway. The rhythmic hum of the rubber tires on the pavement was melodic and almost put Cisco to sleep. It took about forty minutes to reach the city. Street signs illuminated the corners and streetlights directed traffic.

As they exited the expressway and turned onto the city's street, trash littered the sidewalks. The closer they got to the center of the city they saw many workers in blue jumpsuits clearing the rubbish from the streets with brooms and automated sweepers. Freddy noticed Cisco and Arturo staring at the trash.

"Yesterday was May first, *el Día de los Trabajadores*, or a holiday we celebrate for the workers of Venezuela. The workers are given a day off to enjoy their families and to celebrate their contribution to the country. The government always puts on a large parade and fiesta. Hundreds of thousands of people crowded the streets yesterday, so today there is much to cleanup," Freddy explained.

Near the center of town, Freddy pulled in front of a tall hotel. "I made reservations here at the Tamanaco Hotel for you. Just ask for the rooms assigned to the Department of Energy under my name," Freddy said. "You need to clean up and rest. Later this morning, I'll pick you up and take you wherever you need to go. I'll be back at noon. Does that sound okay?"

Cisco was too tired to argue. He really needed a shower and sleep. "Yes, thank you Freddy."

CHAPTER 36

There was an air of panic in the Juarez abandoned warehouse across the Rio Grande, south of El Paso. The old warehouse was in the middle of the derelict garment district of Juarez, where factories owned by the United States boomed in the early twenty-first century. New synthetic materials now created and manufactured in China and India shuttered the once busy factories where cotton-blend products had been a mainstay.

Diego Gomez, second in command of the rebellion, called the emergency meeting after learning of the calamity at Echo Park and the loss of two of the three Venezuelan kidnappers. Apparently, the leader escaped with Maya, taking her to Venezuela. He was out of contact and out of control.

The group of rebellion leaders from the Republic responsible for the kidnapping paid a handsome sum to the Petroleros Venezuelan cartel hoping to force President Torres to step down. They had been waiting for many years for him to step aside or to die. At ninety-two he was still a strong force in the Republic and they decided the waiting was over.

The cartel did not want to wait any longer either. One of the last bastions of oil production, Venezuela refused to convert to the new energy source. Oil was still plentiful and cheap, but the world markets finally stopped needing the black gold. Venezuela allowed modern aircraft to use the international airports, but cars and power plants still ran on local oil. For the past forty years, Venezuela had lived happily off their petroleum resource, but now the economy was a ghost of its glory years.

About seven years ago, the World of Nations began applying pressure on the South American nation to stop their use of fossil fuels. Trade deals were affected and the leaders of the PLV cartel were losing their grip on the Venezuelan government.

Diego Gomez, Under Secretary of Internal Security,

was recruited by the Republic leaders of this perceived bloodless coup. His role in the Department of Security and Information was vital to the success. In fact, each person within this elite rebellious group had been hand picked because of their position in the government or specific talent. They were sworn to a trusted secrecy.

Like Diego, they believed themselves patriotic in their effort to control the use of the particle, so that weapons for the defense of the nation could be created. They believed it was only a matter of time before a rogue nation figured out how to apply the particle to a weapon of mass destruction. It was imperative that the United Central Republic be prepared with a defense. While, President Torres adamantly refused to use the energy for any type of weapon, peaceful or otherwise, this group wanted to ensure the country's survival.

Secretly they and their leaders planned this kidnapping to force the president to step down. The leaders decided the PLV were ideal partners to support the effort and they paid a handsome sum for their part in kidnapping Maya, as well as agreeing to supply the PLV with the particle for their domestic use.

The door of the warehouse opened several times, stopping hushed conversations each time until all seven had arrived. The group arrived sporadically, trying hard to keep the meeting a secret.

Nervously they talked in small groups. Diego Gomez learned the latest developments about the confrontation at Echo Park from Luis Jimenez. Luis was Diego's handpicked security information agent. Not part of the conspiracy, Luis had only been told that an EQA agent had been kidnapped. A long-time internal operative, Diego trusted Luis to perform his work without asking too many questions.

The kidnapping was only expected to apply the proper pressure on the president. No one wanted Maya hurt. It was an explicit demand to the PLV. It was to be a peaceful exchange of power. Once President Torres stepped down, they and the Opposition Party would embrace their efforts and the peaceful coup would change the Republic's political order.

Since the conspirators had tentacles into every major government agency, they counted on their ability to control the rebellion until the president yielded. When he decided to use his godson, Francisco Salaz, as an operative because of a vision, the group both laughed and rejoiced. There was no possibility Francisco could thwart their plans by finding the girl. The president's belief in him was just another indication of his inability to govern the most powerful country in the world.

However, Luis' latest update late last night worried Diego. Francisco called Luis to provide an EQA cover story for his entrance in Venezuela. It was disturbing. The rebellion group thought their connection to the PLV untraceable, especially by Francisco. Now, Diego questioned everything about their plan and concluded the stupid Venezuelans were not as good at their job as advertised.

The rest of the group of seven finally arrived. Four men and three women sat and looked at Diego Gomez in hushed expectancy. Unfortunately, Diego was the spokesman for the rebels, playing go-between the leaders and this group. In the beginning, he thought it a position of trust and power. Now he knew it was a position of scapegoat. The leaders remained anonymous, vowing it was in the best interest of the others to have plausible deniability. Everyone was protected, except him.

Diego stood nervously with all eyes in the room staring at him. "So why was this meeting called?" the outspoken Bianca Munoz piped up before he could speak. In her job as the Republic's Press Secretary, she was used to asking questions and demanding answers. "You know the procedure – never meet together. So, why have you called us here?"

"*Cálmate,* Bianca. My people at Security are scrambling the traffic database to cover this meeting. We are not in danger of being detected," Diego replied.

"Well get on with it then," Leonardo grumbled. "You

called us here for a reason. How bad is it?"

Diego swallowed hard before telling the group of the calamity in Echo Park and the change of plans. "From appearances, a drug-related gang war broke out in the neighborhood where they were holding Maya. One Venezuelan was killed, and two gang members and another Venezuelan were taken to a hospital in Los Angeles. The police have not connected the gang war to the kidnapping, as this type of drug activity is typical for this area in Los Angeles. Several local aeroriders were reported in the area at the time. Our people are working on identifying the specific gang and will be interviewing the hospitalized men when they are out of surgery. The lead kidnapper has taken the girl and we believe he is going to Venezuela. I felt compelled to keep you all informed of the changes to our plans," Diego finished.

"You promised the girl was not to be harmed in any way," Manuel Hernandez grumbled. "If I thought the idiot hired by the PLV would take control into his own hands and take her to Venezuela, I never would have agreed to your plan."

"Calm down, Manuel. We all knew the risks."

"I knew the risk I was taking," Manuel retorted, "but the girl was not to be hurt. She is innocent. I could never forgive myself if she were hurt or worse killed because of our plans. I've known her all her life. She's is friends with my grandkids."

The group supported, but had not planned the kidnapping. Politically, Manuel Hernandez supported the Opposition Party. The OP believed in using the energy particle to create defensive armaments to protect the Republic. President Torres and the conservatives believed the particle had to be protected from any type weapon use, even in the Republic. The president was inflexible, claiming that opening the door to any military use was the beginning of a new world conflict and possibly the end of mankind.

The rebellion leaders had convinced Diego, Manuel, and the others of the president's folly. "It is only a matter of time before a rogue nation creates a particle weapon. We must be prepared and have our own defenses. The president is only making us vulnerable," they had been convinced.

Manuel believed in their position, but disagreed with the method used to topple the president. Now, he shook his head in disgust at himself wondering why he ever thought this was a good idea. He and his family lived well in the Republic. His children and grandchildren flourished in a way previous generations had not, while President Torres guided the nation in peace and prosperity.

"So we don't know where she is?" Julia Cruz asked. "We don't even know if she is alive." A general grumble circulated from person to person. Julia only agreed to the plan if no one was hurt, especially the president's great-granddaughter. The group had been convinced it was the easiest way to get the old president to step down – a bloodless coup, no political upheaval.

"Yes and no. We received only a cryptic conversation from the kidnapper saying he was going to Venezuela. I have people scanning all methods of travel, but they have come up empty so far."

"All of our necks are on the line," Julia grumbled. "If anyone leaks this to the press we are all done. Done!" she emphasized practically screaming at Diego.

"Calm down Julia. Yelling will not help solve this dilemma," Ramon Guzman said. "Have the kidnappers made any new demands, Diego?" His voice was measured, but inside he was elated. He had never cared about the girl. If she disappeared in Venezuela, so be it. All he cared about was the change in power here in the Republic.

"No. Not as far as I know. Two Venezuelans were assigned by the PLV to provide security for the girl, but now the man who was tapped by the PLV to lead the kidnapping, Mason Warrick, has her without supervision," Diego explained. A general grumble continued around the room.

"Let's wait until we know what really happened before we jump to any conclusions," Leonardo Diaz said addressing everyone in the room hoping to impose some order. Leonardo appeared calm, but inside he too was angry. As the Under Secretary of Industry, he had excitedly joined the rebellion. For many years he presented new ideas on how to increase production in the Republic, but felt ignored by the president's administration. His family had fallen apart since his divorce, so he did not have much to lose, though somehow he never fully contemplated the consequences of failure.

"Leonardo is right," Olivia spoke up. "We shouldn't panic. Everything has been going according to plan until now. It is only a small diversion. The PLV still has control over her."

Diego allowed the group to complain and then finally called them to order. "Starting tonight we will proceed with the second phase of the plan, as if nothing has happened. Each of you has been individually briefed."

Phase two of the plan called for major disruptions in the Republic – aerolines, computer systems, traffic, media, and public utilities. The plan entailed enough turmoil to cause the usually peaceful people of the Republic to start questioning the president's rule.

"Bianca, you will continue monitoring the president's activities. With the media and services in confusion, the people will begin to clamor against the government. Allow the media to raise those concerns and fuel their protests. The president will be forced to give in to our demands."

"Perhaps we should wait a couple more days," Olivia suggested.

"Frankly, I don't give a fuck what happens to the girl. If she dies it will be a great shock to the old man. He could even have a stroke or heart attack. If that happens we can move forward with our plans even quicker. Like I said when we started the rebellion, we should kill the president and take over," Ramon interjected.

Diego cringed and the group reacted to Ramon's statement with shock. He was the most radical of the rebels. When first asked to join, Ramon suggested storming the president's residence and killing the old man. Diego warned of his vehemence toward the president, but

Ramon's position in the Department of Commerce was important to the cause. Diego was appalled knowing this entire operation was skittering out of control. He wondered if Ramon really meant what he said. and would have no trouble starting a war within the Republic.

"The rebellion will move forward and on schedule. We must not lose our heads. I hear you Ramon, but many people will die if we start a war. Do not worry, soon we will be victorious and the Republic will be gloriously free from a dying dictatorship."

CHAPTER 37

Blurry images of strange surroundings floated in and out of her perception. Slowly, Maya became more alert and her consciousness overcame the drugs. Opening her eyes, the room was filled with a thin mist and the heat was oppressive. Instinctively using the back of her hand, she wiped at the moisture in her eyes and on her cheeks. Every bit of her felt damp, including the sheets on the bed. The room however was pleasant and cheerful. The large bed, except for the dampness was comfortable.

She suddenly realized she was not bound, her hands and feet free for the first time in many days. Staring above her, a canopy of thin netting covered the bed. The room was large and two French doors stood open on one of the walls. The wooden furniture was massive, although did not begin to fill the room.

Straining for memories, Maya moved her sluggish body. She did not feel hurt, just stiff, sore, and light headed. Only her wrists ached and had purple bruises where they had been strapped together. A dull headache throbbed in the back of her head, making it hard to concentrate. She remembered the kidnapping and then waking in several dirty or smelly rooms. Where? Obviously not here.

Maya heard a door open nearby and a pleasant voice began singing an unfamiliar song, but was singing in Spanish. It was a woman's voice. Struggling off the bed to her feet, she had to hold tight to the bedpost in an unsteady stance. Her head swam and her stomach almost revolted from the spinning. In slow deliberate movements, she staggered to a dresser with a mirror and caught an image of herself. *"¡Dios mío!"* she exclaimed in shock.

Her eyes were sunken into the sockets, tired and vacant, and her cheekbones were prominent on her thin face. Her olive complexion replaced by a sallow look. She tried to pull her fingers through her long black hair only to find clumps of matting. She could not remember when she last went to the bathroom or had eaten.

Beads of sweat dotted her forehead in the heat and humidity. It was difficult to breathe and everything she touched felt damp. She looked around the room and stumbled to a freestanding closet. Inside she found clothes, but they were all men's clothes. Taking a soft man's cotton shirt, she dried her face and arms using it as a towel.

Quietly she tiptoed to the heavy door. Turning the handle she was very surprised it was not locked. Slowing turning and opening the door she stood in the doorway. A tall heavyset black woman with enormous breasts was wiping the furniture in what appeared to be a living room. She looked up hearing the door and greeted Maya, *"Buenos días, señorita."* The black woman's teeth glistened when she smiled.

"Buenos días," Maya replied to the maid's greeting.

The woman did not appear to be surprised by Maya or concerned and continued her work. Cautious because of the maid's enormous size, Maya made no sudden moves. Turning around slowly, she walked across the bedroom toward the large French doors, which were open on the far wall. Stepping through one, it opened onto a small balcony with an iron railing. She soaked in the first sunshine she could remember since the kidnapping. The bright sunlight of the day almost blinded her at first, but felt glorious on her face. The air was warm and humid, but the sun was tempered by a thick hazy cloud. From the balcony, she was able see a wide view.

From her viewpoint, a huge body of water stretched as far as she could see. At first glance, she thought it was the ocean, but then realized that it could be a large lake or harbor. Dotting the body of water were many oil derricks along with some towers spewing orange flames. Some of the flaming towers released black smoke clouds, which flowed toward the sky in spiraling plumes.

Along the edge of the shoreline were a number of large rusted oil tankers. On the side of the gray tankers, large red letters spelling LAGOVEN were faded, though legible. Farther out on the sea, the same large ships floated low on the water, some only small dots on the horizon. A slight petroleum smell in the humid air assaulted her nose.

Peering down and around, she was on the second floor of a large house. Similar balconies protruded from other rooms, eight in all on this side of the house. Below her, gardens surrounded the house. Walkways of flowers and shrubs circled a large fountain and were impeccably manicured. The plants and various palm trees were tall and green, giving a tropical paradise appearance to the grounds. Around the groomed gardens, a high stucco wall curved gracefully enclosing the interior grounds.

Withdrawing from the balcony, she returned to the living room. Much like the large estate's gardens, she studied the lavish furnishings. Heavy tapestries hung on each side of the French doors. The carved wood furniture gleamed from constant polishing. On either side of the sofa, high-backed matching chairs stood like sentries. The sofa and chairs faced an enormous fireplace set in stone. The woman was humming and cleaning a large credenza.

"Where am I?" Maya asked in Spanish. The maid turned at Maya's question and could see an expression of confusion on the young woman's face. *"No te apures señorita. El jefe no tarda de llegar. Vamos a la cocina, yo puenso que tienas hambre."*

The black maid spoke rapidly in Spanish with an unfamiliar accent. Maya did not exactly understand her, but she understood enough to know that the boss man was coming later. She could follow the maid to the kitchen for something to eat. She nodded a response to the woman.

Maya followed her along a long hallway and down a flight of stairs, through a large dining room to the kitchen. Intrigued by her freedom, she followed the woman without hesitation. Food sounded good. She would worry about the rest later.

"Siéntate," the black woman motioned Maya to sit on a stool at the kitchen counter in front of a lavish fruit and vegetable tray. The fruit was large by synthetic standards. The avocados were three times as large as the ones at home, each grape almost the size of a small plum. Plucking several grapes, Maya was shocked as the flavor burst in her

mouth. Even organically grown food in the Republic did not taste this flavorful. In comparison, synthetic food tasted bland. A red strawberry dripped juices down her chin as she bit into it. The fruit tray included several strange fruits she had never seen before. One was sweet with little seeds and another was pink and slightly tart.

Without seeming to have a care in the world, the maid hummed while she sliced bread and cheese at the counter. She placed a huge glass of an iced drink near Maya and sat the tray with bread and cheese near her.

"*Gracias*," Maya thanked the woman.

"*De nada señorita, disfruta,*" she replied with a smile. After telling Maya to enjoy the food, the maid left Maya alone in the large kitchen. Maya's first instinct was to bolt to freedom, but her stomach had seen little food in many days. Sitting at the counter she tried to remember the days of her captivity. She finally realized she had no idea what day it was. Devouring all the cheese and most of the bread, she followed it with the large iced drink. It had a subtle coconut flavor.

While she was still eating, the big woman returned to the kitchen. Patiently she waited for Maya to finish while tidying up the dishes and wiping the counter.

"*Por favor, ven conmigo.*"

Maya finished the drink and followed the woman up the stairs as requested. This time Maya noticed the large paintings gracing the stairwell wall. The upstairs hallway was lined with more large, beautiful paintings and ornate curved brass light fixtures. Like the living room, the hallway had a number of carved wood credenzas topped with heavy brass candlesticks. The hallway was lined by carved wooden doors, all closed.

Pushing in the last door, the woman escorted her into a room with a big bed. Clean clothes, which looked about her size, lay on the bed. Adjoining the room was a bright bathroom. The maid pointed to the large curved bathtub with four clawed feet and told her to enjoy the bath.

CHAPTER 38

In one of the large outbuildings within his estate, Armando confronted Mason. "Where's my brother?" Mason was less than forthcoming last night when he brought the girl. Now, Armando wanted answers.

"Silvio is in Los Angeles," Mason explained. "He's in the hospital," Mason said, hoping it was true and he was not dead.

"You left him? What happened?"

"The safe house was in a bad neighborhood in Los Angeles. Not my choice," Mason gruffed. "Some stupid gang of lowriders attacked us thinking we were drug dealers on their turf. One of them shot Silvio. It was all I could do to escape with the girl."

Armando pondered the story. The house in Echo Park was a place he used as a drug drop in the past. Mason's story sounded plausible, but what about his brother, Silvio?

Armando knew his youngest brother was inexperienced. It was one of the reasons he chose him for the kidnapping. He thought it not overly dangerous. The girl was easy pickings and the kidnapping was planned in every detail. The man who stood before him, Mason Warrick, was one of the best in his trade. Though originally Canadian, not Venezuelan, he had served the PLV well over the years.

"You took a big chance bringing the girl here," Armando complained.

"Where else could I go? The buyer is inept, leaving us holding the goods."

Armando, as leader of the PLV, joined with the Republic rebellion leaders to facilitate the capture and ransom of the president's great-granddaughter. He planned the kidnapping and handpicked the kidnappers, including Mason. The rebellion wanted to put the screws to the Republic's government to make the president step down.

For his part in the coup, Armando was to receive one

billion Bolivars and unlimited access to the energy particle. He and he alone would be responsible for bringing back power and glory to Venezuela. He, Armando Leoni, would be the next dictator of the country. Then, once empowered by the particle, he could run the world.

His control over the Venezuelan Oil Cartel had waned over a decade ago, as evidenced by the rusting ships in the harbor. It reduced the PLV to running drugs to supplement their income, but Armando's true passion was in energy. Energy ran the world; drugs destroyed it. Personally, he never used the stuff.

"You are to stay here until we know the next move," Armando gruffed at Mason. "The girl will not be harmed unless this all falls apart. She is to be treated as my guest and you need to stay away from her. Do you understand?" Armando scowled at Mason.

"Stay? My job is done. You need to pay me and find a new errand boy," Mason growled back at Armando.

"You are done when I say you are done . . . and my brother better be okay or you will pay with your life." Mason held his tongue, knowing Armando was not a man to antagonize.

The bathroom's colorful mosaic tiles were set in a manner to depict sea life. Along the far wall a whale lazily swam under the waves. The blue floor tiles were dotted with tan mosaic tiles to look like seashells. The sun streamed through a large window, lighting up flecks of gold in a mosaic of a large turtle.

Stripping the dirty EQA uniform, Maya stepped into the hot bath water. Gratefully, she sank into its warmth. A bath had never felt so good. Sinking in the tub to chin level, the warm water soaked some of the stiffness from her limbs.

While she bathed, she touched her wrist where her chip had been hastily removed from under her skin. A red scab encrusted over the spot. She picked a little at the scab until a dot of blood popped to the surface. She mused thinking the kidnappers left the chip somewhere to throw the secret police off their trail.

She thought it interesting the maid seemed neither surprised by her presence nor concerned. It was certainly very different from the three kidnappers who kept her bound and drugged. Maya lounged in the tub until the water was cool. Only then did she use the soap to wash and carefully shampooed her hair trying to untangle the knots.

Exhilarated after the bath, she dressed in the clean clothes – a lightweight embroidered *camisa* and a long white skirt. The fabric was soft cotton, not synthetic.

Opening the carved door into the hallway, no one was in sight. Stepping quietly down the hall she decided she would explore. She passed the large maid cleaning a bedroom. The woman looked up at her, but made no move to stop her.

The maid smiled to herself when she saw the young woman sneaking down the corridor. Her *jefe* had explained the woman should be treated as a guest, but she knew the young woman was a prisoner. The blond man brought her last night, almost lifeless. However, she could not escape the hacienda, not without being spotted by the guards on the roof.

Casually Maya walked down the wide stairs to the first floor. A set of large double doors were open to the outside. Peeking behind her to see if the maid followed, Maya stepped outside on the veranda. No one seemed concerned about her movements as she stepped down to the courtyard.

A high wall surrounded the inside gardens. The courtyard was seemingly calm and peaceful. Gardeners were working trimming bushes and tending the flowers. Maya walked unopposed to the fountain near the middle. It was then she looked back toward the house. Around the rooftops of the main house, men with rifles stood guard. Both of the front corners of the house had a small watchtower, where a machine gun and gunner stood ready to protect it.

Suddenly, she realized she was still a prisoner, a prisoner in a bigger cell. Somehow her brain did not react to the revelation. She walked slowly and deliberately around the house three times. Only one large steel gate made an opening on the high wall. The four corners of the roof were manned with guards and several others walked along the parapet. They wore tan uniforms and maroon hats.

The sky overhead was hazy, not clear and bright like in the Republic. When she breathed the fresh damp air, it had a putrid smell. The humidity clung to her skin, but Maya was elated to be free to walk outside. On her third circle of the gardens, one of the gardeners offered her a cut flower and smiled at her. *"Gracias,"* she thanked him.

Besides the maid, the gardeners, and the guards Maya saw no one else. She did not see either the blond cripple or anyone who she thought could be the *jefe*.

Walking in the gardens refreshed her mind and rejuvenated her weakened body. She sat for a long time on a rocking chair on the front veranda. Escape would take time to plan. Returning into the house as the sun dropped above the far hills, she decided to regain her strength and watch the daily routine of the household before trying to escape.

CHAPTER 39

Cisco and Arturo checked into the Tamanaco Hotel. They had adjoining rooms on the fifth floor. When Cisco walked into room 516, the sun was already shining though the curtain and the air conditioner whined trying to keep the room cool. The large bed was covered in a pure white bedspread with colorful pillows. A high backed, overstuffed chair sat in the corner near a small round table. A media center unit faced the bed. Throwing his bag on the chair, Cisco leaned back on the bed, his head propped up against the pillows. He needed to call Gus and let him know they had arrived after he took a shower. He leaned against the pillows and within a few minutes he was sound asleep.

The next thing he heard was a ringing sound in his ears. He wanted it to stop. Insistently it continued. Finally, Cisco's brain registered the annoying sound. Beside the bed, a small pad with a green button flashed a light on and off. Pushing the button he said, "Hello."

"Buenos días," Freddy said hearing the sleep in Cisco's voice. "It's twelve-fifteen. I'm here as I said to show you the city, but if you prefer we can do it tomorrow, *señor.*"

Struggling to shake the sleep from his foggy brain Cisco replied, "No, today is fine. I just need a shower. We'll meet you in the lobby at one. Is that okay?"

"*Bueno.* I will be waiting at the bar by the pool. I'll order lunch," Freddy replied.

Cisco stared at the small pad beside the bed after he disconnected. The green button was now red. Pushing the button a robotic voice answered, "May I help you?" Cisco asked for room 518. Arturo finally answered.

"Meet me and Freddy in the bar restaurant by the pool at one."

After a hot shower, Cisco put on his EQA uniform. He needed to play the part until he and Arturo located Maya. Before leaving the room, he activated Gus' channel on the Pcom.

"How's Venezuela?" he heard Gus' voice after a few

seconds delay.

"Everything is fine, so far. We got past immigration with help from an official named Freddy Mendoza. He's from the Venezuelan Department of Energy. Do a favor for me, run a check on him. He seems legit. He thinks I'm here on an EQA assignment."

"There seems to be a transmission delay on this link, can you hear it?" Gus asked.

"Yes. Freddy says the Venezuelans are about two generations behind on their hardware and software. What do you have on Maya's location?" Cisco asked.

"Well, like you said the computers down there are dinosaurs, so I can't be as sure about the information, but this is what I have. The Carabobo docked early this morning at Maracaibo on schedule. Armando Leoni was last monitored at his hacienda in Cabimas. It's lucky for us the Venezuelan government also tracks Armando's whereabouts. It makes finding him a whole lot easier."

"But what about Mason and Maya?"

"That's a lot harder," Gus replied. "About an hour after the Carabobo docked, a helicopter took off. The flight plan it filed was to Cabimas. It landed there at six this morning."

"Where is Cabimas?" Cisco asked.

"On Lake Maracaibo, about 300 kilometers west of Caracas. Armando has a large operation there and a well-guarded estate on about 500 acres. The only thing I could gleam from the Venezuelan data is some high-level *jefes* from the PLV cartel were seen going in and out of Armando's hacienda last week."

"But nothing on Mason or Maya?" Cisco asked.

"No, I think they were able to stay under the Venezuelan's surveillance. I'm hoping something definitive will pop up soon."

"Hey Gus, how about Arturo's friends in Los Angeles?" Cisco asked.

"Oh yeah, I forgot to tell you. One of them is still in the hospital, the other was released earlier this morning. The police don't seem to be charging either of them with anything, at least not yet."

"Great, I'll tell Arturo. We're going out this afternoon with Freddy, so I'll call you later. I'm going to need a layout of Armando's estate. Can you get that?"

"I can get you satellite views of the area and the hacienda. It won't give you the layout on the inside of the house, but a pretty good external view."

"Great and thanks Gus."

Outside the sun was hot and the air was heavy with humidity as Cisco pushed open a set of double doors toward the cabanas by the pool. Walking toward the cabana bar, Cisco spotted Freddy and Arturo sitting at a shady table. Several kids played in the clear water pool while a couple women sunbathed on lounge chairs. The back of their bikini tops were unstrapped. Two businessmen sat at the bar's high stools. Freddy was reading from a notebook and speaking into a communicator. A tall, half-filled glass sat on the table.

"*Buenas tardes.* Did you rest well?" Freddy asked him as Cisco sat down.

"I slept well, but I'm starving!" Cisco said.

Freddy raised his right arm and snapped his fingers. In a short while a waiter appeared carrying three lunch specials and three bottles of Polar.

"You do drink beer don't you? Polar is one of our finest brews. Here they serve it in ice cold mugs," Freddy said with a smile.

"Beer sounds great to me," Arturo said draining about half the mug in one swig. "Say, that is good."

When the waiter was gone, Cisco picked up a small pocket bread stuffed with marinated chicken and onions. The savory blend of spicy chicken reminded him of his mother's empanadas.

"Each *arepa* is stuffed with a different meat – chicken, beef, or pork," Freddy said holding one of the crispy pocket sandwiches. "It is one of our country's traditional lunches. My favorite is the beef."

Cisco devoured three *arepas* without talking. When he finished and picked up the mug of Polar, he found Freddy staring at him. "I guess I didn't know how hungry I was," Cisco said sheepishly.

"Would you like more?"

"No thank you, but they were great," Cisco said licking his fingers.

"I have a full afternoon planned and tonight we will have dinner with the Director of Energy. He is very anxious to meet you," Freddy said. His superiors charged him with impressing the two *Republicos*. The energy director was thrilled they were here and wanted to entertain them to the highest of standards.

"I am very interested in why your country does not use the particle," Cisco said. He knew it was important to continue pretending to be on an EQA assignment. He longed for more sleep and wanted to get back on Maya's trail, but until Gus could find out anything, he and Arturo would keep up pretenses.

"It is a complicated history," Freddy said. "As you know Venezuela was the last bastion of petroleum production after the Iranians destroyed the Middle East with the nuclear explosion. The economy here was booming when Venezuela was providing the world with oil. Unfortunately, we are a country run more by powerful cartels, than by a robust government."

"But you are a democracy," Cisco said trying to remember his history of Latin America.

"A social democracy in name only. I'm afraid the government is corrupted by the power and money of the oil and drug cartels." Patriotic about his home country, Freddy hated to admit the truth.

"After your country began manufacturing the new energy, Venezuela fought to maintain its status. Your country helped the world to convert to the particle, ruining the oil business for my country." Freddy said it in a matter-of-fact tone, however Cisco wondered just how much resentment simmered under Freddy's calm exterior.

"There are still some places in the world using oil, but the power of new energy is the future. The government here does not allow aerovehicles and all our electricity still comes from petroleum power plants."

"But the AeroLinas plane we flew in on used the particle," Cisco said.

"Yes, the government allows ships and planes from all over the world to dock or land, but otherwise we are entirely dependent upon our oil," Freddy explained. "For several decades our economy has been quite resilient, but the energy department can see an end to our importance in the world and to fossil fuels. Most Venezuelans want to be more like your country and the rest of the world. The people and businesses want aerocars, but the *Petroleros* are trying to keep the new technology out. The department is thrilled you have come to speak to us. The head of the department has setup a meeting for tomorrow morning for you to address all the senior members and department heads," Freddy finished with a big smile.

Cisco tried hard not to outwardly cringe. His EQA cover was now an official visit. "I will be happy to meet your department heads," he replied.

CHAPTER 40

Freddy paid the bar tab and ushered Cisco and Arturo to the parking lot. As he drove them through the streets of Caracas, Arturo was almost giddy seeing all the cars on wheels. For almost fifteen minutes, he kept asking Freddy questions about the petroleum motors, wheel shafts, brakes, and other questions. Freddy seemed impressed with Arturo's knowledge of wheeled vehicles.

Freddy drove for about thirty minutes, winding up into the foothills northeast of the city center. They drove past a sign *Antena De Electricidad Sabas Nieves* and continued to climb. Parking, Freddy led them on a trail ending with a spectacular view of Caracas below them, explaining some history about the National Park while they walked.

The park was busy with families and some tourists. Families carried picnic baskets and the tourists carried cameras. From their vantage point, Freddy pointed to a number of geographical landmarks, including the highest peak, *el Ávila*, an extinct volcano with a distinctive cone shaped top.

Thousands of feet higher than the city of Caracas, the air was still humid, but not nearly so hot. A light breeze blew off the ocean. A brown cloud of smog blanketed the city in a haze, with only the tops of the tallest buildings peeking above. Looking past the city, Cisco could make out a few oil derricks floating in the distant Caribbean Sea. He pointed and asked Freddy about them.

"Those derricks are abandoned. Most of the active derricks are on Lake Maracaibo, where the oil cartel maintains control. Engineers and younger Venezuelans want the government to convert from petroleum to the new energy source. *Políticos* financed by the *Petroleros* and young technocrats studying at the universities have been at odds for years over energy. I think we are finally winning. Our energy department already has plans to import some aerocars next year as a trial," Freddy said smiling broadly.

Cisco paused for a moment wondering how much to

trust Freddy. "Who runs the *Petroleros?*"

Freddy's grin turned dark. "Armando Leoni. *Es un hombre maldito.* He's the leader of the *Petroleros.* I suppose you might call him the kingpin. Armando and his mercenaries are based in Cabimas on Lake Maracaibo. When they are not controlling oil, they are dealing in drugs. He has a huge guarded hacienda on the eastern side of the lake."

Cisco internally grimaced at the description. It was exactly as Gus had described Armando and now he had Maya in his clutches.

"Come," Freddy said. "We better head back. Rush hour traffic will be a nightmare."

Arturo quickly fell asleep in the back seat to the drone of the rubber tires working on the asphalt surface of the road back to Caracas. As they reached the outskirts of the city, Freddy's prediction of the traffic was evident. Bumper to bumper cars inched along the narrow highways into town. Cisco was exhausted, but fought to stay awake. The air conditioner churned and the oppressive heat increased by the petroleum car engines almost lulled him into a daze.

"Freddy, tell me more about Armando Leoni?" Cisco asked yawning and trying to sound only vaguely interested.

"Armando is the son of a wealthy oil tycoon. The family has been powerful in Venezuela for many generations. Much of their wealth was made by buying and exploiting lucrative oil contracts in the early part of the century. He and the cartel under his control have tentacles in every part of Venezuela's economy and government. He surrounds himself with ruthless people," Freddy told him. "You should rest, *Señor.* Armando is not your problem. He is ours."

It took at least an hour to get from the outskirts of the city to the Tamanaco Hotel. Rousing Arturo and Cisco, Freddy told them to take a cab to Maute Grill. He and his boss would meet them there at 10 PM. As Freddy drove away, Cisco turned to Arturo and said, "Come on, we need more clothes."

The downtown streets of Caracas teemed with people. The heat was oppressive and Cisco was dripping under both arms and could feel perspiration sliding down his back. The smell of petroleum car exhaust filled the air. The locals seemed oblivious to both the smell and the heat.

Several blocks from the hotel, Cisco walked into a men's clothing store. After talking to the clerk, he bought several white cotton shirts and dark trousers for both he and Arturo. The clerk explained it was acceptable business attire. Cisco bought a tie, just in case.

Walking back to the hotel Cisco told Arturo to meet him in the lobby at 9:45.

"They sure eat dinner late here. I think I'll go get a beer. You want to come?" Arturo asked, but Cisco shook his head and continued to the elevator.

CHAPTER 41

Well after the sun set, Maya was ushered into a large formal dining room and seated at the end of a long table.

"Buenas noches," a handsome man greeted her as he walked in and sat down at the opposite end. He looked be in his fifties, with gray hair flecking around his temples and through his brown hair. He had a hawkish nose and piercing eyes, though they crinkled when he smiled. He was dressed in a crisp, starched, white shirt with a row of ruffles down the front. Slender, but not skinny, he looked very fit.

Maya noticed the maids and servers of the dinner treated him with a quiet respect, as if they expected to be rebuked, although he was nothing but gracious. They piled the table with enough food for ten people, when there were just the two of them.

He told her his name was Armando Leoni and he owned the hacienda and everything she could see for miles around. She told him her name was Cecilia Juarez and asked him why she was being held against her will, but he ignored her question.

Armando tried not to smile when Maya used her fictitious name, Cecelia Juarez. For right now, the less she knew the better. "Please eat, *señorita*. I have excellent cooks."

"I am a citizen of the United Central Republic and I demand you release me at once." Maya mustered all her bravado.

Armando smiled and replied, "You are my guest, *señorita*. Please enjoy this meal my cooks have prepared for us."

She thought about refusing to eat or throwing the food at him, but something about his demeanor and coldness in his eyes stopped her. Besides, the food looked delicious and she needed to regain her strength. He drank wine and offered her some, but she drank coconut water instead.

"Venezuelan wine is renown around the world," he

said. "Wine, cattle, and oil are our country's exports. You are eating some of the best beef in the world. Venezuela is one of the last places where cattle are not processed in a factory and the beef is allowed to graze on the *llano*."

Maya had to admit it was the best beef she ever tasted. So were the vegetables and fruit. At the end of the meal, a small cup of strong coffee was served with a fruit dessert.

A man entered the dining room, whispered something in Armando's ear, forcing Armando to excuse himself and bid her good night and a pleasant sleep.

He was not worried about locking Maya up. She was free to roam. No one knew she was here. Even if she was located, it would take time for the *Federales* to decide what to do. Armando owned too many of the corrupt government officials to worry about retaliation and the hacienda was well guarded. She could not escape.

"*Buenas noches,*" she replied as he got up from the table and walked out the door leaving her at the large dining table by herself.

Maya returned to her bedroom after the meal. Other than the servants and the armed men on the roof, Maya had seen only a few workers toiling in the gardens. Armando obviously had no wife or children, or at least not here at this house. He treated her kindly, more like a guest than a prisoner, but somehow she knew escape was not an obvious alternative from this tranquil environment.

Standing on the balcony of her bedroom, flames from the distant oil derricks blazed skyward into the dark sky. Stars dotted the inkiness over the dark lake. Tears rolled down her cheeks. She tried to be strong, but the tears flowed. "Why me?" she muttered, but she knew why. She was the great-granddaughter of the president of the richest country in the world. She had refused protection, even when her *bisabuelo* told her she could be a target. She was young and thought the whole world was safe and happy.

As she stared into the night sky, she realized time was lost to her. She heard the maid say something about Tuesday. She was kidnapped on a Thursday in Los Angeles, last week. At least she thought it was last week. The days of being drugged caused her mind to be fuzzy.

Images of her mother and father worrying about her made more tears. They flowed down her cheeks and she wiped them with her sleeve. *"Be strong,"* she mentally told herself. Taking several deep breaths and slowly exhaling, she calmed herself and stopped the tears. Turning back into the room from the balcony, she lay on the bed staring at the ceiling. Her last thought before she fell into a light sleep wondered if someone back home was going to find her here in Venezuela.

Her heavy eyelids closed. It was an odd feeling. Her body felt heavy, but her mind was trying to work. Then suddenly, her body felt light, free, floating, almost like she was flying.

"Mi hijita," a familiar voice called her 'my little one.'

"¿Qué?" she responded timidly.

"No se apuré mi hijita," the voice told her calmly to be ready that help was on the way.

"¿Cuando?" she asked when was help coming.

"Mi hijita," the familiar voice called again, *"Come to me."* It was her bisabuelo, her great-grandfather's voice. Joy flooded her heart and suddenly she found herself standing next to him holding his hand. He looked down at her and smiled.

"Mi hijita, I am glad you came," he said to her. Maya saw herself as a ten year old girl standing next to the rushing river with the popping rocks.

"Bisabuelo, I am scared," she heard herself say. Her voice did not sound ten years old. It was her current voice.

Startled, she opened her eyes. The dream filled her with joy. Her great-grandfather was looking for her. He was sending help. She knew it in her heart, but when. The dream gave her strength and courage. They were looking for her and would find her. In the meantime, she would regain her strength and try to escape the hacienda, if the opportunity came.

CHAPTER 42

Up in his room, Cisco hung his new clothes in the closet, then sat on the bed and activated the link to Gus.

"*Hola*," Gus responded. The connection was better.

"Hey Gus, you got anything new? I just spent the afternoon sightseeing with Freddy and we are going to dinner with his boss tonight."

"I've had some trouble getting information. There was a huge power outage here in Dublán today. The main system had two reboots and the systems are just crazy here, so I don't have anything definitive about Maya, but I checked on Freddy Mendoza. He's a Deputy Controller for the Department of Energy. He works for a man named Elias Lozano. Freddy is squeaky clean. Has worked for the Department of Energy his entire career after he graduated from Simón Bolivar University. He's married with two kids."

"Thanks Gus. What about Armando?"

"I'm downloading a set of files on Armando. There is just so much information on him. The government tracks his every move, so I know he is still at his hacienda in Cabimas."

"Yes, Freddy said it is well guarded," Cisco replied.

"You asked Freddy?"

"It came up in conversation. I guess Armando is a thorn in the Department of Energy's side. Freddy said he is connected in both oil and drugs and has mercenaries to do his dirty work."

"Sounds about right. If Maya is at the hacienda . . . " Gus left the sentence unfinished.

"Oh, and if Mason is still there, he hasn't used his communicator yet. I have a live scan on it."

"Thanks Gus. I have to make a presentation in the morning at the Department of Energy to cover my ass. If you get any bright ideas on how I can get inside Armando's hacienda without being killed, let me know."

Cisco cursed as he put the communicator on the

nightstand. A vision of the blond man who took Maya flashed across his brain. Mason Warrick was one bad ass and Armando by all accounts was worse.

"What the fuck am I doing here?" he grumbled in self-pity at the situation. Out of his league and out of ideas, Cisco cursed himself again. "You're a fuckin' idiot. You're going to get yourself and Maya killed."

Adrenalin flooded his body making his heart pump in his chest. All he wanted was to make everything go away. He just wanted to wake from this nightmare and be back at his mountaintop home. Finally, he got up and began Karate exercises, hoping to calm himself. He could not concentrate on the moves. All he thought about was calling Arturo and getting the hell out of Venezuela.

Opening the portable bar, he retrieved three mini bottles of bourbon and a Coke. He cracked one bourbon and downed it in one long swallow. The amber liquid burned all the way down. Opening the Coke he took a couple of swallows, then followed it with another bourbon. The last small bottle he poured into the can of Coke, then sat in the overstuffed chair.

It did not take long for the hard liquor to take over his brain and calm his nerves. Maya's face came to mind. It was the scene where she was held by Mason at the Echo Park house before he dragged her out. She had been drugged and she was scared. Cisco could see it in her eyes. From somewhere deep inside, he mustered courage and knew he could not fail her and the president. If he died, so be it.

He grabbed his Pcom and scanned the dossier on Armando Leoni. The picture in the dossier was similar to the one Gus had shown him yesterday. A lean, angular chiseled face with brown hair. The dark eyes were hard and cold. According to the information, Armando was involved in numerous shady deals with the oil cartel. He was a suspect as the mastermind of the assassination of two presidential candidates who had anti-oil agendas. He lived on a luxurious estate near Lake Maracaibo, which had been in the Leoni family for generations. There were pictures of his parents, as well as two brothers and a sister, but no pictures or references to a wife or any children.

Cisco pulled the wasp-like G2000 microcom from his bag. Luckily, immigration had not asked too many questions or searched his bags, thanks to Freddy. The voice on the other end answered after a few seconds. "Francisco, I assume you are in Venezuela and the paperwork was sufficient? You need to communicate more often and keep me updated on your efforts." The man's voice was irritated.

"Yes, thank you. Freddy Mendoza met me at the aeroport and has been most helpful in managing my cover story. He works for the Department of Energy and they seem most anxious to have discussions with the Republic on the particle. They want me to do a presentation tomorrow morning to a bunch of big wigs."

"Okay," the voice said with a bit of hesitation. "That is something they are doing without any help from my end."

"Have you found out anything, anything at all?" Cisco asked. It seemed the security people in the Republic had done nothing to help him find Maya. "Do you have confirmation whether she is here in Venezuela?"

"We sent interrogators to Los Angeles to question the Venezuelan who is in the hospital. He is still on pain drugs and not very useful. We do know he is the brother of a drug cartel leader named Armando Leoni. It is possible he is somehow mixed up in this, but we won't know more until we talk to his brother. Hopefully, we can make him tell us what he knows. By the way, the police dropped all charged on the two Española lowriders on our word they were not involved in this matter. It took some persuasion to convince them it was not a drug deal gone bad. One is still in the hospital and the other one was released," the voice told him.

"Thank you for taking care of that. Those two got caught up in this mess by mistake."

"So what is the plan?" the voice asked.

"Tonight and tomorrow I'm an EQA agent, nothing more. After that, I'm not sure."

"You must keep me posted on anything you discover. My superiors are anxiously awaiting your reports," the voice said before disconnecting.

Big fucking help Cisco thought as he tucked the G2000 back into his pocket. Gus was so much better than these security people at headquarters.

Showered and dressed in the attire he purchased earlier, Cisco walked to the elevator about 9:40 PM. He had called the front desk to order a cab. Arturo was waiting near the front door.

"Hey, I have some good news for you," Cisco said as he walked up. "Your friends are not going to be charged in Los Angeles. One has been released and the other is still in the hospital, but they are out of trouble."

Arturo's face lit up in a grin and slapped Cisco on the back. "Thanks. That's good news."

The cab ride to the Maute Grill was short and they were about ten minutes early. Instead of going to the busy bar, they waited until Freddy walked in with a tall, lean man in his early fifties.

"*Señor* Salaz, *Señor* Perez, this is Director Elias Lozano of the *Departamento de Energia* and his lovely wife Gabriela," Freddy made the introductions.

With the introductions complete, the evening started with cocktails and finished with dessert and wine. The main course was a large steak cooked to perfection, seared black on the outside and juicy pink inside. Cisco could not remember when he had such a delicious steak. The meat melted in his mouth almost without chewing. The director smiled when Cisco complimented the beef.

"Venezuela has the best beef in the world," the director said.

Arturo kept quiet most of the evening, listening politely and Cisco was appreciative his manners were perfect. It seemed so odd to Cisco how Arturo easily navigated from lowrider to a formal setting, such as this. The director talked mostly of social issues, asked about life in the Republic as compared to Venezuela, and little of political issues. Cisco noticed Freddy kept a low profile during dinner.

Freddy drove them back to the Tamanaco Hotel and dropped them at the lobby door. "I'll pick you up at eight in the morning. The meeting is at nine. Sleep well."

"You can sleep in tomorrow," Cisco told Arturo, "or hang out at the pool. There is no need for you to go to this meeting."

"Okay," Arturo said. "Come get me when you get back."

By the time Cisco put his head on the pillow it was after 1:00 AM. When the alarm jingled at seven Wednesday morning, he dressed in his EQA uniform shirt and khaki pants. He was ready and had drunk a couple cups of coffee when Freddy pulled up to the curb. They exchanged greetings as Freddy pulled into traffic.

"You look tired," Cisco said noticing Freddy had not shaved and had bags under his eyes.

"Yes, my wife was waiting up for me because one of my boys got into trouble. It was a long night and not too much sleep," Freddy told him.

"Nothing serious I hope," Cisco said.

"No, just got into a fight at school. Usual boy stuff, but my wife was on my case for working so much."

When Freddy got to the turnstile in front of a large glass building, the security guard asked for a signature and allowed them through. By 9:00 AM they stood in front of a large room filled with people. Director Lozano called the meeting to order and introduced Francisco.

It was something Cisco had done many times – speak about the uses and applications for the particle. Still he was nervous. Usually he had a prepared speech, with notes for reference.

"Good morning ladies and gentlemen," he began. For more than an hour Cisco explained what made the particle work. How a tiny speck powered a vehicle and never depleted. Power plants used a bit more of the particle to run the large turbines, but once turning, the turbines would run virtually forever to produce electricity.

During the last part of his presentation, he discussed

some of the issues about traffic control, making the audience laugh. He pulled up a holographic video of the traffic over Dublán. At the end he asked the audience for questions.

"What is the time effort to convert a power plant?" one man asked.

"The Republic has people to assist with these efforts. There will be new technology required to replace the fuel burning engines you use today, but most projects are less than one year," Cisco replied.

"*Señor Salaz,* what do you think our biggest problem will be in the overall conversion in general?" a woman in the back asked.

"Well, that is a very big question," Cisco said and a few people chuckled. "I have only been in your country one day, so I am no expert, however, you will need to update all of your outdated computer systems and technology infrastructure. Traffic control, for instance, will be required for constant tracking of each individual vehicle, instead of ground level traffic control." Cisco could see a number of heads nodding up and down in the audience.

"Some people here in Venezuela will rebel against this new technology and intrusion. We are a proud people and have always been independent. Do you have any words of advice?" another man asked.

"For some time it might be chaos on the streets and in the air, and yes some people might reject the new technology," Cisco tried to couch his words carefully. "Usually the younger generation will embrace the changes. Allow a slow transition until people get comfortable with the change. Convert power plants and public transportation first. Allow older neighborhoods to maintain the status quo." Cisco went on to describe Old Town Dublán versus Dublán City and how Old Town maintained street level driving, while Dublán City was completely controlled by Comsys.

Director Lozano finally stopped the meeting after two and a half hours. "I'm sorry ladies and gentlemen. I'm sure you could listen to *Señor Salaz* all day, but this office must get back to work." Turning to Cisco he said, "*Gracias Señor Salaz*. Your expertise has been very enlightening." The audience gave a hearty applause and began filing out the back doors of the large meeting hall.

After most of the people were gone, Director Lozano asked, "Is there anything we can do for you *Señor Salaz*?"

"Please call me Cisco, sir. Yes, I would like an aerial view of the city and the countryside. It might let me understand the issues you may have converting to aerovehicles." It sounded like a good excuse. Cisco hoped he could see Armando's hacienda in Cabimas along the way.

"Certainly, I will have our helicopter pilot make ready. Freddy, please see *Señor Salaz*, I mean Cisco, is given a full tour."

"Thank you sir."

CHAPTER 43

At a little before one, Freddy, Cisco, and Arturo piled into a yellow and red Department of Energy helicopter at the Maiquetia Aeroport helipad. Freddy sat in front beside the pilot while Cisco and Arturo sat in the back.

When the pilot had made all the preflight checks, he pushed a button and the engine started the blades. The whining of the gas turbine engine as well as the whirling propellers chopping through the air shook the small chopper. A large swirl of dust flew around them as the chopper took off.

"Get ready for the ride of your life," Freddy shouted. The pilot elevated the chopper and swung out over the Caribbean away from the aeroport's busy terminals. As he circled back, the city of Caracas lay before them with a layer of brown smog covering it.

"It would be wonderful to get rid of the smog," Freddy shouted. It is a beautiful city, don't you think?"

The chopper turned sharply and Cisco's stomach lurched with the jerk. He looked at Arturo, who had a grin plastered on his face.

Freddy pointed down toward some construction surrounded by rubble and partially torn-down buildings. "*Universidad Simón Bolivar,*" he yelled over the engine "They are starting to rebuild it. I went to university there," he said with pride. "It was the best technical institute in Latin America for many years, but like our country it has fallen behind the times."

The pilot flew over the city cutting a zigzag path, before he headed inland over a tall extinct volcano. Cisco and Arturo stared out of the small windows. Beyond the mountains, the land was lush and green with rolling hills and blue lakes. Leaving the city of Caracas behind, the land was open and appeared mostly uninhabited. Cisco could see tiny dots against the green grass plain.

"That's the *llano,*" Freddy shouted to them. Pointing down, the pilot swooped lower. As he did, the dots became bigger and bigger until Cisco could discern they were cattle. Men on horseback rode along the edges of the herd.

"Venezuela has millions of head of beef roaming these plains. All the cattle in Venezuela are grass fed," Freddy explained. "The *llano* and the Venezuelan *llaneros* have been raising cattle on this land for centuries. Our beef has always been the best in the world."

"It explains the delicious beef at dinner last evening," Cisco shouted.

"What is a *llanero?*" Arturo yelled out.

"A *llanero* is what you might call a *vaquero,* or a cowboy, where you come from," Freddy told him.

"What else would you like to see?" Freddy asked.

"How about some of the oil production areas, like Lake Maracaibo," Cisco shouted back. Freddy talked to the pilot through a set of earphones and the pilot turned the chopper west.

Soon small oil well derricks dotted the open landscape. Continuing west into the sun, a large lake came into view on the horizon.

"Lake Maracaibo," Freddy shouted. "It is a sheltered harbor outlet to the Caribbean Sea which is why it is so valuable. There are oil deposits beneath the lake." Freddy pointed to oil derricks dotting the huge lake.

Cisco tried to soak in the details of Lake Maracaibo and commit them to his memory. When the chopper descended to a lower altitude, it bounced in the choppy air. The oil derricks looked mostly quiet or unmanned, though some spewed an orange flame. Cisco asked Freddy about it.

"Used to be very busy here, boats in and out constantly. Now many of the derricks are either depleted or not used," Freddy explained. Cisco could see a number of oil tankers looking unused and rusting along the lake's shoreline. Two floated farther out into the lake, near one of the derricks.

The chopper turned again and dropped a bit lower. "Remember I told you about the drug and oil cartel leader, Armando Leoni?" Freddy asked. "That's his hacienda down there. We can't fly too close or his men might start shooting."

"Really? They might do that?" Arturo yelled.

"Yes, he is the most notorious criminal in all of Venezuela. Similar to Italian mobsters in the early twentieth century New York and Chicago, like Al Capone," Freddy said. Cisco looked at him quizzically. "I like to study history," Freddy said and grinned.

"He will be one of our biggest opponents when converting to the particle. It would completely shut down his oil operation," Freddy continued.

A huge expanse of land along the lake's edge was encircled by a wall. The main house looked small from the air, but Cisco knew it was just a perception. Around the main house, a high wall completely surrounded it and the interior courtyard. He could see men walking along the rooftop with rifles. His stomach jumped at every jolt of the chopper, while he mulled over the enormous task ahead. If Maya was down there, she was captive in a virtual fortress.

"Does Armando live there?" Cisco asked casually.

"Most of the time," Freddy answered. "We keep tabs on his activity, so we know he is there right now. He travels some, but not often. He is a wanted man in a number of countries around the world."

The pilot turned the helicopter toward the lake's narrow exit to the Caribbean Sea. Once away from the coastline, all Cisco could see was the blue sea stretching endlessly in all directions. The chopper turned away from the late afternoon sun and about forty minutes later the city of Caracas popped into view with the layer of smog settled over the buildings.

Wandering the expansive grounds of her new prison for the last two days had been a salvation to Maya's body and soul. The fresh air, sunshine, and food energized her. The guards seemingly ignored her, so she studied every tiny detail of the courtyard and house on her walks, trying to commit them to her memory.

From her bedroom balcony, she could see perfect rows of palm trees gracing the long driveway reaching the front entrance to the house. Several miles from the courtyard wall, Lake Maracaibo stretched out to the horizon. Beyond the lush, tropical trees, Maya could see several oil derricks spewing an orange flame. The towers billowed out their blackened oil-smoke toward the sky, which was spread by a willing wind. Low green hillsides stretched for as far as she could see on the inland side of the hacienda.

The house was large and although not new was beautifully maintained. She learned at dinner last night, the hacienda's land covered nearly 500 acres near Lake Maracaibo in Venezuela. The two-story home was built in a square around a small interior courtyard. The first floor rooms, such as the dining room and living areas opened to the interior courtyard. Large floor to ceiling doors remained open to catch the lake air. In the beautiful interior courtyard, vines and flowers of all colors burst with fragrance.

The home was obviously built in a manner to be defensible. Only the large double front door and a secluded kitchen servant's door opened to the exterior courtyard. The second story rooms had small balconies with iron railings or iron barred windows. The balconies clutched tight to the upper story of the main house to provide access to magnificent views. She noticed the balcony doors stayed open to provide ventilation. Even in this hot and humid climate, the hacienda was not air conditioned. Luckily, the thick walls and cool breeze off the lake kept the house cool.

Maya had spent many hours sitting in the interior courtyard enjoying the hummingbirds and bees flitting from flower to flower. Numerous times a day she exited the large front doors and walked the exterior courtyard. Deliberately she worked her legs and regained her strength, while studying the grounds.

The exterior grounds were circled by a high stucco wall. It provided the next line of defense. Maya estimated the wall was at least ten feet tall, higher in some places as it dipped and curved gracefully. Only one large double gate broke the wall's defense. Guards wandered the grounds and guarded from the rooftop. Each carried a high-powered rifle.

While circling the hacienda's outside grounds pretending to stroll aimlessly, Maya studied both the layout and security. She watched the armed guards positioned high on the rooftop corners. The rooftop was monitored constantly. Occasionally armed guards circled the courtyard, and now it seemed to her they patrolled on a specific schedule.

Late in the afternoon, Maya was walking in the exterior courtyard when she spotted a helicopter flying some distance from the main house. It turned and swooped gracefully several times. It was yellow and red with a circle of black on the side. Waving wildly, she prayed they would see her. *"Here I am, here I am, please save me!"* she wanted to scream not caring who was in the helicopter. The chopper never came near to the house and turned away out over the lake. Maya was sure they did not notice her.

Her sudden hope of a rescue crashed. Falling to her knees, she slumped in misery. Why she was here in Venezuela was still a mystery to her. No one knew where she was and from all perspectives, she might as well be on Mars with no way home.

CHAPTER 44

On the drive back to Caracas from the aeroport, Cisco's brain was in overdrive. There seemed no way to find out if Maya was at Armando's compound. Even Gus could not find out.

"Freddy, you said Armando is a criminal and also will try to stop the government from converting to the particle?" Cisco asked.

"Yes, he is an enemy of the government," Freddy said with disgust. "Our country would be much better off without him. He is ruthless and has many friends, especially in the government."

Cisco knew this might be his only chance and he decided to take it. "Freddy, I'm really here from the Republic because a high-level EQA agent has been kidnapped. I think she is in Venezuela and I think she is being held at Armando's hacienda." Cisco let out a long sigh waiting for a reaction from Freddy.

"*Desgraciado,*" Freddy called Armando a miserable wretch. "Why was she kidnapped?"

"She works for EQA and knows valuable information about the particle," Cisco lied not wanting to tell the whole truth.

"So you came here to find her, not to have meetings with my department?" Freddy asked.

"Yes, but I am an EQA agent and everything I told you about the particle is true. Our country wants to work with Venezuela to apply the conversions."

"Are you sure she is at the hacienda?" Freddy asked.

"Not one hundred percent sure, no," Cisco replied. "All I know is Armando's brother Silvio was part of the kidnapping. He was injured in Los Angeles with another kidnapper. The third kidnapper, a mercenary named Mason Warrick, escaped with her and we believe they came here to Venezuela by ship. I think he is here to use Armando's compound for protection and a hideaway."

Freddy processed the information. Cisco held his

breath. "I have heard the name, Mason Warrick. He works for the PLV cartel, a hit man. If the EQA agent is being held by Armando, you are in very big trouble my friend."

"Yes I know. I don't want you to get into trouble or to get hurt in any way. I am just hoping you can think of a way to verify if the woman is at the hacienda. You said Armando is watched carefully at all times," Cisco said.

"Yes, he is watched. I have contacts in the military who I know have access to surveillance. I will make some inquires for you and see if they know anything," Freddy said. "I believe they have contacts inside the compound, a maid and a gardener, who work for the security police."

They had reached the hotel and Freddy stopped the car. "Freddy, I don't know how to thank you," Cisco said.

"I'll get in touch with you as soon as I know something. In the meantime, enjoy beautiful Caracas."

Freddy watched Cisco and Arturo walk into the hotel. As he drove off, he picked up a communicator and said, "Open secure channel ten."

"M52 TIMBER 81," Freddy made an appropriate identification to the secure channel.

"Sir, yes sir. Our intelligence is correct. He took the bait after viewing Maracaibo from the air. He thinks the woman is being held at Armando's compound and asked for my help in determining if this can be confirmed, sir."

Listening to the person on the other end of the conversation Freddy replied, "He only explained she is a high-level EQA agent who is missing. The Republic is keeping very tight about this one, sir."

After listening, Freddy replied, "He followed Silvio Leoni to Los Angeles. Mason Warrick brought her by boat. I believe Mister Salaz is only what he appears and not a rogue agent for the Republic. Our intelligence indicates he is the president's godson."

After a few moments listening to his superior Freddy asked. "Sir, how do you want me to proceed?"

"Sir, yes sir." Freddy disconnected from the secure line.

Walking into the cool hotel after the long drive back from the aeroport Arturo said, "I'm hungry. Let's go get a couple of those Polars and something to eat."

They walked into the hotel's bar and sat at a small table in the corner. The waiter brought two ice cold Polars and they ordered steaks.

"Do you trust Freddy? I was surprised you asked him for help. You just blew our cover," Arturo said after draining half of the cold beer.

"Maybe, I don't know. We have to find out if she is here and I could not think of any other way to find out. Even Gus has been stymied. I had him check on Freddy and he checked out."

"Armando sounds bad, really bad. Did you see all the protection at his house? It looked more like a fortress." Arturo said and Cisco nodded in agreement to Arturo's assessment of what they saw from the helicopter.

When the steaks arrived, they each ordered another Polar. The steak was delicious with fresh green beans, potatoes, and a plantain split and grilled.

Cisco left Arturo at the bar with another Polar. "Don't get into any trouble," Cisco warned him and went upstairs. When he got to the room, he activated the Pcom, but nothing happened.

He waited a few minutes then tried again. This time Gus answered.

"Why didn't you pickup," Cisco asked.

"Sorry, I don't know what's happening, but the Republic has gone crazy."

"What are you talking about?" Cisco asked.

"Communication links are going up and down. Some of the government computer systems have disappeared from the network. The news media is reporting mass disruptions all over the Republic," Gus said.

"That doesn't make any sense," Cisco replied.

"I know. It came out of nowhere and the news media is going crazy. I was downtown and I almost didn't make it back home because Comsys was not responding," Gus added.

"I'm not making much progress here, yet. Do you have anything definitive about Maya?" Cisco asked.

"I can't . . . she . . . " humming filled the link, then nothing.

CHAPTER 45

Armando was in his study when Mason walked in. "What the hell do you want? I told you to lie low and to stay away from the girl," Armando growled.

"You must not be listening to the news," Mason said.

"What news?"

"CRN is reporting major malfunctions in the Republic. Blackouts, computer problems, and Comsys went down for a while earlier today," Mason told him the news. "Two trains collided in Los Angeles with a bunch of people dead."

"So what?"

"The what, is, we have the girl and all hell is breaking out back in the Jalapeño Republic, that's what."

Armando seemed confused by the news. Disruptions were always bad for business, but he did not see how it concerned the girl. Shaking his head he stared down at his desk wishing Mason was not his problem.

"Are you stupid?" Mason asked raising his voice when Armando did not respond. "If they don't want the girl anymore or if we can't make the exchange, we don't get paid! I know you have to have a lot more at stake in this than I do."

Normally, Armando would never allow anyone to call him stupid, but Mason's words stopped him. "Leave me," he growled dismissing the vile hit man.

Armando mulled Mason's words. The asshole had a good point. Without the price on the girl's head and control over the particle, his plans of overthrowing the Venezuelan government would never happen. His contact in the Republic ensured him anonymity by using secure channels and voice distortion.

Armando spoke the buyer's number into the Pcom. After a short wait, the familiar blank screen appeared and a distorted voice answered.

"Moonshot," Armando gave the password. The communication link hummed in the background.

"Why are you calling?" the distorted voice hissed.

"The plans have changed . . . " Armando started to say.

"Yes, the stupid idiots you hired botched the job. What the hell happened at Echo Park and why weren't you paying attention to business?" the voice screamed in his ear.

"*Cálmate,*" Armando said. "We have the package here. That's all that matters right now."

"The police have been questioning one of your men in Los Angeles. If he talks, you are finished," the voice warned him.

"Silvio will not talk." Armando knew his brother would not divulge any information.

"You better hope he doesn't. If you do not hear from me by next Wednesday night, do what you need to do with the girl."

"Hey," Armando cut in. "Our deal did not include killing the girl and . . . " the link hummed and went dead.

Fuming, Armando stared at the communicator. He was in this mess up to his eyeballs and now he was left holding the girl, probably without any payment. It was not a problem to kill her and yet he would take no pleasure killing the young innocent girl. If he did kill her, the rebels from the Republic would have to pay a higher price or he would expose them.

Tapping his fingers on top of his desk, Armando tried to formulate new plans. Monday he had a colleague make inquires in Los Angeles and determined Silvio was alive in Burbank Medical Center. He was recovering, but not yet released. Rico died at the scene at the Echo Park house. Raised in Armando's organization, Silvio would not talk to the police, but they would know he was his brother. *"Mierda,"* he grumbled to himself realizing choosing Silvio for this project left him vulnerable.

Luis Jimenez was frustrated with the limited information he was getting from the security reports. Francisco was in Venezuela, at least he knew that much, or so he thought. Last night the Vette left the Old Town parking garage at 7:34 PM. It left the garage flying west. Luis tracked it to Bahía Kino on the east coast of the Sea of Cortes. It made no sense, but then nothing was making much sense lately.

The computer systems were going crazy throughout the Jalapeño Republic. The Comsys network for the GTCA had been up and down like a yoyo. He was not even sure the information about the Vette was accurate, until he sent someone to check late last night. The Vette was gone. At least he was sure of that. If the Vette left last night then where was Francisco? He made contact late Tuesday from Venezuela, nothing yesterday, but then maybe he tried and had not been able to get a link. Tuesday, Francisco reported he arrived in Venezuela playing the part of an EQA agent. So where was he now?

Grumbling, Luis cursed his position. He had been dishonest with his superior about his ability to track Francisco. He was tracking him blind without the G2000's signal. The only thing saving his ass, were the disruptions within the Republic.

Luis even tried to hack into the computer systems in Venezuela. Their systems were older generations, years behind the times, and though not overly encrypted the methodology made no sense to him. Even basic stuff was missing or the database so convoluted his searches spun on forever and got lost. Using manual methods, he could find no rental car or hotel in Caracas for a Francisco Salaz. The last piece of tangible data was an entry approval for two Republic EQA agents, one for Francisco Salaz and another for Arturo Perez. Who the hell was Arturo Perez, he wondered.

The police in Los Angeles called him back yesterday about the Venezuelan in the hospital. He was Silvio Leoni from Maracaibo. His older brother was a known gangster and leader of an organization called the PLV, a petroleum cartel. Silvio, however had no priors and said he was on holiday with a friend in Los Angeles when some druggies jumped them and wounded him. Echo Park was apparently a well-known area for that type of thing and it did not seem a place to holiday. Without any hard evidence, the police did not plan on detaining him.

Luis could not blame the LAPD. They knew nothing of the kidnapping, so Silvio's story seemed logical. It had been harder to get the police to drop charges against the two men from Española. One of the detectives grumbled at Luis' insistence they were innocent and it was locals who caused all the trouble. Both of the men from Española had minor records, nothing too bad and not connected with drug running, so finally the police decided it was not worth their trouble.

Luis pondered calling his contact in Venezuela, the security manager who said he would send someone to the aeroport to ensure Francisco's entry. What could he say? "I've lost my agent, can you find him?" or "I can't navigate your computer systems while trying to hack data, can you help me?"

The fifteen-minute update started streaming on his screen. Nothing new was listed. Luis shook his head in disgust. Glancing at the time, Luis opened a link to the director. "Sir, I wanted you to know we have no new updates from our agent in Venezuela," he reported.

There was a long pause. "Thank you." the director's voice said without emotion on the other end of the transmission and then disconnected.

CHAPTER 46

Thursday morning the Republic's highest level department heads met at Security Headquarters. President Torres called the group together to discuss the problems affecting the country. For the last two days, disruptions in services, satellites, and the large systems controlling traffic were sporadically interrupted. The news reporters clamored for answers and pressured at the highest government levels for immediate resolution to the problems.

As the Protectors gathered around the large conference table in the room, the president walked in and the conversations stopped.

"Thank you for coming," the president said with a tired voice. Emilio Salaz helped him to his seat at the end of the table.

"I have my best people working on Comsys," Benjamin Aguilar stood up and reported without being asked. We know the system is being attacked by a new virus, something we have never seen before. We fix it and it pops up somewhere else."

"Do you think it's the Chinese again?" Miguel Arias asked. "They write the most ingenious viruses."

"No, I think it is someone who knows the internals of our encryption algorithms. My people have determined it has tentacles into the most secure systems. Only someone on the inside could have access."

"Can you write an antivirus?"

"We are trying, but whoever did this anticipated that move. When we put in a fix, it morphs into another virus. Some of my people have been working nonstop for the last forty-eight hours."

"What about the satellites?" Julia Cruz asked. "Is that also a virus?"

"No," General Castillo said. "Someone is directly interfering with the satellites by hitting them with solar-like flares."

"Solar flares?"

"Yes, they are using some interference which shocks the satellite so it has to reboot. Transmissions caught during the disruptions are garbled, cut off, or just dropped. We are trying to locate the source of the flares?" Castillo continued. "Whoever is doing this is covering their tracks with precision. Just when we think we know where the flare is coming from, it moves somewhere else."

The president let the directors discuss and grouse about the problems in the Republic. He was sure the disruptions were a deliberate move to put more pressure on his administration. Maya had been missing for one week. The clock in his head counting down the kidnapper's threat told him she only had one more week to live.

As the meeting finally ran out of steam with venting, the president spoke. "We need to work diligently to correct the problems, even if it means working 24-7. The disruptions are designed to make the people angry at the government, my government. If it continues the people will be clamoring for my resignation."

"Sir, do you believe insiders are causing the problems? Our own people?" Benjamin asked. "I can't believe that. Even the opposition is not that diabolical."

"I believe the FSA is behind this. They want the stockpile and to regain their land," Miguel added and many heads nodded in agreement.

Valentino Torres knew the kidnappers had not made any new demands, so he assumed Maya was still alive. While he loved his country and always tried to lead it in a benevolent way, Maya was his utmost concern. He would not allow her to be killed over political squabbling.

"No we cannot turn the stockpile over to chaos," General Castillo said. "Let me arrest the high-level opposition leaders and interrogate them."

The old president put up his hand to stop the conversation. "I don't believe they are behind this," the president said.

"It must be Hector de Santos and his ardent followers in the Opposition Party. They have wanted sole power of the government for years. Only they would think to cause chaos in the Republic and have insiders to make it happen," the general insisted.

"You may be right, but in my heart I think we are dealing with something more. Hector and the opposition leaders are still patriots. They love our country. No, I feel sure there is something more behind this or someone who wants control over the energy stockpile."

"I will protect it with my life," the general said looking directly at the president.

There was silence in the room. Emilio Salaz quietly studied each member carefully as they reacted to the president's requests. He had known most of them personally for many years, knew their strengths and weaknesses. Each expressed concern and shock, though Emilio sensed something else, something which made him uneasy.

Finally, President Torres stood and looked around the room. "We need to double our efforts to fix the chaos. Each of us needs to be diligent in weeding out possible people who are undermining the services. Question everything. Trust no one. Review any recent transmissions, absences, and grumblings. We must find those who are part of the conspiracy.

CHAPTER 47

Cisco's room communications port dinged at eight in the morning. "Hello," he answered sitting up on the side of the bed.

"Good morning," he heard Freddy's voice say on the other end. "I have made inquires this morning about the woman you are looking for. Armando's surveillance team will review the data. Unfortunately tomorrow is not a work day, so I may not have an answer for you until Monday."

"Tomorrow's a holiday?" Cisco asked frustrated by the news.

"Not a holiday, a non-work day. Venezuela's government workers are on a four-day cost-saving week. All government buildings, banks, and schools are shutdown on Fridays. Government services and public transportation run with a skeleton work force. All public services are cut by at least sixty percent, including electricity."

Cisco tried hard to control his anger. He did not have three days to waste here in Venezuela while the government shutdown to save costs. He wondered if they shutdown their computer systems, too. Would Gus also be shutout for three days?

"What can we get done today, then," he said resigned to the new problem.

"My cousin is a *llanero*, a Venezuelan cattle rancher. He has a ranch in Maracaibo near Armando's hacienda. He has some men I think will help. We can pose as *llaneros* to get close to the hacienda without drawing suspicion. Do you and Arturo know how to ride horses," Freddy asked.

"I do," Cisco replied. "I'm not sure about Arturo. So what is the plan?"

"I'll pick you up at ten," Freddy said without giving more information. Cisco rang Arturo's room telling him of the plan.

"I only drive lowriders," Arturo replied laughing when Cisco asked him about riding horses. "I want to go. How hard can it be?"

"Okay, meet me downstairs before ten."

Cisco picked up his Pcom and called Gus. He was greeted with humming, then a voice sounding like Gus was in a tunnel. "Hey Cisco, can you hear me?"

"Barely, you're breaking up," Cisco replied.

"Yeah communication is disrupted all over the Republic," Gus said.

"Tomorrow is a cost-saving non-work day here and the government doesn't work over the weekend," Cisco told him. "Have you been able to find out anything in Maracaibo?"

"All I can tell is the security people in Venezuela monitor Armando constantly. He is referred to as a class A target. I guess that means he's a big thorn in their sides."

"Anything on Maya?" Cisco asked.

"Nothing has popped up in their database, except there is a reference to you."

"Me?"

"Yes it was noted you were inquiring about Armando and about the problem in Los Angeles with Armando's brother, Silvio."

Humming interrupted the link. "Gus, we're going out with Freddy to do some surveillance on Armando's hacienda today. Hopefully we'll find out something, but keep looking. Thanks."

Cisco quickly showered and dressed after disconnecting from Gus. He packed a few things into a small backpack including the small knife he got from Juan at Peralta's garage in Old Town and the black beetle-like laser.

Freddy picked them up promptly at ten. He was driving a small jeep, not his official Department of Energy vehicle. About thirty minutes later, he pulled into a small grass airfield with about forty small airplanes parked outside off a runway. Cisco recognized some of the models from air shows and air museums. In the Republic, these were considered antiques. Freddy parked near a blue and yellow twin propeller plane. He led them toward the small plane, where a young man was standing beside the open cockpit door.

"She all ready to fly?" Freddy asked.

"All ready."

Cisco and Arturo climbed in and Freddy followed, shutting the door and assuming the pilot's position.

"You are a pilot?" Cisco asked surprised.

"I rebuilt her while I was learning to fly. A 2025 Cessna 3320," he explained. "She may be old, but she's reliable."

Cisco whistled. "How old were you when you learned to fly?"

"My father taught me when I was a teenager. The territory is large and flying a small plane is sometimes the only way to get around," Freddy answered. "Enjoy the flight."

The short flight to Maracaibo lasted about forty-five minutes. Arturo was glued to the window fascinated with the landscape. Circling south of Lake Maracaibo, the plane landed on what looked to Cisco like a dirt road with a red air sock flowing at the end of the runway.

A man waited on the small airstrip when they landed and greeted Freddy with a big *abrazo*. After introductions, Freddy's cousin Romelio welcomed Cisco and Arturo with a smile and a warm handshake. They piled into his open bed pickup truck. Cisco and Arturo sat in the back.

As the truck bumped along a rutted dirt road, the grasslands of the *llano* stretched as far as the eye could see. About twenty minutes later, a small ranch house popped into view as the truck bounced on a dirt road. Several men were saddling seven horses near the barn when they drove up.

Freddy shook hands with the men and Romelio introduced Cisco and Arturo to the *llaneros*. Each Venezuelan cowboy wore a woven poncho loosely hung over a white cotton shirt and worn-out jeans. A wide sombrero woven of fiber or straw almost covered their eyes. Romelio handed Freddy, Cisco, and Arturo a poncho and hat.

"Don't worry," Romelio said. "From a distance you

will look like a *llanero*."

Instead of cowboy boots Arturo wore black pants tucked into his synthetic high-top boots. "I look like a *pendejo* in this *llanero* getup," Arturo quipped.

"You look more like a *payaso*," one of the *llaneros* joked telling Arturo that he looked more like a clown and everyone laughed.

Romelio and his friends were friendly and jovial, acting like they were going on a holiday ride and not surveillance of a dangerous criminal. Romelio, a man in his late twenties or early thirties, was dressed in lose cotton *pantalones* with a white cotton shirt. His well worn leather boots were the color of the black dirt. He was lean and his skin dark brown from hard work and many hours in the sun.

Cisco walked to where Freddy and Romelio were standing near Freddy's horse. "Thank you for helping me. It could be dangerous," Cisco told Romelio.

"These men," Romelio said nodding his head toward the others, "any of them would be happy to stand up against Armando. Every family on the *llano* has been hurt by the Leoni family, including mine. The Leoni's killed our cattle and drove away the market. Then they stole the land when the families had financial trouble. All because of their greed for oil."

Romelio decided only three of the *llaneros* would accompany the main group, while the fourth man would stay somewhat behind to keep the small herd of cattle moving. More than six men might attract too much suspicion when they approached the Leoni hacienda.

"How far is it from your ranch to Armando's?" Cisco asked.

"About fifteen kilometers," he replied. "We will make the ride in about two hours herding some steer along the way. There is a hillside overlooking the hacienda where we will have a good view without arousing suspicion."

The *llaneros* mounted their horses. Arturo made no move to mount the last horse.

"Arturo," Cisco said. "*Vamonos*." Arturo was standing

beside his horse fumbling with the reins.

"Julio," Romelio called to one of the workers, "go help that *urbanero* onto his horse."

The tall man walked over to Arturo and showed him how to use the leather stirrup to hoist himself up onto the horse. With a big shove Arturo was on the saddle. Julio put the reins into Arturo right hand. He looked as awkward as he looked scared.

"Camilo, stay close to Arturo," Romelio said to one of the men. Romelio signaled to the group and kicked the flanks of his horse. Cisco did the same. Looking back he saw Camilo struggling to help Arturo start the horse to a canter.

Finally the small party, led by one of Romelio's men, headed east. Freddy and Cisco were riding near Romelio, and Camilo and Arturo were bringing up the rear.

"The *llano* is huge," Cisco said looking out as far as he could on the vacant grasslands.

"This is not really the *llano*. The real *llano* is southeast of here. Mine is but a small rancho. The real *llano* is a vast open space with many large cattle ranches, many hundreds of thousands of square miles. The cattle herds on the *llano* equal those you would find in Argentina or Texas in the late 1800s," Romelio explained.

"My cousin's property is considered a *llanerito,* because it is quite small. You see, our family is from Arauca on the *llano,* but his wife is from Maracaibo. She didn't want to leave her family. My uncle solved the problem by helping them buy this small rancho and providing him with a small herd," Freddy explained.

From the rear of the little band of men they heard Arturo curse at his horse, "*Pinche caballo, adelante!*" The rest of the group chuckled at his curses trying to make the horse behave and to move forward.

About two hours later, the guards on the Leoni rooftop saw a small herd of cattle and six *llaneros* crest a small grassy hill. To the guards, the *llaneros* seemed to be moving the cows from one pasture to another, a common occurrence on the surrounding countryside.

Freddy, Romelio, Arturo, and Cisco sat atop their horses ahead of the herd.

"It is a traditional hacienda," Romelio explained. "There are no windows on the first floor opening to the outside. The first floor rooms open into a small interior courtyard. The second floor rooms have balconies. You can see the black railings," he said nodding toward the house without pointing.

Cisco could see the balconies clinging to the upper story and the lower walls appeared to be covered with green vines and trimmed bushes. Around the entire house a large expanse of courtyard was surrounded by a high wall. Behind the house, a large dark blue pool sparkled in the afternoon sun against the otherwise dark green foliage. To the side of the main house were a number of smaller single-story buildings. In addition, one outbuilding looked like a horse barn, the others storage or perhaps servant quarters.

Freddy and Cisco casually broke away from the group of *llaneros* and dismounted behind a patch of scrubby trees to study the hacienda. Freddy produced a pair of high-powered binoculars. Cisco scanned the house noticing guards on the rooftop. The high wall had only a single gated entrance.

Freddy scanned the main house. Above, patrolling along the roof's parapet there were three armed guards. They wore maroon berets and paramilitary camouflage uniforms. Each held a long range, military-style automatic weapon. More guards were located on each corner of the roof. Freddy scanned for guards at ground level, but saw none.

He handed the binoculars back to Cisco. "Guards on the roof with high-powered automatic rifles. What you consider old-style weapons are still very popular here, especially with the oil cartel," Freddy explained.

Cisco scanned the grounds carefully. An older rather plump woman came out of the house and walked to one of the low buildings in the back. It looked like she was carrying a bowl or plate in her hands. A man came out of the horse barn and disappeared behind the house.

"If they have her prisoner, they could have her tied up inside one of the buildings. This is not good." Dejected, Cisco handed the binoculars back to Freddy.

Freddy seemed unfazed by Cisco's comment. "I know from my research the road leading from the gate is the only access in and out of the property. The metal gate is electrified," Freddy said.

They took turns scanning the property with the binoculars for almost an hour. Cisco realized if Maya was being held inside, the house was impenetrable. Freddy was watching the courtyard when he saw a young woman walk out of the house and walk down the front steps toward the courtyard fountain.

"Look over there in the front courtyard. There is a young woman," Freddy said handing the binoculars to Cisco and pointing to a small figure walking around the grounds. Quickly Cisco brought the binoculars to his eyes and pushed the focus button. An enlarged image of Maya's face materialized before his eyes. "Yes, that's her. *Gracias a Dios,*" he thanked God. "She looks okay."

Cisco handed Freddy the binoculars after a few moments. Freddy looked at a young woman with long dark hair walking the grounds. As he watched, she disappeared around the rear side of the house.

As the sun began to dip on the western sky, the small band of *llaneros* moved the dozen cows away from the hill overlooking the Leoni hacienda. Later, Romelio drove Freddy, Cisco, and Arturo back to the airstrip where they climbed into the plane. As Freddy took off, he circled near the Leoni property for one last look.

It was almost dark when they landed back at the small airstrip near Caracas. Cisco noticed several dark cars sat near the empty spot left by Freddy's plane, but thought nothing of them. Freddy guided the plane to a smooth landing and taxied to his spot. As he opened the door, two men in black suits took positions on either side of the fold down stairs.

Freddy exited the plane, with Cisco and Arturo close behind.

"*Señor Salaz*, you will come with us, both of you" one of the men said indicating Arturo.

"Why?" Cisco stammered looking around for Freddy, but he had suddenly disappeared.

"*Señor Salaz*, please just follow me."

Cisco noticed each man, while dressed like a businessman, carried a small weapon at their side. When Arturo started to protest, Cisco gave him a look to be quiet.

"Certainly," Cisco replied. The men loaded Cisco and Arturo into a black car, and sped away from the airstrip. Cisco looked back, but Freddy was nowhere to be seen.

CHAPTER 48

Maya was summoned by the maid for dinner. She spent the afternoon wandering aimlessly around the house, then took a long hot bath and washed her hair. From the bathroom window, she watched a small herd of cattle on the far hill. They seemed a million miles away.

No matter how many times she studied the courtyard and the gate looking for a way to escape all she saw were armed guards and tight security. Though they never threatened her in any way, she knew what their orders would be. Shoot to kill, if she tried to escape.

When she entered the dining room, Armando greeted her, *"Buenas noches, señorita."*

Maya sat at the chair on the far end of the table. "How long are you going to keep me a prisoner?" she asked in reply.

"You are not a prisoner, *señorita*. You are my honored guest. Are you not well cared for, fed, and housed?" Armando almost sneered in a grin.

"Against my will," Maya retorted.

"Ah, your will, well that is a matter of interpretation. Perhaps I am protecting you," Armando said casually waving his right hand.

The maid placed a plate in front of Armando and then another in front of Maya. In the center a precisely formed ball of rice, flattened on the top, was surrounded by black beans on one side and a pile of shredded beef with spices and onions on the other. A half of a large avocado sat beside the rice and a fried egg topped the rice.

"This is one of our national dishes called *pabellón criollo*," Armando said with a smile. "Eat, it is delicious. I had my kitchen make it especially for you."

Maya could see behind Armando's smile. She was not a guest, she was his prisoner, and yet he had been nothing but gracious. She had not seen the blond man with the limp. Perhaps Armando was protecting her from him.

Taking a bite of the spicy meat, the flavor exploded

in her mouth. It had a kick, yet not too hot. She watched as Armando cut a small piece of avocado and took a forkful of rice and meat. She had to admit, the food was delicious. Everything she ate here in Venezuela was fresh and the flavors like nothing she was used to back in the Republic, except perhaps her mother's Christmas dinner.

Armando watched her eat heartily from the plate of *pabellón criollo*. The young woman was perhaps in her early to mid twenties. Young, but had an aura of strength. She had not cried or wailed at her situation. When she talked to him, she looked him in the eye, without fear. He admired that about her. When he was approached to join this rebellion, they told him she was an EQA agent, someone who understood and knew the secrets of the particle – an asset to their cause. She might be, but Armando had his own devices and the young woman sitting across from him was the great-granddaughter of the President of the United Central Republic, and regardless of what happened with the rebellion in the Republic, she was valuable, very valuable.

From his contacts within the Republic, things were quickly spinning out of control. Communication satellites and their traffic grids were a mess. Aeroplanes were sporadically grounded while the control systems spit out garbage. A commuter train crashed killing a number of people in Los Angeles. The banking system was experiencing outages and the people were standing in line at markets unable to buy anything.

Media reporters on CRN were showing people protesting in the streets of Dublán City and Los Angeles. The protests looked small, maybe even staged, but the media was obviously fueling the fire of discontent.

Armando pondered how he could use the unrest to his advantage. His last communication with the rebellion leader left him holding the bag. They seemed less concerned for the young woman who sat across from him, even though they originally told him she was the key.

When she finished the meal Maya thanked Armando, "*Gracias*, the meal was delicious." The least she could do was be hospitable. By watching and listening she had gleaned a few details of her captivity. Her host, as he liked to call himself, was Armando Leoni. She learned the large lake she could see from the balcony was Lake Maracaibo and she was in Venezuela. She knew little of her captor, except he was the *jefe*.

"Why is your hacienda so well guarded *señor?* Are you an outlaw?" Maya asked a provocative question. Armando leaned back in his chair and gazed at the young woman as if pondering what to tell her. He smiled and then said, "I may be considered to be an outlaw to some, *señorita,* but I assure you I love my country. I only have the best interests of my country in my heart. You see, my ancestors discovered oil in the large lake you can see from the window of your room. They and a few men like them risked their lives to start drilling the oil and put Venezuela into the oil business. For many years, oil was this country's main export and supported the general economy."

Maya thought how similar his story was to her own. Her great-grandfather discovered the energy particle and supported the financial turnaround to create the Republic.

"So you are an oilman?" Maya asked. "Those oil derricks in the lake are yours?"

"Yes, they are mine as are many others. I have been instrumental in keeping the oil industry alive here in Venezuela, but now your country has stolen that business away from me."

"Stolen!" Maya exclaimed. "My country has shared the particle with the world to eliminate pollution and to provide the ability for space travel. Your oil could not do that," she ended her statement with a bit of sarcasm.

"No, sadly for Venezuela you are right. Your energy source has helped many countries in the world to revitalize their economies and cleared the air of pollution, but at the expense of countries like Venezuela. Our people are suffering, *señorita."*

"Venezuelans are suffering because your government chooses not to work with my country's government to convert to the particle." Maya knew more history than she wished to share, but could not let his words stand without rebuke.

Armando twirled his fork. The young woman was both articulate and well educated. Her haughty manner amused him. "My country provided the world with energy and then the world deserted us. Your country was determined to rid the world of fossil fuels and claim all of the world's energy resources as their own." Maya could hear intensity in his voice.

She wanted to scream at him, telling him how stupid his country had been to reject the particle, but resisted the urge.

"It is not too late to convert to the particle. I am an EQA agent for my country. Facilitating a conversion of existing operations to maximize the particle is one of my jobs," Maya said.

"EQA?" Armando asked, although he already knew what the letters stood for.

"EQA stands for Evaluation and Qualification Agency of the United Central Republic. I could get in touch with people in my agency to work with your country," she explained.

"Very interesting conversation, *señorita*. I will have to give that some thought. Perhaps we can continue this conversation over another dinner," Armando said.

Suddenly Maya was sorry she had engaged in telling Armando her job. It would have been better to let him wonder who she was. She stood up abruptly and said, "We have nothing more to discuss, *señor.*"

As she walked out of the dining room, Armando said nothing in reply. The young woman was full of knowledge. She knew much about the particle, information he wanted to know. Yes, they would be having many more conversations in the future.

Since his last conversation with the ringleaders of the rebellion, Armando had given thought to his position. Regardless of whether the rebellion in the Jalapeño Republic was successful was of little concern to him. He held a valuable pawn and he expected it to pay off. The woman would be a great resource to him when he got control of the new energy stockpile.

Walking back to her bedroom, Maya replayed the conversation from dinner. She got upset at herself for giving more information to Armando than he gave her. His arrogance made her angry, but at least he did not know her real identity.

CHAPTER 49

The men in the black car did not speak to Cisco or Arturo on the drive. Arriving at a nondescript building outside of Caracas, one man escorted Cisco to a small room, while the other led Arturo down the hallway.

"Please be seated *Señor Salaz*. Would you like something to drink, a Coke perhaps?" the man asked.

Cisco shook his head no. "What is this all about?" he asked the man, but received no answer, only the man's back as he walked out the door and closed it. Feeling trapped and alone, Cisco activated the G2000 microcom, but all he got was a humming sound.

Pacing the small office, Cisco kicked himself mentally for taking Freddy into his confidence. A few minutes later a tall man in a uniform walked into the room. The uniform was military, with ribbons and medals adorning his chest. On each shoulder, a cord circled and hung down the top of his shoulders. The uniformed man sat across from Cisco behind a small desk.

"Please sit down *Señor Salaz*. I am sorry for this inconvenience. You are from the United Central Republic, are you not?"

"Yes sir," Cisco replied sitting in the chair positioned across of the desk. "Freddy Mendoza knows I am with the Evaluation and Qualification Agency of the United Central Republic. I spoke to your country's Department of Energy yesterday."

"I am aware of that. I believe you are here on an official visit for your department, are you not?"

"Yes sir."

"And you are only here in that capacity?" the uniformed man asked.

"Yes sir," Cisco replied trying to focus directly into the man's eyes. "Freddy and Director Lozano asked me to evaluate the situation here in Venezuela in regards to converting to the energy particle."

The uniformed man nodded his head. "And while

you are doing this evaluation you are looking for a kidnapped EQA agent from the Republic, who you think is being held at Armando Leoni's hacienda," the man said as a matter of fact.

Suddenly, Cisco's shoulders slumped. Freddy had betrayed him. Shit. "Yes sir that is true," Cisco said with a sigh. He decided his cover was blown and it was time to tell the truth, well almost the truth.

"I followed the kidnappers to Los Angeles. There was a shootout and one of the injured kidnappers was Armando Leoni's brother, Silvio. We followed a third kidnapper who we believe to be a hit man for the oil cartel here. It was the only lead I had."

"Mason Warrick," the man said.

"Yes Mason Warrick. Another kidnapper named Rico was killed in Los Angeles," Cisco explained.

"Yes, Ricardo Avila was killed in the shootout at Echo Park. We have been tracking them. We were not sure why the three went to the Republic. They were covering their tracks well, but our security team picked up your trail. It was easier for our security to follow you. You are not so good at covering your tracks," the uniformed man chuckled a bit. "Our security agents followed you and Mister Perez here to Venezuela. We can only thank you for eliminating Rico. He was on our most wanted list."

"You followed me?" Cisco asked incredulous at the new information.

"We are not as backward as you might think Mister Salaz. Our security people and their methods are very modern, as are our outdated computer systems. That is what you called them, correct?"

Feeling embarrassed Cisco said, "It was an uninformed statement." The uniformed man chuckled again at Cisco's embarrassment.

"I understand why you might feel this way. Many of our systems are outdated here in Venezuela, just not our surveillance systems."

The door opened and Freddy walked in. He saluted the uniformed man who returned the salute. "Mister Salaz let me introduce Captain Freddy Mendoza of our secret police. I am General Juan Mora."

Cisco sat in stunned silence. They had been following him. He was so worried about the security agents from the Republic following him, and yet the Venezuelans had no trouble tracking his endeavor. Freddy had been a setup all along, obviously to keep tabs on him.

"Am I under arrest?" Cisco asked.

"Oh no, quite on the contrary Mister Salaz, we want to help you rescue the girl. She is very important to your country, is she not?"

"Please call me Cisco, and yes she is very important. She is the president's great-granddaughter." Cisco thought about lying, but they no doubt already knew the truth anyway.

"You will need a diversion to get into the hacienda," General Mora explained. "Tomorrow, Venezuela's electricity is shutoff to many businesses and homes. Armando's hacienda is affected during the conservation. Captain Mendoza and I think it is the best time to try the rescue. Armando's electrified gate will not be operational and his security cameras will be disabled. We think it is an opportune time."

"Wouldn't he have a generator to offset the reduction in power?" Cisco asked.

"Yes, he does, however I have an inside man who will disable the generator to give us enough time for the operation."

They continued talking more than two hours on a plan to attack Armando's hacienda and rescue Maya. By the time Cisco returned to the hotel, he was exhausted. The security police had driven Arturo to the hotel several hours ago and after checking the bar, Cisco assumed he had gone to bed.

Dropping on the bed and propped against the pillows, he pulled out the Pcom and called Gus. All he received on the other end was humming. He tried several times before giving up. He wanted tell Gus about the Venezuelan Secret Police. So much had happened and so much was confusing. He could not fault Freddy. Like himself, Freddy had a double identity – manager at the Department of Energy and a member of the secret police. Weary, he closed his eyes and slept.

CHAPTER 50

Maya tried to sleep Thursday night frustrated at her predicament. Earlier, the maid summoned her for supper. She tried to refuse, but the maid marched her to the dining room where Armando was waiting. She ate in silence, making her captor very angry. By the end of the meal there was an evil look in his eyes.

Finally falling into a fitful sleep, the dream came to her in several versions during the night. In each one, she and her *bisabuelo* were walking near the wide river. He held her hand as they looked across the river watching a young man running on the other side. Behind him, a wild-looking Indian on horseback chased him. The Indian screamed what sounded like war yells and raised his spear. The young man looked vaguely familiar, like she had seen him lately. She heard her great-grandfather call to the young man, telling him to come across the river.

When she woke, she rolled over to look at the clock, but the display was dark. She turned the switch on the lamp, nothing happened. She thought it odd. Perhaps it was not too unexpected for the age of this hacienda. In her wanderings, she could tell the buildings were quite old. The house was meticulously repaired and renovated over the years, although one could see the original building's facade in places not obvious to the casual eye. Armando told her his great-great-grandfather built the original main house.

Pulling the sheet off, she walked to the balcony and pushed open the double doors wider. A cool breeze came in off the lake. Small white caps dotted the lake and it lapped at the beach and pushed at the hulks of the oil tankers rusting along the piers. They swayed gently. The hacienda's grounds were quiet, no gardeners were working which she thought unusual, but she knew the guards would be watching up on the parapet.

For some reason, last night's dream renewed and refreshed her to find a way to escape. Over the past three days, Maya watched the comings and goings at the hacienda. The large metal gate was the only way in and out. Someone, maybe one of the guards controlled the automatic gate, which slid from left to right. The gate itself was not guarded.

Maya was convinced the hacienda was monitored by a surveillance camera system. She saw several cameras on her long walks, some hidden and some like the ones over the front doors and in the courtyard readily visible.

Each morning shortly after eight a delivery truck brought the daily food. It was allowed in through the gate and to the back of the house near the kitchen door. Maya watched it the last two days as the maids and cooks carried packages into the kitchen. The driver seemed friendly to the women. Yesterday, he drank a cup of coffee before he started the truck and drove to the closed gate. The gate opened and he drove off.

Maya dressed and was brushing her hair when she heard the morning truck. She wandered over to the balcony to watch the daily ritual. Two men were standing near the gate. As the truck approached, she watched as they put down their guns and heaved at the heavy gate. Slowly it slid open by their efforts. The truck pulled through and drove to the back of the house.

It dawned on her that the electric gate was not working, just like the lights. Something had knocked out the power to the hacienda. Slipping on her shoes, she pushed open her bedroom door. All was quiet in the hallway. Slowly she worked her way down the hall and then down the stairs to the kitchen near the back of the house.

Inside the kitchen she could hear voices. *"¿Quieres café?"* she heard the maid ask if the driver wanted coffee.

"Sabes que los viernes son mis días lentos. Sin electricidad," the driver complained Fridays were his slow day because there was no electricity.

The cook laughed telling the driver she had to cook breakfast without any lights because the generator was not working.

Maya knew this was her chance to escape. Apparently on Fridays the electricity was cut off, causing a break in the routine of the hacienda. If the gate was not functional, then maybe neither were the security cameras. If she could just get to the delivery truck without detection, perhaps she could crawl inside and hide. It did not matter where the truck went once it was outside of the hacienda's walls.

Hurrying through the hallway, she headed to the front veranda. The guards were used to her walking the grounds. When she reached the wide front door, she pulled one side open and walked out into the morning sunshine. Casually, she walked down the veranda steps and strolled toward the fountain, not making any hurried moves. One of the men near the gate looked at her and she waved as she had been doing on her walks. He raised a hand in response. Slowly, but deliberately, she headed around the courtyard toward the back of the house.

It was hard to control her excitement. She wanted to run, but kept a slow and steady pace. Near the side of the house in visual range of the guard by the gate, she bent over a rose bush and pretended to smell the flowers. As she rounded the side of the house, the truck was still parked near the kitchen door, its back panel doors open.

Maya stopped. Quickly she scanned the yard for guards. She knew it was not time for their morning rounds, but everything was different today. Timing her moves so the driver and the cooks did not see her, she cautiously stepped closer and closer to the truck. Suddenly the driver exited the kitchen door. She stopped, sucking in her breath. He jumped into the back of the truck, then jumped off the tailgate and picked up a large carton. Quickly she tiptoed closer, ducking across the front of the truck and around the side away from the kitchen. She held her breath, peeking around the end of the truck she focused on the kitchen door. She could see neither the driver nor the cook.

Suddenly a strong arm encircled her waist and another covered her mouth.

"Shutup and you will live," the voice said. The strong arm pushed her up into the back of the truck and toward the far front. She was pushed into a corner and covered with a tarp. The strong arm held her and she did not resist.

Was the strong arm the person her *bisabuelo* sent to rescue her? Maya stayed quiet and calm. Several minutes later, she heard the rear doors to the truck close and the driver get into the cab. The engine grumbled as the truck started to move. She heard the driver yell something to one of the guards as they exited the compound, and felt the truck bump down the lane. Elated, she was free.

From the kitchen door, the cook saw the blond man with the limp grab the young woman and throw her into the delivery truck. She could do nothing until her shift ended tonight. She thought about trying to stop them, calling for Armando to stop the truck before it drove off. He would no doubt kill Mason for defying him, but the girl was not safe here either. She vacillated trying to figure out what General Mora would want her to do.

Generally her job was undercover work only, not actively participating in any activity here at the hacienda. She had been placed as a cook to funnel information to the secret police more than two years ago. Her job was to report unusual activity, guests, Armando's whereabouts, and general information about the hacienda. She reported the young woman and Mason's arrival. She made sure the young woman was being well fed and the maid was attending to her personal well being. Armando seemed to be treating her as a guest, although she knew the girl was a prisoner. The cook turned away from the door as the truck drove away. She would call General Mora tonight and let him know the girl was gone.

CHAPTER 51

Waking several times during the night, Cisco was unnerved by the plans they made last night with the general. In the morning, he did a few karate exercises to relieve his tired brain and took a long hot shower. Neither did any good to dispel the dread he felt. Even with the assistance of the Venezuelan secret police, the scheme to storm Armando's hacienda fortress was daunting. When he dressed, he put the small laser in his pocket along with the knife.

Last night, General Mora had photo surveillance pictures spread across his desk. "We need to get you inside while the fence is not electrified and will need a diversion to draw the guards away from their posts," General Mora had explained.

"Maybe we can drive the cows close to the fence," Freddy had said. "It might cause them to open the gate and come out to investigate. They would not be overly concerned by a group of *llaneros*, hopefully not enough to start shooting, but it might give us some cover."

"We need a bigger distraction, something not ordinary and not threatening," the general had said.

"I think the best spot to go over the fence would be on the west corner away from the gate. It has pretty good cover with short trees and bushes. If a diversion was on the other side, it would draw the guards away from the west side," Cisco suggested pointing to the picture of the gated compound.

"There's an oil derrick east of the main gate near the dock. Most of the derricks are defunct. I could send two of my men around from behind and set it on fire," Freddy added figuring the burning oil derrick would cause alarm at the hacienda.

Cisco unzipped his belt and extracted a long thin band, handing it carefully to Freddy. "That's enough explosive to blow the thing into the lake," he said with a grin. Freddy examined it and nodded. "Very ingenious," he replied.

These were the details of the plan. Romelio and several *llaneros* would drive a small herd of cows close to the front gate. Two men would sneak along the lake and blow the oil derrick when the guards were distracted by the cows. Freddy, General Mora, Cisco, and two security police would scale the fence on the west side when the guards were occupied.

Cisco and Arturo were waiting when Freddy picked them up at the hotel at 8:00 AM. An unmarked helicopter waited at the La Guaira helipad with a young pilot in military gear. Freddy told them the general and men had left earlier to limit any suspicion.

"Armando has many eyes in Maracaibo and Cabimas. We must be very careful not to tip him off," Freddy reminded Cisco.

During the flight, Cisco was too nervous to talk and Arturo seemed lost in thought. The pilot made a wide circle away from Armando's compound, before landing on a hill near Romelio's ranch.

It was late Friday morning when they joined the general's men. Romelio and his men were ready to go. After last minute instructions from the general, the group made their way toward Armando's hacienda. Romelio's men pushed a small herd of cows ahead. The general was hoping no one would notice the others as they diverted to the west side of the hacienda.

It was after 2:00 PM by the time all the parties were in place. Romelio's cows were within shouting distance from the front gate. Cisco could hear one of the guards yelling down from the parapet.

"Okay," General Mora said as they waited on the west side of the hacienda's wall. "Let's hope that old derrick still has some oil in it, enough to make a good burn." As they waited, Cisco pulled out his tiny laser gun.

"*Chévere,* I want one of those," Freddy said. Cisco asked Freddy what the word *chévere* meant.

"Oh, *chévere* means 'it's great'. I guess that's some of

our slang," Freddy said.

"Could that tiny laser pick off the guard up there?" Freddy pointed to the guard on the western parapet about 150 meters away.

"Yes," Cisco replied.

"As soon as we hear the explosion, and if that guard doesn't move, take a shot." Freddy said wanting to see the power of the tiny weapon.

Time ticked by slowly as they waited to hear the explosion. Meanwhile, Cisco studied the hacienda. On the second floor, the balcony doors of two rooms on the west side of the house were open. He pointed to them and Freddy nodded.

"As soon as we're over the fence, I'll try to get to that window and into the house. Maya must be in a room on the second floor. I'll find her and exit from the back kitchen door," Cisco said.

A tremendous explosion literally rocked the ground. Freddy watched the roof and the guard on the west corner moved toward the front. "The guards took the bait. Let's go!" Freddy shouted.

General Mora wished them luck. *"¡Buena suerte!"*

Freddy, Cisco, and two security police scaled the stucco wall. From the front of the hacienda another explosion shook the ground. Guards were yelling and then gunfire erupted. Cisco said a short prayer hoping none of Romelio's men would be hurt or worse.

Reddish sunlight bathed the front of the white stucco hacienda from the burning oil derrick. Flames licked high into the sky, spewing dark smoke. As usual the wind blew off the lake and smoke was drifting toward the compound courtyard. With weapons ready, the guards ran toward the eastern side of the rooftop to view the trouble.

Armando was in his study when he heard the first explosion. Quickly he grabbed the papers off his desk and stuffed them into a wall safe. Grabbing a pistol, he headed toward the front of the house. Armando had plenty of trained and loyal men, but he was not afraid to defend his property and his livelihood himself. In fact, he enjoyed a good fight and he always won.

Reaching the front door, Armando watched as flames soared skyward, shooting over the derrick and up into the sky. Suddenly the veranda shook as another explosion boomed in the background.

Armando ran into the courtyard toward the front gate. "What happened?" he asked the closest guard.

"*Quien sabe, jefe,* the oil derrick just suddenly blew up. A small herd and some local *llaneros* are up there on the hill. Maybe they did it," the guard said pointing to Romelio and the small herd.

"*Llaneros desgraciados.* Open the gate and go after them," Armando screamed at the guard.

"*Sí, jefe.*" The guard yelled at two others to open the gate.

Orange and gray shadows from the intense fire danced on the white stucco walls. Armando watched the guards move through the open gate toward a small herd of cows and a couple *llaneros* up on the hill away from the hacienda.

Realizing the *llaneros* were probably not at fault, he yelled after them. "Forget about the stupid cows," he shouted. "Get that fire out before the entire dock burns!"

Romelio and his men had moved away from the main house after the derrick exploded. The gate was now open and their job was done. Two guards exited the gate and came their way. Although willing to fight, he did not want any of his friends killed. He told his men to be ready.

Quickly Cisco and Freddy ran toward the side of the main house. Hugging the wall for a moment, they caught their breath, before Freddy swung a triple hook up over the railing on the balcony. Surprisingly, he easily climbed the wall up to the black railing. He attached the rope securely before Cisco shinnied up.

Crouching on the balcony, Cisco nodded and they burst into an empty room. Without saying a word, they moved toward the door. Behind them one of the security police followed, while the other stayed on the ground to defend their position.

Freddy and Cisco worked along the second story bedrooms only to find them empty. Downstairs they heard loud voices from the courtyard. A male voice was shouting orders.

"Freddy, she must be somewhere in the house," Cisco whispered. "Maybe she's hiding?"

"Come on, we'll check downstairs," Freddy said leading the way toward the staircase at the end of the hallway.

Cisco followed Freddy down stairs. The stairs ended in a large entryway and the front doors stood wide open. A mist of smoke drifted through the open doors and outside they could hear voices shouting. Turning, they checked the large dining room and headed toward the back of the house. Halfway down the hall, a door opened and a large black woman carrying a bundle stepped out. Seeing the two strangers, she screamed, dropped the bundle, and started running down the hallway toward the kitchen.

Cisco aimed his laser, but Freddy pushed his hand down shaking his head back and forth.

Embers from the burning trees near the edge of the lake were raining down, igniting several small fires in the garden courtyard. Larger brush fires were burning on the expanse of land between the house and the burning derrick. Armando gave several sharp orders to the guards to put out the garden fires first.

From behind him inside the house, he heard a loud scream. Only then did he remember the young woman. Turning back toward the house, he walked up the veranda steps. The fire from the burning oil mixed with the sun gave an eerie orange glow on the front doors. In the distance he heard the shrill sirens of the Lake Maracaibo Fire Department responding to the fire.

"*Mierda*," he cursed at the chaos.

Freddy and Cisco stood on either side of the kitchen door with their weapons drawn, before they burst into the room. The large black maid cowered behind a counter trying to hide her enormous figure. The cook stood by the stove, wielding a large knife in her hand.

Armando bounded up the stairs to the second floor passing large paintings of his ancestors, his father, grandfather and great-grandfather hung on the stairwell wall. When he reached the top of the stairs, another explosion shook the house, this one even louder than the other two. It nearly knocked him off his feet.

Panicked by the sudden turn of events, Armando became torn between saving his hacienda and saving the girl. She was worth a fortune, but his heart was here in Cabimas. Reaching Maya's bedroom he yanked the door open. He expected her to be cowering at a corner, but the room was empty. Checking the closet and behind the draperies, he quickly moved along the hallway checking each room. Where the hell was she?

Freddy moved beside the cook and spoke to her quietly. She lowered the knife and whispered something Cisco could not hear. Freddy shook his head at the information. Grabbing Cisco's arm, Freddy pulled him toward the kitchen door. "*Vamonos*, the girl is gone," he said.

"Gone?" Cisco hissed. "What do you mean gone?"

"Come, now. We must get my men to safety."

Armando searched the house. One of his guards found him and yelled at him, "*Jefe*, you must leave now. The police and fire departments are coming."

Moments later, a large black car rumbled through the gate. The driver wasted no time, while Armando watched out the bulletproof windows. The fire department boats surrounded the burning derrick. Several fires burned in the yard and one of the outbuilding's roof was on fire.

Freddy and Cisco quickly scaled the stucco wall. Once outside the compound Freddy yelled into his communicator to alert the others to pull back. The Lake Maracaibo Fire Department's sirens wailed in the background.

When they finally reached the general, Freddy explained, "The cook is one of our operatives. She saw Mason grab the girl this morning and they escaped inside a food delivery truck."

Cisco slumped on a nearby tree at the news. All this was for nothing. Maya had been here and now she was gone, again.

"Why didn't she report that to you?" Cisco asked.

"She can't make any communication from the hacienda," Freddy said. "She can only communicate after her shift. It is not her fault."

"What about Armando?" Cisco asked.

"He just left in his car," the general said. "Only a few of his guards are left at the compound. My men have surrounded them and Romelio shot one guard who chased them up on the hill. Your *amigo* was thrown from his horse in the fray and is injured."

"Arturo?" Cisco asked.

From the bulletproof car, Armando opened the car's communicator and groused to someone on the other end. *"Vamos,"* he barked at the driver. The black car sped east with Armando fuming in the back seat. The girl was hiding, but the security police would find her. The Republic rebellion leader would never honor the agreement and now his plans to use the girl for his gain were gone.

CHAPTER 52

By the time Cisco and Freddy reached Romelio and the *llaneros* up on the hill overlooking the hacienda, the Lake Maracaibo Fire Department was busy dousing the fires and more sirens were announcing the arrival of the Maracaibo Police. When Cisco looked back, the derrick spewed black smoke, drifting and blanketing Armando's house.

Cisco found Arturo stretched on the ground when he and Freddy walked up the hill to where Romelio and his men rested.

"His leg is broken. We've got to get him out of here and get him to a hospital," Romelio told Cisco.

"Hey," Cisco said kneeling beside Arturo. He winced at the sight of Arturo's leg, which bent at a crazy angle. "I'm sorry you got hurt. Don't move. We have to get you to a hospital," Cisco told him.

"Funny, *ese*," Arturo grinned using street slang. "My leg is busted in pieces, and you tell me not to move." Arturo grinned and then grimaced. Cisco patted his shoulder.

"Hey, where's the girl?" Arturo asked suddenly aware she was not part of the group returning from the hacienda.

Mason grabbed her this morning and they escaped in a delivery truck. Armando left before we could capture him, too. The police and firemen are cleaning up the mess.

Just then, the sound of helicopter blades reached them. "There's the chopper to take Arturo to the hospital," Freddy said.

The medics lifted Arturo onto a stretcher after carefully wrapping his leg. As they lifted him, Cisco put out his hand and took Arturo's. "Amigo, everything is going to be okay. Freddy will keep an eye on you and he'll get you back to the Republic. I'll try to come see you at the hospital, but I have to follow Mason and Maya."

"Eh Cisco, we sure kicked some ass, huh?" Arturo beamed. "When we both get back to Old Town, we'll go split a bottle of tequila."

"It's a promise, amigo" Cisco assured him.

As the helicopter lifted off with Arturo, Cisco found himself slightly lightheaded and in a daze. He walked away from Romelio and his men. He could not believe Maya was gone. The cook reported she was treated well at the hacienda, free to roam around, and appeared unhurt. Armando treated her like a guest, but now Mason Warrick had her again.

Freddy put a hand on his shoulder. He reacted with a start. *"Cómo estás,* Cisco?" he asked concerned.

"Bien," Cisco replied. "I'm okay."

"There is nothing more we can do here. Lieutenant Ayala and his men will finish up here. I'll have a driver take us back to the Romelio's ranch."

The *llaneros* crested the far hill headed to the ranch by the time Freddy and Cisco arrived. Romelio's wife Benita greeted them. She was relieved to hear everyone was safe. Her cheekbones and long jet-black hair characterized some Indian heritage. Two toddlers clung to her plain cotton dress hiding another child on the way.

Seeing her and the children, Cisco was overwhelmed by the courage of Romelio. He had so much to lose, yet he gladly joined the fight at the hacienda. It humbled Cisco, but Romelio and the *llaneros* seemed buoyed by the experience.

Romelio kissed his wife and children, swinging his youngest daughter up into his arms. The men excitedly related the story to Benita, embellishing parts while she set out plates of spicy beans with meat and a large pot of potatoes. Humming quietly, she sliced a stick of hard crust bread and put it along with a bowl of butter on the table.

As Cisco wolfed down three servings of food like a starving man, he listened to the men relate the stories of the ongoing power struggle with the Leoni family. Today was considered a victory.

As the food began to disappear, the men laughed and drank the local beer, Cerveza Zulia. The stories escalated the adventure until Romelio brought out a bottle of Old

Par scotch to celebrate the victory over Armando. With the scotch poured into tiny glasses, the story telling started again. Benita listened intently to the men and smiled.

A tiny satisfied kitten slept on her lap. Cisco watched the tiny kitten sleeping and wished he could be home now and away from all the madness. Nothing made sense anymore. Images of the fire at the hacienda, Maya's terrified look as Mason took her at Echo Park, and the pain on Arturo's face flashed through his head in a jumble. The cook said Armando treated Maya well, but now she was back in Mason's clutches. What would he do to her? Twice Cisco found her and twice he failed to rescue her. Was it bad luck or fate?

Walking outside, Cisco breathed deeply of the cool evening air. It smelled of fresh cut grass and not the burning oil near the lake. A few bright planets hung in the clear evening sky. What about the Republic? Gus said there was mass chaos and fighting in the streets. Had the whole world gone mad? Reaching into his pocket, he pulled out the communicator.

"Gus," Cisco said, actually not expecting to hear Gus' voice on the other end. It had been over a day since he talked to him because of the communication disruptions in the Republic.

Gus answered. "What's up? Where are you?"

"Well right now I am on the *llano*. We attacked Armando's hacienda this afternoon."

"Oh, I've had his compound under my surveillance since last night. I saw a big explosion and fire and lots of vehicles at the hacienda a little while ago. A helicopter landed on a hill nearby."

"It's a long story," Cisco replied. "The vehicles are the local police and fire departments. Arturo's been hurt, broke his leg in several places. Freddy had him transported by chopper to the local hospital."

"Did you get Maya?"

"No, Mason escaped with her again, this morning."

Gus could hear the dejection in Cisco's voice. "Hey, I'm sorry. How about Armando?"

"He left in a black car in the middle of the fray. Hey, this connection is much better, what's happening in the Republic?"

"Communications are better. Comsys has been relatively stable for the last twenty-four hours. I can communicate with the international networks again. But the media analysts and opposition party officials have been fueling anger against the government. The president gave a long speech last night trying to calm the people and explain how things will get restored. He looked really old and tired, though."

"Gus, I need you to review the footage of the hacienda from this morning. According to the cook, Mason kidnapped Maya sometime in the morning and they escaped in a delivery truck."

"Okay, give me about ten minutes to set that up and I'll call you back." The communicator went dead and Cisco put it into his pocket. From inside the house, Cisco could hear Romelio and his friends singing a drinking song. For them life was simple and they were celebrating a small victory.

Cisco stared into the star-filled sky. *"Ayúdame Dios,"* he prayed to God for help.

Freddy walked outside and found Cisco staring toward the direction of Lake Maracaibo. A small stream of orange fire still spiraled into the dark sky.

"I'm sorry about the girl. We have people looking for her," Freddy said.

"What about Armando? Why did you let him drive away?" Cisco asked.

"We could not charge Armando without finding Maya. Can't arrest a man for living in his own home," Freddy replied.

"How long have you been a secret agent?" Cisco asked.

Freddy smiled and then laughed. "We don't call ourselves secret agents, just internal affairs agents, but I guess you could say I've been an agent my whole working life. After college General Mora recruited me. He wasn't a general then, though, just a colonel. With my degree in electrical engineering, he set me up in the Department of Energy," Freddy explained.

"How about you? How long have you been undercover?"

"What day is today?" Cisco asked.

"Friday, why?"

"Six days, then," Cisco replied.

Freddy doubled over in laughter. He put a hand on Cisco's shoulder and they both laughed heartily. "Six days!" Freddy laughed again. "Do you want a job? I'm sure General Mora would want to hire you. You must be a really quick learner."

"Maybe just stupid or lucky," Cisco replied.

"When I read your EQA portfolio, I couldn't find any discrepancies. It was why it took us so long to try to figure out just what you were really doing here. Now I understand," he said.

Cisco's Pcom buzzed. It was Gus. "I followed the delivery truck this morning. It made four stops, but I can see Mason and Maya exited near at a bakery store at a marina. The marina is in a place called Altagracia. He walked with her to the marina and onto a boat moored there. I can't make out the name of the boat from the satellite angle, but it is a big blue and white boat. Not much more I can give you except the boat is still moored there. I've got a scan on the boat, so if it moves I'll be able to give you the make and model."

"Gus, can you contact my father? I mean, do you think you could get a message to him somehow?"

"Sure, what do you want me to say."

"Tell him," Cisco paused wondering what to say, "Tell him the spirit is strong."

"That's it?"

"Yes, thanks Gus. Keep me posted if the boat moves." When he disconnected, Freddy looked at him puzzled.

"Who's Gus?"

"He's an InfoAgent from the Republic." Freddy still

looked puzzled. "He's like an undercover expert in communications, satellite imaging, and tracking people electronically."

"He's a security data analyst then" Freddy said.

"No, yes, well except he doesn't work for the government. He works rogue."

Instinctively Freddy seemed to know what Cisco needed to do. "Camilo will drive us to the marina and we'll go find the boat," Freddy said.

"Gus said it's moored at a marina in Altagracia. Where's that?"

"Altagracia is northeast of here on the lake. Armando and the PLV have several boats moored there. It's late but hopefully we'll find something," Freddy replied throwing his bag into the truck.

Cisco thanked Romelio and Benita for their hospitality, giving Romelio an *abrazo*. *"Gracias,"* he told Romelio several times. How could he possibly thank these people enough for their help?

The truck bounced along rough dirt roads across the *llano* and Camilo did his best to control the truck. Even with the bouncing and jarring, Cisco dozed on and off over the next hour. Before long, the bumpiness of the dirt road gave way to smooth blacktop. Cisco saw lights from the marina blinking ahead. Finally, Camilo stopped near the dark marina.

Glancing at his watch, Cisco was surprised to see it was almost eleven. "Let's go check the marina and find the boat," Cisco said after they climbed out of the truck and thanked Camilo.

"I booked us rooms at a small hotel across the street from the marina area and left orders to have my plane serviced and flown to Altagracia in the morning. It's late and everything is closed for the night. Let's get some shuteye." Freddy said.

Frustrated Cisco started to say, "But the boat . . . "

"It's still there," Freddy replied. "I have my people watching it."

"Well let's go storm it," Cisco said. "Maya's in there."

"Not tonight," Freddy said. "That boat would be stocked with enough ammunition to fend off an army. It would be suicide for us and death for Maya. It will be there in the morning and we need more help. I requested several agents to come with my plane. Besides, the marina is closed for the night. The boat's not going anywhere."

CHAPTER 53

Cisco awoke in the morning to his Pcom alert. Only the barest of light filtered thru the window's drapery and the clock near the bed shone 4:51 AM.

"Hello," Cisco answered.

"Cisco the boat is on the move," Gus said on the other end.

"What?" Cisco bolted up in bed.

"Freddy said the marina was closed until morning. Are you sure?"

"Yes, it's a thirty-two foot Nomad cruiser. I have it on my tracking system."

"Mierda," Cisco cursed.

"A black car arrived about four-forty this morning and the boat left at four-forty-eight. It's heading north out to the Caribbean Sea."

"Could you tell who was in the black car?"

"Only one person got out and walked to the boat. In the dark I couldn't make a positive ID, but I'm guessing Armando. The boat is registered to one of his PLV subsidiaries."

"Gus, keep tracking them. I have to wake Freddy."

"Cisco, your father said he is praying for you. He also said to tell you the soil protectors are bad," Gus said. "What the hell does that mean?"

"I don't know. Keep an eye on that boat and let me know where it goes," Cisco disconnected the communicator, angry at Freddy for not storming the boat last night and now it was gone. Maya was gone. He shrugged on his shirt and picked up his pants. His hand stopped in midair thinking about his father's words. "The soil protectors are bad." Suddenly his father's words made sense. Some of the Protectors were part of the rebellion. His father had told him, "Trust no one, not even the Protectors, but which ones?"

Cisco banged on the door to Freddy's room until he got an answer. He told Freddy what happened and to get dressed. Ten minutes later they met in the lobby.

While Freddy fanned out asking questions about the boat, Cisco casually slipped down the marina walkway to where the boat had been moored. Nothing seemed out of place, except the boat was gone. Four cigarette butts lay scattered on the walkway. The mooring ropes were casually wound around the U-shaped cleat where the boat moored earlier.

He walked out to the end of the dock and looked back at the town. Altagracia looked like a small resort town with lots of boat masts reflecting in the lake's calm inlet. Older but well kept hotels dotted the shoreline stretching along the beach. Its location on Lake Maracaibo was ideal, or so read the vacation travel guide he found in the hotel room.

He looked out toward the lake. The light of the pending morning was just beginning to illuminate the water. Somewhere out there Maya was on a boat with Mason Warrick and most likely Armando. Standing alone on the dock in a small town he never heard of, defeat churned in his stomach. He should have overruled Freddy and they should have stormed the boat last night.

A squawking flock of sea gulls followed a fishing boat coming into dock. Breathing deeply, cool air filled his lungs. He stretched his arms high above his head and twisted his torso left to right then right to left several times. She was alive. He had not failed and he would not give up. She was out there somewhere, waiting for him to find her. Turning back he saw Freddy walking out of the marina office. He strode on the dock to meet him half way.

"Everybody knows the boat belongs to Armando's PLV organization," Freddy said, "so they won't talk much. I did verify it left early this morning before the marina opened. The marina master saw it leave out his window. No one saw the girl, but it made the marina master's wife very nervous when I asked about her."

Cisco pondered the information. "My hunch is Armando left the country. Knowing the *policia* moved on the hacienda yesterday, I think he'll get out of the country as fast as he can," Cisco said.

"Perhaps. The range of the boat is not more than 500 kilometers. General Mora has agents keeping track of it. I also found out the Cafe de Mares has the best *desayuno* in town. Let's go have breakfast," he said with a grin. "My airplane should be here by seven."

Cisco wanted to yell at Freddy, wanted to complain how he thought Freddy was taking this complication too lightly. Thankfully, something stopped him. Freddy and General Mora were more than helpful. Instead, he followed Freddy down the dock and across the main street into the town.

The aroma in the Cafe de Mares definitely lived up to the reputation. The tiny cafe was busy even though it was quite early. They waited in the jammed doorway for an open table. Some locals seated near the entrance stopped their conversation and one of them nodded toward them. Two fishermen at the counter turned and stared. A heavyset young man sitting alone in the back was definitely studying them. Cisco could feel the young man's unfriendly eyes watching them. Two men got up and left and Francisco sank into a booth glad to be away from the staring eyes.

"Did you notice the man in the back?" he asked Freddy.

Freddy whispered, "Don't talk, just eat."

The waitress poured two small cups of coffee without asking. They both ordered the Saturday breakfast special. Grunting the waitress turned and left. Freddy shrugged his shoulders before he picked up his coffee. Cisco took a sip. It was very strong, but smooth, not bitter. When the waitress brought their breakfast, they wasted no time in devouring it. No one spoke to them, but the unfriendly eyes, let them know they were unwelcome.

After Freddy paid, they left and walked briskly back to the hotel in silence. Freddy was obviously nervous. "I'll call a cab. Meet you back down here in ten minutes." he told Cisco. "Hurry."

When the cab arrived, they jumped into it and Freddy

told the driver, "La Jolla Airpark."

"Good idea," the cab driver responded. "I'd get out of town if I were you two. The quicker the better." The driver watched for Freddy's expression. "Don't worry," he continued, "I'm not one of them."

"One of whom?" Cisco asked.

"One of Armando's *pistoleros*. The morning news headlined the bust at Armando's hacienda. Then you two show up in town making inquiries about his boat. It makes people very nervous. Armando owns this town," the cabby told them.

"And you? You're not one of them?"

"*Coño*, I'm just a cab driver. Nobody owns me, but I try not to make too many enemies."

The small airpark was just ahead. One plane was taxiing on the runway. An orange single engine was warming up several slots down from Freddy's blue and yellow Cessna. Two dark sedans were parked next to the small building that housed the flight school. He stuffed a handful of bills onto the seat as the cab pulled up beside the plane.

"Let's go," Freddy said to Cisco. "*Muchas gracias,*" he thanked the cabby.

They ran to the plane. "Get in!" At the controls, a young man sat fiddling with some switches and another man sat in the other front seat. Cisco and Freddy sat in the rear. "Get us out of here Ruben," Freddy yelled to the pilot.

"Freddy, what's wrong?"

"Armando's *pistoleros* were waiting for us at the flight office. Hopefully they're still trying to find out which plane is ours. We have to get out of here before they figure it out."

Ruben steered the plane to the end of the runway. Cisco looked back. Four men stepped out of the flight office. One man pointed at the plane and started running. All of the men were armed.

"They've seen us. Here they come!" Cisco yelled.

Ruben pushed the throttle forward and the little

plane rolled down the runway. At the end of the runway, he pulled back on the stick and the plane nosed upward toward the eastern morning sun. They could hear gunfire behind them getting more distant as the plane climbed. Finally, the little plane climbed into the bright morning sky above the smog, hugging Lake Maracaibo.

CHAPTER 54

It was dark when Maya woke with the sound of the engine and the movement of the boat. Yesterday the blond kidnapper pushed her into the delivery truck. He pulled her out of the truck at a marina and took her to the boat. She wanted to scream and run, but the point of his laser pushed tightly against her back. Once on the boat, he tied her up and gagged her. At least he did not drug her.

After pretending to be asleep, she tried to wiggle her hands loose, but they were tightly bound. She heard him snore several times during the night. They both woke when the boat's engine came alive. She looked over expecting the blond man to have started the boat, but he too was just waking up to the sound.

Mason heard the engine jump to life, waking him. Looking beside him, the girl was still bound and also awake. Who the hell was driving the boat? Quietly, he rose and sneaked up the stairwell to have a look. Peeking topside, he saw the back of the driver's head. It was Armando.

Yesterday Mason saw his opportunity to leave Armando's estate. He knew the delivery truck came each morning, so he decided to hitch a ride. As he approached the truck, he caught the girl trying to hop in the back. Grabbing her, he hid her behind a number of crates, thinking how lucky he was to have her again.

As the morning delivery truck made its rounds to the local establishments, Mason saw it stop at the marina in Altagracia. Hiding in Armando's boat seemed like a good idea. After all, dragging the girl around was a bad idea. She was his paycheck. He had only intended to use the boat to keep her hidden overnight until he formulated another plan. Confused, Mason wondered why Armando was driving the boat alone. Usually, one of his men would be driving and Armando would be in the cabin. Something seemed very wrong.

Moving slowly, Mason return to where Maya was tied

up and covered them both with a quilt. Soon the engine sounded louder and the movement faster. Mason could tell they were away from the docks and headed out to open water.

The engine droned for several hours, before cutting off. He heard voices, shouting from outside. After a few minutes, the voices faded and the boat rocked gently, banging slightly against a dock. As soon as the voices faded, Mason was up and headed topside.

When he returned, he ripped off her gag. "You scream, you die," he growled.

"I have to use the bathroom," Maya asked nicely. Mason pulled a long knife out of a drawer and cut the ties to her hands and feet. "Back there," he said.

Maya took some time in the bathroom. In the little mirror her face looked weary even after she washed it and she ran some water over her teeth with some toothpaste she found in the drawer. Mason was sitting at the small kitchen table eating handfuls of dry cereal. He pushed the box toward her.

"What's your name," Maya asked. While she was thinking in the bathroom, she decided to try sweetness instead of anger toward the blond man. She knew he was dangerous and would kill her without a thought, but there was a reason she was still alive.

Mason looked at her hard. "Why do you care?" he grumbled.

"I thought as long as we are stuck here together we could at least be civil," she replied.

"Mason," he said after a few moments, then grabbed another handful of cereal.

"Where are we?" she asked.

He did not see any reason to be secretive. The stupid girl would not be able to relate the story to anyone after he got his money. "Orchila Island," he told her.

Armando left the boat docked at the old southwest marina and went to a small cafe.

"*Buenos días Señor Leoni,*" the proprietor greeted him.

Armando was well known on Orchila. "Would you like come coffee? Breakfast?"

"Just coffee and then I need a ride to town. Have my boat serviced, change the oil and gas it up and have it cleaned." Armando usually docked the boat at the hotel, but when it needed servicing he brought it here.

"I'll have it done this afternoon. Is that okay?" the man replied.

"Sure," Armando agreed. He knew he would be here a couple days.

Last night he holed up at his father's old hunting cabin in the mountains west of Lake Maracaibo. He slept little trying to piece together the events of Friday. When the power was cut off, they could not get the stupid generator running. His man told him the ignition was burnt and needed to go to town to get a part. It left the hacienda security system down and vulnerable. Then the derrick exploded. He pondered if the Feds caused the explosion as a diversion.

It was not the first time the Feds raided his compound, usually looking for a cache of drugs to pin a charge on him. They knew they would not find anything at the hacienda, but the exercise gave them credibility. It was all part of the game. It had been some time since the last raid, but the timing of this one bothered him because of the girl. Were they looking for drugs or for her? Had stupid Mason led the Feds to the hacienda? After their last shouting match, he would not put it past the blond asshole to have called the Feds himself.

Armando grumbled under his breath. He could not find the girl in the house before he left. She was hiding and was now almost certainly in the hands of the police. His leverage was gone, and all his plans to take over the particle were gone too, up in smoke. Last night hiding in the old cabin, he decided to take the boat to Orchila. He could be safe and comfortable here on the PLV's private island for as long as necessary until things calmed down in Maracaibo.

About twenty minutes later, Armando was riding a

cab to Puerto Orchila, the largest town on the island. The Hotel Magdalena, run for the pleasure of the PLV, always had rooms with no reservations necessary. Maybe he would do some deep sea fishing to pass the time. Sitting back in the cab, he closed his eyes and tried not to think about anything.

Mason had been to Orchila Island often. It was the PLV's playground, their private island in the beautiful Caribbean Sea. The PLV took over the island from the Russians, who used it as a similar playground for their military officers. A deserted Russian military installation was the only remnant of the Russian occupation of the island.

The PLV enjoyed the same isolation as the Russians. Two hundred kilometers from the coast, the island was completely defensible. From his many trips here, Mason knew the security measures employed on the island. No one could approach the island without detection, unless they swam here. Twenty-four hour surveillance kept visitors safe, but now Mason was stuck there.

He was sure Armando captained the boat, recognizing his profile and his voice when he called to the dock attendant. Luckily, Armando was oblivious to the fact he had stowaways aboard. Outside Mason heard voices nearby, then an engine. Another boat was coming in. Mason waved the laser toward Maya, reminding her to be quiet. The boat docked nearby, its wake gently rocking them for several minutes.

CHAPTER 55

"Are we going back to Caracas?" Cisco yelled.

Freddy yelled back over the engine noise, "Yes, Maiquetia Aeroport."

Conversation was almost impossible, so Cisco stared at the emerald Caribbean Sea from the window. The Caribbean shimmered in several shades from emerald to aqua blue. Dark green edged the coast of Venezuela to the right. Ruben was flying low allowing the clear Caribbean water to magnify the sandy bottom. Several sunken ships were clearly visible. The wrecks looked fuzzy and he realized the sunken ships were covered with seaweed and coral. Movement waved underwater as schools of fish darted in and out of the wreck's hulls.

Cisco could see larger fish, which looked like large shadows, moving near the surface. As he watched, he realized they were not large fish, but sharks. He shuddered thinking how easy it would be to throw Maya overboard, making her a tasty meal for one of the large predators.

Leaning back in the seat Cisco tried to make sense of the latest developments. Mason kidnapped Maya, this time escaping the hacienda. Why? He and Armando were *camaradas*. If not, then why had he come to Armando's hacienda? Mason was a mercenary for the PLV, Armando's oil cartel. Silvio, Armando's brother, was also involved in the kidnapping so assumedly Armando hired Mason for the kidnapping job.

If he and Armando were comrades, then why would he need to escape? Was he also a prisoner at the hacienda? Mason and Maya's escape was hours before the attempted rescue, so there could be no connection. Those acts were purely separate, and yet Mason and Maya hid in the boat later captained by Armando. Or was the dark figure someone else? In either case, where would they go? Perhaps Mason did not kidnap her, and she went with him willingly.

Over and over he analyzed the possibilities like a

scientific experiment. Each time he came to the same conclusion – he had no idea. The pieces just did not fit together.

Leaning back in the seat Cisco closed his eyes listening to the low whine of the turbine engine, then suddenly all was quiet. He found himself next to his godfather by the river. The child Maya was beside the old man holding his hand. It was early morning and pink sunlight bathed Maya's face.

"Nino," Cisco heard his own voice. *"I am in Venezuela looking for Maya, but there she is with you."*

"De acuerdo mi hijo," his Nino agreed. *"She is with me and I am protecting her."*

"Como Nino, she is still in danger. I don't know where she is."

"You must trust your feelings, mi hijo. You will find her."

"What do you mean trust my feelings?"

"Cálmate mi hijo. You found me didn't you?"

"I didn't find you Nino. I don't understand."

"Listen, she is calling to you. Her spirit is strong. Trust your feelings."

"Tower, this is four, charley, baker, tango, niner requesting a clearance to Maiquetia," Ruben's voice jarred Cisco from his dream as the pilot spoke to the air tower at Maiquetia Aeroport for landing instructions. The tower's voice gave a scratchy response and Ruben banked left beginning to descend.

After two turns, the triple runways were straight ahead and Ruben aligned the little plane to the far right runway. The tower's voice sounded over the radio, "Four, charley, baker, tango, niner, you are cleared to land on two niner." Quickly the ground was rising to meet the plane. Effortlessly Ruben landed the Cessna on the smooth runway with hardly a jerk. Freddy patted the pilot on the shoulder.

Cautiously, Ruben taxied the small craft near a low building with *Terminal Privado* emblazoned on its large sign. Freddy ordered service for the Cessna, while Cisco walked, stretching his legs. When the plane was secure, they gathered their belongings and walked into the terminal building. A large clock near the door read 10:14 AM.

As they walked past a SATComm, abruptly Cisco remembered he could connect with his XA200 Corvette from anywhere. "Freddy, I'll meet you at the cafe."

He voiced the Corvette's Comsys number into the public SATComm. *"Tío,* are you there?" Cisco almost whispered when he heard the other end beep.

"Space cadet," he heard Charley's voice reply. "Where the hell are you?"

"Well, would you believe Maiquetia, Venezuela," Cisco replied.

"Venezuela! What the fuck are you doing there? I thought you were in Los Angeles. Your mother is worried sick about you. Especially with all the crap going on in the Republic. You better give her a call, *pendejo.*"

"I can't, not yet. I shouldn't be calling you, but hopefully they won't track the Vette's link."

"They? Are you in some kind of trouble, space cadet?"

"No *tío.* Where are you?"

"In Albuquerque. Mercedes wanted to find her friends. She's been acting very strange. She stopped using makeup, cut her hair and is using her real name, Tiffani. Apparently, she changed her name when she was kidnapped. She's driving me nuts. I think she wants to stay here and . . . " Charley let the sentence hang.

"I saw how you two were with each other." Cisco said.

"Frankly I'm too old for her. Guess she just grabbed at the first person she could, to get away from those *vatos.* I knew it, but didn't want to admit it. Well, it was fun while it lasted. I guess I'll go home and leave her here and get on with what I do best, gambling, drinking and chasing women."

"You're serious aren't you?" Cisco asked.

"Yeah, I'll be leaving tomorrow. I need to get back and find out what's going on in the Republic and in Old Town."

"Tío, do you remember the *vato* you won the lowrider from?"

"Sure, why?"

"His name is Arturo Perez and he's in a hospital in Maracaibo. He helped me through some pretty rough stuff and got busted up for his efforts. Without him, I'd be dead right now. He's not really a bad guy and in fact he loves Mercedes, well Tiffani. He tracked me, because he thought I was you."

"He followed you to Venezuela?" Charley asked.

"No, I brought him with me to Venezuela. It's a long story, but he really helped me and now I need to make sure he gets back to the Republic."

"Que chinga, and he's in a hospital, where?"

"In Maracaibo. I have to leave him behind. Make sure you and Gus get him back to the Republic and his *ranfla* is parked in the long-term parking garage at LAX. Please *tío,* help him."

"Where are you going?"

"I can't tell you and if you talk to my mother don't tell her you talked to me. Its better she doesn't know."

"Okay space cadet. I'll do what I can for Arturo."

"I'll pay you back when I get home. If you need money, ask my father."

"No problem, space cadet."

"Bueno," Cisco said and terminated the call. He knew it was a risk to call Charley, but he could not leave Arturo stuck here in Venezuela without someone to help him.

He pulled out his Pcom and opened the link to Gus.

"Freddy and I are in Maiquetia," he said.

"I know. I've been following you," Gus responded. Cisco smiled thinking he should have known Gus was keeping a close eye on him.

"Armando took a boat to Orchila Island. It used to be a military base used by the Russians, but now it is a private island owned by the PLV. Parts of it are run like a tourist island, but I'm thinking the tourists are all friends of the PLV," Gus told him.

"How far is the island off the coast?"

"About 200 kilometers," Gus told him.

"Do you have visuals of the island? Did you see Maya get off the boat?"

"The PLV has obvious scrambling methods to interfere with communications. The satellite images are not so good. It's not a place where my satellite connections can watch closely. I can download some basic images of the island and where the old military base is located, but not much else. Sorry, but the PLV keeps the island off the grids for obvious reasons."

"Will this Pcom work if I get to the island?" Cisco asked.

"Yes, but I would not trust that they don't have the capability to detect the signal. My scrambling and encryption algorithms might not work there. It might be just an open line. I just don't know."

"Okay. Do what you can. Thanks Gus."

Walking along the terminal's hallway, he spotted Freddy drinking a cup of coffee at a small cafe. Freddy waved at him.

"My people have tracked the boat to *Isla la Orchila*," he whispered when Cisco sat down.

"Yes, I just talked to my source. He couldn't tell who disembarked the boat. He said his satellite images of that island are not very good."

"Well, mine are better. The PLV bought the island from the Russians in the late 2040s. They use it as their Caribbean playground and as a drug drop point. My intelligence saw Armando dock the boat at the southwest marina near the old military facility."

"Great," Cisco replied.

"Well, not that great. We monitor it, but getting to it and getting ashore is a difficult problem. If you think Armando's hacienda was well guarded, think of it surrounded by vast blue water." Cisco's chest visibly fell.

"Cheer up," Freddy said. "We have operatives on the island. General Mora is already working on a plan."

CHAPTER 56

Luis Jimenez had been monitoring the reports for a week. They provided little information about Francisco's whereabouts. Luis' twenty-four hour on-call status, cafeteria food, and lack of sleep had become more than annoying. In fact, he had thought about calling his boss and telling him to go to hell. Nothing, not even the large bonus they promised for doing this and keeping quiet was worth it to him anymore.

Without the G2000 monitoring device working, he was completely blind to Francisco's whereabouts and he had not been calling in. The director was mad, but Luis could do nothing.

Luis knew the Corvette was in Albuquerque, New Mexico. Several days ago the Corvette left Old Town, flew to Bahía Kino, and then to Albuquerque late Thursday. Luis knew Francisco was not driving. He was also monitoring news from Venezuela. Yesterday afternoon, reports started coming in from Maracaibo. Armando Leoni's hacienda was raided after a large fire erupted near his compound. He scanned each fifteen-minute report in detail. Pulling up Venezuelan databases, he was monitoring the situation, but the data was not coming through. Apparently, Venezuela went on an electricity shutdown on Fridays and most systems were not operational. By early Saturday morning, the reports once again were responding but with only minimal data.

Weary, almost sleeping at his desk, Luis expected the same short fifteen-minute report at 10:45 AM and almost ignored it. The report made Luis perk up. There was a call to Francisco's Corvette's Comsys number to someone called *tío*. The uncle addressed the caller as 'space cadet.' Luis wondered if they were code names. Reading on in the transcript, the caller said he was in Venezuela. It had to be Francisco.

The uncle was in Albuquerque and finally Luis understood who was driving the Vette. Francisco wanted his uncle to help a man named Arturo Perez who was at a hospital in Maracaibo. They discussed a girl named Mercedes, though Luis was sure it was not a code name for Maya. The call ended without any other useful information.

Well at least Luis was sure Francisco was in Venezuela, Maiquetia to be exact. It was not much to go on, but at least he could give his boss something. Maybe the asshole would get off his back. Thursday night Luis had admitted the G2000 monitoring device was not working. He blamed it on the electronic disruptions and his boss seemed to buy it.

Luis punched Maiquetia, Venezuela, into his computer and read the results. It was both a coastal town and where the large aeroport for the city of Caracas was located. Luis guessed Francisco made the call from the aeroport and put out a search for airline passenger lists to anywhere under the name Francisco Salaz. Then he called his boss.

"Sir, the operative is at the Maiquetia Aeroport in Venezuela," Luis said.

"Does he have the girl?"

"I doubt it sir, it was not part of his conversation. He would have called me if he had her," Luis said.

"So how do you know where he is if he didn't call in?" his boss' irritated voice asked him.

"I tracked a conversation with his uncle, sir." After several seconds of silence Luis continued, "Maiquetia is where the large Caracas Aeroport is located. I'm tracking all departures, sir."

"Good work. Keep me posted." His boss, Miguel Arias, disconnected the call.

Miguel thoughtfully sat his Pcom on his desk after terminating the link from Luis. Finally, some small shred of this mess had a crack. The president's godson, Francisco, was in Venezuela. The last communication several days ago from the kidnappers indicated the president's great-granddaughter was alive.

When the voice on the other end grumbled hello, Miguel related the news.

"You're sure she's alive?" Roberto asked.

"Not absolutely, but I believe Francisco would have called in if he found her dead," Miguel answered.

"Let me know as soon as you reach him. I want verification the girl is alive."

Thinking Maya was alone and in the PLV's clutches in Venezuela infuriated him. She was to have been safe and secluded here in Los Angeles, unharmed.

Armando paced the hotel room after the call he placed to his hacienda. Gonzalo, his trusted bodyguard, told him the Feds did not find the girl or Mason Warrick on the property. It would have been impossible for them to hide. Gonzalo said the Feds searched methodically for hours. Armando told Gonzalo to spread the word to all PLV members to find Mason. He could not have gone far.

Armando knew Maya was at the hacienda Friday morning. The maid checked on her and let him know she was awake. The cook said Mason accepted his breakfast at the cabana by the pool where he was staying at around 6:30 AM. It had been Friday morning, when the government forced an electricity reduction. His generator had malfunctioned, leaving the hacienda vulnerable, otherwise nothing seemed out of the ordinary before the explosions. Armando rubbed his chin thinking. Mason could have damaged the generator in order to escape with the girl and then called the Feds on him. It seemed the only logical scenario.

"Damn fucking government and their electricity plan," Armando cursed to himself. He could only surmise Mason had the girl and swore to himself when he found the blond cripple he would kill him.

CHAPTER 57

Mason and Maya heard several boats docking nearby.
They heard engines, men shouting, and then quiet. Mason
knew all of the boats docking here were PLV members or
workers. It was Saturday and Orchila Island was a safe
place for PLV members to enjoy fishing, snorkeling, or just
relaxing. It was the PLV's Caribbean playground. Mason
also knew most of the boats would arrive in the morning,
so the people could enjoy the full weekend on the island.
Larger yachts, supply boats, and the fishing rentals were
allowed to dock at the Puerto Orchila Marina, but scrutiny
was extremely tight as part of the security measures used
here on the island.

Maya watched as Mason seemed to be checking
something topside. He poked his head through the opening
at the top of the four steps leading topside several times.
After one of the checks, he approached her, tied her hands
and feet firmly to the table, and gagged her tightly. He
climbed the four steps, looked cautiously again, and
disappeared from sight into the sunlight. When he was
gone, Maya struggled with all her strength to wiggle from
the ropes until her wrists screamed in pain.

Mason hopped off the boat casually. He was hungry
and desperately wanted a beer. He had been to Orchila
many times. While he did not want to be noticed, it did not
matter. If anyone saw him they would not be alarmed. He
was not a PLV member, not one of the elite, but had
enough credentials to be on the island.

The inner circle of PLV businessmen and drug lords
used the island to have a vacation or a fishing weekend. It
was a place they used without fear of harassment or arrest.
There was one large hotel which catered to PLV families.
The PLV members were all Venezuelans by birthright, the
influential families long bound by money, greed, and status.
Mason managed to be tolerated by the PLV only because
of his ruthless ethics. He and others like him did the PLV's
dirty work – killing, intimidating, and making people

disappear, for a price. The elite hardly ever soiled their hands in such ways. Like Armando, they lived in lavish homes and drank the best Venezuelan wines.

Mason walked the short distance from the old dock to a group of shacks called Southgate Orchila. Walking into a cantina, he ordered a beer. A few heads nodded his direction, but otherwise ignored him. Sitting at the end of the bar, he guzzled the cold beer, and ordered a second.

At thirty-nine, Mason knew he had no real future in the PLV, just another killing, or some other job to ensure the PLV's power. One day he would be killed and no one would care. He had stashed money in a bank account on Aruba for the last five years. It was not a lot, but with this job he planned to take the money and leave Venezuela. He had scouted small seaports along the Chilean coast not too far south of Bisabella. He thought the area ideal for his needs. Once this job was done, he planned on disappearing far from the reaches of the PLV forever.

The trouble at Echo Park changed everything, because of some fucking drug dealing gangbangers. It forced him to bring the girl to Venezuela and to Armando's hacienda. He was reluctant, but had no choice. Armando was furious, especially when he told him about his brother being injured in L.A. His plan to escape on the boat this morning with the girl also fell apart and now he was stuck on the island.

At first, Mason cursed his bad luck. Obviously, Armando knew the girl had escaped. Armando would also realize he was gone and would suspect he had kidnapped her, though seemed oblivious to the fact they were his stowaways. Mason knew Armando would stay at the hotel in Puerto Orchila and also thought perhaps Armando might be planning to kill him before the deal was done. He saw only two options – steal a boat and hide in Aruba, Tobago, or one of the other islands in the Lesser Antilles, or find Armando and trade the girl. Both had risks, but only the second choice might produce a paycheck.

Mason ordered another beer and two orders of beef *arepas* to go. Maya heard footsteps and then a large sway of the boat as someone stepped topside. She prayed for it to be anyone other than the blond cripple.

Mason dropped two bags on the table, untied Maya, and removed the gag.

"I brought food for you," he grumbled.

"Thank you," Maya replied.

While Cisco and Freddy waited for General Mora to inform them with a plan, the minutes ticked by like hours. To pass the time, Cisco and Freddy made small talk.

"Freddy, don't you have a family? I thought you had a wife and kids. Where do they think you are when you're . . . working?" He finished with the only word he could think of to describe what he now understood about Freddy.

"I have a virtual family," Freddy said. "On all my formal documents, I have a wife and two sons, but they don't exist."

It hit Cisco hard. Was that a life? Was that a life he would want? He lived alone and never seemed to mind, and in fact enjoyed it, but the past week had changed him. It made him think differently about life and death.

"Did you ever want a family?" Cisco asked him.

Freddy looked down. "Yes. I fell in love once. I thought about marriage, but I had to make a choice. There is no way I would get married and continue being an agent. It would be too dangerous, both for me and my family."

"Why didn't you quit and get married. General Mora would understand," Cisco said.

"It was hard, a really hard decision, but I believe in what I do for Venezuela."

"And the girl, the one you loved?" Cisco asked.

"She hated me at first, but she met someone else. Sometimes I do wonder if I made the right choice. I know you are not married. Your bio said you live alone on the side of a mountain northwest of Dublán City. Do you have a girlfriend?" Freddy asked.

Cisco thought about Vivian. She may have been calling his Pcom and thinking he was just not calling her back. So, she would not be talking to him by the time he got back to the Republic, if he got back. Then the image of Monica enticing him in her Mars pod popped up. Her lovely firm breasts with pink nipples and the moist nest between her legs had been fun. He quickly shook the images away. "I don't really have anyone serious," Cisco replied catching his breath.

Finally, General Mora called Freddy, who listened and nodded to whatever the general was saying.

"Yes sir. We'll meet you there at 9 PM."

Freddy motioned for Cisco to follow him outside. Once he was sure they were away from any prying ears Freddy said, "General Mora has arranged for a small submarine. We will have to travel at night because the Caribbean is so clear we would be easily spotted. We should get to the island by the early morning hours tomorrow. We meet Mora at the old Maiquetia wharf number fourteen at nine tonight."

On time, Freddy and Cisco waited on wharf number fourteen hidden on the side of an old building. It was eerily quiet. The top of a small submarine popped near the surface of the dock. The hatch opened and General Mora climbed out.

Freddy saluted and the general returned the salute. The general shook hands with Cisco.

"You ever been in a sub before?" the general asked.

"No sir," Cisco replied.

"I hope you're not claustrophobic," the general smiled at him.

"No sir. I've been in some pretty tight spaces in my space travel. I've just never done it under water."

"Good, you can tell us more about space travel. It will take us about six hours to get to Orchila."

"I thought it was only 200 kilometers away."

"It is, but we have to take a circuitous route, like a whale or dolphin might take, to throw off their sensors," the general explained.

Freddy, Cisco, and the general climbed through the small hatch and into the tiny submarine. Besides the three of them, the skipper and a Venezuelan Marine sat at the controls, filling the sub to capacity. The general closed and sealed the hatch and ordered the skipper to submerge.

In less than a minute, the sub was cruising in complete blackness. At first the blackness closed in on Cisco. It was a strange feeling even his space travel did not replicate. In space, the sun, moon, planets, and stars always reflected light somewhere in the universe.

After the small sub was safely out of the harbor, the general asked Cisco about space travel. Everyone was entranced by the stories about space and Cisco talked for several hours. He also explained how the energy particle made space travel possible. The skipper was excited to think about a submarine powered by the particle.

Cisco explained how the power of the particle was almost unlimited, if controlled. Space travel allowed the power to be maximized, while car travel had to be throttled at a much slower speed. "If the speed is not throttled, there would be chaos in the sky. It is not the power of the particle, but the problem of managing the people," Cisco explained.

"So it is the same problem as our gasoline engines. If there are no speed limits or stop lights, the people would drive crazy," Freddy said.

"Yes, once the computer systems are in place to control the airborne traffic, your beautiful city of Caracas, for instance, could eliminate pollution problems and you could run as much electricity as you need every day of the week," Cisco said.

"Officially, Venezuela wants help from the Republic to get the particle technology. However, the PLV has the government under its control and has been resistant to the change," the general explained.

"I'm sure the Republic will work with you to adapt the technology and they will work out the money issues as they have with other countries."

"If we can crack the oil cartel's hold over the government, then the new technology can take over. I hope to see that in my lifetime," Freddy interjected.

"We better try to rest," the general said looking at his watch. "Tomorrow will be long day."

CHAPTER 58

Mason waited for the late afternoon siesta when the town was relaxing in cool places inside or in the shade. He was taking a big chance, but the town was far enough away and no dockworkers were about. Tying the girl's hands tightly behind her, he forced her up the four steps to the top deck. He thought about gagging her, though it would look too conspicuous if anyone spotted them.

"You scream, you die," he warned her.

They walked slowly on the dock, Mason keeping his good arm wrapped around her shoulders as if they were a couple. He led her along the beach away from the small huts that made up the shabby town. Mason made sure to walk close to the water's edge so their footprints would get washed away. For the most part the girl seemed compliant, however he kept a tight hold on her arm. Toward the end of a long stretch of beach, a man-made rock jetty extended into the sea.

Maya filled her lungs with the cool sea air as they walked. It had been hot and muggy in the boat, and cool sea air refreshed her. The days spent at the hacienda near the lake had rejuvenated her body, so she walked steadily along the sand. As they walked, Maya scanned the beach. She pondered if she could outrun her captor. He limped because of a deformed or damaged leg, but had a laser and would use it. Besides, her hands were tied tightly behind her. Ahead of them, a rock jetty formed from volcanic boulders blocked their way.

"Up there," he grunted at her and gave her a shove toward the jetty.

Mason pulled at her elbow to climb the volcanic boulders. Not able to catch herself, Maya fell against the sharp edges on her knees almost knocking Mason down.

"Ooowwww," she cried out as she tried to get her footing.

Not only was the jetty a mass of jumbled rocks, it was wet and slippery. Mason had never walked this part of the beach, although knew it led to the old military base. They could have walked the road to the abandoned base, but Mason worried they would be visible to anyone passing by. Pulling at her arms, he untied the binds.

Jerking her to her feet, "Now get up there," he grumbled.

As they crested the rock jetty, Maya saw a large compound of low dark buildings ahead. Groves of palm trees swaying in the gentle sea breeze. Some low foliage of scrubby bushes and wild grasses grew along the ridgeline.

"Come on," he said and pulled her arm. On the far side of the jetty, he found a secluded spot nestled in the volcanic boulders where they could not be seen from the town or from the sea. He thought it was adequate cover until nightfall. Pushing her to the sand, he tied her feet.

Maya curled herself on the soft sand and closed her eyes. The sound of the sea lulled her asleep. Later, she was wakened by Mason jerking her feet to untie her.

"Get up," he barked.

She was surprised is was almost dark and stars were popping out in the clear sky. Mason led her away from the jetty and headed directly to the abandoned Russian military base. It took them a while walking along the beach in thick sand. Mason had explored the old military buildings when he spent time on the island. The buildings had not been in use for at least thirty years and a good place where he could hide the girl.

The old buildings made of metal and wood were shabby from the battering of the salt winds, the glass windows mostly broken or gone. Passing several buildings, he finally found what he was looking for, the jail. Every military base had a brig. It would be the perfect place to hide the girl until he could find Armando and make a trade – his life and money for the girl. The heavy metal outside door groaned and scraped as he pulled it open. Inside it was almost pitch black.

Maya watched in horror as Mason opened the old door. Grabbing her tightly, he pushed her ahead of him. It was surprisingly warmer inside the jail than the cooler night air outside. She tripped over something in the dark and stumbled. The floor stunk and she heard something scurry in the dark. She wanted to scream, but took Mason's warning seriously. Mason shoved her into a small cell. The cell had a single window. She could see the dark sky through the window, but the cell itself was pitch black. Mason tied her hands from behind then gagged her with a handkerchief. She wanted to struggle, to fight him and escape, but knew she had no chance against him. When he finished, he pushed her to the floor.

"I'll be back," he told her, turned, and clanged the metal cell door behind him. He had specifically used a cell door which still had a key in the lock and after he twisted it, he pocketed the key.

Mason walked away, satisfied the girl was secure and no one was likely to find her. Walking back outside, he gathered his bearings and headed back toward the dock using the road. Quietly he slipped past the shabby town. A few lights, hanging on makeshift cords, lighted his way. Leaning against a wall, an old rusty bike was illuminated in the dim light. Feeling the tires, Mason decided it could be ridden and quietly pulled it along. He walked it out of the town, and hopped on. He knew it was maybe ten or eleven miles to the main town of Puerto Orchila.

After Maya heard the old jail building's door creak, she quickly got to her feet. Blackness surrounded her. Inching along the wall she found the door. Starting to her right, she slowly shuffled her feet, inch by inch. Her shin connected with something metal and hard. Carefully using her knee, she determined it was an old metal cot. Moving on, her hip ran into a metal sink hanging on the wall. The rest of the room was empty, except for a couple rocks or small pieces of concrete her feet kicked along the floor. Reaching the door again, she estimated the jail was about ten feet square. A small window was on the wall opposite the door. She could not see anything but the night sky and felt the cool ocean breeze blowing through the broken window.

Finally, her eyes adjusted slightly in the dark. It was

an odd sensation to be able to see dim shapes, not visible before. She shuffled across the room again, allowing her eyes to focus in the darkness. Below the sink, she saw broken pipes where faucets used to be attached. Bending down awkwardly, she tried to catch her gag on the end of a broken pipe. She pushed the rag with her tongue, trying to push it out of her mouth, but it was tightly wound through her teeth and tied at the back of her head. She tried again, scratching her cheek with the metal.

Something scurried nearby. Goosebumps broke out on her arms and a shiver went up her spine. "It's only a mouse or maybe a lizard. Nothing more than that," she told herself. She tried again to move the gag. It would only move a bit. She worked on the gag until she was exhausted, finally sinking down on the floor under the sink.

From somewhere in the darkness she heard a far off voice, "Don't give up." She strained to hear the voice again, or was it the wind and her imagination? Renewed by the voice, she looked under the sink. Vaguely she could make out the sink shutoff valves sticking out of the wall. One was twisted badly with sharp jagged metal edges, the other just a piece of round pipe. Scooting over on her butt to the twisted valve she finally found a position where her hands could feel the jagged metal behind her. Carefully, she positioned the ropes holding her hands over the jagged metal and moved the rope back and forth in a sawing action. If she went too far, the sharp metal pricked her wrists.

The slow work was exhausting and she had no idea if it was doing anything to cut the ropes. Her hands still felt tightly bound. Concentrating, she tried to work the exact same position on the rope. Push, pull, push, pull, she tried to make methodical movements against the jagged metal. Several hours later, a dim light coming through the small window illuminated the cell floor. Dawn was approaching. Dawn would mean Mason would return. Furiously she started working harder – push, pull, pull, pull.

Her shoulders ached from the awkward position and her wrists stung from the tight scratchy rope rubbing them raw as she sawed. Sometimes she had to bite on the gag because of the pain. Suddenly, she felt one of the strands give way a little. With renewed effort she sawed her binds against the metal. In a few more minutes, it gave way completely and her left hand was free. Exhausted she fell against the cell wall and stretched her arms.

"Gracias a Dios," she thanked God several times while she loosened her right hand and removed the gag.

CHAPTER 59

Cisco closed his eyes and tried to relax. The hum of the sub's engine was soothing, but he squirmed on the cramped seat. He tried to control his breathing, methodically relaxing each part of his body, but his brain would not stop replaying the events of the last week. He stared out the small window beside him into complete darkness. There was no up or down, no visual horizon to make one feel grounded, no light at the end of the tunnel for reference.

He prayed to God for help. "Show me the way and be my light," he prayed internally. Sometime later, he fell into a deep sleep. Deep in his dreams, a melody of clicks and pulsating sounds surrounded him. It was like listening to a symphony of wind instruments – the haunting sound of an oboe followed by the higher sound of a clarinet. A sharp series of clicking brought him fully awake.

Cisco opened his eyes to an eerie light surrounding the sub as the morning filtered through the clear Caribbean's water. Freddy pointed out the window where a pod of whales swam nearby. The huge animals swam alongside the sub, maybe about twenty adults and several calves.

"Are we almost there?" Cisco asked.

"Yes. There's a small cove on the south side of an old military base. We don't think it will be guarded this time of the morning," Freddy responded. "We will use the military barracks for shelter until General Mora gets more details on Armando.

The small submarine surfaced in a cove just as the sky lightened slightly from the coming morning. Freddy popped the hatch and pushed his head topside with a set of binoculars. "All clear sir," he said to General Mora.

"One of our operatives here on the island will meet you with dockworker clothes in the Administration Building at the old base. It will also be our fallback position. He says it is abandoned, but defensible." General

Mora saluted Freddy and then shook Cisco's hand and said "Good luck, son."

Freddy and Cisco climbed from the tiny sub, swam to the beach, and scurried across the sand to a patch of trees. On the trip, General Mora explained when they were on the island, he would not be in communication. One of the many security measures of the PLV was highly monitored communication on the island. Once on the island, they would be on their own.

"Do you know the operative?" Cisco asked Freddy.

"No. He's been on Orchila for a number of years."

Last night General Mora explained Leo would be their guide on the island. He had been an operative on Orchila for many years and knew every inch of the island. Freddy led the way to the old military base. Cisco had to watch his feet in the dim light. Tree roots stuck out of the sand along with rocks and debris. After about fifteen minutes of walking, the buildings of the old base popped into view.

Finally free from the ropes and gag, Maya grabbed the metal door handle with both hands and shook it with all her might. The metal jingled a bit, but was securely locked. *"Aaayyii,"* she grumbled. She had wasted all her strength to loosen the ropes just to be stuck anyway. Tears flowed down her cheeks. She had tried not to cry since she had been kidnapped, not wanting to let her kidnappers see her scared or weak. Here, alone in the cell, the tears cascaded down her face and she let herself cry. The sobs finally subsided after venting her frustration. Picking up the gag from the floor, she wiped her face and blew her nose.

The sun was sneaking in more and more as morning approached. The small window became clearer. It had jagged pieces of glass still sticking out of several parts around the edges. Maya stared at it. The window was small, less than two feet square. A grown man could not squeeze out of it, but she was smaller. Looking around she picked up a small chunk of concrete rock from the floor. She smashed the concrete against the glass sending it splintering to the floor. Furiously she worked. Shards of glass cut her hands. Grabbing the gag, she wrapped it around her right hand for protection and started again. In short order the window was clear of the broken glass.

With her hand still wrapped with the gag, she tried to pull herself up. Her exhausted shoulders did not have the strength. Looking around the cell, the only item was the old cot. Grabbing one end, she pulled it across the floor and leaned it against the wall at an angle, the top just below the window. It took several tries to get the old cot at the correct angle to not slide when she tested its use as a ladder. Halfway up her head stuck out the window. A cool breeze from the ocean greeted her. Collapsing her shoulders she wiggled them through. Edges of glass from around the window ripped at the outsides of her arms. Ignoring the pain, she pulled her arms through and her tiny waist followed.

Balanced with her hips on the window's edge, she looked down. Sand and rocks lay beneath the window where she would fall, head first. Her feet were at the top of the cot and at one point she felt sure she might be stuck like this when Mason came back, half in and half out. With a renewed reserve of energy, Maya used her feet to push against the cot. She fell forward out the window toward the ground.

She hit the sand on her left shoulder, the rest of her weight jarring her knocking the wind from her lungs. Looking around after she caught her breath, all was quiet. A number of old buildings stretched in both directions. The rundown buildings were all single stories except for a tall, thin tower. Gathering herself, Maya ran across the open sandy road toward the trees. She ran until the jungle surrounded her and her sides screamed from lack of oxygen.

Freddy led them toward the old military base from the ocean side. The administration building was near a jail at the center of the complex. Working their way along buildings, they hugged against the old walls until they reached a door marked *Administratsiya* and pushed it open. Cisco was surprised the Russian word was so similar to the Spanish and English words. Inside one of the offices, clothing lay on a desk. Beside the clothes were two leather belts with long sheathed knives. White seaman's hats also sat on the desk. Cisco noticed the clothing was well worn and looked unwashed. Drips of what looked like blood smeared the front of the pants. Freddy and Cisco stripped from their wet clothes, donning the grubby dockworkers uniforms.

"I see you two made it on time," a voice startled them. A young well-tanned man of medium build stood in the doorway. He too was dressed in the white shirt and pants with a seaman's hat. He reached out a hand. "My name's Leo Garcia."

After a brief greeting, Freddy and Cisco finished dressing and pushed their wet clothes into the old desk's drawer. They picked up the belts with the knives and wrapped them around their waists.

Before slipping out of the administration building's door Leo warned them, "Act naturally. Laugh and walk like you own the place, but if anyone stops us, I will do the talking." Leo took off in the lead with a bit of a swagger in his step. Freddy and Cisco followed.

Maya rested against a palm tree. Several not too rotten dates she found lying in the sand tasted good. The intense sugar gave her system a much needed jolt of adrenalin. The sun was just peeking over the eastern horizon of the Caribbean giving hints of orange and pink tinges along puffy gray clouds. Maya had a fairly clear view of her prison. Now free, she had no idea what to do.

Suddenly three men dressed in white caps walked from between two buildings and headed down the sandy road away from her. She jumped up and started to run in their direction. Getting to the edge of the trees, she was almost ready to scream at them when she saw a long knife sway against one of the men's trousers. Jumping back, she wound back into the trees as the men disappeared down the road.

Realizing her position was fragile, Maya sat beneath a palm and assessed her situation. Mason would return finding her gone. In the morning light, the old buildings which included her prison looked like an old military base. A five-story airplane control tower at the end of the sandy runway looked dilapidated, but sturdy. When Mason dragged her here last night, she had not seen anything resembling a town, just a few old buildings near the dock.

Her final assessment – she needed shelter, food, water, and rest. She needed these things somewhere Mason would not easily find her until she could find a town and the police. Looking around, she noticed the sandy footprints where she walked. Cursing herself, she realized she left him an easy trail right to her position. Picking up a fallen palm frond, she quickly erased her footprints dragging it behind her and walking in circles. Using the bloodied handkerchief, she picked up as many dates as it would hold tying the top to keep them inside. Quickly she headed toward the old air tower. Skirting the end of the runway by staying in the trees as long as possible, she scurried to the tower door covering her tracks by swishing the palm branch.

She pushed against the door and was surprised when it creaked open. Carefully she closed it and tiptoed up the tiny stairwell. Reaching the top, she had a beautiful view of the ocean in three directions. To the east the sandy runway stretched to the end of the buildings. She had a wonderful view to the entire area and would be able to see anyone coming, but the tower was also a prison with the only escape five stories down.

Most of the glass in the tower windows was missing and a cool breeze blowing off the ocean fanned her face. Needing a break, she had to scrape broken shards from the floor with her foot to give her a place to sit. Opening the handkerchief, she sat and ate four dates. Without any water, the sweet dates stuck in her teeth.

Leaning back against the tower's wall, she closed her eyes. Concentrating she tried to recount the days of her captivity. By her reckoning, it was Sunday morning. Clasping her hands together she prayed. She thanked God for helping her gain her freedom and prayed he would keep her safe until she could find her way home. She prayed for her parents and her great-grandfather who would be frantic with worry. She ended with "Amen."

Closing her eyes, she let the ocean breeze fan her face and listened to sea gulls squawking in the distance. She let the sounds lull her into a light sleep.

Across the river Maya saw a young man running for his life. Dust flew forming a dust cloud behind him. He tripped and fell. As quickly as he fell, the man was back on his feet desperately trying to outrun a ferocious Indian warrior on a big black horse. The warrior reared back on the horse and aimed his lance at the young man. Maya could see his face clearly.

"¡Mira bisabuelo!" Maya heard herself scream. "He is going to be killed." She tugged on her great-grandfather's arm and pointed to the young man across the river.

"No se apure mi hijita," her great-grandfather told her not to worry. "Francisco is on his way to find you. Don't be afraid. Call to him."

Maya jolted awake from the dream. Perspiration soaked her body and breathing was short and hard. Struggling to her feet, she steadied herself. Below her vantage point in the tower nothing moved, except the palm trees swaying slightly in the breeze.

The dream was so real. She could still feel her *bisabuelo's* arm. He called the young man across the river, Francisco. Did he mean Francisco Salaz? Shutting her eyes she tried to recall the dream and remember Francisco's face. Before she went to college, he had been an inspiration to her career. Her great-grandfather was his godfather and followed Francisco's career at the EQA. He used to tell her about Francisco's assignments to the space colonies and his work with the particle.

She had not seen him for maybe five years, since her cousin's wedding. Francisco was sitting with his parents and his older brother's family. She smiled remembering his unruly dark hair and infectious grin. They had danced one dance at that wedding, encouraged by her *bisabuelo*. Almost a foot taller than she, Francisco had soft hazel brown eyes. They danced awkwardly, but she remembered he bowed to her after the dance.

Suddenly she remembered the face of the *vato* in Echo Park – the *vato* who shot Mason in the arm and looked at her with worry in his eyes, hazel eyes. He was dressed like a *vato*, but it was Francisco, she was sure. He had come to rescue her, but Mason dragged her down the hill. Tears welled again in her eyes realizing her chance to be rescued at Echo Park had been foiled. In the dream, her *bisabuelo* told her Francisco was on his way. Was it possible he could find her again? She was lost and didn't even know where.

CHAPTER 60

After leaving the girl secured at the old jail, Mason rode the rickety bike to Puerto Orchila. When he arrived, the little port town was mostly asleep except for a mangy old dog wandering the main street looking for scraps. Mason knew Armando would be staying in the Hotel Magdalena, the only hotel in town. There was no registry, no way to know his room number, but Mason guessed it would be on the top floor with the best view of the ocean.

There were no guards in the town, no guards at the hotel. Mason knew the PLV felt secure here on the island. It was one of the few places the PLV members could relax. The docksmen made sure only invited boats landed. Unlucky fishermen, tourists, and especially any type of law personnel were not allowed. If any of these types did come they would never be seen again.

Finding a side door, Mason climbed the stairs to the top floor and waited in the stairwell with a view of the hallway. He slouched down to the floor with his back against the wall. It would be several hours before Armando got up and headed for breakfast. Dozing lightly, Mason peeked around the corner each time he heard a door open and close. It seemed a long time before he was rewarded. Armando exited a room down the hallway and headed toward the elevator. Mason waited until the elevator departed, walked to the room's door, and picked the lock.

The drapes of the room were open slightly letting in some morning light. The bedspread was thrown casually off the end of the bed. A small overnight bag was open near the bathroom. Mason closed the drapes and sat on an overstuffed chair to wait for Armando to return. He put his laser in his lap.

Freddy, Cisco, and Leo walked to the small town near the south dock. Armando's blue and white boat swayed evenly in the gentle movement of the sea. It was one of the bigger boats docked here. They walked slowly past the small shacks, which made up the tiny town until they reached the dock. Leo knelt and rolled up some rope and pretended to double check the lines to another boat. Freddy told Cisco to act casual. No one else was on the dock. As they moved toward the large blue and white boat, Cisco prayed Maya was inside. They could grab her and go.

When they were alongside Freddy said, "Stay here, I'll go check it out."

Leo motioned Cisco to keep moving down the dock, so as not to draw attention to Armando's boat. They were almost to the end of the dock, when they heard the whine of an engine. Cisco froze. Coming toward the dock, an open top boat carrying men dressed similar to them pulled alongside. Leo quickly grabbed the line they threw, twirling it expertly around the cleat when the boat slipped beside the dock.

Leo called to the men in the boat. The Spanish lingo was unfamiliar, but the men smiled and responded.

¿Alguien quiere regresar al continente?" the skipper asked if anyone wanted to return to the mainland.

Leo shook his head and threw the line back. The small boat started the engine and backed from the dock, turned, then revved the engine and accelerated out to the open sea. The waves it generated rocked Armando's big blue and white boat.

"Workers coming for their weekly shift," Leo said quietly. "They work for a week straight, and get two days on Aruba or the mainland. These men were coming from Aruba." When Leo and Cisco reached Armando's boat, Leo whistled softly. Freddy popped up from below and quickly jumped to the deck.

"Did you find anything?" Cisco asked.

"Nothing specific. Someone used the bed, ate cereal, and used the bathroom, but I can't tell if it was Maya."

"Now what?" Cisco asked.

"Now we wait. There are only two ways off this island, one is by boat the other is by chopper. General Mora will be hearing from our operatives soon. They should be tracking Armando's whereabouts and someone will try to get word to us. In the meantime we need to blend in," Leo answered.

Mason waited, shadowed by the high backed chair in Armando's room. Finally, the door opened, Armando flipped on the light, and shut the door behind him. Only then did he see the shadow rise with a laser pointed at his chest.

"What the fuck?" Armando growled. "How did you get here?"

"Ha, you were kind enough to give us a ride," Mason retorted.

"What?"

"You never even looked below deck."

Armando cursed under his breath. "Where's the girl?"

"She's at a safe place. So let's talk money," Mason said with a forced grin.

Armando's anger at the filthy mercenary almost brought him to action, but keeping an even voice he said, "You'll get your money when the girl is released, not sooner, and not from me. That was the job you agreed to."

A wicked grin spread on Mason's face. "Well, the job and the terms have changed. You will give me two million bolivars. You get the girl and I get off this island, alive."

It was really a small amount to get the girl back. She was worth so much more, but then Armando knew Mason did not know her real identity. He thought about dickering, but decided the dickering would come later. "The banks are not open on Sunday. I will not be able to transfer the money to you until tomorrow. I need proof the girl is unharmed," Armando said calmly. "You must take me to see she is okay."

Mason nodded in agreement and waved the laser at Armando. "Let's get going."

Armando picked up the intercom and ordered a cab. By the time they reached the lobby, a cab idled outside the front steps.

Orchila Island was shaped like a fat boomerang, with

the old military base covering the southwestern end of the boomerang. The island was only ten miles from tip to tip of the boomerang shape, in nautical miles. Driving around was more like fourteen miles from Puerto Orchila to the abandoned Russian base. Along the road, the cab passed several groups of workers walking the distance from the west dock to the town of Orchila. Part of the island's security demanded all visitors and workers to enter and leave the island by the old west marina and not directly to Puerto Orchila.

As a cab with two passengers passed them on the main road Leo hissed, "That was Armando. We need to turn around and go back."

"And the other man was Mason," Cisco said seeing the face he had seen at Echo Park. "I'd recognize that face anywhere."

Leo stopped and walked toward a stand of trees along the side of the road. Pretending to tie his shoe, he looked up and down the road. In the distance behind them, another group was walking toward Orchila. "Fall down," Leo barked at Cisco. "Pretend to be drunk or sick."

Cisco did as he was told, lying beside the road holding his head and groaning. As the four workers came nearer, Leo spoke to them and they laughed. Leo waved them on. The only word Cisco understood of the odd Caribbean Spanish slang was *borracho*, meaning drunk. After the four were out of view, Leo pulled Cisco to his feet. "Come on," he said and led them back following where the cab was headed.

By the time they walked back to the old town dock, the cab was nowhere to be seen, and Cisco was thankful Armando's big blue and white boat still floated lazily tied to the dock.

"Where do you think they went?" Cisco asked.

"Only one place to go, the old base," Leo said. "Only we can't be seen heading there on this road."

CHAPTER 61

The cab stopped on the old dirt runway near the middle of the complex as directed by Mason and they got out and walked toward the old buildings. Mason kept the laser ready walking behind Armando. Knowing Armando's reputation, Mason would make no mistakes. Pulling on the old jail door, they walked into the long hallway stretching straight ahead. Some of the metal doors of the cells were standing ajar, some closed. The putrid smell of mold and rot filled the air.

Maya heard the engine of a car outside. Keeping hidden in the tower, she waited while two doors opened and then slammed shut. Peeking over the tower wall, she watched two men walking into the compound toward the jail. One was Mason and the other Armando. She knew where they were going.

Slumping down, she tried to calm her breathing. They would find her gone. Her brain whirled with fear and doubt that she had covered her tracks. Hearing a small noise, she peeked over the wall again to see the cab driver quietly getting out of the cab and walking toward the jail. Her heart beat wildly in her chest, thumping so loud she thought it could be heard in the quiet.

Mason led Armando to the cell where he left Maya and pulled out a key from his pant's pocket. The old key scratched in the lock and the door clicked. He ushered Armando into the small cell expecting to find Maya hunkered in the corner. The cell was completely empty. The small cot turned upside down on the floor.

"What the fuck," Mason cursed.

"Where's the girl?" Armando growled.

Flustered Mason spun around the room disbelieving his eyes. "She was here I tell you, bound and gagged." Mason shoved the cot as if believing she might be hiding under it then scanned around the empty room.

"And now she is not," Armando grumbled. Mason pointed to the small window and said, "She escaped through there." The small window about five feet above the floor did not look big enough for escape.

"Bound and gagged, she escaped through that small window?" Armando sneered.

"Yes. She must have. She was here I tell you." Mason's voice had a pleading sound to it. "Look at the blood on this rope. She must be somewhere on the island. I'm telling you the truth. I locked her in this cell." His plan to exchange the girl for money had now disappeared.

"You have failed me again," Armando growled the words and stepped toward the wall of the cell. Before Mason could respond, the cab driver's body filled the doorway. Hearing Armando's key words, the pistol in the cabby's hand fired directly into Mason's chest.

Surprise registered on Mason's face moments before he fell forward. Blood poured in rivets along the uneven sandy floor. The cabby calmly walked to the body and kicked it several times, then shot Mason in the head. Mason's body jerked from the blast, and settled with a large gaping hole in the back of his head.

"You did well, Rodrigo," Armando patted the cabby on the shoulder. "We must find the girl. Get as many men as you can, find her, but do not hurt her. Make sure they all understand."

"Yes *jefe*, we'll find her. She's still on the island."

"When you find her, take her to my boat," Armando ordered.

It was several minutes after the cab driver sneaked toward the jail before the sound reached her ears. Several seconds later another shot echoed. Peeking from her vantage point, Maya saw two men walk out from the jail building, Armando and the cabby. Carefully Maya bobbed up and down for only seconds to see what they were doing. They walked to the small window where she escaped. The cabby stopped and pointed to the sand and then to the trees where she had hidden. Armando shrugged and made a wide arc with his arm. They walked back to the cab, got in, and drove off.

Maya scampered down the tower stairs. She knew they would be back looking for her. She knew finding a new hiding place was imperative, but could not leave before she made sure Mason was dead. Once down the concrete tower steps, she ran the distance to the jail building across the dirt runway without worrying about leaving tracks.

Mason lay in a puddle of blood on the jail cell floor. The back of his head oozed a pulpy mass of blond hair, blood, and brains. Crouching, she patted his pockets looking for something, anything she could use as a weapon. His pockets were empty except for a few bolivars and a cigarette lighter, which she took. Holding in her natural reflex to gag, she rolled him on his side. Under his body, was a laser covered in blood. Picking it up carefully, she wiped it on the front of his shirt as best as she could, then let the body roll back into position. Holding the laser in her left hand, she stood over Mason and cursed him, "Rot in hell."

Leaving the cell as she found it, she ran down the hallway and out into the open air. The laser gave her hope she could at least defend herself when they came for her. Now she needed a better place to hide.

She knew from the panoramic view from the tower, the trees were sparse and offered little protection and she could not hope to cover all her tracks in the sandy soil. The buildings of the old compound were all single story, except for the tower. They would search here first. Her only option was the sea. If she could reach the water and rocks, her trail would disappear. Maya scurried toward the sagging chain link fence. Finding a small opening, she wiggled through and headed for the shoreline.

Leo led Freddy and Cisco along the beach to circumvent the main road leading to the old military compound. Trudging through thick sand and scrambling over rocks, they walked in silence. A gunshot sounded from a distance. Leo held up his hand.

The sea lapped against the beach and rocks. Two

seagulls cawed above the sea as they flew above the water. Then they heard another shot. Cisco cursed under his breath. "Let's go, it could be Maya."

Scrambling at a faster pace, Leo led them along the rusted chain link fence on the leeway side of the compound. Finally finding an opening, they wiggled through, running along the fence until they reached the old military base. The compound had many outbuildings, barracks, chow hall, officer quarters, workshops, the tower, a jail, and the administration building.

Peeking around each building, they worked toward the central area. Nothing but the wind in the palms and the seagulls broke the quiet. Leo pointed to tire tracks in the sandy runway.

"They're gone. See the tire marks go both ways." Leo waved Cisco toward the administration building and Freddy to the barracks. Leo headed for the jail with small windows, some broken, some barred.

"Whistle if you find anything," he instructed.

Cisco headed back to the administration building where they had left their clothes, while Freddy headed toward the barracks. Cisco was almost to the end of the long hallway checking the rooms, when he heard a whistle. Running, he pushed the door to the building with a bang, no longer caring about any stealth. Freddy was coming around the corner and waved him to the jail.

Ducking into the door at the end of the jail, all was quiet. Down the hallway, some doors stood open or broken off their hinges, some closed.

Leo heard the jail door and yelled, "Down here."

The beating of Cisco's heart stopped and caught in his throat when he saw Freddy staring through the jail cell door. Peeking over Freddy's shoulder, he saw Mason lying on the sandy floor in a pool of blood. Flies were starting to nibble at the bloody, pulpy mess which had been his brains. Cisco sank against the wall in relief.

"Armando did this," Freddy said. "Mason must have kept Maya here and they came to get her. Looks like Mason lost out."

What had been relief for Cisco turned to anguish. Cisco turned and cursed his bad luck. He had failed Maya again. She was here and now back in Armando's clutches.

"Cálmate," Freddy told him. "She is not here, so she is alive. Armando only has one way to get her off this island. We must get back to the dock and be ready."

They headed down the main road away from the abandoned military base. Leo set a fast pace, almost jogging.

CHAPTER 62

Maya scampered across the sandy dunes. She could hear the waves beating against the coastline as she got closer. All was quiet except for the sea gulls screeching and flying above the clear blue water. Looking up and down the beach, she saw no one. Happily she ran to the water's edge and splashed the warm Caribbean Sea on her hands and arms. Mason's blood on her hands washed away. She desperately wanted to jump into the waves and clean the sand and sweat from her body, but knew getting far away from the jail was more important.

Mason had pulled her along this beach last night when they came from the boat. It had been very dark and she could not pay attention to details, but she remembered the ocean was on her right side. That meant the dock and Armando's boat was behind her. Maya followed the water's edge away from the compound until her breathing was ragged and a pain pinched at her side.

Cisco, Freddy, and Leo were almost to the edge of the old port town when two cars came racing toward them. Cisco wanted to turn and hide in the small trees at the side of the road, but Leo held to their course. The first car sped by, but the second slowed and stopped. The driver yelled at Leo, "*Jefe* needs every man. Get in," he ordered.

They squeezed into the car carrying three men. Cisco practically sat on top of a large man who stunk of BO. The driver jammed the accelerator and drove the sandy road back to the abandoned Russian compound. When they arrived, three men from the first car were waiting.

The driver of their car seemed to be the leader. Cisco kept his head down, hoping no one would recognize him as a stranger.

"*El jefe* needs to find a young woman who has escaped," the driver said. The man's words uplifted Cisco soul. Maya was alive. She had escaped, obviously before Armando killed Mason. His mind swirled with relief.

Someone in the group snickered and said, "*El jefe* must be having trouble in bed, if they are running away from him." Everyone laughed heartily until the driver barked, "She is his property, not a *puta*. He will pay handsomely for her return. Do not hurt her. She is to be found alive and unharmed."

They all quieted. Cisco casually peeked around noticing the men were not armed with guns, only long machetes or dock knives. He patted the tiny laser in his pocket knowing it gave him an edge.

"Spread out in groups of three. Search the compound first, every inch. If you find her, whistle," the leader instructed.

"Leo, you and those two check the administration buildings and the officer's quarters. Jorge, you take the dormitories." The leader led the others to check the old tower.

Leo headed toward the Administration building. Once away from the others Cisco whispered, "Does that man know you?"

"Yes, I've worked on the island for several years as an operative for General Mora. I know most of these men, so they think I am one of them. The lead man is Rodrigo, a trusted Armando bodyguard. Don't let his appearance and demeanor fool you. He is a killer."

"What about us. Don't they wonder who we are?"

"They would assume you are PLV because they know me," Leo said. "Just, don't do anything to call attention to yourself."

Leo led them to the Administration Building. Cisco took the left side of the hallway, Freddy the right. Most of the doors were already open and the rooms empty except for some old broken furniture. Cisco had looked inside the rooms just a little over an hour ago, but this time they searched more carefully.

"Maya," Cisco whispered in each room. "Maya, it's me, Francisco." No one replied.

Freddy struggled to open the next to the last door on the right. It would not budge. Knocking lightly he called softly, "Maya, if you are in there, we are friends." Only silence greeted him.

Exiting the administration building on the far end, Leo led them to the officer's quarters. They repeated the search, quietly calling to Maya. Cisco pondered what they would do if they found her or worse if one of the other groups found her. The odds were three against six, not too bad, but still not good.

Finally, a shrill whistle sounded in the quiet air. Walking outside, another sharp whistle came from the jail. Leo, Cisco, and Freddy knew what had been found – Mason's dead body. Soon the others were assembled outside the cell door.

Most of them knew Mason. The blond mercenary with a limp had a bad reputation. "This is what happens to anyone who fails *el jefe,*" Rodrigo barked. "We will not fail him."

In just the few hours since Mason was killed, flies hungrily fed from his brains. It was definitely a sight which encouraged the searchers to find the girl.

Rodrigo picked up a few shards of glass from the floor and picked some threads from the edge of the window. "She must have escaped from the window," he said. They all walked outside and assembled under the window. Rodrigo studied the ground, where more glass shards stuck in the sand. Several had small amounts of dried blood on the edges. Footprints led off across the old sandy runway to the trees.

"That way," he yelled. "Spread out."

Freddy quickly jumped up and took a central position, heading directly across the sandy runway. The other two groups took the left and right sides. Cisco desperately hoped his group would be the ones to find Maya. How far could she go? When had she escaped? Hours? More? His brain swirled with questions as they sprinted across the runway.

Maya caught her breath and started jogging instead of running. Most important to her was leaving no trail. By staying at the water's edge, the waves erased her footprints quickly, however she was visible and it bothered her. Every couple of minutes, she stopped and looked behind and forward. She saw no one. Rounding the corner, a small cove lay ahead. Splashing at the edge of the cove, her footprints were immediately erased.

CHAPTER 63

Armando took a long hot shower after Rodrigo left to round up a group of men to search for Maya. There was no way she could escape the island. He alerted the docks men here in Puerto Orchila to spread the word. Her only way off this island was by boat.

The stupid blond cripple thought he could make a bargain. He forgot Armando owned the island and the men here were loyal to him and the PLV. At least now, he had full control over any new negotiations with the Republic for the particle.

He had mulled over his situation in the shower. Orchila was an ideal place to hold the girl hostage, even better than his hacienda while he negotiated new terms for her release. However, he had other responsibilities in Maracaibo. Now that the Feds had searched his compound and found nothing, taking the girl back seemed a better idea.

Dressing, Armando packed his small bag, but left it on the bed. Walking downstairs, he arranged a driver to take him back to the old port and his boat.

Nine men searched the overgrown area away from the seaside of the old military compound. After a while they were going in circles tromping over each other's tracks. The palm trees offered little protection for anyone to hide. About an hour later, Rodrigo reassembled the searchers into a group.

"She could be anywhere," one heavyset man complained. Sweat dripped down his arms and his shirt was completely drenched. It was mid afternoon and the heat of the afternoon sun oppressive. Everyone else looked about the same, hot and weary.

Rodrigo pulled out a gun and pointed it at the heavyset man. "You too tired Julio?" he sneered. Julio shook his head no and the others looked away in silence.

"We head toward the sea. You three go back toward

the marina," Rodrigo said pointing to Jorge and two others. "Leo, you start where the compound fence ends, that way toward Signal Rock. She will not be able to past it."

Leo, Freddy and Cisco went down the sandy runway. "What's Signal Rock?" Cisco asked when they were out of earshot.

"*Isla la Orchila* is shaped like a fat boomerang. The northwest corner of the island is all volcanic rock with a tall outcrop called Signal Rock. The sea crashes into that corner of the island. It was used by pirates to deliberately lure ships aground to be looted."

"How did they do that?" Cisco asked confused.

"Pirates would build a fire on the top of the rock as a beacon signal. It was a pirate's method of creating a lighthouse. In bad weather, the light signaled a safe harbor, but instead the boats were destroyed on the rocks. The pirates salvaged the cargo."

"So if Maya reaches Signal Rock, she won't be able to scale it?" Cisco asked.

"Unlikely, the shoreline is impassable. The waves crash against the rocks and there is no beach area. We must hurry."

Finally stopping for a break, Maya was sweating profusely even with a slight cool breeze blowing off the sea. Her empty stomach growled for food and water. Sitting on a nearby rock, she dug in her pocket and retrieved the handkerchief with six dates. Plopping one into her mouth, it was a feast. Slowly she sucked on the sweet, sticky pulp of the date, trying to force her dry mouth to absorb any moisture. She looked out on the clear blue of the Caribbean Sea. If only her chip was still working or she had a Pcom. Numerous satellites circled the Earth providing communications services everywhere, even here. How simple it was, just pick up a Pcom and call anywhere in the world. It had been the only world she had ever known, until now.

She thought about a picture from a high school history class. It was of a group of people stranded on an island. They dug the word HELP into the sand hoping someone looking from the air would see. She tried to remember the story and could not remember if the people were rescued.

She ate two more dates and tucked the rest back into her pocket. Most of the coastline here looked as if the tide would devour the sand each day. A little way back she remembered passing a more protected beach where the sand looked unperturbed by the sea. The area was not too far back, after the cove. Turning back, she quickly walked along the edge of the water.

Keeping a sharp eye out for boats or people, Maya finally reached the sandy beach. Along the way she picked up a smoothed piece of driftwood. She pondered which direction to write, toward the sea, or toward the land. She finally decided toward the sea. Starting on her left, she dragged the piece of driftwood behind her to create the word. It took about ten precious minutes to write the word HELP in large letters in the sand.

She felt stupid looking back at the word and almost went to destroy it. Help from whom, from where? How could she signal someone even if they saw the word? What if Armando used it to find her? Dropping the piece of wood, she started back on the edge of the water the way she had come.

"Great-grandfather, if you are sending Francisco let him see the word," she said almost as a prayer. It seemed stupid, but the dream and her great-grandfather's words made her believe. She had to believe they were looking for her. It was her only hope.

Armando reached the old port where his blue and white boat was docked. He strode down the dock and jumped onto the boat. Ducking down through the hatch, he saw the evidence as Mason described where they hid while he drove the boat to the island. How could he have been so stupid not to check the boat before he took off? He had no idea why Mason hid with the girl on the boat. It seemed an unlikely place to hide. Armando had only thought of escaping to the island on the spur of the moment.

Shrugging, he decided it was now a godsend. The girl was stuck and she could not communicate with anyone. She was isolated and eventually would be found.

Leaving the mess below, he went topside. The midday sun was beating unmercifully on the deck. Jumping back off the boat he headed down the dock.

"Get my boat gassed up," he hollered at two men working down the dock.

"Already done," one of them replied. Walking into the old port, Armando headed for the cantina. At least he could get a beer and something to eat while he waited for Rodrigo and his men to find the girl.

Cisco fell behind Freddy and Leo. Not used to humidity, he felt lightheaded. Leo was searching the edge of the brush for footprints. Freddy walked even further into the beachhead. Soon they arrived back at the cove where they had exited the sub.

Near the tree line, small fresh footprints were clearly visible. Putting his foot beside the small print, it looked definitely small like a woman's shoe print. The prints led through the tree line and off along the edge of the water. With renewed vigor they headed on calling "Maya" into the wind every couple of minutes listening for a reply.

CHAPTER 64

Maya had finished the word in the sand and was retracing her steps along the sea's edge when she thought she heard voices. Someone was calling out, but she could not make out the sound. Panicking, she regretted writing the HELP in the sand. It was like a huge beacon saying – here I am, come find me, come kill me. Running along the edge of the surf, she cursed at herself over and over for making such a blunder.

Maya reached the beach where she had turned around. This time she kept running, scanning for any place to hide. The beach was narrowing and on her left side, the ground became rockier. She rounded a corner to find herself staring up at a large rock formation jutting far out to sea. The beach abruptly ended and the jagged volcanic rock blocked her way. Seawater smashed and exploded against the formation with each wave.

She sank to her knees. This was as far as she could go. She was completely stuck. The sea was certain death. Heading back the way she came meant running directly into the voices she heard a little while ago. They would see the writing in the sand and know she was here. Looking up, the steep, jagged volcanic rocks seemed her only hope. Gathering courage, she slowly picked her way up the black cliff.

Freddy and Leo searched along the tree line as they walked along the beach. Cisco walked closer to the shoreline in the sand. He yelled, "Maya," but it was lost in the wind and the crashing waves. He walked near the shoreline hoping to find her small footprints.

The beach opened up slightly, with the beach unperturbed by the ebb and flow of the waves. A slim rivulet was dugout perpendicular to Cisco's gait, then another. The sand created little hills on either side where it was scraped away. He jumped over another rivulet and walked to the edge of the water. He looked out toward the horizon where the Caribbean Sea met the teal blue sky. It was impossible to see where the two met. It blended into a blue blur.

Cisco turned around to head back across the beach. Ahead of him, the word HELP scraped into the sand jumped out at him. The word written in the sandy beach was undeniably fresh. "Over here," he yelled.

Freddy and Leo reached him and saw the word written in the sand. They all started to yell Maya's name, over and over. If she was hiding nearby, surely she would hear them.

Leo shuffled his feet over the word written in the sand. Cisco thought it was a good idea and quickly helped him erase the word he believed was written by Maya.

"Come on," Leo said. "Signal Rock is not too far. She can't get past there and will have to turn around. We'll find her."

Cisco began yelling "Maya, Maya where are you?" over and over.

Maya slipped on a loose piece of lava rock and fell onto her knee. Blood dripped from the wound down her leg and stained her trousers. The going was hard. Behind her, she thought she could hear voices yelling. Painfully she inched her way up the steep rock wall. Below her, the waves violently crashed against the rocks, above her the cliff got steeper. A wrong move could send her falling down the face of the jagged rocks into the crashing sea and surely to her death.

The late afternoon western sun was burning into the volcanic rock. Each time she tried to use the rock as handles to pull up, the hot black rock burned or ripped at her hands. Once she though she heard voices, then the waves crashed. Finally, she reached a nook in the cliff with a large boulder big enough for her to crouch behind and hide. About halfway up the cliff, she was now able to turn and look below her without falling. Settling behind the boulder, she got herself comfortable in her hiding place.

The voices seemed to be getting closer, louder. Maya

pulled Mason's laser from her waistband. Most of her training for the EQA department used lasers, but Mason's older model was heavy and awkward. Suddenly a white sailor hat popped into view coming down the beach in her direction. Then, two more followed behind. The man in the front was pointing into the sand and calling to the others. They had found her footprints leading directly up to the rocks.

"You will never take me alive," Maya muttered to herself. Aiming the laser at the lead man, she held her breath and fired.

The hiss of a laser shot came from above them. Cisco watched Freddy buckle as his pants leg sizzled. Quickly he and Leo grabbed Freddy and pulled him to the base of Signal Rock. Another hiss exploded beyond them in the sand as they dragged Freddy and themselves to safety.

"Damn, where did she get a laser?" Leo asked.

"I don't know," Cisco said. "She thinks we are the goons hunting her."

"Maya," Cisco yelled. "Maya, don't shoot."

The waves crashed against the rocks and Cisco could not tell if she heard him. He cupped his hands around his mouth and shouted again. Leaving Leo and Freddy, Cisco inched his way to his left away from the sea and waves. He was sure it was Maya, scared and confused. Her instinct to protect herself was understandable.

"Maya," he yelled again in intervals. Slowly working his way around the base of the cliff, he found where footprints packed the sand between the tumble of rocks. Carefully he started to climb, checking ahead before making a turn.

Maya could no longer see anyone below her. She saw one of the men stumble and the others pull him to safety out of her sight. That would make them think twice before trying to scale the cliff, but she was stuck here halfway to the top. The western sun told her it was late afternoon, maybe four or five o'clock. Once night fell, she would lose both her advantage and ability to climb up or down.

Below her Cisco climbed the lower portion of the

cliff steadily. The going was not hard, but the sun-baked rocks were hot and sharp to use for handholds. He was listened to the waves crashing below him and detected a rhythm. Using the break in the sound, he called out again, "Maya!" Between each break of the waves, he yelled her name and waited for a response.

Maya heard a voice below and then behind her. One of the men from below was trying to circle up to her. Panic filled her chest. Her first instinct to run was obviously impossible. Her only logical move, wait and have the laser ready. She heard a rock tumbling down the cliff nearby, hitting others as it fell. Maya gripped the laser and pointed it toward the small path she used to reach her spot.

Cisco was about to turn a corner when he heard Rodrigo's voice nearby. "Put down the laser, *señorita*. Slowly. No sudden moves."

Rodrigo held Maya in his sights, pointing a gun at her, while two others climbed down to her and grabbed her arms. She had no way to struggle or run.

Peeking around a boulder, Cisco saw three white hats poking above the rocks further up the path. Quickly, he ducked out of sight and made his way down to where he left Freddy and Leo.

"Rodrigo found her. They're up there about half way," he told them. "Should we take them as they come down?"

Leo pondered their situation for a few moments. "No, we need to get out of sight. It's getting dark and they'll be taking her to Armando," he said.

Cisco was disappointed. He did not want Maya slipping away again, but had to submit to Leo's decision. It would be three against three, but he did not want Maya hurt in the crossfire. "What about your wound?" Cisco asked Freddy.

"It's just a burn, I'm okay. We better get over the lava wall. They'll be coming down from that side," Freddy said and pointed to the left.

CHAPTER 65

Moving back into the trees, they waited until they could see the three men and Maya carefully working their way down the volcanic rockface. Rodrigo carried a small laser, while one of the other men kept a tight hold on Maya. Finally, they reached the sand.

"Armando, we have the girl." Rodrigo spoke to an open Pcom and reported their success. "Where do you want us to take her?"

Cisco could see the defeat on Maya's face and it broke his heart. She looked shaken, red eyed, and disheveled. One shoe was missing and dried blood covered her trousers at the knees. Bloody hands hung at her sides, but she was not crying.

"He wants us to take her to the hotel," Rodrigo spoke to the others and started down the sandy shoreline.

When Maya and her abductors were well down the beach, Cisco grumbled, "We should have taken them. Once they get her into town, it will be harder to get her."

"Rodrigo is a killer. I'm counting on Armando wanting to keep the girl alive. Come on, we need to get back to town before dark," Leo told him.

Armando was elated with the news from Rodrigo. The girl had been found. Downing the last of his beer, he hurried from the cantina, down the dock, and onto his boat. The sun was almost touching the horizon and would soon be gone. Although he would have preferred getting off the island with the girl today, the trip was not one he wanted to make in the dark. Besides, it gave him time to negotiate with the rebels for a new arrangement. Revving the engine of the big blue and white boat, he backed it from the dock and headed east to the main town of Puerto Orchila.

A half hour later, Armando had secured the boat at the private dock at the hotel. Up in his room, he poured himself a scotch on ice and sat on a comfortable chair to wait for Rodrigo to deliver the goods. His spirits were high as he initiated a call to the Republic rebellion's leader.

Cisco, Freddy, and Leo followed down the sandy beach, keeping well behind Rodrigo. When they reached the cove, Leo suggested a plan. "Freddy, signal the sub and have it pick you up. Get that leg attended and tell him what has happened. Cisco and I will take the shortcut to the town. Tell General Mora to take the sub out to sea far enough to use the ComLink, yet close enough to help if necessary," Leo said.

"Leo, you must know how dangerous this may be for you. It will blow your cover here on the island. Are you ready for that?" Cisco asked. He thought he should go at it alone, but he also needed Leo's help.

"My cover here on the island may already be compromised, besides saving the girl is what is important. Everything else is secondary."

Cisco had also resigned himself to either saving Maya or die trying. He admired both Leo and Freddy for their heroics. He just hoped neither would be killed in the process.

"Come on," Leo barked at Cisco and took off running into the tangle of trees away from the sea. It was not long before Cisco was panting trying to keep up with him. Sharp branches of the local shrubs and palms ripped at his arms and face. They scrambled over volcanic debris and it was dark before they reached Puerto Orchila. Leo stopped in a dark area within sight of the main part of town.

Cisco was completely spent from the workout, but Leo was only breathing hard.

"How do we find Armando?" Cisco asked.

Leo pointed. "He's at the hotel and I know what room he'll be in."

"How do we get in?"

"We wait and watch. Nobody is going anywhere tonight."

Armando's Pcom buzzed. Setting down the glass of scotch, he answered, but waited before speaking.

"You better have good news," a man's voice spoke.

"I have the girl. She is unharmed."

"You altered the plan without authority. It cost us plenty to cover your mistakes." The man's voice was terse and angry.

"There were no mistakes, only unavoidable modifications to the original plan. The question is whether you want the girl returned safely and how much it will cost," Armando replied.

The voice on the other end did not immediately reply. "How much?"

"Another hundred million Bolivars and I will personally deliver her safely."

"You're loco. We can't manufacture that much cash. You've already been paid well." The voice grew brusque.

"You want the girl unharmed. Your country is rich and mine poor. A hundred million dollars is chump change for the Republic," Armando scoffed.

"Where are you? Where is the girl? Are you still in Venezuela?"

"We're safe and the girl is with me. We're on Orchila Island."

"I need to contact my resources and I will call you. Make sure the girl stays safe," the voice grumbled and the Pcom link shut off.

It was not long before Cisco and Leo saw the small party arrive at the hotel. In the dim lights of town, Cisco saw Maya's small form pushed up the steps and into the hotel.

"There they are. Let's go," he said to Leo as he started to rise.

"Cisco, these men are ruthless. There is a reason she is still alive. We must bide our time."

"I was given an assignment to find her and bring her home safely. The entire Republic's future depends upon it. If there is a chance to do that, I must take it. We have the advantage, because Armando doesn't know we are here."

"You are dealing with one of the most ruthless killers on earth. He has many men watching out for him. Eyes are everywhere and someone will notice you are a stranger. You will not get past the lobby at the hotel," Leo pleaded with him.

"I can with this," Cisco told him holding out the tiny laser. "It gives me an advantage."

General Roberto Castillo activated his Pcom's secure channel. The Republic's Commander of the Military waited for an answer.

"You have news?" a woman's voice asked without a greeting.

"They're on Orchila. He has the girl secure, but he wants another hundred million."

"Only one hundred? I expected more," she laughed softly.

"This is getting out of hand. He'll continue to extort us more and more for the girl. Maybe he does not even have her. We have no proof."

"Have we had any news about Francisco?" she asked.

"No, nothing. He has not called in for two days. He could be dead."

There was a pause on the Pcom. "We need to go to Orchila. We'll take the hundred million with us and exchange it for the girl. Armando will do as I wish, but no girl, no money," she said.

CHAPTER 66

Finally relenting to Leo's insistence it was too dangerous to storm the hotel, he and Cisco stayed hidden overnight, sleeping in shifts while they kept watch. As dawn barely began to lighten the eastern sky, Leo roused Cisco.

"Follow me," Leo said and led Cisco to a shed. They ducked inside where gardening tools were stored. "Change into those clothes and sombrero. Take some clippers and go to the garden. Tend to the flowers. Stay far away from the paths where people will pass in and out of the front door and keep your head down," Leo told him.

When Cisco began to complain, Leo continued, "I will see where they are holding Maya."

Accepting Leo's expertise here on the island, Cisco followed his orders and began to change his clothes.

Maya woke up bound to the bedpost of an opulent room. It reminded her of the room at Armando's hacienda, but a little smaller. They tied and gagged her last night, but did not drug her. For that, she was thankful. Although she knew Armando was on the island, she had not been taken to his room as she expected.

She lay staring at the ceiling thinking about her almost escape yesterday. The scene replayed in her brain. Three men were below her rocky position. She was sure she hit one with a laser shot. She was waiting and listening as one of the men was climbing up to her position, and she thought he was calling for her. So focused on him, she did not hear the men above. If she had it to do over again, she would have jumped into the sea.

The door to the room opened interrupting her thoughts. A man with a pistol at his side came and untied her. He pushed her along down the hallway and opened a door to a large bathroom. Without a word, he pushed her inside and she heard the door lock click.

Two elderly women were folding towels and one was filling a large claw-footed tub.

"Desnuda," one of the women told her to undress. Maya gladly stripped the dirty clothes and sank into the tub of hot water.

The woman gently scrubbed her body with sea sponges. Her injured knee stung a bit at first, and one of the women was very careful to clean it tenderly. After scrubbing her head to toe, one of the women shampooed her hair and rinsed it. Through it all Maya relaxed, letting the warm water soothe her skin and body.

Armando was again treating her as a guest. It seemed so crazy to see this obviously ruthless man treat her with kindness. She had escaped and he had killed Mason, so she expected his wrath, not kindness.

Stepping from the tub, a large Turkish towel wrapped her nakedness. It felt good to be clean. One of the women hummed while Maya sat on a chair and she worked on drying and untangling her hair with a blow-dryer.

When she finished, Maya's long dark brown hair was brushed silky smooth. They dressed her in a flowered sundress and placed a purple orchid behind her right ear.

"There *señorita,* you are beautiful," the maid complimented her.

"Gracias," she thanked them feeling greatly refreshed for the moment.

The woman escorted her to a room with a view of the Caribbean Sea. A cool ocean breeze ruffled the curtains of the opened sliding doors. Outside the door, an armed guard stood on the right side of the balcony. When the maid left, she heard the click of the door lock – the room was just another prison. A large bowl of fruit and a pitcher of fresh juice sat on a table. She picked at a few pieces of the fruit and downed a large glass of juice. Stretched out on the bed, she immediately fell asleep.

Cisco knelt near a bed of flowers across a path and he had a clear view of the front door. He had lost track of days. Orchila was not a place where time mattered much. Cisco believed it was Sunday, but maybe it was Monday. Either way he only had a few days to rescue Maya and get back to the Republic to save his *Nino's* presidency.

"Cisco, Maya is in a room with a guard on the balcony and one outside her door. She's on the third floor," he heard Leo's voice. Leo had stopped and was pretending to lace his shoe. "I've heard some scuttlebutt Armando is waiting for a helicopter from the mainland."

"If he's planning on taking off the island by helicopter, we need to get her now," Cisco hissed.

"I believe he has called for a high-level PLV meeting. Nothing will happen to her for now. Keep working on the gardens. I'll get you if there is a way to get to her. Right now it is impossible," Leo informed him.

"Okay, but we have to get her before they take her off the island. We should have stormed her room last night," Cisco grumbled.

"Stay calm. We cannot fight them all. Oh yes, Armando brought his boat to the hotel dock and it is serviced with a full tank of gas. We may be able it steal it for our escape, if we live."

Desperately Cisco fought an urge to open the secure channel and call in the Republic's security guy. "Send in the Special Ops," he would tell him. Cisco wondered if they could extract Maya from the island. Gus had warned him that all communications on the island were monitored. If his cover was blown, Maya's life could be in danger as well as his.

Cisco kept low, snipping dead flowers and trimming the shrubs around the garden. When he could, he studied the third floor room with the armed guard. While people wandered about the small town, Cisco never saw Armando. He watched Leo working near the docks, talking and laughing with some of the other men.

It was early afternoon when Cisco heard the sound of helicopter blades whooshing and the gas turbine whine. It swooped down and steadied before it came down for a three-point landing at the helipad. Before the blades stopped completely, three men stepped from the large door of the chopper, followed by a woman. She wore a scarf over her hair, but still had to hang onto it under the chopper draft. One of the men held on to her arm and escorted her down the walkway toward the front door of the hotel.

Two men looked Venezuelan. The PLV honchos, just as Leo predicted. The man escorting the woman looked familiar. He was carrying a large briefcase. Cisco edged along where he had been working to get a better view. He was studying the man's face, not paying attention to the woman. When they got near the doorway, a large exotic bird swooped nearby and cawed. The woman jumped and looked up. Cisco caught her face in the full sunlight. It was Vivian Bejarano.

"What the fuck!" was all he could mutter to himself before the three men and Vivian were ushered inside the hotel.

CHAPTER 67

"Querida, I have missed you," Armando nuzzled Vivian's neck after they were alone in his private suite. The PLV escorts and General Castillo went to their rooms to relax and freshen up. They were to meet later in the downstairs restaurant to discuss the business at hand.

Armando ran his hands down Vivian's back and they came to rest on her butt. He pulled her to him.

"Is that all you can think about at a time like this?" Vivian groused. "Where is Maya?"

"She is in a room on the third floor, well-guarded. Come here *querida* and relax."

"Huh! I've heard that before. Francisco Salaz is on the island. He also found Mason Warrick at the Echo Park house, starting this entire fiasco. It was he, with the help of General Mora, who attacked your hacienda," Vivian told Armando in a huff.

"Who the hell is Francisco Salaz?" Armando asked.

"He is President Torres' godson. He's an EQA agent and I've known him since we were in grade school."

"You are flustered over nothing. How could an EQA agent do all that? My plans were impeccable. Mason said it was a drug deal gone wrong in Echo Park. How do you know this?" Armando resented Vivian's anger.

"Our Republic's security people were supposed to be tracking him, but they are useless. Finally, I had to arrange for an InfoAgent to find him. My source confirmed General Mora is nearby and we believe he got Francisco onto the island," Vivian told him.

Armando was about to contradict her, then remembered how Mason played stowaway and brought Maya here. Perhaps the security on the island was not as good as he thought. Instead, Armando opened his communicator and alerted security to be on the lookout for anyone not recognized. Vivian took the communicator and gave them a description of Francisco.

"My men know everyone on the island. He can't be

here, but if he is, they will find him."

"Have Maya brought up here to your suite. We cannot take any chances," Vivian demanded.

"Don't worry, my love, the hotel is secure. No one who doesn't belong here can get through. Now, come to me." Armando hugged her and would not be put off.

As the late afternoon sun bore down on the island, Cisco found a shaded hidden spot away from the front of the hotel, but within view of the large helicopter, which stood still on the helipad. He sat on the edge of a small hill facing the Caribbean Sea deep in thought about Vivian. From his vantage point, he could see Armando's big blue and white boat bobbing near the dock.

His brain fired over and over trying to make the latest developments make sense. Leo told him high-level PLV members were expected. Two of the men fit that description, but Vivian and the other man did not.

His first instinct was to believe she was here to negotiate Maya's release. He finally recognized the man who escorted her into the hotel. It was General Roberto Castillo. Dressed in street clothes and a panama hat, Cisco did not recognize him at first. Trying to fit the pieces in his weary brain, he kept reanalyzing the facts.

He had not reported Maya's existence on Orchila to the security gurus in the Republic. His last report on the secure channel only told the voice he was in Venezuela. Wearily he replayed the events of the last several days. He had communicated with Gus about Orchila, but Gus would not have told any Republic authorities. So why would General Castillo and Vivian arrive on the island? How did they know to come here?

Gus swore he disabled the location beacon on the secure G2000 communicator in his pocket. Perhaps Gus was wrong and they had been tracking him all along. If so, they could be here to negotiate Maya's release. However, he could not make sense of how Vivian would be selected for such a dangerous role.

"Cisco, I've been looking all over for you. I thought

maybe you had been caught," Leo's voice startled him.

"Caught?"

"The men have been instructed to look for you all over the island. Something blew our cover," Leo said.

"Mierda," Cisco swore.

"I have a new plan on how we can get to Maya's room, but we may have to fight our way out. Are you ready?"

"Leo, a woman arrived this afternoon."

"You mean the woman who came on the helicopter?"

"Yes. She's from the Republic. She may be here to get Maya?"

"No, that's Vivian. She's Armando's lover. She's been to the island often," Leo replied.

"What! Armando's lover? It's not possible. I know her. I've known her since we were kids. There must be some mistake," Cisco almost growled at Leo.

"She has come here with him off and on for several years. A maid in the hotel says she can be mean and vicious, if she does not get what she wants. Some think even Armando is afraid of her," Leo replied.

Bile tasted in Cisco's throat as he digested the news. Vivian? Here and part of this kidnapping. Then General Castillo was also involved. His father's words came ringing in his brain, "We're having concerns about one of the old crop protectors." It had nothing to do with crops, but with the Republic. The general was a turncoat.

"Come we must go, now. Armando's doubled Maya's guard, but the rest of the men are spread out looking for you. We must strike now."

Cisco followed Leo to the garden shed. He and Leo changed into gray jumpsuits and Leo handed him a toolbox. Leo smeared a bit of grease on Cisco's face.

"These are the keys to Armando's boat. Whatever happens, if we pull this off, take Maya and head out to sea and contact General Mora. Don't worry about me, just get her off this island," Leo told him and handed Cisco the keys.

Cisco pocketed the keys and felt for the laser. As he slipped it over his finger, he wondered if he could kill Vivian, if he had to. The revelation of her betrayal befuddled him. It did not compute to anything he knew about her or thought he knew about her. His brain flashed back to their night in her apartment for dinner and then fantastic sex. His father's words flashed across his brain, "Trust no one."

Leo led Cisco toward the back door of the hotel. Per Leo's instruction, they walked along the road acting normal. In the lights surrounding the hotel, they could see guards walking the perimeter and posted at the door.

"*¿Quién eres tú y qué haces aquí? Levanta las manos,*" the security guard asked them who they were and what they were doing here. The guard told them to put their hands up.

"It's me, Leo and Alberto, the plumber. There's a plumbing problem on the fourth floor," Leo told him. "Why are you so jumpy?"

"Armando says we have to search everyone," the guard replied. He frisked Leo and then Cisco, finally searching the toolbox. The tiny laser in Cisco's palm was invisible.

"What's happened? Is it the honchos who arrived in the chopper?" Leo continued a casual conversation with the guard.

"I don't know. Okay, you can go on up," the guard said.

Leo led the way down a long hallway past several doors. At the end of the hall, they reached the service elevator. He used the passcode and pushed the third floor button.

"Get ready," he said as the elevator doors closed. When the doors opened on the third floor, a guard pointed a rifle at them until he recognized Leo.

"Who is that with you?" he asked. Cisco did not give Leo a chance to answer. He pointed his finger and zapped the guard. Leo's eyes went wide as he did not hear the laser, yet the guard was on his back. They pulled the guard's body to the side of the elevator.

"Come on. Let's go get Maya!" Cisco hissed.

CHAPTER 68

Vivian accepted Armando's advances. He was attentive and sexy, paying special attention to her secret desires. Although a bit older than she, Armando was in prime physical health, with a lean body and a deep passionate Latin nature.

They met when she was on a ski holiday in Switzerland. Initially his machismo attracted her, however later she realized the power he commanded. When the rebellion needed an ally, she brought Armando into the group.

At first, she thought only of his ability to muster the kind of treachery needed by tapping his mercenaries who controlled the drug cartel. It was only later he shared his vision for a takeover of the particle energy by Venezuela. It was pure genius and she planned on being by his side as the Republic buckled to their demands.

After a shower, she sat drying her hair with a towel. Armando swept the hair from the nape of her neck and began gentle kisses.

"Armando, call to have your guards bring Maya up here. I need to see her before we have our meeting," she demanded. A few minutes later, there was a knock on the door and a guard led Maya inside.

"Thank you, Rodrigo. Wait outside," Armando said.

"Welcome, *señorita*. You have caused me a lot of trouble, however there is a friend of yours from the Republic here who may keep you from dying," Armando spoke deliberately.

Joy filled Maya's heart. Finally, someone from her great-grandfather's security police had found her and a way to trade her life for a large ransom. A woman sat in front of the dressing table finishing her makeup. When the woman turned and spoke to her, Maya looked at her with confusion. The beautiful woman was a stranger.

"Hello Maya. My name is Vivian Bejarano. I suppose you thought I was one of your great-grandfather's men or

Francisco. No, but I am here to purchase your release, but only if you do as we instruct. Please sit down."

Cautiously, Leo turned to the right and headed down the hallway. He took out a laser and held it in front of him, ready to shoot. Cisco followed, checking behind frequently to see if anyone followed. As they turned a corner, two guards were walking down the hallway toward them.

"What the hell, Leo? What are you doing?"

"We are checking on a disturbance reported up here. The guard is dead at the elevator," Leo said with a concerned voice.

"What? Lorenzo?"

"Yes you better go. We'll keep checking this way," Leo told him and pointed down the hallway.

As the guards hurried off, Leo and Cisco almost ran the rest of the way to Maya's room. Leo muttered as they reached the doorway. It was slightly ajar and no guard was posted.

"They've taken her."

"Where?"

Leo pondered a second then said, "Probably Armando's suite. Let's go. Follow my lead." Leo did not take any time to explain his plan. Instead of the elevator, they took the two flights of stairs to the top floor and Armando's suite.

Pushing the door from the stairwell, Leo grabbed Cisco by the arm and began yelling.

"I got him. Don't shoot! I got the man," he yelled.

Rodrigo came running down the hall and stopped them. Cisco kept his head down and let Leo pull him along.

"Take me to Armando," Leo demanded pulling Cisco by the arm.

Armando heard the commotion in the hallway. First voices and then a knock on the door.

"*Jefe*, we've got him," Rodrigo's voice accompanied the knock.

"Vivian, your friend Francisco has been caught. Go

get dressed."

Retreating to the bathroom, Vivian dressed in a lightweight cotton sundress she kept here on the island. She found it was more comfortable than the Zortex clothing in the humid heat. Armando unclipped the pistol in his shoulder holster, then slowly and cautiously opened the door.

"We've frisked him. He's clean," Rodrigo said. "Leo caught him."

"Good job, Leo. Rodrigo, go and call off the search. Leo stay here and keep a hold on him," Armando ordered.

As Armando ushered them into the room, Cisco saw Maya sitting in a plush chair. She looked unharmed.

Maya looked up and saw the face of her dreams. It was the same face she saw in the kitchen in the old house in L.A. It was Francisco Salaz. He had found her on this tiny island in the middle of the Caribbean. He was here, but he was also caught. She wanted to scream with frustration.

"Welcome, *señor*. I have many questions about how you managed to circumvent the security on the island. Apparently, we need to increase our efforts," Armando spoke with a chuckle. He sized up Francisco as he spoke. At about six feet with a lean body, Francisco did not present a large threat. He was dressed in the island work clothes.

"Your security is not as good as you think. Neither is it at the hacienda." Cisco played him hoping to keep Armando talking while he formulated a plan. He tried to keep his eyes off of Maya, focusing only on Armando.

Armando struggled to keep control. What an arrogant fool, but then he always enjoyed an unfair fight.

"There is a friend of yours here who may keep you from dying quickly," Armando spoke deliberately.

"Let Maya go. She is innocent. You can keep me here, but let her go. Your plans will not work. The security people in the Republic will not allow you to win," Cisco said still seeking to incite a response.

"Ha! You are worthless to me. She is the grand prize. If it were not for your friend, I would kill you right now."

Armando sneered at Cisco.

"Or perhaps I might just kill you now," Cisco warned him. Leo, who had been holding his arm, lightened his hold and Cisco could feel the tiny laser on his fingertip.

"With what? Your bare hands?" Armando laughed at him. The bathroom door opened and Vivian walked into the living area of the suite.

"Hello Cisco. I suppose you are surprised to see me?" she asked as she went to Armando and put her arm around his waist.

Cisco was not as surprised as he was when she stepped off the helicopter. That shock had long past. Now he was mostly curious. "Why are you doing this Viv? Why are you tied up with this gangster?"

"Gangster? No, Armando is more gentleman than many. He understands power and how to get it."

"He's a heartless killer. He and the PLV have been raping the country of Venezuela for years and corrupting the government," Cisco replied.

"Pinche pendejo." Armando cursed at him and rose to his full six foot two inch height. In a fast move, he backhand slapped Cisco's face. Cisco staggered, but did not fall, but he could taste blood on his tongue.

"A gentleman, Viv? This is your idea of a gentleman? Why are you doing this?" Cisco asked Vivian again looking in her eyes.

"The Republic is to blame for my father's death. He told me that particular gold mine was played out, but they sent him and his crew down to make sure. He went because Valentino asked him to do it personally. It caved in and no one could reach them in time. Every one of them died and I swore I would make the Republic pay for my father's death. Now we have Maya and the president must step down or he will feel the pain of losing her." Venom and bitterness affected her voice as she spoke.

"Viv, it was an accident. I remember everyone was devastated. The president asked him to go because he was the most experienced," Cisco tried to reason with her. Her passionate bitterness against the Republic and the president made little sense.

"No one cared, not even you," she sneered at him.

"Of course I cared, everyone cared. He was given a state funeral," Cisco reminded her. "You must not do this Viv. This is not you. Please let her go. She is innocent. She was only a child when that happened," Cisco pleaded.

Cisco thought he saw her face soften. She was not a killer, at least not the Vivian he knew. She cared about people, children.

"Don't listen to him," Armando groused. "He is only trying to soften your resolve. We need the money and we need the particle to change Venezuela and gain influence in the world. He is nothing. Nobody will ever even know what happened to him after we throw his body into the sea."

Vivian's eyes widened. It never occurred to her she would be face to face with the prospect of killing Cisco. They had a history and as her first love, he always had a place in her heart. Was there any other choice? Maya was the key to this operation. All was not totally lost as long as Maya was in their possession. Francisco was just baggage.

"Kill him," Vivian said to Armando and turned away.

"No!" Maya screamed.

CHAPTER 69

It happened in an instant. Cisco made the split second decision not to kill Armando. Killing him was easy, but he thought the Venezuelan government might want him alive. He might also be their ticket off this island.

Armando moved his hand to raise the pistol with no qualms to killing the unarmed young man. Normally, he let his guards or henchmen do the dirty work, but he took pleasure in killing this thorn in his side. Besides, he wanted to look strong in front of Vivian.

Cisco raised his right hand defensively against the incoming blast, or so Armando thought. Suddenly, his right arm and side burst in pain and Armando's weapon fell to the floor. Leo moved in and grabbed Vivian from behind and pinned her arms.

"Don't try anything Vivian. I don't want to hurt you," Cisco warned her.

"What the fuck?" Armando cried out.

"That was only a small taste of what I can do to you, if you fuck with me, Armando. We are going to your boat. Vivian, take his arm and stay right next to him. If you make a wrong move, I will not hesitate to kill both of you. Now, let's go."

"You'll never make it past my men," Armando groused.

"Maybe, maybe not, but you will die first," Cisco warned him in response.

Armando stepped out of the room first, Vivian beside him, then Cisco with Maya beside him and Leo taking the rear. Out in the hallway, Leo pointed his laser at Rodrigo and two other guards who were waiting for orders.

"Armando, tell your men to stay back," Cisco ordered.

"You men, go ahead of us and don't try anything," Armando ordered after Leo relieved them of their weapons.

The elevator in the old hotel was too small and Leo

suggested they take the stairs. He pushed Rodrigo ahead of him.

"You will not get away with this," Armando said again. "My men, and there are many of them, will shoot you without my command. Give yourself up now and I will let you live," Armando tried to bribe Cisco.

"Just don't you try anything asshole. I would like nothing better than killing you, both you and Vivian for what you have done. I will get Maya out of here safely," Cisco told them.

Shots came at them as they exited the stairwell. Leo pushing Rodrigo ahead, put the guards in the line of fire and they went down. Pushing the small level on the tiny laser, Cisco set it for spread mode and with one shot four security guards glowed and went down.

"Go on. Keep walking," he told Armando and Vivian. They walked down the hallway and across the foyer to the main doors.

"Leo, keep Maya safe. I'll go first." He pushed Armando and Vivian in front of him.

"Tell them to keep their distance," Cisco ordered Armando.

"Stay back, don't shoot!" Armando shouted loudly to whoever might hear him.

A shot came near them from the left. Leo quickly took the armed guard down.

"Cisco, you cannot get away with this. Armando has too many men and they will be positioned where they will pick you off. Both of you," Vivian tried to scare him.

"Are you afraid to die Viv? You have seen what I can do."

As they reached the end of the pathway, Cisco scanned the area. Ahead he could see the dock and several boats. Armando's big blue and white boat bobbed in the water.

To the right near the corner of the hotel he expected guards might be hiding, waiting. He looked up behind them, up on the balconies where several snipers could be stationed, but saw no one. Still, their position did not look good. It was open ground to the docks. Snipers could easily pick them off. He pulled Armando by the belt closer to him.

"What the fuck. What are you doing?" he asked Cisco.

"You men," Cisco yelled. "I will kill him if you try anything."

Cisco lifted his hand and sent the unseen laser at Armando's left arm. Armando buckled a bit and screamed. Both arms were paralyzed and he helpless.

"Tell them Armando. Tell them what I can do," Cisco hissed in his ear.

"Don't shoot. He'll kill me. Stay back," Armando yelled.

"Louder."

"He'll kill me. I order you to stay back," Armando screamed as loud as he could.

"Vivian, you go out first. Maya stay close to her. Armando, stay close to me. Leo, cover us from behind." Armando shuffled near Cisco. Cisco knew it would not completely cover them, however it was the only idea he had. He kept his thumb near the trigger on the tiny laser.

Slowly they marched. Vivian stumbled, but Maya had a hold of the back of her dress. When they got about twenty yards Cisco told them to move faster. At almost a run, they got to the boat. "Vivian, Maya get in and go below!" Cisco yelled out when they got to the boat.

He grabbed the helpless Armando and used him as a shield while he untied the rope from the cleat. Several shots hit the dock nearby from his left. With a touch, Cisco sent a spray of shots toward that direction. Leo unloosed the ropes from the cleat, while Cisco pushed a struggling Armando aboard. Once on the boat, he slipped the key in and the engine sprung to life. Pushing Armando to the floor of the boat, he did his best to maneuver the boat quickly away from the dock.

Shots came from behind them. He heard Leo shout just before a searing pain stung his upper shoulder as a bullet grazed him. He jammed the throttle down. More gunshots sounded from behind them from men standing on the dock.

"I'm hit," Leo cursed as a shot hit his upper thigh.

"Is it bad?"

"I'll live," Leo replied.

Cisco pointed the boat out to sea and crouched on the starboard side. He was unsure of the laser's distance, but remembered Javier saying the distance was less when the laser was in spray mode. Repeatedly shooting toward the docks, Cisco watched his shots fall short as Armando's men jumped into another boat and gunned it to follow.

He heard a scream from below deck and then a thud. Vivian's head popped topside. "The girl is dead, Cisco. You failed," she sneered.

Cisco felt the pain in his soul. Everything he had done had been for naught. Maya was dead.

The boat suddenly lurched as it hit a wave. The jerk sent Vivian sprawling over Armando. Cisco heard gunshots nearby as the PLV guards were gaining on them. He pushed on the throttle, but it was already at the max. Pain shot through his shoulder with every jerk of the boat.

More shots hit nearby from the boat behind them. He clung to the wheel with his left arm trying to steer away from incoming waves. The boat bounced crazily in the chop of the sea.

"More speed Cisco," he heard Leo shout. "They're gaining on us."

The big blue and white boat was larger than the speedboat gaining on them and not as maneuverable. The bow hit another depression in the water and lurched before speeding on. Vivian pushed up from the deck and headed toward him.

"You've ruined everything!"

She reached out to grab Cisco. He could see hatred in her eyes. Gunshots sounded from behind them. Vivian's body jerked and her face took on a surprised look. Blood spurted from her blouse. Her hands fell to her sides and she crumpled to the deck. Cisco watched in disbelief as she died before his eyes. He tried to feel remorse, but thought she got what she deserved.

"Vivian!" Armando cried out as she fell near him.

Gunshots rang from behind them in rapid succession. The boat jerked and slammed the water as it bounced along at full speed. Cisco turned his eyes at intervals to keep tabs on the boat that followed. Armando and Vivian were a pitiful sight. Armando was trying to cradle Vivian's lifeless body in his useless arms.

Cisco wondered if the boat following them caught up, whether they would take chances with Armando on board. He thought they would circle or maybe ram them to try to stop him. He wondered if he could stop them with the tiny laser. The situation was growing more dire as each second ticked by.

Suddenly, it all seemed so useless. Vivian said Maya was dead. Nothing else seemed to matter. Eventually, the big blue and white boat would run out of gas in the blue Caribbean Sea. Regardless of whether they outran the PLV, he had failed.

A surge of gunfire erupted. He heard the bullets hitting the hull of the boat. They made an odd sound as they hit the fiberglass hull. He knew it meant the pursuers were close. He turned to fire the laser. The men in the PLV boat were close enough for Cisco to see their faces. One was pointing an automatic weapon. As if in slow motion, he saw the man pull the trigger and the bullet fly through the air. It caught him below his right shoulder. The pain seared through his entire chest as he returned a spray from the tiny laser.

Suddenly, the scene became oddly quiet. All the engine noise and gunshots evaporated into nothingness. Over the mayhem, he heard his *Nino's* voice. "Come with me. Come with me and Maya," his godfather's voice said. Cisco wondered if he was dying.

It was a loud explosion, which shook the boat and brought Cisco back into the present. A second loud boom sounded behind them as the pursuing boat exploded into pieces and burst into flames. Leo jumped up and caught Cisco as he sagged near the helm. He slowed the boat to a stop. On the horizon, the sub had surfaced and a man holding a large bazooka waved to Leo.

CHAPTER 70

He was looking across the river at the Indian warrior gesturing at him with his fist above his head and yelling unintelligible screams. A spear was stuck on the ground where he had been standing when the warrior caught up to him. Even from the opposite side of the river, the fierce screams of the warrior threatened him deep in his soul. Beside him, Maya and his Nino were standing watching the warrior rant.

"Why does the Indian want to kill me, Nino?" Cisco asked his godfather.

"Cisco, wake up." He heard Maya's voice speaking to him.

Struggling to bring himself awake, Cisco opened one eye and saw white. His brain wondered if this was heaven. He heard his name again. Opening both eyes, he looked around a white room with a curtain around him. He was hooked up to an IV and his mouth was dry. Maya's face came into focus.

"Where am I?"

"You're at an army hospital in Caracas."

"You're alive?" he croaked at her vividly remembering Vivian's words.

"Yes, thanks to you. Vivian hit me and knocked me unconscious, but I am quite fine."

Maya pressed the alert to fetch the nurse. After taking his vitals, the nurse asked, "Can I get anything for you?"

"No, thank you."

As the nurse left, Freddy limped into the room. "Welcome back," Freddy said and grinned. They proceeded to fill Cisco in on how Leo was able to reach the sub on a Pcom and they positioned the sub to take out the PLV boat. Armando was in a secure hospital and would be turned over to the authorities for kidnapping when he fully recovered.

"He'll be in prison for the rest of his days, if he lives that long," Freddy said and laughed. "Vivian's body is lying in a morgue here in Caracas, until the Republic decides what to do. Your General Castillo has already been extradited to the Republic."

The details swirled in his brain as he remembered commandeering Armando's boat away from Orchila Island.

"General Mora wants to know when you're signing up to be a Special Op?" Freddy said with a grin. "He's mighty impressed with you." The friendly banter and smiling faces were great medicine. After a while, the talking or the drugs for the pain were making him tired. He turned to Maya.

"Maya, why are you still here? You should be home with your family, especially your great-grandfather," Cisco told her.

"I will not leave without you, Cisco. You saved me. Now it's my turn to take you home," she said and blushed.

"I tried to send her home. The president wanted to send a plane for her, but she refused. So now, I am watching out for both of you," Freddy said.

"Thanks Freddy. By the way, what happened to Leo?"

"He was injured, but was treated and released. He told me to pass on his regards," Freddy said.

"Freddy, Leo is the real hero. Without him, I could not have rescued Maya. I will have our president reward both of you."

"Don't worry about that. We were glad to help. Because of you, we finally have Armando Leoni on charges that will stick. Hopefully, you will come back and help us convert to the particle," Freddy said.

A week later Cisco and his father, Emilio, walked into President Torres' private office. The old man got up from his chair and took Cisco in a warm *abrazo*. "Welcome home, *mijo*. You did well, as the Spirit told me you would. Come sit with me," he said and led Cisco and Emilio to a sitting area. He asked a man to bring refreshments.

"I don't understand the spirit *Nino,* but I had dreams of a warrior trying to kill me. You were always on the other side of a river, beckoning me to cross over. You and Maya were in the dream. What does it mean?"

"The warrior was there to help you overcome your fear. Only your own fear could defeat you. The lesson served you well. You escaped danger at every turn and found Maya." President Torres said and smiled at him.

After the man brought glasses of iced tea and left them alone again, the president began speaking again.

"Maya told me how you found her several times. She told me you were dressed as a *vato* in Los Angeles. She did not recognize you at the time. I would like to hear about that," he said.

Cisco explained how he borrowed Uncle Charley's red *ranfla* and followed clues to Los Angeles. The president laughed heartily hearing Cisco's description of the *Japovato* gangs. "You told me to go under the radar to evade the kidnappers."

"Yes, you certainly took our suggestions to heart."

For the most part of an hour, Cisco related all of the events of the past week. He did not leave out Freddy Mendoza, General Mora and his special ops agent on the island, Leo. Neither did he leave out telling his *Nino* about Gus de la Garza. The president was intrigued by the explanation of how the InfoAgent had been able to be such a pivotal part of this operation.

"They all deserve medals or commendations," Cisco told him.

"The President of Venezuela called me to thank us and to ask for you to return and help them with a conversion to the particle. This time you can take your Corvette," he said with a chuckle.

"I have to admit, many times I was not sure I would find Maya and save her. I was lucky," Cisco told him.

"Luck had nothing to do with it Francisco. You had the Spirit on your side," and when he said it his eyes twinkled.

Toward the end of their conversation, Valentino looked at Cisco with a smile. "Francisco, you remind me so much of your grandfather, Salvador. He was like a brother to me and a very brave man. He too got me out of scraps, more times than I can remember. When we were first locating the particle, the Rio Oro Gold Mine was tainting the water of the local Indian tribe. It was your grandfather who realized cyanide was making the children of the village sick. One night when we were camped at the meteor site, Salvador anticipated the miners would try to harm us. We had called the authorities on them for their ecological misuses and they were angry. While I was asleep, two men came to the camp. Your grandfather had laid a trap and they got caught up in it. It killed one and broke the other's leg."

"My father never told me about that," Emilio spoke, shocked at the story his father never related to him.

"Yes, your father didn't want anybody to know he killed a man, but he saved our lives," he responded and looked directly at Cisco, knowing the heroic efforts and the death he caused might be weighing on him.

As they parted, Valentino hugged his godson tightly. The Republic would never know how he saved it from ruin. The efforts and the Protectors would go on in secrecy. A chair at that table would be reserved for him when the time came.

"Te amo, Nino," Cisco said and released him from the embrace.

Cisco's Vette was parked on the landing pad at his parent's house. Before going up the path into the house, he strolled once around his baby. Charley had taken good care of it.

"Mamá," he yelled as he walked into the kitchen with his father. "Where are you?"

"I'm in the kitchen," she answered.

"Mamá, I'm hungry."

"You're always hungry. You and your father must not have had a very good hunting trip. You are both thin," she admonished.

"The trip was a bust for wildlife. We only bagged a couple of scrawny rabbits. It is why I built such a big greenhouse for you. Whatever would we do without you?" Emilio said and wrapped his arms around his wife. A warm embrace and his father's lies created a smooth diversion of the topic of where they had been for most of the last week and his mother grinned at the attention.

Cisco could barely keep himself from laughing. His adventure and almost death at the hands of PLV mercenaries was classified information. The disruptions in the Republic blamed on solar flares, and nothing was archived about Maya's kidnapping. As far as his mother knew, he and his father had gone hunting in the mountains.

Francisco wolfed down three plates of his mother's cooking. He thought about Maya. Somehow he felt lost without her. She had slept most of the way home on the military plane in the curve of his arm.

"Francisco? Francisco?" his mother said. "Are you alright?"

"*Sí, Mamá,*" Francisco said. "I'm just dead tired. Now that I've had your home cooking, I feel as if I could sleep for two days."

As he was flying home, the secure Pcom buzzed and he heard Gus' voice.

"*Hola.* Welcome home," Gus said.

"Gus, I can never thank you enough for all you did. I told the president you deserve a medal."

"I got better than a medal, Cisco. General Bustamante called me in for an interview after he heard the name Agustín de la Garza in connection with finding Maya. I've been reinstated with Special Operations including a promotion."

"Congratulations Gus. You deserve it."

Gus seemed elated, but said he would not be in touch. "Going undercover again," he told Cisco.

Cisco flew the Vette over his property twice in manual mode. It was calm and quiet. Landing on the pad, he walked up and into the house. No dreams came to him when he drifted into a pure, restful, and well deserved sleep after Maya's image flashed across his brain.

END

Glossary of Spanish Words:

The following is a glossary of *italicized* Spanish words which are used repeatedly throughout the series which do not have an English counterpart, such as important = *importante* or Mama = *Mamá*. Other infrequently used words, phrases, and sentences written in Spanish are immediately explained within the text itself.

abrazo: a hug
abuelo; abuela: grandfather; grandmother (m;f)
adios: goodbye
ahijado: godson
amigo(s); amiga(s): friend (m;f)
aprovecho: enjoy, appreciate, take advantage of
ayúdame: help, asking for help
baboso(s): drooling idiot (a slang or curse word)
bisabuelo; bisabuela: great grandfather or grandmother (m;f)
bueno: good
buenos días; tardes; noches: good day; evening; night
bienvenido(s): welcome
cabrón: asshole or bastard (a curse word)
caballo(s); caballero(s): horse; horseman or gentleman
cállate: shutup or be quiet
cálmate; cálmese : be calm or calm down
caramba: curse/slang for 'Holy Shit'
Chicano: term to describe persons of Hispanic origins
chica: term for a young girl
chingado: shit or fuck (a curse word)
cojones: slang for a man's testicles
camaradas (s): comrades, friends
culón: a chickenshit (a curse word)
desgracia, desgraciado: unfortunate, miserable wretch
Dios: God
drogueros: drug pushers, drug cartel, or slang for druggies
ese: Chicano street slang meaning man, dude
farolito: Christmas decoration of a lighted bag; luminaries
gracias; muchas gracias: thank you; many thanks
hacienda: a large plantation or estate
hola, horale: hello greeting
huaraches: sandals

jefe: the boss man

llano, llanero(s): ranchhands, cowboys of South America

machismo: very manly

maldito: bad; describing a person

mañana: tomorrow or the sometime later

mierda: same as shit (a curse word)

mi hijito; hijo; mijo; hijita; hija; mija: my son; daughter (m;f)

muchacho(s); muchacha(s): like saying 'the guys' (m;f)

nada: no or nothing

Nino: short form of padrino, nickname for a godfather

pantalones: pants

payaso: clown

pendejo(s); pendeja(s): slang for asshole (a curse word) (m;f)

peso(s): Mexican money

picaro: a womanizer

pinche: fucking (a curse word)

poco loco; loco: slang for a crazy person

primo(s); prima(s): cousin (m;f)

pulque: a milky alcoholic drink

que?: what or why

querido; querida: affectionate meaning my dear (m;f)

ranfla: vehicle of Chicano style, lowrider

señor(es); señora(s); señorita(s): like saying Mr. or Mrs. or Miss

sentar: sit down

sí: yes

Te amo: an expression of love

tío; tía: uncle; aunt (m;f)

tontos: in reference to a man's testicles

urbano: city dweller

vámonos or vamos: let's go, get out of here

vaquero(s): livestock herder or cowboy, i.e. *llaneros*

vato(s): slang for Chicano gang member

www.ingramcontent.com/pod-product-compliance
Lightning Source LLC
Chambersburg PA
CBHW070632180626
46817CB00006B/2103